A Beautiful Satan II

By

RJ Champ

Published by DC Bookdiva Publications

Copyright © 2013 by RJ Champ

ISBN-13: 978-0-9887621-0-7

Library of Congress Control Number: On File

Publisher's Note

This is a work of fiction. Any names historical events, real people, living and dead, or the locales are intended only to give the fiction a setting in historic reality. Other names, characters, places, businesses and incidents are either the product of the author's imagination or are used fictiously, and their resemblance, if any, to real life counterparts is entirely coincidental.

Edited by: Jenell Talley

DC Bookdiva Publications

#245 4401-A Connecticut Ave

NW, Washington, DC 20008

www.dcbookdiva.com

facebook.com/thedcbookdiva

A BEAUTIFUL SATAN II
NATASHA'S WRATH

By
RJ CHAMP

Chapter 1

Dr. Alverez traced his fingertips along the white linen. "I also found something very peculiar." He gazed down at Angel as spit formed in the corner of his mouth. He surprised her when he stopped abruptly and grabbed her by the wrist.

"I also found a bloody vial inside your bag with a woman's clitoris floating around inside, so don't play games with me, bitch! Give me what I want, or I'll have the whole fuckin' DC police department crawling up your ass faster than you can scream daddy," he hissed with lust brewing in his eyes.

Angel's lips trembled with contempt. "I don't know what the hell you're talking about, but you better get your dirty-ass hands off me!" Angel cringed when she felt his onion-tainted breath on her face. The dirty grin on his face made her want to vomit.

Dr. Alverez leaned in closer. "I don't have time for this shit," he hissed bitterly as he ripped the iPhone from his waist. "Let DC police handle your ass." He pressed the screen icon marked "security."

"Corporal Monroe. How can I assist you?" a monotone voice said.

Two seconds later someone knocked on the door.

"Dr. Alverez? Nurse Lewis. Are you in there?"

Beads of perspiration broke out on Angel's forehead. It was already too late. The nausea and butterflies were churning in her stomach, and the light in her hazel eyes grew dim.

Angel was claustrophobic all of a sudden as she watched the pitch-black shadow engulf her mind. Angel's conscious faded as the wicked nature that is Natasha emerged.

Her facial expression simmered with rage, the muscles in her jaw twitched violently and her eyes overflowed with hatred. Natasha was straining to control herself from tearing his wide, bumpy nose off his ugly, pockmarked face.

Natasha forced an awkward smile as she reached out and grabbed the doctor's crotch. She gave a devilish grin and muttered, "Do we really need to bring the police into this, doctor? We're two hot-blooded adults, are we not?" The desire to end his life grew with every breath.

Dr. Alverez snickered quietly. "That's what I've been waiting to hear. Now you're talkin'." He wiped the saliva from the corner of his mouth with the back of his hand, then turned off the iPhone and slipped it in his pants pocket.

"Shhh ..." He licked his lips, motioned toward the door and whispered, "Don't worry about the nurse; she doesn't know that I'm in here. As soon as she leaves, it's just you and me, Mrs. Rising." He made a disgusting slurping sound as more drool formed in the corner of his mouth.

"Mrs. Rising has left the building, doctor," whispered Natasha. The creepy tone in her voice touched a nerve. "Natasha is the woman you'll be dealing with for the remainder of your time here."

"What?" he said confused. A troubled look jumped across his face when he looked her in the eyes. He hesitated for a split second, but his mounting lustful cravings got the better of him. Dr. Alverez palmed her ass and quickly dismissed the warning echoing in the back of his head.

"Natasha, huh," Dr. Alverez breathed. "Who's she? I suppose that's the, uh, nickname for your sexy, secret dark side?" He stopped short. His eyes fell to her chest, and he leered at the nipple imprint pressing against the white fabric. "Fuck this," he grunted, unable to control himself any longer.

"Doctor!" Natasha scolded. "Get a hold of yourself," she commanded, while fighting off his sexual advances. Natasha winced when she felt his rough, pockmarked face press hard against her neck. Her insides boiled when he began to molest the base of her neck with his cold lips and wet tongue. She was a microsecond away from biting off his nose.

"Doctor!" Natasha seethed. "We need somewhere more private…"

"Huh?" His head popped up. "More private? Where else would we go?"

Natasha sighed. "Well, doctor, you work here, so you should be the one to make the call. But first, before we go any further, I'm going to need Angel's belongings."

It struck Dr. Alverez as odd that she spoke of Angel as if she were a third party. He looked her in the eye.

"Okay. That's no problem. My car is parked downstairs in the garage."

Natasha's lips curled into a wicked grin. "Is there a delivery elevator on this floor that we could use?"

This late in the evening, the hospital garage was practically deserted. A teal-colored Mercedes-Benz was parked in the far corner of the garage. Dr. Alverez's name was prominently painted on the concrete wall above the sedan.

Inside the vehicle's spacious rear cabin, Natasha squatted down in between the doctor's legs. She quickly undid his pants and pulled them down around his ankles. His brow stretched upward as eager anticipation swirled in his eyes.

"What's the matter with this little thing of yours?" she said. "It looks sick, like it needs some medical attention." Natasha's tone and demeanor was unmistakably facetious. She reminded him of his dry-ass bitchy wife. Her face flashed in his head, then on the floor between his legs. He was totally annoyed with her looks, her mouth, and her presence.

Dr. Alverez snapped his head toward her and shot Natasha a wild glare. He was seething mad now. "You dirty whore!" he spat angrily. "Who do you think you're talking to?"

Natasha met his hostile leer without flinching. She laughed loudly and obnoxiously, causing the hairs on the back of his neck to stand.

"Whore!? You calling me a whore, and you're the one out here cheating on your wife! You no good son of a bitch! You're no better than these sluttish women out here fucking around with married men! You're the fucking whore!" she spewed venomously. Both her hands closed with remarkable strength around his scrotum.

"Ooowww!" he cried like a bitch.

Natasha smiled, enjoying the look of pain on his face. "You pulled your little dick out on the wrong bitch tonight, and this will be the last time that you try to stick your little penis in any other pussy besides your wife's. Matter of fact, you won't be sticking your dick anywhere ever again," she growled, grinning sadistically.

Dr. Alverez' eyes grew wide. Fear and loathing overcame him as he began sobbing uncontrollably.

Natasha took several deep breaths. Her evil spirit pumped fire into her veins. Like a crazed maniac, her hands gripped his scrotum and sprang apart with a powerful heave.

"Mother of God!!!!" he shrieked at the top of his lungs. Mind-numbing pain engulfed his body, paralyzing him. He felt his testicles and their juices spew from the hideous gash in his groin!

Dr. Alverez stared in shock and watched his world swirl into complete darkness right before his very eyes. Natasha loved every minute of it, laughing wickedly, pleased with her dark deed. As the doctor's soul departed his body, she could feel her sadistic spirit surge forward and bloom.

Natasha stuffed a cloth in the car's gas tank, then set the cloth on fire. The fire destroyed the car's interior. It took only seconds for the flames to mix with the flammable gas fumes and turn Dr. Alverez's car into a fire bomb.

Kaboom!!!

The teal sedan exploded like a fireball and rocked the entire lower foundation of the garage. The explosion sent shockwaves throughout the garage, destroying everything within the vicinity that was made of glass.

In the background, a cacophony of fire alarms and sirens erupted throughout the hospital.

Within minutes, fire, rescue, police, and paramedics swarmed the hospital grounds. Bright flashing lights lit up the dark landscape, while helicopters hovered, crisscrossing the skyline.

Several miles away, the effects of the devastation were apparent—a major catastrophe had taken place tonight, and somewhere within the burning rubble a life was lost

Chapter 2

Detective Clark helped himself to the coffee fountain inside the hospital cafeteria, and then strode back through the first-floor lobby on his way back to the fire-ravaged garage.

He couldn't see a connection between this crime and the serial predator case the department had been working on. A physician burned to death in a car explosion in a hospital garage?

Looks to me like old Doc was probably doing a few too many house calls. I'll bet anybody my paycheck that's what's going on here, Clark said to himself while taking in the crime scene.

Louis emerged from a group of CSI techs busy scouring the crime scene. He spotted Clark and waved him over.

"Anything?" asked Clark, sipping on his steaming cup of java.

Louis shrugged, forcing a tired smile. "I'm not totally sure what we have, but there is an indication that this could be our guy."

The uncertainty Clark detected in his partner's demeanor irritated him.

"Spit it out, Rich," Clark directed dryly. "Let me analyze the facts and the evidence. Because if you ask me, I think we're wasting our time."

Louis motioned to the report in his hand. "Well, we already know about the body in the backseat. And we have a name here. Dr. Alverez was the only physician who was unaccounted for, so we can pretty much pencil him in as our flamed-broiled corpse over there." Louis hesitated. "What the team has discovered," he began, frowning, "is the doc's scrotum was disemboweled." He watched his partner's reaction.

The lines on Clark's forehead deepened. "Some nut case cut his nut-sack open?!?" The thought made him cringe.

Shaking his head vigorously, Louis replied with a staunch, "No. That's not the case. Someone ripped it open!" he said emphatically.

Clark's face contorted painfully. "What? Why the sick fucker," he muttered sourly.

Tony Woo was keeping a close eye on the pair. He casually strolled over to the men and acknowledged them with a slight nod.

"Well," Woo began, "if this is our guy, fellas, he's made a peculiar move in this slaying here."

Clark frowned. "Okay, Woo, what are you getting at? Let's hear it."

Woo folded his hand behind his back. "Well, for starters, the victim's scrotum was torn open and the testes removed," he said. He held up his hand for silence when Clark started to interrupt. "Our suspect collects trophies. Here, check out this." He handed Louis a specimen vial. "This suspect left us his calling card."

"What's in the bottle, Woo?" Louis inquired, holding up the clear vial. He studied the strange bodily remains floating inside. *Looks like a couple of walnuts,* he said to himself.

Woo huffed. "What you're looking at is our victim's testicles," he answered plainly. "We found them shoved in his mouth. I also believe the car was set ablaze in an attempt to cover our culprit's trail and to destroy any crucial evidence."

Clark inhaled deeply. "So what are you saying, Woo? We got us a copycat on our hands? Is that what you're getting at?"

Woo quickly shook his head. "No idea," he said. "Until I upload every piece of evidence from this crime scene into my criminal analysis database and make an in-depth comparison from every angle possible, I'm not going to jump the gun. I would advise you two to do likewise."

Chapter 3

The following day, Angel felt utterly spent as she was wheeled through the automatic sliding doors by her attending nurse. Jovan was following close on their heels, his wife's belongings cradled in his arms.

The strong winter sunlight was blinding. Angel had to shield her eyes and allow her eyesight to gradually come into focus.

"That's me right there, Beauty," Angel said, pointing in the direction of her husband's shiny black Mercedes SUV.

Beauty looked surprised, then impressed, as she pushed Angel's wheelchair over to the passenger door.

"Excuse me, nurse. I'll get the door for you," Jovan said, stepping around both women. He could feel Beauty's eyes burning a hole in the back of his head. *What could I say? I was just as surprised as she was when I walked in the room to pick up my wife and saw her standing there at my wife's bedside. What an awkward moment! But as long as she keeps her mouth shut, everything will be all good.*

When Jovan turned to Beauty, her innocent gaze demanded an explanation that he couldn't provide at the moment. The expression on her innocent face made his guilt soar.

Damn, he said to himself. He felt bad about the whole situation.

While Jovan helped his wife into the vehicle, Beauty stood beside him, staring. When he was finished, he secured the door, took a deep breath and turned to face her.

"Thank you for all your help, miss," he said, extending his hand. Beauty framed him with a fervent stare. "You're welcome, Mr. Rising," she said quietly. He sighed inwardly, thanking God, and blessed her with a sly wink and a smile before making his way around the truck.

It didn't take long before the black SUV was speeding along the wide 395 interchange. The glossy Benz truck caught the outside lane and stayed there.

Out of nowhere, Angel blindsided Jovan with an off-the-wall question.

"So what's going on with you and that red bitch? Are you fucking her, too?"

Jovan looked mystified. "What in the hell are you talking about now?" he protested. "You know damn well I ain't fucking that bitch! I don't even know that bitch!" he huffed. "You need to get a fucking life, 'cause you getting on my goddamn nerves with that bullshit! Every time I turn around you're accusing me of fuckin' some bitch!"

Angel eyed him suspiciously. "I saw the way you were looking at one another. If y'all not fucking, the look I saw said 'let's fuck,'" she sneered.

Jovan responded with a dry-sounding laugh. "Girl, you crazy, you know that? I'm convinced you've lost your goddamn mind 'cause you just pluck shit out of thin air to fuck with me about. What is it? You get off on that kind of shit?" He was angry now. "Because if you're going to accuse me of something, then you need to come correct. Get your facts straight before you come at me with the bullshit, or don't come at me at all. You got that? Shit, what kind of fucking drugs they got you on anyway? You're not even healed completely, and here you are starting some bullshit! Get a fucking life!"

Angel shot him a scathing look and turned away. She glanced up at the mirror, searching for a moment of quiet reflection. It was clear to her that Jovan was being deceptive, but she felt drained right now. She'd deal with him later. She allowed her mind to wander. Angel sighed heavily and sunk into the soft leather seat, the last shreds of doubt withering away as she drifted off to sleep.

Chapter 4

The next afternoon ...

A group of young children were playing tag, running through the barren, dirt-strewn courtyard of the 640 Lorton-Morton projects on a cool, sunny afternoon.

Jovan and Ray appeared in the front entrance of a drab-looking brown brick apartment building. Blazing sunbeams flooded their eyes the moment they stepped out into the dusty courtyard.

The cell phone on Ray's hip squawked suddenly. Jovan paused for a second when he heard the voice speak. He thought he recognized the timbre in the man's voice emanating from the speaker. He tried to place the voice. The name was right on the tip of his tongue, but he couldn't recall who it was.

Ray needed to speak in private. He turned and walked in the opposite direction.

Jovan stopped in the middle of the project courtyard. His eyes panned across the cul-de-sac of the infamous projects. This area was urban blight in its rawest form. Cliques of armed 640 head-bustas were lounging on fences and loitering outside of apartment buildings, pushing work, and trolling their territory.

Today, Jovan had journeyed into the belly of the beast. He met with the devil face to face. He sat down, shook his hand, and proceeded to work a deal with the devil himself.

Jovan was very cognizant of the situation. The move he made today had major implications. What he did today was break a promise he made to himself. He swore once he took his wedding vows he would back off of the drug business and break the stronghold that the drug game seemed to have on him.

But today Jovan did the complete opposite—he backslid. He let Ray talk him into going with him to meet with Dutchy Hans, Uptown's most prolific drug lord.

The larger-than-life drug figure was much cooler than Jovan pictured he'd be. The meeting went to the letter, just like Ray said it would. Dutchy Hans welcomed Jovan into the ranks and gave his blessing. The gesture was the equivalent of a mafia underling meeting with a Don and being allowed to become a made man.

This major connect would automatically catapult Jovan into the upper echelon of DC's drug underworld. He wasn't sure that he was even ready to make that kind of commitment.

Ray startled Jovan when he brushed past him. "C'mon, playboy," he said walking toward his Beemer. "Redman ready to dip out."

Sliding behind the wheel of his black SUV, Jovan started feeling an uncomfortable sensation in his gut.

The deadly twins, Dank and Psycho, were paired up with two other heavy gunners, Biggie and Dude. Together, the four men represented a potent killer force with ample firepower. Their arsenal included .40- and .50-caliber Smith & Wessons and Desert Eagles and M-5 submachine guns. The men were strapped to the teeth with enough hardware to scare the bejesus out of a S.W.A.T. team.

Ray hit the twin's cell phone and ordered them to move out. The raven-black Dodge Magnum they were pushing was blocking Redman's candy-apple red Cadillac CTS. Redman was Dutchy Hans' sergeant at arms, a rising force in the business.

The plan was for them to follow Redman across town to a secret stash house, where ten bricks of pure Colombian snow were awaiting their arrival.

The black Magnum rolled out first, followed immediately by the red Caddy. Ray's white-gold BMW fell in line, and Jovan brought up the rear in his black ML-500.

The small procession of vehicles exited the projects and came to a stop at the intersection of Morton Street and Georgia Avenue. When the traffic cleared, the vehicles turned right on Georgia and headed north.

A separate group of automobiles quickly exited a small strip mall parking lot at the same intersection. A burgundy conversion van with tinted windows sped off after the small group of cars with its own crew in tow.

Approximately a quarter mile up Georgia Avenue, Redman hit his right turn signal and sounded his horn, alerting the crew riding ahead in the Magnum to make a right turn.

At the intersection of Georgia and New Hampshire avenues, the black Dodge veered right on New Hampshire, the procession of cars following suit like boxcars on the rear of a locomotive.

After turning off Georgia, Jovan reached adjusted his rearview mirror. His eyes shifted back and forth, from the road to the mirror.

The burgundy van came speeding into view.

"WTF!" Jovan's eyes jumped wide. He immediately fumbled at his waist to get a hold of his BlackBerry.

"Ray! Ray!" Jovan blurted urgently. "Can you hear me, Ray? Check it, I think we're being followed!"

Ray answered back immediately, "C'mon, J, ain't nobody following us, dude. That's you being paranoid. You might need to slow down on the Purple."

Jovan's eyes shifted from the rearview to the road to the driver's side mirror. He repeated the process over and over in five-second intervals. "Ray, nigga, I'm not being paranoid," he voiced sternly. "There's a fucking van on our ass, and the bitch been on us since we past the House (Penthouse was hottest strip joint on Georgia Avenue).

"Alright, playa, let's see if you know what you talking about." Ray sounded patronizing. "Follow my lead."

The BMW abruptly broke from the group, slowed down and pulled to the curb. Ray popped out and waited for his man to park. He stood scrutinizing the oncoming traffic and didn't see a single van in sight.

"Look, playa," Ray said approaching Jovan's truck, "do you see a van anywhere around? What I tell you, huh?"

With a reluctant face, Jovan admitted weakly, "Yeah, I guess you right." He was glaring hard at the flow of traffic moving toward them. A van finally rolled by, but he knew that wasn't the one he had seen earlier.

Both men agreed that nobody was following before they climbed back in their cars and continued on their way.

Dank hit Ray on his cell and let him know they had already gone around the traffic circle. The Magnum and Caddy were parked three blocks from the circle in front of the cemetery on New Hampshire Avenue, waiting for them.

The Beemer slowed just before entering the traffic circle. Jovan wasn't paying attention to the road; his eyes glued to the rearview. When his eyes hit the windshield—

"Oh shit!!!" he gasped, and stomped on the brake pedal. The black SUV skidded to a stop only inches from a collision. "Muthafuck!" he yelled, realizing he almost fucked up. He shook off the rattled nerves and gathered his composure.

The traffic inside the circle resembled a motor speedway. Automobiles raced around the circle as if they were in competition, jockeying for position as they entered and exited the nonstop traffic surge.

A two-lane gap opened up. Ray punched it. He mashed hard on the accelerator. The Benz truck entered the circle right on his heels.

Three seconds later, Jovan's mouth fell wide when he looked in the rearview. His heart was pounding in his chest as he watched the burgundy van thunder into the circle, trying to catch up.

"Ray! Ray! Look behind you, nigga! It's that fucking van! That bitch is on our ass!" Jovan sounded fearful and furious all in the same breath.

"Shit!" Ray hissed. "I see 'em, J! Who the fuck are they?"

Both vehicles continued around the circle. They bypassed their turn off, and rode completely around the circle, exiting back out on New Hampshire. They headed back toward Georgia, driving through the first traffic light before deciding to pull over and park.

This time neither man got out. They sat and waited and watched. The dark van appeared at the crest of the hill. Suddenly, the van accelerated down the slope.

Jovan and Ray were riveted to their side view mirrors, watching as the van quickly closed the distance. The vehicle rolled up and skidded to a wheel-screeching halt five feet past Ray's BMW.

A wave of panic hit them both. They sat stunned as a trio of charcoal-colored Dodge Chargers raced into position behind the van and blocked them in.

The men emerged from their cars toting M-5 submachine guns. Jovan's and Ray's first inclination screamed robbery. Or maybe it was a kidnapping or a hit.

Those thoughts dispersed instantaneously from their minds the moment they heard one of the men bark, "Freeze! Hands in the fucking air, dirt bags!"

The hectic scene became crystal clear as the task force leaped from their cars with tactical precession and spread out into a formidable circle around both vehicles. The task force wore dark-colored clothing. Their backs of their flak jackets were emblazoned with three gold letters: D.E.A.

Both men were hustled out of their vehicles, frisked, then told to lean against the side of the hoods as agents converged on their cars, eager to search for any signs of criminal activity.

"What's this all about?" demanded Ray. "We ain't break no muthafuckin' laws! So what the fuck is this shit?!?"

The unit commander, Agent Blake, tapped the shoulder of the officer standing guard over Ray. He waved the subordinate out of the way.

"What's that you shooting off at the mouth about?" Agent Blake asked, towering over Ray, glaring down on him as if he wanted to bash his face in. "I advise you to cool your boots, son," urged the brawny commander as he adjusted his belt and pants.

"What?" Ray snapped aggressively. "You ain't advising me of jack shit! I know my goddamn rights! Fuck this shit!" He mugged the muscle-bound man, then straightened his brown cardigan and smoothed out the wrinkles in his jeans. When he finished attending to his clothes, Ray sneered and flipped the brown-haired man the finger. "For that matter, fuck you too!"

Agent Blake's wide yellow face turned beet red. "So that's how you wanna play this out? You think you Mr. Tough Guy, huh?" he grumbled, before pouncing.

Ray didn't have a chance to respond before the lieutenant reached down and snatched his frame off the hood, twisted his arm behind his back and tossed him, head first, in the back of the van.

"Y'all boys deal with that one there," he ordered, eyeing Jovan. "This big-mouth tough guy right here is all mine." A dark grin fell across his lips as he hopped in the van and slammed the door.

Jovan watched intently.

"What you looking at?" asked a short Caucasian agent with a receding hairline and bad attitude. "You gotta problem with what's going on here, huh? Speak about it!" He tossed his hands in the air like he was itching for a fight.

It was quite obvious to anyone in the presence of the short man, that he was a poster child for the Napoleonic Complex.

Jovan had to restrain himself from laughing in the man's face. He was definitely a funny little dude who used his position in law enforcement to help him cope with his shortcomings.

"Agent Dent," called a fellow agent, rounding the front of the black SUV. This agent looked fresh out of the academy. He was young, spirited and full of zest. His name was Agent Aim, the newest recruit to the task force. He motioned for the sergeant to step to the side so they could speak in private.

"Sir, our informant must've supplied false intelligence. We came up empty-handed in both vehicles."

The little guy groaned, then whirled on his heels and continued with a contemptuous twist. He pivoted, then stopped and stared at Jovan.

"What's going on here?" he asked bitterly.

Jovan shrugged and gave a callous look. "I dunno. I'm still trying to figure out why a gang of DEA agents was following us around from the get go."

Agent Dent waved his finger as he approached Jovan. "I think I've got a good enough idea of what went down and where our misstep took place," he said, grinding his teeth. He leaned in close to Jovan. "We tailed the wrong two vehicles, didn't we?" he asked grimly.

The men eyed one another. "If that's what you feel, then who am I to say otherwise?" Jovan said, his tone frosty.

"Well, Mr. ..." Agent Dent grinned drily and produced Jovan's driver's license. "What's this say? Umm ... Jovan Rising?" He held the card at eye level. "You and your partner there, uh, Mr. Ray Leon, you two wannabe big shots ..." Agent Dent paused, eyeing Jovan with a look of disgust. "If y'all boys break wind the wrong way, we gonna be on y'all ass so fast and hard you won't know what hit you. We know you dirty. All we gotta do is catch that ass. So it will behoove you to get the hell out of our city!"

Jovan watched the agent steadily. They couldn't do a damn thing to either him or Ray; that was a fact. They were both clean as a whistle. Thanks to the system Dutchy Hans had in place. You paid for your product at one place, then traveled clear across town to another destination to complete the transaction. No large amount of cash or any amount of a controlled substance was found in either of their possession.

Jovan responded with a hearty chuckle. "Man, you a funny-ass dude." He cracked up and bounced off the hood. "Anybody ever tell you how funny you are? Take it from me, you're in the wrong line of work." He snickered and flashed a crooked grin.

Acting out of sheer compulsiveness, Agent Dent sprang into attack mode and shoved Jovan against the hood. The little man was surprisingly strong for his size.

"Oh, shit!" another officer yelled.

Other agents jumped up, surprised, and converged on the pair as they scuffled.

"Yeah, you son of a bitch!" Agent Dent said, his voice cracking in the heat of struggle. "Am I funny now? Do I look like a fucking joke?" He was flustered, fighting against his men and the suspect, trying to get his hands around Jovan's neck.

With some maneuvering and quick thinking, Jovan rolled out of Dent's clutches. He immediately started laughing and taunting the angry man.

"Funny muthafucka you are," he said, standing out of harm's way. "Can't help but to laugh at your little ass!" Jovan snickered and flipped him off.

"Let go of me!" Dent wailed. "That son of a bitch don't know who I am! But I got his bad ass! Yeah, I got your number, buddy, and you are fucked!"

A young agent stepped between the two men, grabbed Jovan and forced him backward. "Look, man, cut the bullshit." His voice was firm. "You and your man, y'all in the clear, so you need to get out of here before something else jumps off."

The words he spoke seemed to register with Jovan. He scanned the area for Ray, who had just stepped out the van.

"You good, champ? Everything all right?" asked Jovan, surveying the scene.

Ray turned and gave an odd look over his shoulder. "Yeah, J, I'm good. Let's get the fuck outta here. These muthafuckas are crazy!"

Jovan wheeled around and headed for his ride. He noticed the angry little agent glaring his way. He hesitated at the passenger side door before pulling it open, then sneered at the agent, matching his look with scorn before climbing in the behind wheel. Inside, Jovan pressed the keyless ignition. He let out a deep sigh of relief when the engine came to life.

Jovan and Ray rolled out, leaving the DEA task force agents to linger and ponder their misstep.

Jovan and Ray knew they weren't out of the woods yet. Not with the Feds sniffing at their heels. They had to make sure they were on point at all times. One slip up, one fumble and their ass would be handed to them on a platter. In the drug game there was an unwritten rule of thumb that hovered at the back of every mans' mind: The Feds weren't to be fucked with, Point Blank!

Chapter 5

Later on that evening, as night settled over the city, the dark landscape floated outside the BMW window as the X-5 cruised along the road. The beautiful Malaysia looked perfect behind the wheel, driving the quiet countryside. She relished the tranquility; the calmness helped soothe her chronic anxiety.

Suddenly, Malaysia saw Ray's Potomac mansion come into view. The palatial structure glowed brilliantly in the dark distance. With her sights set on a clear destination now, thoughts of seeing Jovan made her heart flutter excitedly. His handsome face floated through her mind, spurring the Thai model to move with a little more haste. She pushed the pedal to the floor and the sleek ride roared along the narrow strip of country road like a missile.

The first floor of the mansion was empty except for the two college cuties hanging out in the spacious kitchen. They were seated at the dark granite island whispering and giggling and trading shots of Patron.

Wale's "That Way" resonated from the lower level of the pool house:

> *I don't recollect your name*
> *Let me tell you that those heels*
> *Really complement your frame*

The atmosphere inside the pool house was sexy and mellow. Outside, fifteen half-naked honeys wearing skimpy thong bikinis and stilettos pranced around the pool and danced and lounged on cream-colored sofas half -naked.

Ray, donning a plum-colored smoking jacket, was comfortable in his usual spot on one of the sofas by the pool. A trio of attractive honeys—one dark chocolate, one caramel, one vanilla—kept him company. If his boys didn't know any better, they would swear their man was trying to imitate that bamma Prince.

Over in the far corner, on the opposite side of the pool, the twins Dank and Psycho were bunned up. The twins' taste in women was identical, just like them. Each man had a pretty cocoa-brown doll baby cradled under one arm and a cute snow bunny under the other.

Biggie's massive frame sat on the poolside sofa adjacent to the twins, a broad smile plastered across his face. He had this pixie-faced rump shaker doing the snake in front of him. Her body was so vicious it was obvious the thick little number had danced her way into many a man's lewd dreams.

Biggie's partner Dude was probably the happiest of the crew. Because of his chronic acne problem, he wasn't used to partying with such beautiful women. Dude was used to freaking the neighborhood rats. The fact that he was actually being groped and seduced by a pair of nasty Columbian bombshells was crazy. Dude felt like he was on top of the world! His tall, lanky, nappy-headed tail was moving and grooving on the floor with the ladies.

Damn, life was never this good! I owe you one, God, Dude thought.

Suddenly, the French doors to the adjacent room swung open. Jovan emerged, grinning like Chester Cheetah, cloaked in a gold terry-cloth Gucci robe. He tied his belt as he walked across the room, a look of pure satisfaction on his face.

Two gorgeous honey-toned Puerto Rican mamacitas strutted behind him. The salacious duo had curves for days and firm, perky breasts. Their hard nipples protruded through their sheer white bikinis. Just the sight of the hot Latina pair could give a man an instant hard-on.

"Ay, J!" Ray yelled abruptly, sporting a cheesy grin, his fist held high. "You lookin' good, my man, real good!" he said with a fake Hispanic accent.

Jovan nodded with a smug look and mimicked the accent when he replied, "Ay, Ray! I'm feeling good too, my dude, feeling real good!" His head started bobbing in rhythm to the music. He was feeling it—the music, the cognac and the triple-stack ecstasy.

Jovan took off his robe and let it fall to his feet. His black Armani boxer briefs was all that he wore.

Every woman in the room couldn't help but stare. The brother had a chiseled physique with an enormous, eye-popping bulge that seemed on the verge of bursting through his underwear at any moment.

Jovan started doing this lewd dance. The women seemed to let out a collective sigh as they watched in delight, hoping and waiting for his unbelievable organ to be released.

Then, without warning, the action surrounding him seemed to pause. All eyes shifted to the entranceway directly behind him.

Jovan immediately sensed another presence enter the room. He looked at Ray and was startled by the apprehensive look on his face.

He spun around. When he saw Malaysia and the leer she was giving him, Jovan could swear he felt the ground move under his feet. He looked shocked.

Malaysia was fighting for control when she asked in a disgusted tone, "What's your problem, baby? What is it? You need something? Attention? Affection? What? Why are you performing a damn striptease in front of all these horny-ass bitches?" She was furious. Her piercing gaze swept the crowd of half-naked women. The glock holstered beneath her cherry-colored suede suit jacket flashed in her mind. It took every ounce of willpower not to whip out her pistol and let off a couple rounds.

Jovan shook his head and laughed at the accusation while slipping on his robe.

"Baby girl, it's nothing like what you talking about. I'm just having a little fun, that's all. Come on over here and give your man a hug." He spread his arms and flashed his award-winning smile.

He quickly ran through the greeting process, excused himself from the crowd and escorted his angry girlfriend upstairs. He rushed her into a private bedroom, closed the door and stripped.

"Here. Is this what you want?" Jovan grabbed hold of his meat. "You come busting up in here like you own this. What the fuck is your problem? Huh?" He spoke in a hushed tone, gritting his teeth.

"I wish you would," Malaysia protested defiantly, waving her hand. "Don't even try that reverse psychology on me. That's an insult!" she said, walking across the plush pomegranate-colored carpet. She gave Jovan a frigid stare when she passed him.

Jovan glared at her, but he could see her rage was mounting, so he cautioned himself to be cool.

Malaysia stood across the room, the winter moon filtering in through the floor-to-ceiling windows, dancing in her long, silky hair. She looked out at the sprawling landscape.

"Hey, precious," Jovan said, breaking the uncomfortable silence. He attempted to change the subject before sparks really started to fly. "How did you know I was out this way?"

Uncertainty flashed in her emerald gaze. Turning away from the window, Malaysia shrugged and said nothing, apparently unwilling to give him an answer.

She swayed toward Jovan and brushed against him provocatively on her way to secure the door. Then she slapped him viciously across the face.

Instinctively, he drew his hand back to backhand her but caught himself at the last second when she grinned, taking the sting out of her assault.

"Bitch! Have you lost your fucking mind?" he lashed out.

A wild sensation overcame Malaysia, and she quickly took off her suit jacket and tossed it aside. "I don't know what the hell it is about you." She threw her arm around his neck and smashed her lips into his. Five seconds later, Malaysia pulled away and said in a breathless tone, "But I will blow this muthafucka off if you break our covenant."

The unexpected feel of cold steel pressed against his groin rattled him.

"What-the-fuck!" Jovan looked down. When he saw the gun aimed at his dick, his eyes bulged. "What's up? What the fuck are you doing?" he demanded. "Huh? What?

You gonna shoot my joint off? You don't wanna do that!" His reflexes had sharpened. Without thinking, he snatched the burner from her hand and grabbed her by the neck. He pushed her up against the wall with one hand while holding the gun at her head with the other.

"Are you outta your fucking mind?!? Huh, girl?" he scolded vehemently.

A faint smile crossed Malaysia's lips. She provocatively slid her hand between his legs and began stroking his penis.

"C'mon, baby, wouldn't you rather make love than war?" she whispered in his ear.

Jovan scratched his head, looking perplexed. "I don't know what kind of games you're used to playing or what kind of bammas you're used to fucking with, but you need to get it straight in your head: I ain't to be fucked with," he said. The cadence in his voice grew fierce.

Suddenly Malaysia drew a short breath and conceded, "Oooh, yeah ... looks like your thang is ready for me." She winked and dropped to her knees.

"But I thought ..." Jovan hesitated, then closed his eyes and exhaled. "Oh my God," he said. He was savoring the sensation of her delicate mouth devouring his male organ. "Goddamn you!" He shuddered as the feeling of euphoria swept through his body.

Chapter 6

DC homicide detectives and CSI agents converged on a swath of wooded land behind the Fort Totten Metro station in NE, DC.

The sound of wind whistled through the wooded brush, rustling the cold, dry landscape as the thick forest of birch trees swayed. Their bare branches trembled under the windy assault.

Yellow crime-scene tape stretched the length of the park. Groups of detectives and CSI agents outfitted in light-blue translucent suits were busy poking, prodding and scrutinizing the wooded terrain in search of evidence.

Detective Clark nodded tiredly as he walked over to the edge of a hill. As he gazed at the wooded valley below he almost lost his footing.

"Whoa there, buddy!" Louis said, helping his partner regain his balance. "You okay?"

The valley below him seemed to spin. Clark, now alert, gripped his partner's wrist and stepped away from the edge. He squinted at the dimly lit distance below.

Nestled at the base of the valley was a small utility shed.

"Who discovered the body?" asked Clark.

"One of those, uh, CSX train workers," Louis answered, eyeing his partner closely. "You are aware that this here is the dump site, right?"

"There's only one set of prints around the site where the body was found." A CSI agent interrupted politely.

Clark spun on his heels. "The CSX worker, no doubt," he stated flatly.

The agent agreed. "That's who discovered the body and made the call." He paused and motioned to a young boy walking his dog. "The kid over there says he spotted one of those Dodge Magnums rolling out of the park with its lights out a couple of nights ago."

The duo turned to one another. "What's the kid's name?" Louis inquired. Clark was already making a beeline to intercept the young witness.

"The owner of the Mag was doin' the damn thing, know-what-I'm-sayin'?!" The frail, curly-haired teenager had spunk. He was extremely animated as he recalled the events with amazing detail. "Them dudes had the whip wet! I mean that joint was wet-n-rollin' on Lebrons!"

Clark chuckled to himself—the quizzical expression on his partner's face tickled him.

"Okay, let's get this straight," he said, clapping his hands. "What you're saying is the Dodge was clean and had a nice set of rims, right?" He knew the kid's hip street lingo had Louis lost in translation.

The teenager rolled his eyes. "Man, that joint was rollin' on Lebrons, rose-gold 23's, wet black, limo tinted up, bangin'-ass sound system and a tight-ass rose-gold grill! Man, I ain't never seen a Mag that raw. Ever!"

Louis's and Clark's brows shot up in surprise. "Rose-gold grill? Is that what you said? Are you sure about that?" Clark didn't want to get his hopes up too high, but the kid seemed sure of his description.

"Man, I know what I saw," he retorted smartly. "That's my new dream car, dawg. Here—take a look at it." He whipped out his cell phone.

The kid had a picture of the black Dodge Magnum with the rose-gold grill and rims as his screen saver. He had taken an amazing picture of the car as it rolled by under a bright streetlamp.

The Dynamic Duo was overjoyed. They wanted to hoist the kid on their shoulders and parade him around the neighborhood.

Clark motioned to the CSI agent. They needed the photo downloaded immediately.

"Thank God for the creation of camera phones, " Clark sighed.

Chapter 7

72 hours later ...

It was early evening in the city. A gray overcast finally gave way to sunshine.

> *My gun dirty, my brick clean*
> *I'm ridin' dirty, my dick clean*
> *She talk dirty, but her mouth clean*
> *Bitch, I'm MC Hammer*
> *I'm about cream*

Rick Ross' "MC Hammer" boomed from the interior of the glossy black Dodge Magnum with the rose-gold grill and rims. The car was rockin'-n-rollin' in rhythm to the beat, swerving from lane to lane, balling down 16th Street. The car roared past the entrance of the Carter Baron Amphitheater, almost mowing down two young ladies. The pair managed to sprint to safety as the speeding automobile went thundering by.

Dank and Psycho were cruising the city without a care. A thick cloud of weed smoke saturated the air inside the car's cockpit. The twins were puffing on thick Dutch Master cigars stuffed with the crucial Purple Haze and downing glasses of straight Patron.

"Psycho, you wanna see what's jumpin' off at that pussy joint over in Adams Morgan?" asked Dank, gripping the wheel with his left hand while toking on the blunt with his right.

Psycho gazed at his brother. His red-tinted irises gave him an eerie look. "You know I'm down for that, D," he shrugged, taking a long, hard pull on the blunt. "Nigga, if pussy involved, I'm there," he said as he held his breath, his voice tight.

Dank drained the Patron from his glass. "Oh, yeah!" he roared energetically. "That's what I'm talkin' 'bout. Say no more 'cause we gonna be knee deep in pussy by the time you finish that smoke," he stated, flipping his dark Aviator shades down over his eyes.

The Magnum lurched forward, zipping through a red traffic signal. Up ahead, at the intersection of 16th Street and Columbia Road, the car made a hard right turn and raced around a lane of slower-moving vehicles.

The Dynamic Duo was on the prowl, trolling through the streets of DC with a purpose. The steel gray Crown Victoria cruised along the 14th Street corridor. Clark noticed the mounting traffic jam up ahead. The sedan slowed at the corner of 14th and Chaplin and bust a right turn onto a steep, hilly incline.

At the top of the hill, a crew of block hustlers mingled in the middle of the street. Two lookouts spotted the Crown Vic rolling up the hill.

"Get low! Busters on the block!" The warning echoed up and down Chaplin, and the crew dispersed immediately, resembling a throng of roaches scattering hit with a bright light.

"Check out the lames," Clark grumbled sourly, then mashed the accelerator. He grinned crookedly as he drove by the paranoid bunch of drug dealers. He nodded and winked at a couple when he caught them looking his way.

"They're lucky we got bigger fish to fry than dealing with their petty, pedaling asses."

Louis asked suddenly, "You don't think it would do any good to rough a couple of their feathers? See what kind of information we might get?"

Clark shook his head. "I'm not in the mood to deal with any petty hustlers today, Rich," he admitted with a smirk.

The Crown Vic continued to the end of Chaplin, where Malcolm X Park appeared. The lush green landscape expanded for a couple of blocks in both directions. The sedan stopped. Clark could turn left or right. He decided to go right.

Proceeding along the edge of the park, Clark made a left at the far end of Malcolm X and rode along the east edge of the park, bust another left on 16th Street, rode another fifty yards and turned right on the narrow block of Kalarama Road.

Clark navigated the side streets in an attempt to avoid the growing rush-hour traffic, but he knew eventually his luck would run out with the side streets. What he yearned for now was a fresh cup of hot coffee and what better time to take a coffee break than rush hour.

The Crown Vic reemerged at the corner of Champlain Street and Columbia Road, the heart of multicultural Adams Morgan.

"You know it's my coffee break time, Rich," Clark said casually, checking himself out in the rearview mirror. He made sure that his stylish London Fog hat sat atop his clean-shaven head just right. "We gonna stop down at that nice coffee house on 18th Street since we're right around the corner."

Louis jumped suddenly, like someone had went upside his head. "Oh, shit! Tell me what I'm seeing is real!"

Clark was startled. "What? What'cha talkin' abo—" His voice trailed off mid-sentence. Clark snatched his shades off and peered through the windshield with utter disbelief in his eyes.

Dank was blowing smoke in the air when he noticed the red and blue lights flickering in his rearview mirror.

"Aww, shit!" He tossed the blunt out the window. "Ain't this a bitch!" he spat, pissed. "Toss the smoke, Psycho, we got bustas on our ass!"

Psycho frowned. "What?" He looked in the side-view mirror. "What the fuck are they fucking with us for? We ain't breaking any traffic laws." He hit his blunt two more times before tossing it.

"You right," Dank answered, his voice dry and harsh. "So what the fuck are they pulling us over for, huh?" The twins faced each other, their jaw muscles twitching violently.

"Let's play this shit by ear first, alright?" Psycho spoke up, his gaze wild and unstable. "Might be some traffic shit, know-what-I'm-sayin'?"

Dank was hyperventilating. "Alright. That's a bet. As long as they talking traffic shit. Other than that, we gotta scratch 'em."

"Without a doubt," Psycho agreed, gritting his teeth.

A bullhorn sounded abruptly. "Turn your car engine off, and place both your hands out the window! Do it now!"

Clark stood with the driver's door open, talking into the bullhorn. Louis emerged from the passenger side with his service weapon drawn. He looked potent with his gun trained on the suspects' vehicle. Both men were unconsciously holding their breaths. They despised tinted windows, but the tint on the Dodge was particularly troubling. Its highly illegal limo tint made it virtually impossible to get a handle on what was happening inside the car.

Dank shook his head vigorously. "Bets off, champ," he growled, fumbling beneath his seat. "This ain't no fuckin' traffic stop!"

His brother nodded. "That's a bet. Let's scratch these bammas!"

The sound of automatic gunfire erupted inside the Magnum. Bullets exploded from the dark rear windshield as an army fatigued–clad Dank leaped from behind the wheel, letting fire spit from the M-5 submachine gun.

The surprise attack caught Louis and Clark totally off guard. Both detectives dove for cover. Clark's heavy frame slammed across the front seat, just as a wave of bullets tore into the Crown Vic's windshield. He clenched his eyes shut as shards of glass sprayed him in the face. "Fuck me," Clark breathed, frantically searching the floor for his weapon as bullets exploded all around him.

Louis dashed between two parked cars just as bullets exploded behind him. "Clark! You okay? Are you hit?" he asked crouching between the cars for cover.

"I don't think so," Clark grumbled, staring at his partner. "Don't worry about me," he barked, cocking his gun. "Get those scum bags!"

"Call for backup! I'm on 'em!" Louis took a deep breath. He could feel his pulse surge as he gripped his pistol. He popped up and started blasting.

The twins scrambled back into the car. Dank glanced back, then floored it. The Magnum peeled out, smashing into cars, forcing them to make way.

Fuming, Clark bolted to his feet. He was thoroughly amused to see the suspects attempt to flee in their car with a tight traffic jam blocking their path. He felt a wry pleasure inside as he and his partner locked eyes.

"Let's get these sons of bitches!" The duo took off running down the hill with guns at the ready.

The Magnum's wheels were burning rubber, struggling to push a path through a virtual wall of metal.

Psycho looked back over his shoulder. A shiver of panic swept through him when he saw the two detectives running toward them. He flung open the passenger's door, leaned out and sprayed his M-5 recklessly.

A cacophony of tear-filled shrieks and screams emanated from the violent fracas as pedestrians caught in the midst of the deadly running gun battle dove for cover, attempting to stay out of harm's way.

Louis and Clark both ducked for cover and returned fire.

"C'mon, D! Them bammas on our ass! Let's bounce!" Psycho said frantically.

Dank laughed mockingly. "Fuck 'em!" he snapped. "You just keep 'em off my ass while I get us outta here!" he said mashing the gas, the car's wheels spinning in place.

Psycho caught a hint of something in his brother's expression. He watched him curiously until his concentration was broken by the sound of bullets whizzing by his head. Psycho dove hard on the ground and rolled, returning fire as he moved.

"Dank! Dank! Get the fuck outta there, now!" he cried out. But his brother wouldn't listen. It was as if he were in another mindset.

Dank watched the two detectives in the rearview as they approached cautiously from behind.

Yeah, this my time to shine, he said silently. Dank looked possessed as he clutched the submachine gun. Foaming at the mouth, he leaped out of the car in a blind rage and opened fire. His angry bark was indecipherable as he took the full blast to the chest. Dank was instantly cut down by the Dynamic Duo's swift barrage of gunfire.

Dank's body slumped over the door, then crumbled to the street in front of a terrified rush-hour crowd of onlookers.

Chapter 8

A cool night seemed to bring a measure of calm to the area after a hectic day. Beauty strutted across the moonlit hospital parking lot with a peppy bounce in her step. She stood outside of her plum-colored Navigator, fished inside her brown Louis Vuitton purse and let out a small sigh of relief when she found her car keys. Beauty didn't waste any time. She quickly peeled off her pink scrub top and climbed in her vehicle.

She could breathe easier now that her workday was finally over. She snatched off the pink scrunchie holding her hair in place. Beauty's long blonde mane cascaded below her shoulders, outlining her pretty red face in a soft gold frame of bone-straight hair.

Ever since the fiery explosion in the employee section of the garage, Beauty made a conscious effort to park her ride outside in the parking lot. She'd rather take her chances with the elements of nature than some wacko and his home-grown terrorism.

The purple SUV coasted to a crawl as Beauty guided the Navigator toward the exit. She yielded to oncoming traffic. While she waited for traffic to clear, she retrieved her BlackBerry and quickly skimmed through her new e-mails.

A sudden knock on the window startled her. Beauty jumped away from the window, and her BlackBerry slipped through her fingers. She stared for a minute at the honey-blonde woman standing outside her window like she had a serious mental problem.

Beauty cracked the window. "Yes? May I help you with something?" she asked with a cautious look.

"Go 'head, girl," Natasha chimed with a sly smile. "I know you not getting brand new on a bitch now!"

"Angel?" she said, uncertain. She hesitated. "Girl, is that you?" she asked, frowning warily.

Natasha was amused. She grinned as she twirled her blonde locks around her finger. "What, you forgot about me already? Honey, you know you ain't right."

Puzzled, Beauty unlocked the passenger's door for her. "Girl, what are your doing out here at the hospital at this time of night?" she inquired with a curious eye, watching her lover's wife slide in next to her. Beauty couldn't see it coming, but a violent storm had just invaded her life.

"This time of night?" Natasha let out a sigh. "Honey, it's not late. Matter of fact, it's not even nine o'clock yet. What you mean late?" She winked. "In my book it's still early."

Beauty wasn't sure what she wanted, but she gathered from her friendly disposition that she was still in the dark about her and Jovan. So what did she want? More importantly, where in the hell had she come from? That was the million-dollar question.

"You know I didn't recognize you right away. I thought you were some stranger trying to bum a ride. Girl, I was about to floor it on your ass," she admitted. *What's up with the honey-blonde wig, blue contacts and skin-lightening make-up? She's so light, she almost looks like a white girl,* she said to herself. She wondered what the disguise was for.

She didn't let on to her true feelings, which told her to high tail it out of there the moment she realized Jovan's wife was standing outside her window.

Beauty let out an ominous sigh, and said, "It's nice to see you again, Angel. Looks like you've made a very speedy and marvelous recovery. I take it that you haven't had any problems, no, uh, reoccurring ailments or anything from the accident?"

Natasha shook her head.

"Well, that's good to hear," Beauty lied. "You looking all hot and sassy with that honey blonde. Where you on your way to?" she probed tactfully.

"Oh, nowhere in particular." A mischievous twinkle flashed in her eye. "I just happened to be in the area and thought I'd stop by and say hi."

Beauty wasn't buying that. *What's her angle?* "Well, that was very nice of you to think of me," she replied politely. "Maybe you could give me a call next time and you and I could go have a drink somewhere." She felt anxious all of a sudden, like she needed to be out of this woman's presence.

Natasha turned to Beauty. "Beauty," she huffed, "now come on, honey. You know damn well you're not doing anything else tonight but taking your ass home. So there's nothing stopping you from joining me for a little drinky-drink right this minute." She patted Beauty on the thigh.

Beauty rolled her eyes. "But I really do need—"

Natasha raised her hand, cutting her off. "I don't want to hear it, honey." Her expression was adamant. "We can go to a bar right down the road. Besides, I'm treating tonight." She smiled.

It was obvious to Beauty that saying no wasn't an option. She figured, *Oh, what the hell. A couple of free drinks, then I'll be rid of her ass for good. What harm would that do? Might as well since she acting so pressed.*

Beauty made a solemn promise to herself: *If Angel gives me one smidgen of suspicion that she knows anything about the relationship between her husband and me, I'm outta of there faster than she can bat an eye. She'll be catching a cab back to her car ... wherever that may be.*

"So which bar are we going to for drinks?" Natasha asked with a twisted grin.

The purple Navigator drove south along Wisconsin Avenue. The SUV sped past a Saks Fifth Avenue department store on the left just before crossing the city limits into DC.

"Oh, shit!" Natasha cursed. "I dropped my damn keys." She leaned over and started fumbling around at her feet and under the passenger's seat. "They must've slipped in the back because I can't seem to find them up here." She unfastened the seat belt and crawled in the backseat. "Here they are," she whispered, more so to herself.

"Well, you found them right on time," Beauty responded, glancing to her left. "We're here," she announced, sounding relieved. The bright neon sign that said "Zodiac" seemed to beckon her.

Fifty yards beyond the bar, there was a dark, narrow one-way street, Cedar Place. Beauty didn't waste any time getting there. Her foot fanned the accelerator anxiously when she noticed a break in traffic. She whipped the wheel hard to the left and stomped the gas pedal.

Coasting along Cedar Place, she could feel her muscles start relaxing. She searched for an empty parking space. She spotted one on the left under a thick elm tree. In no time, Beauty pulled the rolling hunk of metal over, gave the wheel a couple twists and turns and her ride was parked.

She snatched her brown LV bag off the floor, pulled out her Bobby Brown lip gloss and applied a fresh coat, instantly making her lips moist and enticing. She glanced over her shoulder and sighed.

"Well, you ready to get going, Angel?" She flashed a plastic smile. "You know I can't be hanging out too late."

"And why the fuck not?" Natasha scowled, a look of total disgust etched in her face. "What else you got going on tonight? You got a hot date? Need to run off and fuck some other woman's husband? Is that it, you freak-ass-bitch?!"

Beauty froze. *OMG! This bitch was playing me all along!*

"Fuck you!" she scoffed and twisted in her seat. "Evidently, the bitch you're referring to isn't doing what she supposed to be doing at home to please her man. Otherwise he wouldn't need to find pleasure in another woman's pussy, now would he?" Beauty tossed her a snide look, but her expression was a false indicator of how she really felt. She wanted out of there so badly. Beauty was ready to abandon her own vehicle just to get away from this crazy-ass woman.

Natasha gave Beauty a noxious look. Her gaze was deadly, psychotic. "You nasty-ass slut!" she growled in a sinister tone. "Bitches like you don't deserve life!"

Beauty looked up in the rearview mirror. She was terrified and astonished when she caught the flash of a blade twirling in Natasha's hand.

OMG! the voice in the back of her mind screamed. *I knew I should've left this bitch at the hospital!*

"It's unfortunate for you that you chose the wrong woman's husband to fuck!" Natasha said, lunging from the backseat. She threw her arms around Beauty's neck.

A horrified shudder shot through Beauty's core. "Lord, help me!" she cried as a sharp, burning pain tore through her neck.

"You fucking slut!" Natasha snarled in her ear, raising the blade in the air. "No more fucking for you!" She brought the blade down with a powerful swing, plunging the twelve-inch serrated steel deep in Beauty's jugular. "Yeah, that's it honey," she groaned sadistically as she watched the dark crimson goo spew from the gash in her throat, splashing the front dashboard and windshield.

The moment seemed surreal. Beauty's mind refused to comprehend the travesty unfolding upon her. *This crazy bitch is killing me!* Her mind struggled to accept the reality of death as her life slowly began to slip away. Beauty continued to put up as much of a fight as she could to save herself, but the woman's strength was incredible, and she had already injured her gravely.

Beauty was pinned to the seat. She could feel the dark force of death coming for her. Slowly, death engulfed her soul. *Oh, Jesus, please ... I take you as my Lord and savior!!!* With her last dying breath, Beauty tried to save her soul.

Chapter 9

It was early morning in the Nation's Capital. An overnight ice storm had blanketed the city with a thin layer of ice, putting a damper on the morning commute as Washingtonians ventured out across the slippery urban landscape.

DC Homicide and CSI teams swarmed into the Friendship Heights neighborhood. They quickly roped off the entire block of Cedar Place as teams of agents scoured the vicinity for evidence. The scene was becoming an all too common sight on the streets of Washington.

News crews from every station in the DMV were posted at either end of Cedar Place, hungry for any tidbit of information pertaining to the grisly murder spree.

The elusive serial predator was the top story on every local newscast and covered the front page of all local newspapers. The mounting murder count and the sadistic manner in which the murders were carried out, along with the crafty evasiveness of the infamous serial killer, made for sensational news. Washingtonians were captivated by the continuing bloody saga that held the entire region in its hellish grasp.

An intensely poignant look covered the face of Tony Woo as he emerged from inside the purple Navigator. He gazed the length of the block, his eyes focused on the massive influx of news crews gathered along Wisconsin Avenue.

A young CSI tech donning a navy windbreaker with the hood pulled snugly over his head was moving along the slick pavement like he had some serious business to settle. He was flipping pages on a small notepad, skimming his material.

"Excuse me, sir," he began, his voice brimming with confidence and fortitude. "From what I've gathered so far from my interviews with the three employees at Zodiac, our victim here never made the trip inside. The doorman swears that she never stepped foot inside their establishment."

Tony Woo nodded. He sighed and said, "I sort of felt that would be the case." He pulled his specks off his face. The cold drizzle felt good on his skin as he watched the energetic young tech and shook his head. There was an obvious cloud of discontent and uncertainty hovering in Tony's eyes. He paused pressed his palms together and took a deep breath.

"You know, Tommy, this is the very first time in my career that I feel at a total lost," Woo admitted with a woeful gaze. He went on, "I actually feel hurt and sorrow for that young lady lying in there. It pains me, Tommy. She was so young, so innocent. She never got a chance to really experience what her life could've been." He hesitated and rested a hand on Tommy's shoulder. Woo added with a look of disgust, "Look at all those hungry-ass vultures standing around down there. They don't give a rat's ass about the victim or her family as long as they get a nice juicy story to report!"

Tommy nodded his head toward Woo. "I understand your grief, sir. I really do, but—"

Woo cut in. "Do you really understand?" he grumbled, squeezing Tommy's shoulder. "She didn't deserve that, Tommy! He gutted her like a hunter guts his kill!

What are we dealing with here? He's worse than a monster, Tommy! What we're looking for can't be human. It can't be!"

Tony Woo's eyes fluttered suddenly, and his knees buckled under him. Before either man could react, he collapsed, taking a knee on the icy cold pavement.

"Sir! Are you okay?" Tommy looked surprised as he dropped his notepad and helped his supervisor to his feet.

Out of nowhere the Dynamic Duo appeared.

"Is that Tony?" Clark asked. "Hey there, fella. Are you okay?" He offered his assistance, but Woo quickly waved him off.

Without uttering a word, Louis rushed to Tony's aid. He grabbed his free arm, and wrapped it around his waist. He and Tommy made sure that Woo was steady on his feet.

"What's going on here?" Louis questioned with obvious concern. "Did you slip and fall on the ice, Tony?"

The CSI supervisor's usually sturdy bearing was absent. That in itself struck Louis as odd. The detective sensed instantly the uncharacteristic chink in Tony's armor. The unstable nature he was exhibiting was not the man Louis had come to know and respect. Something deeply disturbing had to have touched the man for him to have regressed to such a point.

Louis and Tommy walked him over to one of the paramedics working the crime scene.

"Lord have mercy!" Clark muttered when he looked inside the SUV. The sight of the carnage outraged him. "He's a sick, demented scumbag! To do something that twisted … Somebody, somewhere has to give us something more to go on so that we can take this sick fucker off the streets!" The frustration on his face was intense.

"What does it look like in there, Bill?" Louis asked, moving into position as he prepared to examine the kill zone. He recoiled, clenching his eyes tightly. "Son of a bitch!" Louis cursed as the horrible sight caused him to gag. He suddenly felt the sensation of asphyxia overcome him. His equilibrium faltered. Louis staggered backwards, bent over and grabbed his thighs to steady himself. He forced himself to breathe. His stomach was balled into a tight knot. Detective Louis allowed every able-bodied person within earshot to know just how he truly felt about the destruction of the woman's body lying disemboweled inside her purple Navigator.

A ferocious wail of heartfelt grief erupted from deep inside the detective. Rich Louis broke down emotionally. He suffered a fit of hysteria on the spot.

Chapter 10

The pitch darkness inside the room was absolute. Jovan could sense the physical world invading his thoughts. He also felt something evil resonating within the interior of the room. There was something ungodly moving in the darkness with him.

Taking a deep breath, Jovan forged deeper into the black abyss. With each step, he felt his confidence waiver.

Then he felt it---something brushed up against him. He hesitated briefly, shivering with fear. He pretended not to feel anything, but as he pushed on, the feeling of trepidation was growing with every step he took.

A soft whisper drifted in the air. Seconds after hearing the voice, a bright beam sifted through the darkness. Out of nowhere, a creepy shadow appeared in the doorway. Jovan froze, his eyes riveted to the dark form slowly floating towards him.

Jovan shuddered when he recognized his new boo, Beauty, coming his way. She seemed to be pulling something from her torso. Jovan strained to see what it was she was twirling in her hands.

Suddenly, Beauty was upon him. The dire look on her face was unnerving. She paused, leaned over and breathed heavily in his ear. "I hate you!!!" she spewed. Her outrage was crystal clear. "Look what your Angel has done to me!" she hissed hatefully.

Jovan looked down. "Oh my God!!!" he shrieked, the blood drained from his face as if he had just seen a ghost. Beauty's hands were drenched in blood up to her elbows. She was twisting and pulling on a mangled, bloody mess:

her intestines! The gory bundle dangled from her exposed torso in a ghastly display. The horrible sight made Jovan gag. He stumbled backward, looking vexed. His head started pounding as the room swayed beneath his feet.

Beauty was sputtering something unintelligible, her mouth twisting grotesquely.

"I hate you! For what you feared, you've created. Your wife is your demon! Your wife is your death!!!" she said.

Beauty's cryptic tirade echoed in his head over and over.

Jovan's eyes popped open. He shivered when he looked up and found Angel hovering over him. She was gazing at him with a deadpan look on her face, as if she were in some kind of trance.

Suddenly, the shimmer of steel caught his eye. Jovan shook his head violently, bolted off the sofa and blared, "Angel! What the fuck are you doing?!? Standing over me with a goddamn knife in your hand?! What the fuck's up, huh?" His tense facial expression was filled with worry and fear.

The sound of Jovan's voice roused Angel from her trance. She shot him a lackadaisical look as she emerged from a confused state. She gazed at her husband, her brow crinkled deeply. She watched his face gradually come into focus. The knife slipped from Angel's fingers and tumbled to the carpet, landing beside her foot.

"What?" she jeered. "What are you complaining about now?"

He looked incredulous. "Complaining?" Jovan mocked drily. He bent down and scooped the knife off the floor. "This what I'm talking about right here!" He held the steak knife in front of her face. "Why were you standing over me with this in your hand, huh?"

Angel gave a noncommittal shrug. "I don't know. I was looking for something to eat." She blew him off, walked in the kitchen and opened the refrigerator door.

Jovan rushed in the kitchen behind her and slammed the refrigerator door shut.

Angel glared at him like he was crazy. "What's your problem? Have you lost your damn mind?"

Frustration seized his face. "Have I lost my mind?" he retorted, grinding his teeth. "Ain't you the fucking pot calling the kettle black!" He looked over and tossed the knife in the sink, then folded his arms across his chest. With a condescending leer, he inquired casually, "Tell me something—when was the last time you seen that nurse broad ... umm ... what's her name?"

"What damn nurse?" Angel smirked.

Sucking his teeth, Jovan eyed her shrewdly. "You know what nurse I'm talking about. The one that released you from the hospital."

The question struck a nerve. Angel propped her hands on her hips and tilted her head to the side. "You got the fucking nerve to ask me about that hot-in-the-ass-blonde-headed skank?!" Indignation hung from her face like a heavy burden.

"Hold the fuck up!" Jovan's expression was tight and grim. "You need to pump your fucking brakes! I asked you one simple goddamn question. All it deserves is one simple goddamn answer! Nothing more. So stay in your fuckin' lane, a'ight?"

"Stay in my lane?!" Angel sneered, matching the fervor in his voice. "Muthafucka, you got the nerve to ask me about some hussy that I believe either fucked my husband or wants to fuck his dirty-dick ass!" Suddenly, Angel had a virtual meltdown right on the spot. She gave Jovan a tongue lashing that made his head spin. By the time she was finished with him, Jovan was utterly speechless. All he could do was drop his head in defeat and roll out.

Angel's hellfire tirade followed him out into the hallway as he bounded up the stairs. He wanted away from his wife. At the moment he didn't know what to think or say. The ghastly dream continued to replay over and over in his mind. Beauty's ominous declaration resonated in his thoughts and weighed heavy on his mind. Jovan was torn, conflicted and confused.

This is a need to know situation if ever there was one. Is Beauty dead or alive? That was his immediate concern. Jovan feared the worst—his pretty young sex partner was probably dead.

Why did she come to me in my dream? Did Beauty's ghost come to warn me about my wife? Damn, her words sounded so crazy! "Your wife is your demon. Your wife is your death!" Those exact words continued to haunt his mind.

"Oh, God," Jovan shuddered. "This some spooky-ass shit!" he said to himself while preparing to leave.

Chapter 11

Friday night ...

There was a full moon shimmering in the midnight sky above our Nation's Capital. It was a couple minutes after midnight. Over in NE, DC, one block south of New York Avenue, on Okie Street, a profusion of glitz and glamour clogged the roadway and sidewalks outside of Love, Washington's ultra-hip nightclub.

A colorful envoy of stretch limousines lined Okie Street. Each vehicle waited patiently in line for its turn to pull up to the VIP entrance and unload its flamboyant passengers.

A raspberry-colored stretch Hummer limousine with glistening chrome rims pulled up. It stopped at the VIP access entrance. A chauffeur dressed in all black hopped out, strode around to the rear passenger cabin and opened the door for his group of flashy ballers.

Jovan and Ray were first to emerge into the spotlight. The dapper pair was a picture of power and wealth. Their navy suede Valentino suits were the perfect backdrop for their iced Jesus pieces. The diamonds sparkled brilliantly against the expensive fabric.

The men each slipped on a pair of platinum Valentino shades, then led the way through the VIP entrance. They strode up the red carpet exuding power and confidence, matching one another step for step.

Trailing close on their heels was their potent killer squad. Psycho was the top dawg of the hit squad now, filling the void his brother's untimely death had left. Next in line was Dude, then Biggie. A new addition to the crew had just been sanctioned by the team. He was a bona fide hardcore gangsta who went by the name Nutso. He was a mountain-size gangsta, standing 6'10". He was bald, and his head was tattooed—a virtual Birdman lookalike. His resume was stamped in blood. Nutso was lethal, a thoroughbred killer.

Love was ultra-swanky. The décor had flair, panache. Four elegant levels of unadulterated entertainment for the trendy up and coming, the movers and shakers, ballers and high rollers.

The crew headed straight for the VIP lounge. At the velvet rope, a heavyset Nigerian wearing a crisp gray Christian Dior suit was manning the entrance. His name was Dobie. He was a longtime friend of the two bosses.

A broad, welcoming grin broke out on Dobie's shiny dark face when he recognized the flashy pair approaching.

"My friends," Dobie said pleasantly, extending his hand. "I'm so glad you've joined us tonight." He unlatched the velvet rope and waved the men inside. "Any special accommodations you gentlemen need, I'm here to serve you."

The crew rolled up in the lounge and carved out their own private enclave. It didn't take them long before they were in their comfort zone, popping bottles of Cristal and Ace of Spade like they had just won a championship.

The boss men, Jovan and Ray, looked like predators on the hunt. Their eyes prowled the floor for fresh meat.

Over by the bar, a small group of ladies had piqued Jovan's interest. There was one in particular amongst the group that caught his eye. Her name was Eujami, E for short. She was a stunning Ethiopian goddess. Sexy. Exotic. Chocolaty. Luscious and busty beyond belief.

Eujami was the spitting image of the hot new supermodel Imani. She had soft, brown, captivating eyes and long, silky jet-black hair that fell to the small of her back.

With a playful elbow to Jovan's rib, Ray muttered, "I can see you got your sights locked and loaded on something over there at the bar, huh, playa?"

Ray was sizing up the potential prospects gathering around the bar too. He licked his lips, excitement swimming in his eyes.

"Mmmm ...tasty bun-buns just waiting to be plucked and fucked," he voiced bluntly.

Without taking his eyes off his intended target, Jovan shook his head. His expression was smug, his voice conclusive when he said, "Yeah, some pretty-ass pussy that I'm getting ready to add to my stable, ya dig?"

Ray was intrigued. He leaned over, grinning. "Is that a fact? So which bun-bun do you have in mind? You gonna add her to your personal stable or the party stable? What'cha gonna do with her?" A deceptive glimmer flashed in Ray's eyes.

Jovan's gaze flickered as he leaned back and gave his partner a skeptical look. *That's odd. What kind of question was that to ask,* he thought.

"What I'm gonna do with her? What you wanna know that for?" Jovan shot back smartly. "Baby boy," he snickered, "you know what women are to me—something pretty, some ass and some pussy. Nothing but meat for male consumption. Nigga, you already know my flow." Jovan's witty remark put a big cheesy grin on Ray's face. He turned his attention back toward the bar and the hot looking Ethiopian honey wearing a body-hugging ivory Gucci dress and matching boots.

Jovan heaved his suede-suited frame off the sofa, looked down at Ray and said flatly, "I got business to take care of. You gonna assist me in closing this deal or what?" He peered over his Valentino frames, waiting for a reply.

Ray bounced up, still grinning. "Meat for male consumption, huh? I'm feeling that," he admitted, taking a sip of champagne. "Hope you don't mind, playa, but I'ma have to steal that one from you and add that to my playbook."

Stroking his chin with a thoughtful gaze, Jovan turned and said, "Well, in that case, I suggest you take out a pen and pad. A pussy-gettin' nigga like me gots plenty more shit for your playbook," he boasted while primping himself. "C'mon champ," Jovan motioned, stepping off, "let's go handle this pussy."

A buzz of excitement emanated from the group of women watching the flashy pair approach the bar. Jovan and Ray walked directly over to where the women were seated, and casually staked their claim.

Jovan took a seat at the bar next to Eujami, a deliberate move on his part. A shrewd, cunning look materialized on his face as he sat listening to the Ethiopian beauty and her friends whisper and cackle amongst themselves.

He smiled and laughed inside. It was quite clear to him that he and Ray were the topic of the ladies' conversation. The ladies quickly confirmed his thoughts with a number of admiring looks and smiles, beckoning for the men's attention.

"Excuse me, ladies," Ray began, "but, uh, what's the special occasion tonight? If you don't mind me asking."

"Special occasion?" an Indian shorty quipped. "What makes you think this is a special occasion?"

That was Jovan's cue. He smoothly inserted himself into the conversation. His hand rose in the air, attracting all eyes to the dazzling show of rocks glistening on his wrist and fingers.

"Allow me to clarify what my man here is trying to say," Jovan said charmingly, making eye contact with the chocolate bombshell. *Whoa! h*e sighed inwardly. Her beauty thrilled his manhood. "What he meant was that it has to be a special occasion for so many lovely, beautiful ladies like yourselves to be gathered in one setting." The beautiful Eujami was openly eyeing him with interest.

Eujami felt that the handsome, sharply dressed man was talking directly to her. Her heart started doing backflips when she heard his velvety-smooth voice speak to her.

Jovan could feel the chemistry between them building. He fought back the smile that was about to explode across his face when he noticed the swooning, spellbound look in Eujami's pretty brown eyes.

Jovan leaned into Eujami's ear. Her sweet Chloe Love fragrance excited him. "We've got our own private party going on over there," he said, gesturing toward their semi-private area.

"Why don't you come chill with me for a little while, have a few glasses of champagne, get acquainted with one another." He paused briefly for effect, taking a purposeful whiff of her hair and neck. Jovan added, "I can tell that you like the finer things in life. That alone makes us a perfect match."

Eujami felt his charm was irresistible. His aura was smooth, thuggish and raw—totally intoxicating! She suddenly felt her loins bubbling between her legs.

Eujami held her breath and gazed into his eyes. She exhaled, then asked coyly, "Is there something special going on over there that I should know about?" When she finished, Eujami tried to contain herself, but she failed. A warm, inviting smile spread across her pretty brown face.

Oh, okay, baby girl wants to play a little hardball, Jovan quickly surmised. *She doesn't want to come off as being too easy. Well, I can respect that ... as long as I'm bangin' that back out tonight,* he voiced silently with a devilish grin.

Jovan took his index finger and lightly traced the back of Eujami's hand, ascending her wrist and arm with a feathery touch. Immediately he felt her shudder.

"You and I are what's gonna make it special," Jovan said coolly, his voice trailing off as he took her by the hand. Eujami couldn't help herself. She blessed him with a smile that was infectious, and he knew she was putty in his hands. "So c'mon, baby, I'm gonna show you the time of your life tonight."

You could tell by the gleam in her eyes Eujami was love struck, utterly captivated and intrigued by Jovan's persona. He was a top-flight nigga and he knew it, her kind of man. She could definitely see herself with this man for the long haul. She was dreaming.

The hit squad looked on gleefully when the bosses returned with a gang of grade-A pussy.

"Hey, where's Dude?" asked Ray, scanning the area.

"Huh?" Biggie, the oversized brute, looked dumbfounded. "Oh, that bamma yaked up off the Henney, running around here somewhere."

"Well, ladies, you all make your selves comfy. This here is all ours," Jovan announced with a wave of his hand. "So drink until you're content, chill and get acquainted with the fellas." He stopped short and focused on Eujami. She just finished applying her M.A.C lipstick. Her lips were scarlet ribbons, and she was breathtakingly beautiful. Jovan swore he felt himself melt on the spot.

Share my world, don't you leave, promise I'll be here
Whenever you need me near
Share my world, don't you leave, promise I'll be here
So baby don't you have no fear

Soulful songstress Mary J. Blige's heartfelt ballad, "Share My World," created a hot, sensual atmosphere all across the floor.

Jovan was chilling, bunned-up with Eujami, who snuggled tightly at his side. Together the two of them made for a very cute couple.

"You know you want this," Jovan boasted, arrogance billowing in his voice. "Them bammas you fuck with is ash. Baby, I'm a rich lotion."

Eujami giggled like a love-struck adolescent under his spell. His confident swagger had her insides doing cartwheels.

"I can tell life with you is just full of surprises," she said, grinning sheepishly. "Not a dull day on the calendar, I bet."

Jovan chuckled lightly, running his hand through her long silky hair. "Hey, my motto is to live every day to the fullest, like there's no tomorrow." He hesitated. "Is there anything wrong with that? Let me know 'cause I've come to realize that there's only two types of people in my life: lovers and haters. So, huh, what category should I file you under?" He watched Eujami's eyes climb slowly toward his. Her warm gaze billowed affectionately when their eyes met.

Could he actually be the one? Eujami wondered. "Live your life how you see fit; it's your life." She gazed at him dreamily.

"Hold up," he said, placing his finger to her lips. "You didn't answer my other question."

"Check this out, girl!" her best friend Olivia said, interrupting their conversation. With excited glee jumping off her face, she showed off a chunky iced-out bracelet glistening on her wrist. The expensive bauble was a gift from Ray—that was how he marked his territory. Olivia was his piece of ass for the next month, maybe longer.

Jovan glared at Olivia with heat in his eyes. She was fucking up his vibe with E, and he was hot!

Springing to his feet, Jovan looked down at E. With a forced smile, he mumbled, "I'll be back." He whirled on his heels and strode briskly across the lounge.

Both women could feel the heat radiating in his wake. They stared after him, looking baffled. "Oooh, girl! He's a testy one," Olivia commented, then got back to admiring the ice on her wrist.

"He might be," Eujami responded, standing. She took her friend by the wrist. "Remember girl, they're only men. We hold the key, we have the power." With Eujami's declaration, both women shared a moment of light laughter.

After freshening up in the restroom, Jovan stepped into the hallway. He was busy with his BlackBerry, flipping through the numerous e-mails, all courtesy of Malaysia.

Damn! What in the hell has gotten into her? he wondered. *She's starting to get out of hand, and I'd hate to let that pretty piece of ass go. That would hurt my fucking manhood,* he confessed.

"What's going on now? Are you too good, or is it you're too busy to return my calls? Which one is it?" Malaysia asked in a disgusted tone.

The sound of her voice made the hairs on the back of Jovan's neck stand at attention. He looked up and the jubilation on his face shattered when he caught sight of his Thai girlfriend glaring his way.

She was standing in the hall looking like a high-class model in her gold Chanel suit, her arms folded across chest. She was waiting for an answer.

Jovan felt uncertain how to explain. Then another thought occurred to him. Befuddled, he asked, "How in the hell did you know I was down here at Love?"

Malaysia's BlackBerry rang. She huffed, then snatched the device out of her gold Chanel bag. After reading the message, she slammed the BlackBerry down in her bag.

"Is everything alright, baby?" Jovan asked. He could see the discord in her demeanor. He wasn't sure if it was the message she had just received that was causing her bad mood or if had she witnessed his actions in the VIP.

She smiled and applied another coat of lipstick, putting on a big charade. "Well, I've got an emergency that requires my immediate attention," she said calmly. "When I finish, I'd like to spend some time with you tonight. So I would appreciate when I call you if you show me some respect by answering my call." Malaysia paused and fumbled around in her bag. She caught Jovan off guard when she looked up and said offhanded, "What, your Versace wife not around, so whoever is around, you better put 'em in check and answer my call."

Malaysia was shrewd. She slipped her gold-framed Chanels over her eyes, slung her bag over her shoulder, walked up to Jovan and gently palmed his face.

"Think about what I said, love," she whispered before planting a wet, juicy kiss on his mouth. "Show a measure of control. Please don't disappoint me." She spun around and disappeared into the crowd.

The last words she spoke lingered in the air, and Jovan knew he better take heed to the look Malaysia gave him.

A moment later, Jovan stepped inside the VIP area. He looked around with a sneer, like something was wrong. He walked over, pulled Ray to the side and told him about the run-in with his girlfriend. They both decided it would be best to round up the group and take the party out to Potomac.

Jovan addressed the crowd, explaining to the women their plan to move the party to a more exclusive and intimate location. The ladies were more than happy when they were told they would be driven in a limo to a flossy crib in Potomac.

Eujami slid around the table, rushed over to Jovan's side, giddy and full of excitement. She wrapped her arms around his waist, smiling up at him.

"Wherever you wanna go, whatever you wanna do, I'm down for it!" When she spoke, there was a hint of a slur in her tone. Eujami held him tightly, resting her head against his chest.

Jovan glanced down at her with a seedy grin singed on his lips. He placed a light kiss on her forehead. "Welcome to the good life, baby. I'm gonna show you how true ballers play, and tonight I'm gonna make you a star."

Outside on Okie Street, traffic jams consumed the late-night hours. Parking attendants and ushers served as traffic guides on both sides of the street, directing vehicles to and from the curb as they picked up their awaiting parties.

The club's owner, Marc Jakes, stood on the red carpet just beyond the club's wide staircase. He was a friendly, charismatic man. At 6'4", Marc, dressed in a tailor-made suit, hovered above the fray, watching the flashy sea of patrons spill out onto the street.

At the top of the red-cloaked staircase, Jovan and Ray emerged through the glass doors. Marc recognized the pair immediately. He turned to the closest parking attendant and waved him over.

Jovan, Ray and Marc exchanged a few pleasantries while waiting for their limousine to arrive.

The stretched Hummer rolled to a stop in front of the group, and the chauffeur, Dave, alighted from the vehicle. He walked around and opened the rear cabin door, delighted to see the sexy throng of shortys accompanying his party. By the expression on Dave's face, you would've thought he was gonna get a piece of ass.

64

Dave was extra attentive to Olivia as he helped the ladies into the limo. She was the last of the women to make her way inside. Dave beamed, admiring her shapely rear end. He was startled when suddenly, out of the blue, he was accosted from behind.

A task force of homicide detectives materialized from the crowd. The suits grabbed hold of Dave, pushed the limo door shut and surrounded the group.

"Everybody, chill! Let's not cause a scene. We need to speak with Mr. Angelo Whimple. Now!" Detective Clark voiced, his sharp authoritative bark echoing in the air.

Hearing his government name announced out loud like that made Psycho cringe. He instinctively took two steps back and made a half-hearted attempt to slip off into the crowd. But he was immediately pounced on by two dark-suited detectives.

"Hold your horses there, buddy," said a wide-body agent, putting a crushing bear hug on the suspect as he tried to escape. "I guess this is our guy. Hey, buddy, we got some questions that we need you to answer downtown," the detective advised him, then rustled the suspect through the crowd of anxious onlookers.

Jovan removed his shades. He looked nervous. His piercing gaze swept the face of each detective. He took mental snapshots of each man's face.

Louis noticed the unscrupulous look in Jovan's eye. The look set off warning bells in his head.

"You got something you need to get off your chest, buddy?" The detective stood eye to eye with the man, their intense glares locked in a heated face fight, neither man giving an inch.

"Don't let these folks play you out of position, playa," Jovan heard Ray say just before he felt his arm on his shoulder. "That's what they want you to do so they can haul your ass down to Central Cell for the night."

With a curt snicker flying from his lips, Jovan shot the detective a look like he was insignificant.

"Yeah, you right, baby boy." Jovan eyed the man from head to toe. He replied, "I look too good to be going that route tonight with these bammas."

Detective Clark cut in. "Need some assistance, Rich? Are these boys giving you any problems?" Clark and Ray exchanged fleeting glances. Louis and Jovan were too busy face fighting to notice the silent exchange.

Louis nodded, looking harsh. "Yeah, this one here," he began with a tight smirk. "I think he might be suffering from a bad case of that Superman disease."

Clark chuckled lightly. "C'mon, Rich." He patted him on the back in an attempt to downplay the situation. "I doubt that either of these boys wants any parts of you—or me for that matter. We got who we came to get, so let's get ready to move out. Y'all boys continue on as you were." Clark stood waiting for his partner. It was obvious to him that Louis had it in for the other guy. He made a mental note to address the subject later.

The crew stood by helplessly watching the task force cuff Psycho and stuff him in the back of a dark Crown Victoria sedan. Then the officers disappeared just as quickly as they appeared. Red and blue lights flashed silently in the sedans' grills and windshields as the cars maneuvered through the thick mass of traffic lining Okie Street.

"C'mon, J," Ray voiced urgently. "Let's get the fuck outta here, playa! We got some regrouping and planning to do, ASAP!"

That was some fucked-up, embarrassing-ass shit! Jovan thought. He was trying to save face. *For that shit to go down in front of Love was fucked up!* His eyes swept over the crowd with a fierce look. He could hear the buzzing in the air.

"What?!? What the fuck y'all looking at?!?" He lashed out at strangers, boiling with outrage.

"C'mon, big dawg," Nutso's deep baritone billowed over the clamoring. His massive hand rested on Jovan's shoulder. "Let's blow this scene. What, you forgot? We got company waiting on us."

The jolly expression on big Nutso's face helped to ease the growing rage that was eating Jovan up inside. The thought of smashing Eujami helped him get over what had just happened.

The crew piled inside the Hummer to the relief of the anxiously awaiting groupies.

Dave the chauffeur was more anxious than anyone. He wanted out of there, and fast wasn't fast enough for him.

Chapter 12

Soft rays of tinted moonlight sliced through the darkness inside of Jovan's newly adopted love den. He and Eujami were nude, lying atop bronze-colored satin sheets, embracing and touching one another in anticipation of their sexual nexus.

Eujami's soft purring sent exciting tingles racing into Jovan's groin as he placed his hands on her skin. The tips of his fingers lightly traced the subtle contours of her skin, sending excited ripples through her entire body. She felt like fireworks were going off inside.

She loved the way Jovan's hard, chiseled frame felt, rubbing against her as she slowly explored his anatomy with her probing fingers. Eujami's tightly clinched eyes shot up when she gripped his engorged penis.

She glanced down, stunned. "Oh, my goodness!" she gulped with her eyes staring widely. She was fascinated by the enormity of his maleness, standing at attention like a massive flagpole.

Jovan grinned triumphantly. "You like what you see?" he asked while stroking her hair. A sense of calmness surged inside of him, and he attributed that to the easygoing aura of his new friend.

Eujami nodded, looking very impressed. "I think you might be a bit too much for me to handle," she whispered, spellbound.

"Aww, c'mon now," he voiced in a mellow tone. "You can't possibly know that until you've tried, now can you?" His hand eased down between her legs. Slowly and delicately, he began to massage her clitoris. "What did I tell you earlier?" he whispered in a husky tone, watching her eyelids close.

Eujami was enjoying the sensation of his fingers on her love spot. Sensual moans floated off her lips as she squirmed under his touch.

When Jovan climbed on top of her and parted her legs, Eujami felt a rush of euphoria sweep over her and her eyelids began to flutter.

"I told you I was gonna make you a star tonight," Jovan spoke softly as he hovered above her watching her facial expressions bloom.

Eujami swallowed hard when she felt the head of his penis force its way between her lips, like a fist invading her love canal. She winced, clutching at his back, feeling the pressure build inside. She began to shiver uncontrollably as the breath left her body. Eujami's eyes rolled back in her head, and she shuddered and stuttered all in one breath, practically speaking in tongues.

For a moment, Eujami was entirely devoid of thought, her senses succumbing to erotic body-numbing orgasms.

Soon after rocking E's world, Jovan sauntered into the pool house looking carefree, clad in his favorite bathrobe and slippers. He hesitated when he caught a glimpse of himself in the gold-framed mirror just beyond the pool's edge. He looked so satisfied when he stared himself in the eye. He winked, then walked over to a vacant lounge sofa and flopped across it. All eyes were on him, and he loved it.

Ray, Dude, Biggie and Nutso were gathered pool side with a thick cloud of smoke drifting in their vicinity. The men passed around thick blunts of Hydro and downed shots of straight Goose. A couple of ladies were sitting on the edge of the pool with their feet dangling in the water.

Nutso extended his arm in Jovan's direction. "Here ya go, big dawg," He grinned, "I know you wanna hit this crucial."

Jovan paused for a split second, then sighed and hopped off the sofa. The girls playing footsy in the water smiled and waved to him. Jovan winked and blew them a kiss.

Ain't nobody break them off yet?" he inquired, sizing up the two shortys. "What's going on? Y'all know we got a reputation to keep." He smiled as he puffed on the blunt.

"We all taking a break, just like you," Ray said in defense, taking a gulp from his glass. "Shit, you here now, Mandingo, you can handle that too."

The sound of Ray's iPhone interrupted the exchange. Rick Ross and Lil Wayne's "I'm Not A Star" blared from his robe pocket.

"Unknown" flashed on the screen. Ray cringed. "Yeah, who this?" he said, sounding annoyed. His hand went up to silence the group as soon as he realized who was calling.

"Man, these bitches trying to set me up, Ray!" Psycho said, trying to stay cool. "They saying me and my brother was running around town slumpin' broads! You know that ain't us. Man, get the lawyer on top of this shit, and get me outta here!"

Ray looked apprehensive. When he spoke, his voice was deceptive. "Dawg, I got a call that this shit's gonna be on the fucking news and in *The Washington Post*! What the fuck's going on? You ain't know them folks were on you like that? C'mon, man, keep it real with a nigga!" Ray glared across the room, emotionless.

A loud exhale emanated from Ray's cell. "Ray!" There was obvious pain in Psycho's voice. "We ain't got nothing to do with this shit! Slaying women? You know me better than that! This shit is bogus! Straight bullshit!"

Ray groaned. "Soldier, I don't know what to think." He paced the edge of the pool, looking tense. "I gotta big-ass question mark stamped across my fucking forehead right now. First, I had to deal with this Mike shit. Now I gotta deal with you and your brother's hot-ass shit! Where you think all this shit y'all dumb asses getting into is flowing, huh? Lemme tell you—right to my ass! In a minute, all that hot-ass shit y'all doing is gonna blow up in my face, and I'm gonna be the one paying the price for y'all's fuck up!" He stopped in front of the mirror and stared at himself. "I worked too hard to get where I am, and I can't let y'all bammas bring me down." Ray shook his head. His eyes narrowed as he vaguely recalled an earlier conversation with his nemesis Detective Clark.

"I had your back and saved your ass when your ass needed saving," Clark said, sounding high-strung and full of himself. "The time has come. I need you to reciprocate some of that love over this way. Somebody out of your crew gonna have to bite the bullet. My job and my reputation is on the line. I need a fall guy to pin these serial murders on, just for the time being."

Ray was speechless. Give up one of my folks on a serial-murder beef? That shit sounded unreal.

"You can't be serious, B," Ray answered reluctantly. "That shit wouldn't hold water. Somebody would see right through that shit!"

His fears were instantly confirmed. "Let me worry about that. It's like this—you wanna roll like a big dawg, then you gotta pay like a big dawg." Clark's voice was steely. "You can either give us one of your boys' asses to serve up, or we can take a nice chunk out of yours. You make the call." A loud, haughty laugh resonated over the line just before it went dead in his ear.

The last words Detective Clark spoke hung like a dark cloud.

Ray took a deep breath, then said, "I'm sorry, baby boy, but you gonna have to bite the bullet on this one. Just hold strong, soldier, you'll be alright." There was no questioning the doom in his words.

He slumped, put away the cell, and turned to the crew with a look of discontent.

Jovan immediately figured something wasn't right. "So what's going on, champ? Psycho good? When he getting out?"

"I'm not sure when he'll be getting out," Ray replied with a withering look. "I gotta touch bases with this attorney tomorrow. He'll let me know something."

Jovan sensed deceit coming from Ray. He regarded him with a sideways stare as he walked over to rejoin the group.

Ray glanced up, looking uncertain and then immediately concerned. "What's the deal, J? Something on your mind?" Weed smoke spewed from Ray's nostrils while he held Jovan with a cold stare.

Dude turned around on the sofa. His acne-riddled face looked confused. Then Biggie burst out laughing next to him for no apparent reason.

"What's a party without the music!" yelled Nutso from the adjoining room. You could hear him shuffling around inside, trying to figure out how to operate the sound equipment.

Jay-Z's "Big Pimpin" suddenly filled the pool house. The live, energetic beat instantly dispelled any unsettled vibe swirling in the room. The men happily began bobbing their heads and pumping their fists in the air to the hard bass beat. It wasn't long before they melded into a rambunctious chorus, rapping verbatim along with the song.

The rowdy choir's musical antics drifted beyond the confines of the pool house. Outside, in the cold, dark night, at the top of the glazed concrete driveway along Lake Potomac Drive, Malaysia's dark SUV was hidden in the shadows.

Leaning on the steering wheel, she peered through a set of powerful infrared binoculars, surveying the mansion and its occupants from the roadside.

Malaysia's night goggles were riveted on the second-floor bedroom window. She had her sights set on a nude woman sitting on the edge of the bed talking on her cell phone in the dark. She instantly recognized her as the same woman who had her paws all over Jovan earlier in the club.

Well, love, will you be paying her another visit before the night is through? Malaysia wondered. *I warned your ass.* She seethed silently at the wheel.

Chapter 13

In DC...

A silver CTS bent the corner at Riggs and South Dakota so hard the tires screeched. Jo Jo clutched the wheel, swerved from lane to lane and dipped around vehicles with reckless disregard.

Jolly laughter filled the Cadillac's cockpit. Angel giggled merrily in the passenger's seat, her right hand glued to a bottle of Hennessy Paradise.

Their girlfriend Ronnie, a nail care specialist in Jo Jo's salon, was laughing in the seat behind Angel. Ronnie was from SE. She was a cute, high-yellow honey with a perfect Halley Berry hairdo and a hellified body that resembled the super video vixen Maliah.

Their heavyset home girl Nina sat next to Ronnie laughing so hard she had tears in her eye. She was a natural at finding the funny side in any situation.

The sleek Caddy veered to the left suddenly and whipped into a strip mall parking lot. The car sped through the entire lot. At the far end, Jo Jo snatched the wheel hard to the right, slipped in the vacant slot directly in front of her shop and stopped on a dime two inches from the curb.

"Goddamn, bitch!" Angel said, giggling. "Who the hell you think you are, Speed Racer?"

Nina added with a boisterous roar, "Naw, that bitch too black to be Speed Racer! She's Racer X ho, Black Trixie!" The entire car erupted in laughter.

Jo Jo slid the key in the dead bolt on the salon's door Muffled voices and laughter briefly seeped through the glass door before it opened. The light from outside spilled across the black tiled floor as light laughter followed the intoxicated group of women inside the hair salon.

Nina pushed passed her girlfriends. "Can y'all move y'all fat asses!" she urged. "I have to go!" She rushed around the black marble reception counter and flung open the glossy pink restroom door with such force it was a miracle the door didn't come off its hinges. "Ooooh, shoot!" she said. She exhaled a loud sigh of relief that resonated throughout the shop.

The trio proceeded into the main salon area. Jo Jo turned on the lights while Ronnie stepped inside the break room. She found some cola and ice in the refrigerator, a perfect chaser for their cognac.

Angel was being nosey, checking out the empty stations. The different photographs decorating the stations piqued her interest.

"Damn, who's ugly, fat child is this?" she laughed jokingly and held up a picture of someone's overweight 5-year-old boy.

Jo Jo slung her curly tresses back and tossed Angel a scolding glare. "Girl, you know that ain't right," she scoffed as she slipped off her black full mink and flung it over the back of the chair at her station. "Here, lemme hang up your chinchilla before you melt."

Angel snickered, then put back the photo just the way she found it. She shrugged the grayish-blue fur off her shoulders, imitating a striptease routine. "You like don't you, blackness?" She puckered her moist, silvery-coated lips in a playful sneer and winked.

Jo Jo understood that Angel liked feeling pretty and irresistible all the time, so she played along by taking a step back. She placed her hands on her hip and gave Angel a hard, scrutinizing leer.

"Yeah, bitch, you're just flawless in every way conceivable. If I had a dick, I'd slam your phat ass over the counter and fuck you every which way but loose!" They both cracked up laughing at each other.

It didn't take the ladies long to settle down with a nice, strong cognac while they sat around chatting about everything and nothing.

Angel got upset with Nina when she asked about Jovan's job title. Anyone close to Angel knew that her husband's profession was a sensitive subject that was better left alone.

"My man and my man's business affairs is none of your concern!" Angel said, shooting Nina a look. "So keep his name out of your mouth and off your mind. You need to learn how to keep a damn man!" she retorted in a nasty tone. "Don't be worrying about other bitches' men. That's your goddamn problem!"

"Girl, I think you need to pump your damn brakes," Nina hissed, looking serious, "and come down off your high horse. I don't know who you think you're talking to like that, but I ain't the one!" She hesitated, then added, "I ain't no bamma-bitch like Tina!" The moment she said Tina's name she regretted it.

Jo Jo was in the mirror combing her hair when she heard Nina mention Tina. She instantly became worried.

"Nina!" Jo Jo scolded. "That shit ain't right, and I'm not gonna let you sit here and bad mouth my best friend. God rest her soul." She looked skyward and mouthed a silent prayer before continuing. "That's blasphemy, and I'm not gonna allow that in my presence!"

Nina back peddled. "Yeah, I know I shouldn't have gone there, but Angel be tripping sometimes with her prissy, high-and-mighty ass." She looked over at Angel, rolled her eyes and turned her nose up.

Mentioning Tina triggered a torrent of painful memories for Angel. Her eyes suddenly rolled back, like she were possessed. Her body grew rigid, as if she were on the verge of having an epileptic seizure.

Suddenly an explosion of heartfelt emotions erupted from Angel. Painful sobs rocked her body. Then, out of nowhere, she exploded into a heated tirade.

The women sat motionless, gawking, flabbergasted. Was Angel experiencing an emotional breakdown?

Jo Jo hopped up looking worried. She rushed over to Angel's side.

"Tina didn't deserve what happened to her! That was some foul shit!" Angel voiced scathingly with a twisted sneer perched on her lips.

"Look at me, Angel!" Jo Jo demanded, palming her face with both hands so they were eye to eye. "What in the hell is your problem? Don't you know we've all been devastated by Tina's death. But the way you're carrying on, this isn't helping anyone, especially not Tina. Yes, she isn't with us anymore, but she's in a better place. You know that."

Out of nowhere, horrible images of Tina's death flashed in Angel's head. She could see the terrified look on Tina's face a split second before the sharp edge of a blade plunged deep into the base of her neck.

Startled by the horrible vision, Angel jerked away from Jo Jo. "Get off me!" she shrieked. The image in her head seemed so real. Angel bent forward, rubbing her head in frustration as tears clouded her eyes.

Suddenly, the sight of a blood-soaked blade reeled across her mind. She could see a thick crimson flow of lava gushing from the deep gash in Tina's throat as she lay naked on the kitchen floor. The blood-soaked blade seemed to drift directly in front of Angel's eyes, and then it disappeared. In its wake, a sadistic voice echoed in her head: "Whore! Bitches like you don't deserve life!" The blade floated into view and hovered menacingly, in a state of suspended animation. Angel jumped when the blade suddenly swooped down and plunged deep in Tina's throat, slashing her from ear to ear. The grotesque scene played out in Angel's mind like a real-life horror flick. She shrieked in agony and buried her face in her hands.

It took Angel a few minutes, but she was finally able to clear her mind. When she opened her eyes, she realized she was bent over with her face cradled in her hands. Slowly, she gripped the arms of the chair and sat up straight.

She was surprised to see her girls all staring at her like something was wrong.

"What's going on?" Angel asked. "Why y'all looking at me like that?"

Ronnie was holding her hand over her mouth while shaking her head in disbelief. She flopped in her seat and pulled her hand away.

"Who's the whore you were screaming about, Angel?" she asked with a cautious look.

A confused and flustered expression flashed on Angel's face.

Nina hesitated, glaring at Angel with wide eyes. "What the fuck was that shit all about?!?" she said, baffled.

Jo Jo's brow creased with worry. "Angel," she whispered carefully, "you were screaming some crazy-ass shit, girl. You said 'whores and bitches like you don't deserve life.'" She paused, before adding, "You mean to tell me you don't recall saying any of that?"

Angel thought deeply for a moment, and then her mood turned progressively dark. She huffed, feeling her spirit overcome with frustration.

Without warning she sprang to her feet. "I need to get outta here. I need some air." She threw her chinchilla around her and rushed toward the door.

Jo Jo, Ronnie and Nina watched as she made a hasty departure from the room. The women looked at one another, totally perplexed by the bizarre episode.

"Damn," Nina voiced sullenly. "Our girl is losing it!"

Chapter 14

Two days later ...

Jovan stood along the Washington Tidal Basin, gazing across the Potomac River, lost in thought and enjoying constant stream of commercial planes departing and landing at Reagan National Airport.

When he was a kid, his father would bring him to Haines Point, and they would enjoy quality time together, fishing, eating crabs, cooking out and watching the nonstop parade of planes until the sun set.

As Jovan got older, he learned his way to the park on his own. This was where he found his solace when times got hard or he needed to clear his mind.

At the moment, the cover story splashed across the front page of a week-old *Washington Post* newspaper was troubling him. The front page read:

Vicious Slaying in Friendship Heights
Congressman Laruix's Daughter Found Mutilated
Another   Victim   of   DC's   Serial   Predator?

There was a photo of Beauty. The caption read: *Daughter of Congressman Demitri Laruix found slain. The body of Beauty Laruix, a 24-year-old graduate of Howard University's nursing program, was found early yesterday morning.*

Jovan couldn't stop thinking about the dream he had. He couldn't get the frightening image of Beauty or her cryptic words out of his head: "Your wife is your demon. Your wife is your death." Disturbed, he pushed away from the safety railing and began walking toward his car.

Jovan stood outside his Mercedes-Benz truck and removed his jacket. He threw the Claude Montana jacket on top of newspaper on the passenger's seat and climbed behind the wheel. Concerned and slightly puzzled, Jovan huffed, then pressed the ignition button.

The growing tide of uncertainty was gnawing away at his conscience. He wanted answers, he needed answers. The uncertainty was killing him.

Jovan peered up at the rearview mirror. "What the fuck is going on with the women in my life?" he wondered aloud. He hesitated, took a deep breath and sat up straight. "I know what I gotta do," he conceded, seemingly drawing strength from himself the more he spoke. "Fuck beating around the bush anymore. I need straight answers. Point blank." His facial expression was firm.

He leaned slightly to the left and peered in his side mirror. *All clear*, he thought. With no hesitation, the black SUV eased away from the curb, caught the open lane and powered forward.

The evening rush hour was in full gridlock, and Jovan was smack dab in the middle of it, attempting to navigate downtown DC. While silently brewing in the gridlock, Jovan felt his BlackBerry vibrating on his hip and welcomed the distraction.

He took a quick peek at the screen. *Malaysia. Damn, she never did call me after the club.* The thought just occurred to him when he realized he hadn't spoken to her since that night in Love. *Well, baby girl probably still tripping over the scene at the club,* he told himself. *That's alright. One dose of this bomb-diggity and she'll catch amnesia. She'll love me like nothing ever happened,* he boasted smugly, then blew a kiss to a cute cinnamon honey pushing a hot pink Range Rover in the next lane.

Jovan casually activated the hands-free Bluetooth connected to his ear. "What up, precious?" he answered coolly. "You must've read my mind 'cause I'll be damned if I wasn't just about to call you," he lied. "As a matter of fact, I was just thinking to myself, saying 'Damn, what happened the other night?' You never called me after you left the club, and that's not like you, baby. You usually prompt with yours, like clockwork." He bit down on his bottom lip to keep from laughing.

"I know, love," Malaysia breathed easily, "but my work that night had gotten way out of hand. The scene was a lot more complicated than we had anticipated. By the time I was finished surveying the crime scene it was much too late, so I called it a night," she said sweetly.

Malaysia's ultra-easy demeanor didn't go unnoticed by Jovan. He was prepared for some backlash, expecting it even. But his Thai girlfriend's mild-mannered behavior threw him for a loop. *I guess she's finally catching on to the program,* he admitted silently. *Go with the flow and everything will be sweet and easy.*

"It was too late, so you called it a night?" he repeated, sounding doubtful. He was turning her words over in his mind. "That's strange for you," he said skeptically. "No matter how late it is, you usually hit my up anyway."

Self-absorbed, examining her French manicure, Malaysia said, "You're right, I can't dispute that. But you can't dispute the fact that I was under immense pressure that night. By the time I finished working the scene, I was totally drained. I know you understand, knowing the line of work I'm involved with. Besides, I know you and your friends had a ball partying and singing and only God knows what else you were doing. I'm sure you had your fun, right?" Her tone was laced with a twinge of deceit.

Jovan could sense something wasn't right. He nodded unsteadily, looking ahead into the distance. "Umm … yeah, I was good, but I would've been a lot better if I would've gotten a call from you." He tried to disguise the doubt in his voice but failed terribly.

Malaysia looked up from her nails. A sly grin touched her lips when she realized Jovan was fishing. *Isn't he the pot calling the kettle black,* she thought.

"If I called," she began before stopping herself. "Well, I'm calling now. So what are you doing, love? Are you too busy to, uh, stop by my house and spend some much-needed time with your precious baby? We have some making up to do, and I've got an itch that's burning for you to scratch." The naughty innuendo was crystal clear.

Jovan flipped his wrist to check the time on his diamond-faced DiBur. "Get that body into something silky and sexy for me," he ordered with a cheesy grin. "I'm on my way as we speak, so be ready."

Malaysia set the phone on the computer table next to the monitor. She was silent for several seconds watching the detailed street map of DC glowing on her computer screen. Moving at a snail's pace, deep in the heart of downtown DC, at the intersection of Constitution Avenue and 7th Street, blinked a tiny white dot.

"That's it ... come to me, " she whispered, peering at the screen. "I can't wait to see how you like the special surprise I got for you."

Chapter 15

Meanwhile ...

Louis and Clark entered Tony Woo's office in the Homicide Division Command Center at DC Police Headquarters. Clark was holding a manila folder in his hand, sporting a pompous overconfident look.

"Tony. Just the man we've been looking for," Clark said easily. "We got something that I'm sure is gonna put a great big Kool-Aid smile on your tight ass." He tossed the folder on Tony's desk.

Without moving, Tony peered over his wired frames and eyed Clark's naked head. He took the folder off his desk and started skimming through the contents. He handed the folder back to Clark. His expression was bland. He was unimpressed.

Tapping the side of his wired frames, Tony muttered, "Angelo Whimple?" He kicked back in his chair. "So he's the serial predator we've been searching high and low for all this time, huh?" He regarded both men with suspicion. "This your suspect? A young drug-dealing thug? Where's the evidence connecting him to the crime?" Tony said, looking amused.

Smiling at his partner, Clark covered his head with his favorite hat. "We found aniline all over the interior of that Dodge Magnum we towed in here from the Adams Morgan shootout." He gloated smugly and scooped the folder off the desk. "The Whimple twins are our suspects in this ongoing investigation. That special chemical you gave us to go on really helped us identify the perpetrators." He stopped short and turned to Louis. "Ain't that right, Rich? Without that chemical name and makeup to go on, we'd still be chasing our tails around in the dark."

With a weak nod, Louis concurred. He looked away when Tony tried to make eye contact.

"Hey," Clark spoke up, "who's to say these two won't lead us to more culprits that could be involved in this murder spree?"

Tony Woo snickered. He couldn't believe they were actually going through with this unbelievable story and that they had the audacity to try and push the bullshit his way.

"What are you suggesting, Clark? You two think you may have uncovered a violent gang of serial killers? Is that what you're telling me?" He pushed his wire frames snugly on his face. "If that's the case, what are the two of you waiting for? File your report with the chief. Let's see what happens."

A hearty chuckle erupted from Clark. "It's already been filed with the chief," he said nonchalantly. "This here is just some extra copies for our personal files."

Loud chatter could be heard outside Woo's office. Something about Potomac, Maryland, caught Clark's attention as a trio of DEA agents went rushing down the hall.

Clark stuck his head out. "Hey, fellas!" he shouted. "Where y'all rushing off to in such a good mood? Let us in on the action." He stepped outside the office.

Lieutenant Tanner, the blonde beach bum and team commander obliged him. Unable to conceal the excitement on his face, Tanner spoke quickly.

"We're on our way over to the court building to see if we can catch up with Judge Howard. We need to get this search warrant signed off on." He paused, then said with a haughty grin, "Your suspect in there just confessed to the victim found over there in Fort Totten Park. He admitted to his involvement and supplied us with a short list of names who also may have taken part in the murder of Mike Lewis."

Clark looked apprehensive. "What the hell are you talking about? We've got evidence linking him and his brother to our serial case. What's this bull crap he's giving you? Sounds like some shit that'll have y'all chasing your own tails around town," he voiced drily. The mounting irritation in his tone was obvious.

Sergeant Nuygen placed his hand on Clark's shoulder. "Mr. Whimple says he doesn't know a damn thing about any serial murders. But he did tell us with intricate detail how he and a few of his associates carried out the murder." The sergeant hesitated, allowing the full gravity of his words to sink in before he continued. "They murdered Mr. Lewis in one of those extravagant estates out there in Potomac."

Smiling joyfully, Lieutenant Tanner jumped in. "And guess who's the ring leader." He waited for a reply, then blurted, "The Teflon Don himself, Mr. Ray Leon! Yeah, we've been trying to get his ass for quite some time. If what he says holds water, then we got his ass!"

Sgt. Nuygen gave Clark an enthusiastic pat on the back.

"Yeah, we gotta body to pin on his ass. But you and your partner can come along for the ride if you'd like." The sergeant started walking away. "But right now we have this warrant for Lake Potomac Drive that needs a signature."

Dejected, Clark watched the trio move toward the exit. He felt a gut-wrenching pang of frustration as he envisioned their case crumbling right before his eyes.

Louis joined his partner outside Tony's office. With obvious concern, he stated, "If what they say is true, then our case just got flushed down the goddamn toilet."

Clark was straining to hold his composure. He could feel Tony Woo's eyes burning a hole in the back of his head. Without looking back, he tucked the folder under his arm and motioned to Louis as he stepped off. That was all he could do at the moment to keep from allowing the forensic chief the satisfaction of seeing him grovel.

Just as Clark had thought, Tony Woo eyed the pair intently. Tony felt the bubbles of elation stirring about as the men departed his company. He turned, picked up the phone and dialed the appropriate extension. A metallic voice answered. "Internal Affairs. How can I direct your call?"

Chapter 16

The evening rush hour gridlock seemed unending as Jovan moved amongst the traffic.

He looked around at the other drivers, annoyed. He knew better than to travel around town during rush hour, especially downtown.

"Fuck!" Jovan hissed when he felt his BlackBerry alerting him. "Who is it this time?" The word "wife" flashed on the screen.

"What are you doing?" Angel asked sweetly.

He huffed, irritated. "Well, right now I'm not doing a damn thing! I'm stuck downtown in this fucked-up traffic! Why?"

"You son of a bitch!" a strange voice spat harshly. "Who the fuck you copping an attitude with? You better pump your damn brakes, nigga!"

"What-the-fuck!" Jovan said, grimacing to himself. "Who the fuck is this?!?" he fired back hotly.

"It's me, Da," Angel replied quietly. "You know it's me, stop playing."

Jovan's brow furled tightly. "Hold the fuck up," he grumbled sourly. "Angel, what's going on? What kind of games are you playing, huh?" Laughter erupted in his ear. The obnoxious sound sent a wave of chills to his core.

"Ain't nobody playing no goddamn games with your dirty-dick-ass!" the strange feminine voice snarled with unbridled contempt. "You're the gamer, and I've warned you before. But you're the type of nigga that thinks his shit don't stink. But I got something for your ass!"

Jovan gritted his teeth. "Who the hell is this?" he demanded, "Give me a name! You got all that fucking sense! Tell me who I'm speaking with!" He paused for a split second. "Who this? Black-ass Jo Jo? That's you playing on my fucking phone? Y'all bitches better stop playing with me 'cause it's not a game!" Jovan noticed a Bozo the Clown–looking dude pushing a red Maxima daydreaming. The black SUV cut in front of him. Jovan grinned and flipped Bozo the finger when he blew his horn in protest.

"Dumb bitch! This Natasha you talking to, nigga!" Her voice dripped with venom. "And I doubt that you'd want to fuck with me. I take that back. I know goddamn well you don't wanna fuck with me in no way, shape or form. Fuck with me if you want, and you' won't have that dirty dick to fuck around with ever again!" she warned, laughing.

"Bitch!" Jovan retorted sharply. "You must not know who the fuck you talking to or who the fuck I am! I don't know who the fuck Natasha is, and I don't give a fuck! But Angel knows I don't take lightly to muthafuckas making idle threats. So I advise you and her to suck on my dirty dick, bitch!" He thought for a second, then added, "Angel too damn stupid to know when she's being played by a freak-ass bitch that's really trying to fuck her man! Dumb bitch! Both of y'all can go eat each other's pussy as far as I'm concerned 'cause y'all bitches not gonna see this big dirty dick, not today!" He laughed out loud before he hung up.

A victory smile slid on his lips when he looked up at the mirror. "Play with me," Jovan spoke to himself. "Bitch, you won't see me for a few days now. See how you like that shit," he chuckled as he made a right turn.

Upstairs in the Rising home, Natasha sat at the computer desk, glaring at the screen, twirling her blonde locks. "You don't know what we've become," she voiced grimly. The reflection staring back at her was a strong she-devil.

"But I love my husband." Angel's protest sounded so weak, in total contrast to the simmering animosity brewing within her alter ego, Natasha.

"You can love him all you want, but that nigga don't wanna be loved!" Natasha sneered. Her distaste for Jovan grew with every breath she breathed as she sat in front of the computer monitor and watched the blinking black dot proceed along the digital road map.

Jovan seemed to be heading Uptown. Natasha wasn't one hundred percent sure, but she had a pretty good idea of his intended destination. She reached down into the Louis Vuitton duffle bag resting at her feet. A second later she produced a dark orange medicine vial. The label on the bottle read: Oxyline – Authorized for J. Rising.

Chapter 17

Malaysia was sitting by the bay window in her bedroom, overlooking the front lawn. She loved sitting by the window, watching the sun set at dusk.

Jovan's black Mercedes cruised along 5th Street. At the corner of 5th and Jefferson, he paused at a four-way stop sign before making a left turn, then coasted halfway down the block and pulled up beside Malaysia's dark blue X5. He could see her in the window looking down on him.

She watched him park his truck. When he alighted from the vehicle, Malaysia felt her heart soar. She loved this man, adored every inch of him. But his good looks and intelligence were overshadowed by his arrogance and deceit. That part of him she rebuked, wholeheartedly. She closed her eyelids tightly and exhaled. She stood up, smiling faintly.

After parking his SUV, a strange thought abruptly jumped to the forefront of his mind—something Malaysia said earlier: "I know you and your friends had a ball partying and singing and only God knows what else you were doing."

How in the hell did she know we were singing? Jovan wondered. *We weren't singing in the club. The only place we sang was down in the pool house.*

The thought gave Jovan an uneasy feeling as he rounded the Mercedes and bounded up the red brick stairs.

He walked into the empty foyer and closed the door behind himself. He could hear music playing upstairs. A mellow rhythm cascaded down the long carpeted staircase.

Its soothing melody was a welcoming antidote to his ears. He could feel it working to calm his growing anxiety.

Jovan moved across the foyer. His gaze swept the vacant living room. He noticed the fireplace burning and an empty drinking glass on the mantle above it. Marshia Ambrosia's "Late Nights, Early Mornings" seemed louder as he moved toward the bottom of the stairs. He grabbed hold of the banister and made his way upstairs.

Jovan paused in the bedroom doorway, allowing his eyes to focus on the dimly lit room. The air inside the master bedroom was enhanced with rose-scented candles and sweet touches of Malaysia's signature fragrance: Michael Kors.

Suddenly, the bathroom door swung open and light spilled across the plush carpet before Malaysia turned off the light and began to work it. She sashayed across the floor, her sexy ivory lace thongs and yummy hips in tow. A matching pair of Kate Spade stilettos adorned her feet.

The sight of her derriere and dimple-decorated smile—so erotic and sweet—gave Jovan goose bumps.

"What's the matter, lover boy?" Malaysia inquired, her tone drenched in sultriness. "Don't tell me the cat got your tongue." A devilish grin parted her lips.

He could see her sparkling emerald irises studying him affectionately. Jovan took three long strides. He was on her. The delightful aroma of Gold perfume filled his nostrils. She stared him in the eye, wrapped both arms around his neck and greeted him with a hot sunset smooch.

Jovan wrapped his strong hands around her naked waist and kissed her passionately. His hands slowly traced down her soft, silky backside. His touch sent chills throughout her body. She closed her eyes and enjoyed the feeling. She knew what he wanted and was eager to submit to his sexual whims.

Outside, the temperature plummeted as night fell over Washington, bringing to an end another day in the Nation's Capital.

The entire house appeared to be dark, save for the windows of the master bedroom and living room. Inside, the rooms glowed ominously, seemingly beckoning the deadly, sadistic presence stalking the grounds under the cloak of darkness.

A frosty northwestern breeze blew through the bare maples trees, whipped around the house and blasted Natasha's exposed face, causing her to smile and grimace at the same time.

Gazing up at the ceiling, trying to catch her breath, Malaysia's mind and body were totally satisfied and full of rapture. She was blown away by the sexual eruption she just experienced, compliments of Mr. Rising.

A few moments later, after regaining some of her strength and bodily senses, Malaysia rolled over and rested her chin on her elbows.

"You alright, precious?" Jovan asked coolly. He was busy grooving to the sounds of the music while staring up at the ceiling, motioning with his hands like a maestro conducting an imaginary symphony orchestra.

Shaking her head, eyes lost in thought, Malaysia answered sweetly, "The way you do my body ... mmmm ... I can't help but be alright. Mmmph, mmmph, mmmph."

Smiling confidently, Jovan replied, "Yeah, I know that's right." He reached down and cupped her naked ass. "Whenever you ready for another round, just say 'daddy'."

His eyes roamed her body lustfully. Her lady lumps were simply impressive.

She giggled. "I swear, I have never met a man who's more full of himself than you."

"Ain't that the truth," he responded smugly. "That's why you love me so much," he added with a playful slap on her ass.

"Me and the whole wide world," she mumbled under her breath.

He frowned. "What's that?"

"Nothing," she said, quickly dismissing her comment. "You know I could use a drink, and I know you could too for that matter, so would you mind getting us both something to drink … Daddy?" Malaysia leaned over and kissed him tenderly on his chest, then gestured toward the window. "Your bathrobe is folded up on the chair by the window." Her voice suddenly sounded precarious.

Jovan didn't notice. He rolled out of the bed, plucked his burgundy Ferragamo robe off the chair and blew her a kiss as he slipped it on. Malaysia watched him silently as he moved about the room. His hard, masculine physique was a treat to the eyes. She had to admit Jovan was her kryptonite. She was weak and vulnerable in his presence, like a puppet under his control.

Lying across her gold satin sheets, Malaysia's eyes trailed his every move. She didn't twitch or utter a sound until he walked out. She waited a few more seconds, then eased her naked frame to the edge of the bed, stood up and walked over to the walk-in closet. She hesitated briefly in the doorway. She was calm, but her nerves were tingling uncontrollably.

"Loving you is like a taste of hell," Malaysia said as she turned on the light in the closet and disappeared inside.

Downstairs in the living room Jovan sounded like he didn't have a care in the world, singing "12 Play," one of his favorite R. Kelly, while he stood at the bar mixing their drinks.

When he finished, he waltzed around the bar with his drinks in hand, threw his head back, downing a glass of cognac in one gulp, then scooped another glass off the bar and continued across the room.

Pure hate radiated a few feet away, in a dark, shadowy corner of the room. Natasha was seething quietly in the dark, watching him. It took everything she had in her not to pounce on him right then and there. She visualized Jovan's death by her hands. Seeing him die provided her with a weird sense of calm—the calm before the storm.

In her hand, she twirled the blade of death and eyed him as he walked across the floor nonchalantly. He paused in the foyer, his gaze swept the area and made one cautious sweep before proceeding upstairs.

Jovan froze at the top of the stairs. He could hear someone moaning close by. He moved cautiously along the wide carpeted hallway and paused outside the first door he came upon. He turned the knob and pushed it open. Inside, the air was stale, like the bedroom hadn't been used in a long time. The moment he entered the room, the sound of breathing became more pronounced.

Jovan set both drinks down on a dark oak nightstand beside the door. His gaze focused on a queen-size canopy bed with a black sheer veil draped around the entire frame. His eyes slowly panned the room, and he detected movement behind the black veil on the bed. Carefully, he made his way towards it, his body tense with anticipation. He stopped in front of the bed and held his breath as he cautiously pulled back the covering.

With utter disbelief splashed on his face, Jovan had to blink twice to make sure his eyes weren't deceiving him, but they weren't! Eujami, his Ethiopian shorty, was staring up at him with wide, terrified eyes, her mouth gagged. She was splayed across the bed, her hands and feet bound to the oak bed columns, like a sacrificial lamb for slaughter. Jovan stared, unable to move his eyes away from the startling sight.

"What the fuck?!" he gasped, bewildered. *She's wearing the same Gucci dress she had on the other night! My God! Has she been here tied up like this since then?* He cringed at the thought.

Malaysia slipped in the room unnoticed and noiselessly glided into position behind him. Jovan sensed a presence shadowing him. The look in Eujami's eyes confirmed his feelings when he saw the whites of her eyes expand suddenly, registering alarm.

He felt his muscles tighten and his heart race. Jovan shifted his weight as he moved to turn. He felt a sharp pain explode across the back of his head. He wobbled unsteadily, wrestling against the pain. He glanced back as he reached for the bedpost and caught a startling glimpse of Malaysia as she brought the slap-jack down on his head a second time. Jovan's body stiffened for a split second before the blow sent him crumbling to the floor.

Chapter 18

In Potomac, Maryland, things were just getting started ...

Party sounds resonated across the dark lush expanse outside the palatial estate on Lake Potomac Drive. On the lower level inside the hip pool house, an intimate party gathering was underway.

The voice of the Louis Vuitton Don, rapper, Kanye West, reverberated through thick clouds of weed smoke, permeating the entire pool house as bikini clad honeys popped their booties as if they didn't have a care in the world.

Ray was wrapped in his signature smoking jacket, his legs crossed. He was leaning back on a plush lounge sofa beside the pool with a thick blunt dangling from his mouth. He was in rare form, grinning from ear to ear. He was surrounded by a bevy of honeys, looking like a true Don.

Suddenly, he felt his iPhone vibrating in his pocket, disturbing his groove. Smoke spewed from his nostrils as he whipped out the phone.

"You can fuck up a good piece of pussy, you know that?" Ray voiced sarcastically. "What the fuck is it now? Damn."

On the other end of the line, Detective Clark clenched his jaw, fighting back the urge for a sharp reply. "I think you better chill out, 'cause what I'm about to lay on you is gonna fuck your head up." He waited, making sure he had his undivided attention before he went on. "I hope you're not in Potomac, 'cause your boy Antonio turned rat. The Alphabet Boys just secured a warrant for you and your crew on murder charges, so I advise you to get ghost because, as we speak, the Alphabet Boys are moving in on your Potomac spread."

Ray's eyes blinked wide and his jaw fell open. "Psycho flipped the script?" he muttered incredulously. "Naw, nigga, you must be trippin'!" He bolted to his feet and began pacing the floor, drawing concerned looks from his crew. Ray's serious demeanor instantly upset the mellow flow in the room.

Clark smugly retorted, "If I'm mistaken, then how is it that I know you gave the okay for your crew to take out your man Mike? And the fact that the murder took place at your Potomac hideout? Look, I warned you about the body count. I can keep the dogs at bay when it comes to the drug beefs, but when you start spilling blood, then it's out of my hands. I warned you about this, so you don't have nobody to blame but yourself."

The reality of what Clark said rocked Ray to the core. The gravity of the situation made his head spin and made him nauseous at same time.

Biggie, Nutso and Dude all crowded around him.

"Ray, what's going on?" Dude asked, a look of earnest concern splashed on his face. "I can see something got you real fucked up."

Ray stood silent for a moment, regarding each man with a hard, roguish stare. He sighed deeply. "Man, Psycho switched bitch on a nigga, and the Feds mobbing up right now to take us all down." He rested his hand on Dude's shoulder and looked him square in the eye. "I want you to get all the bitches outta here. Bag up all the dough—everything we got on hand in this joint. We taking flight," he voiced adamantly. "I don't know about y'all, but me, I can't stand to do a bid. I'd rather hold court in the streets than spend one day up in the joint." Ray paused and made eye contact with each man. "Are we clear on this? Are we all rolling in the same ride? 'Cause if not," he gestured strongly with his hand, "then you can roll out with the bitches!"

Outside in the cold, dark night, DEA and ATF agents were moving into position, surrounding the Potomac estate. Operating as commander of one DEA task force team was a familiar light complexioned character with long reddish-orange cornrows. His name was Special Agent Cordel Smith. He couldn't wait to see the look on Ray's and Jovan's faces. He could finally tell Jovan that the two cars he sold him were now being used for undercover sting operations, like the one he worked on to get them. Cordel laughed at them silently.

Chapter 19

Slowly, Jovan's eyelids began to slide open. His vision was hazy and he had a splitting headache. He felt groggy and disoriented. When he realized his hands and legs were incapacitated, the troubling image of Eujami bound to a bedpost popped in his head.

"Oh my God!" he said as a floodgate of disturbing images went cascading through his mind. Jovan made a futile attempt at getting loose. Then something hard slammed across his back. "Muthafuck!" he groaned in agony. The smooth saxophone melody drowned out every verbal complaint he spat.

He quickly realized he was lying on the floor, able to move only his head from side to side. When Jovan looked up, Malaysia's lace-clad crotch stared down at him from the edge of the bed.

"I don't think you want to piss me off any further because I have had it with you," Malaysia muttered, casting an evil look. Her mood was dark and intense, something he never witnessed before.

"What the fuck do you think you're doing, huh? What's this shit supposed to accomplish?"

She glared at him with heat in her eyes and slid off the bed. She squatted next to his head. "I warned you not to break our covenant," she said, grinning wickedly. "But you did it anyway. Not only that, but you're just a man whore. You meet women in clubs and fuck them with no regard for the people in your life, let alone regard for yourself and the spirit that dwells within you. When you lay down with someone, don't you know you allow that person's spirit to come into you?" She stopped when she saw his eyes close.

"Look at me when I'm talking!" Malaysia palmed his face roughly, suddenly becoming furious. "When you lay down with people, you mingle spirits, and you shouldn't take that lightly," she warned, her lips curled in a tight sneer. "I don't take what you did to us lightly at all. I wanted so bad to raise this baby with you, marry you, have a life with you. But you have made that virtually impossible now."

Nervousness flashed in Jovan's eyes. "Wh-wh-what in the hell are you saying?" he stuttered, trying to jerk loose. "Baby! What damn baby?"

Malaysia was a bit hesitant. She looked at him with tears in her eyes. "I'm with child," she spoke in a hushed tone. "I'm carrying your baby!" she cried, tears streaming down her cheek. Her hand disappeared. A second later she yanked out her Desert Eagle and swung it around.

Jovan's eyes moved immediately to the gun in her hand, and a lump the size of a grapefruit jumped in his throat. Absolute fear overcame him.

"Now you've forced my hand," she whispered, tracing his lips with the barrel of the gun.

This bitch has lost her fucking mind, Jovan silently voiced, watching the wild, hazy look in her eyes. He read her every gesture and tick, as if he was inside her head. All her sordid talk was starting to scare him.

Malaysia strained to hide her emotions, but failed. She felt her world crashing in on her as her emotions hit the ceiling.

"You made me do this!" she screamed, tears coursing down her face. She gripped the gun handle and pushed the barrel hard against his cheek. "How does this feel?" she growled with a sinister look dancing in her eyes. She applied more pressure.

Struggling against the pain, Jovan hissed, "Bitch, if you don't get the fuck off me!"

After some hesitation, Malaysia conceded. She sighed, stood and walked over to the window. She paused for a second, staring down on the dark, quiet street.

"Jovan ," she began, wiping her eyes, "you really messed up the life we could've had together. And now it's all gone." She reached down, took off the safety and cocked the gun.

The sound echoed around the room, sending a wave of chills that seemed to radiate deep in Jovan's bones.

"What are you doing?" he asked, struggling to stay calm. "Precious, we have a child to raise. You wouldn't want to deny our child the chance to have a father in her life. Think how you would've felt." He was trying to tap into the emotional bond she shared with her father.

Malaysia frowned and turned to him. "I know what you're trying to do," she said, looking him dead in the eye. Her face showed no emotions as she walked toward him.

"Jovan, I majored in psychology, so that shit doesn't affect me." She took a knee and placed her mouth to his ear. "You should've thought about that before you stuck your dick in your little freak girlfriend in the other room."

At the mention of Eujami, Jovan decided to change gears. "So what are you gonna do with her? You work for the police department, and you're running around the city kidnapping people. What do you think she's gonna do, let this shit blow over and not say a word?"

Malaysia let out a wicked laugh. "I think it would behoove you to worry about your own well-being. Because your girlfriend isn't saying anything to anyone ..." she stopped short. "How should I say this? Oh, I know," she said with a cunning smirk. "Your girlfriend has left the building."

Jovan looked at her with his nose scrunched. "What's that supposed to mean?"

The smooth sound of Marsha Ambrosia's voice slowly began to dissipate, leaving the room silent.

"We can't erase what was meant to be," she mocked drily. "What a crock of shit! You're so full of it, and I can't believe I was that gullible to believe in your fairy tales. I despise your ass!" she spat. "Take a good hard look at what you let slip through your fingers because of your promiscuity." She stood with her legs spread eagle, her hot crotch deliberately hovering above his head.

"Because you couldn't keep your dick in your pants." She took dead aim at his penis. "For the blatant violation of our covenant, you don't deserve to have that monster serpent of yours do any more harm. I won't allow it."

Jovan's eyes bucked wide with fear. "What the fuck are you doing?!?" he cried out franticly. The high-pitch alto in his voice revealed how scared he was. "I know you better stop this bullshit, for real! Lemme go! I ain't for this shit, Malaysia!" His puffed up male bravado crumbled on the spot.

Finally, something pierced his tough-guy exterior. She smirked, glancing down at him.

"Awww ... don't cry now. You can dish out the misery, but you can't take it?" There was an obvious tone of indifference in her voice. She let him know how she felt when she spit on him. "Fuck you, Jovan!" she snarled, aiming her weapon at the head of his penis. She took a deep breath and held it.

"Noooo!!!" Jovan bellowed, looking terrified.

The sound of the door cracking echoed around the room and broke Malaysia's concentration. A sharp shrill cut the air. Malaysia looked up. A deep searing pain tore through her thigh, and she cried out like an injured pig, gaping in horror at the large blade protruding from her leg. Blood gushed from the wound like a water sprout.

Natasha melted from the shadows and sprang through the doorway like a crazed maniac. Operating off sheer impulse, Malaysia swung the pistol up to eye level. Just as she pulled the trigger, she felt her wounded leg buckle. The gun roared, missing its target. The bullet landed in the wall, just to the right of the door frame.

Jovan gave an astonished look as he watched Angel charge in the room. Every muscle in her body seemed tuned to one objective: Malaysia. *Angel?!? Is that my Angel,* he thought.

Like a powerful linebacker bearing down on a defenseless quarterback, Natasha vaulted violently across the room and knocked Malaysia clear off her feet. She landed on her back, the wind knocked out of her. She gasped for air.

"Oh, God!" Malaysia breathed in pain, trying to gather herself. *Get up!* the voice in her head screamed. Immediately, she rolled to her left, and not a second too soon. Natasha swung the machete, and the blade slashed the empty space on the carpet.

"Dirty bitch!" Natasha hissed.

Jovan couldn't believe his eyes. *But what's up with the blonde wig and blue contacts,* he wondered, looking perplexed. *How in the hell did she find me? Something ain't right,* he thought. *This is some crazy-ass shit!* He fought like hell to free himself as the women squared off.

Malaysia's adrenaline was pumping in overdrive as she bounced off the floor. A painful expression leaped off her face when she landed on her feet and struggled to steady herself.

My gun! Where's my gun, she shouted as her eyes searched the floor frantically. She spotted the butt of her gun poking out from under the chair.

"Bitch!" Natasha growled. "You like fucking married men!" Her face twisted into a mask of anger as she wielded the machete with fire leaping from her eyes.

Lord, no! This can't be happening, Malaysia voiced to herself when she realized who the woman standing before her was. She felt a chill rise through her body, and an unexpected apprehension surged within her. *Angel,* she concluded. *Jovan's wife had stalked them, and now here she was to get revenge!*

"Look here, I can understand your pain. Believe me, I do," Malaysia said, invoking a diplomatic approach to the situation, trying to defuse it. "Look, I work for the DC police, and that man lying there isn't worth you going to prison."

Natasha's eyes narrowed. "You hoes are all alike," she voiced bitterly, her breaths sounding more erratic. "You think you can fuck another woman's husband and not suffer any consequences behind your dirty little secret." Her demeanor intensified. "Bitch, I'm here to collect; I'm not here to listen to your excuses. In my eyes, bitches like you don't deserve life!" She lunged toward Malaysia like a wild panther, swinging the blade with pure hatred surging from her body.

Instinctively, Malaysia morphed into a defensive stance. Her body turned rigid, preparing to counter her attack.

The blade flashed across her eyes, slashing Malaysia's forearm slightly before she was able to deflect the blow. Both women collided hard, then crashed to the floor. They tussled violently, kicking, thrashing and screaming across the carpet.

For an instant, Malaysia felt a surge of fear. *Lord, help me!* she cried inside. *This woman is too strong for me. She has the strength of a mad man!*

"Please ... please ... stop this! He's not worth it!" Malaysia cried as the woman overpowered her.

Natasha rolled on top of her. "Don't cry now, bitch! Ha ha! Ain't that what you said to him?" she snapped sharply.

"Please, let me go. No man is worth this! No man is worth throwing away your life!" she insisted, her voice brimming with emotions as she fought hard to escape the woman's clutches. "I don't want your husband!" she yelled, fear etched in her face. "You can have him! Please, just let me go!"

A harsh laugh tumbled out of Natasha's mouth. "He's not my husband." Her tone hardened instantly. "I don't want his dirty dick ass! That bitch is dying right along with you."

The finality in her voice was unmistakable. Jovan heard the exchange of words, but his brain was having a hard time assimilating the full meaning of what she was saying. Then it hit him.

Beauty's cryptic words floated to the forefront of his mind. *"Your wife is your demon. Your wife is your death!"*

Fear coursed through him. *Who the fuck is this bitch? That's not Angel talking like that!*

Jovan froze when he saw her arm rise above her head, her hand gripping the machete firmly. His body stiffened involuntarily, and his breath froze in his chest. Time seemed to stop. When he blinked, the machete disappeared from the air.

Malaysia let out a muted croak of a scream, just loud enough to make Jovan cringe when he heard her. He knew Malaysia was gone.

Natasha sat gloating over her kill, watching the thick lava-like flow of blood seep out of the her neck, and creep down the stainless steel surface. Natasha had pierced Malaysia's throat with such force, the machete sliced clear through her flesh, and stuck in the carpeted floor where it now rested, jutting sickly from her throat like a upsetting horror scene.

Jovan's palms began to sweat. He could hear his heart pounding rapidly as he watched the blonde imposter rise to her feet. He tried to respond, but she cut him off.

Natasha's head snapped around. "Don't say shit!" she warned, her expression toxic. Her icy blue glare rattled him.

Those eyes ... He thought long and hard. Then the memory jumped in his head. He remembered waking up at the house covered in black soot a while back. He had seen those wicked-looking eyes in his dream. *Was it a dream?*

Jovan's gaze shot around the room. He sat silently, telling himself not to panic as he watched her suddenly concerned when she pulled the bloody machete from Malaysia's corpse. The sight made his skin crawl.

Natasha was moving systematically. After removing the blade, she crossed the room and disappeared in the closet. A few seconds later she reemerged carrying a bundle of clear cellophane in one hand and the blood-soaked blade in the other. She moved past Jovan like he wasn't there and stood over the body, before kneeling beside it. She placed the machete on the carpet next to her. Natasha bowed her head, and a jumbled murmur spewed from her mouth. Her lips were moving fast and furiously; she was speaking some form of tongue.

For a moment Jovan felt a spark of hope when he witnessed her bow her head in what he assumed was prayer. But his hope was quickly dashed—any sign of remorse from this woman faded when the murmuring ceased.

He watched the blonde imposter's head rise. Without a word, she reached for the machete. She wrapped her hand around the black leather handle and picked it up from the floor.

Natasha enjoyed the look of shock and pain on Jovan's face when she held his girlfriend's decapitated head in the air. Demonic laughter echoed from her throat as she watched him go into an emotional meltdown before her.

"God help meeee!!!" he shrieked.

Chapter 20

Nutso volunteered to escort the ladies to their cars to send them on their way. He gathered all the women in the pool house, then took a seat at the bar and sipped a cold Heineken while he watched the ladies slip into their tight-fitting jeans and skirts.

"Damn!" he cursed under his breath, turning up the bottle. *Why does this shit have to go down tonight out of all nights? Why tonight when I had two bad honeys' backs to bang out? Damn!*

Meanwhile, Ray was in the master suite on the third level of the west wing emptying out the main safe. He was stuffing stacks of twenties, fifties and hundreds into a brown leather Mark Cross duffle bag.

He shed his smoking jacket and put on a heavy black leather Byblos jacket and cap. He dropped the Mark Cross at the foot of his bed and strolled toward the walk-in closet. Reaching inside, he retrieved two .50-caliber hand cannons and a stack of fully loaded clips. He sat on the edge of his sleigh bed, loaded both weapons, slammed a slug in each chamber, then pocketed the loaded burners. The inside pockets of his jacket seemed like they were made specifically to conceal weapons; each gun fit snugly inside.

Ray stood in front of the full-length mirror and admired his swarthy style—it gave him that ruthless appeal that he liked.

"Yeah, let a bamma try me tonight," he said to himself, shrugging his shoulders, feeling cocky. "They ass will be in for one helluva surprise fucking with me." He patted the outer shell of his jacket. "Perfect," he grinned. There wasn't the slightest indication that he was carrying a weapon. "Shit, if I didn't strap up myself, I wouldn't know I was toting," he said as he turned away from the mirror.

On the estate's east end, Dude and Biggie were inside the second master suite. Both men were busy unloading a cash and weapons stash from another safe.

"Man, where are we going?" Biggie asked with a look of concern, lugging a dark camouflage duffle bag weighted down with an arsenal of guns and ammo.

Dude was focused on counting the stacks of money he was loading into another army fatigue bag.

"What? Did you say something, Big?" Dude asked, looking up.

Biggie placed the artillery bag in the hall outside the room. "Yeah, cuz," he answered pulling his forest green North Face parka over his shoulder. "Where we going from here? The Feds ain't coming tonight. Shit, we didn't have to send them honeys home just yet. I wanted some pussy."

Dude snickered. "Go 'head with your fat, black, freak ass," he said playfully. "You act like the pussy going somewhere."

"It is, cuz," Biggie interjected. "The pussy walking out the door. What you talking about?" he said as he walked over to the window.

"So what," Dude retorted. "We'll be knee-deep in pussy this time tomorrow, so put your freaky black ass on ice, alright?"

"Aww, man," Biggie said as he peered out the window. "We are seriously fucked!" he scoffed, clearly disturbed. "The Feds got this joint surrounded!"

Dude's gaze shifted to the window where Biggie stood. "Man, what the fuck you talking about?" he demanded. He quickly moved toward the window and nudged Biggie aside. "Nigga, stop play—" Dude began, then bounced back from the window and grabbed his chest like he'd been shot. "The fucking Feds!" he groaned.

Ray's cell phone squawked. An anxious-sounding Dude rambled, "R-R-Ray … the Feds outside this joint! What we gonna do?!?"

Downstairs, Nutso was just clearing the pool house. He ushered the women into the main room, and spotted the pair he was supposed to hook up with. They were standing off to the side, whispering and giggling.

Feeling cocky and confident, Nutso approached the hot pair. He walked up to a cute red bone with long sandy locks, freckles and a tight physique of a gymnast. Her name was Toya, and she eyed the big fella with interest as he moved in.

Toya turned to her friend Nicole, a leggy chocolate honey with an eye-popping 38-DD rack. She wore a pair of geeky eyeglasses, but she was a hardcore freak on the low.

"Y'all still trying to hook up and do that tomorrow?" Nutso asked coolly, silently praying they both said yes.

The women eyed him from head to toe, then smiled at one another, an undercurrent of heat in their look.

"Sure, we can hook up, big boy," assured Toya, smiling. "Are you sure you're ready for the both of us? 'Cause we've got appetites that will blow your mind."

Nicole threw her arm around Toya's shoulder. "Yeah, so I hope you know what you doing," she began, licking her lips, "'cause we ain't got time for no inexperienced new jacks taking a dip in the pool for the first time. You know what I'm talking about?" she winked.

"Oh, it's on!" he said excitedly. "The number you put in my phone, that's where I can reach y'all?" he asked, not waiting for an answer. "Oh, I'm gonna show y'all how I gets down and dirty." He laughed and turned to the group. "Okay, ladies, y'all probably will hear something from Ray either tomorrow or the next day," he advised walking toward the smoked glass entrance.

Nutso eased the door open. The crisp night breeze smacked him in the face. A split second later bright flood lights exploded across the front of the house. Nutso's enormous frame eclipsed the lighting in the doorway. He froze in place, stunned.

"Freeze! Stay where you are!" a commanding voice boomed over a bullhorn. "We have you totally surrounded. Don't make a move!"

"What in the hell is going on?!?" asked Kitty, a thick cocoa honey with a feisty attitude. "Who the hell do they think they're talking to like that?!?" She pushed two girls aside and squeezed right by Nutso and out the door. "I don't know who in the hell you muthafuckas think you're talking to!" she railed, hands flying in the air, head twisting and turning like a snake ready to strike. Kitty stood her ground and yelled just beyond the entrace, "I know my damn rights! So y'all can kiss my black ass!"

"Hold you fire! Hold your fire!" the commander's voice shouted from behind the bright glare of the lights.

Nutso knew a golden opportunity when it was presented, and he wasted no time springing into action. He quickly extended his left hand, leaned down and scooped the short, thick Kitty in one swoop. He used his right hand and ripped a chrome-plated S&W .45 semi from his waistband. Nutso used Kitty as a shield and let the .45 bark as he retreated inside and slammed the door.

Inside, ear-piercing screams filled the main room. The women were cowering in fear, in a state of shock— except Kitty, who was kicking and screaming in a fit of rage.

"Nigga! Get your fuckin' hands off me! Have you lost your damn mind?!? You could've got us both killed!"

Nutso blew her off. "It wasn't going down like that," he said frankly.

Ray, Dude and Biggie came flying down the stairs. "Is everybody alright?!?" asked Ray, marching in the room. "Who was just shooting?"

Kitty was riled up. "It was that crazy-ass nigga right there!" she responded tartly. "He almost got our ass killed!"

Nutso grinned facetiously and mocked her by placing the barrel of his gun to his lips. He blew on it and said, "Stop bitching."

He turned to Ray. "What's next, playboy?"

The loud bullhorn squawked. "Ray Leon! We know you're in there! So why don't you save yourself, your friends and all of us out here the pain and aggravation and give yourself up!"

Hearing the Feds announce his government like that was a serious blow to Ray's mental state. He was good under pressure—"never let them see you sweat" was one of his favorite clichés. But he was never confronted with a situation of this magnitude, and Ray could feel the pressure building inside as he tried to conceal his emotions. This was something far beyond anything he could've anticipated.

Slowly, Ray scanned the faces around the room. The women were all huddled together, scared. Except for Kitty. She looked like she was enjoying herself.

His crew was ready to rock and roll. They were just waiting for him to give the word. But was he ready? The question made Ray's heart thunder in his chest.

Ray drew his .50 caliber from his jacket. A wave of fear swept through the room as the women watched him walk to the front door, open it slightly, stick the gun outside and fire off five rounds. He paused, listening to the stunned silence in the distance.

"Muthafucka! C'mon, try your hands! We got hostages, bitch!" he shouted with obvious contempt before he slammed the door shut.

The air in the room was full of trepidation. Ray's actions only served to intensify the mood as he walked to the center of the room brandishing the smoking gun at his side. He glared around the room, shock and despair was splashed across every woman's face. Ray paused for a second, a look of contemplation swirled in his eyes as he looked on. "I want all the women to head downstairs," he directed, while contemplating his next move. "Nutso, you're responsible for the women."

Grinning with the look of a slippery-sly fox, Nutso was more than happy to oblige, and he wasted no time escorting the women back downstairs. Shit was getting ready to kick off at any second. He could feel it.

Dude and Biggie sensed the stress in Ray. That was an emotion he seemed to be immune to—up until now. It was evident to them that Ray was experiencing deep distress.

"What do you have in mind, Ray?" Dude inquired carefully. "You know them folks ain't letting us outta here."

His words seemed to strike a nerve. Ray started rubbing his temples in frustration.

"What the fuck do you think!" he scoffed, fighting hard to maintain his composure. "I told you what time it was. So go get the heaters and bring all that shit down here. Now!"

As Ray watched Dude and Biggie scramble into the room with the weapons stash, a dreadful feeling rocked his core. He knew the possibility of them making it out was very slim.

"Ray Leon!"

Ray cringed at the sound of his name being called.

"This is your last warning! Give yourself up! Lay down your weapons and come out with your hands in the air! I repeat, this will be your last chance to comply!"

There was a sudden ominous look about Ray. His frown hardened as he agonized over the voice on the bullhorn. The timbre in the man's voice was familiar. He tried to place it.

"No ... it couldn't be," Ray said, breathless.

Seeing the astonishment on Ray's face, Dude and Biggie looked at one another.

"What's the deal?" asked Dude, eyeing him closely. "You got something else in mind?"

"It's that bamma on the bullhorn," he answered curtly. "Fuck me. That's the Miami bamma Cordel!"

An uncomfortable silence filled the room as the stark revelation offended the men.

"Cordel?" uttered Biggie, looking surprised. "You talking about the bamma with the red cornrows who always talking that big-willy shit?"

Ray nodded with a sour smirk. "Yeah, that's the bamma." He made a motion with his hands and ordered, "Get the guns out!" His disposition intensified as he stormed toward the staircase leading to the pool house. He flung open the door. "Nutso! Get your ass up here. Now!" Ray spun around and caught Dude and Biggie off guard.

"Dude, toss me one of those M-5s. I'm going up top. Y'all hold the fort down here," he commanded, heading for the stairs. He hesitated, turned and said, "They not coming in here as long as we got these hostages. Them bitches ain't crazy," Ray assured them before sprinting up the stairs.

Nutso rushed in just in time to see Ray bounding up the stairs.

"What's the deal? Something about to jump off?"

Dude looked uncertain, but he wasn't backing down, no matter what. "Not yet," he responded seriously. "We gonna hold the fort down here while Ray control shit from upstairs." He leaned over the artillery bag and started doling out M-5s and Tec 9s. "Nutso, you got the main room. Big, you take the left wing. I got the right."

Toting a weapon under each arm, Dude stopped in front of the light switch. He turned and eyed his partners, Big first, then Nutso. "Y'all ready?" he asked calmly. "Okay, let's do this."

Dude pressed the light switch. Light gradually dissipated, blanketing the entire first level in total darkness. The armed trio spread out and maneuvered easily under the cloak of darkness.

Chapter 21

The police radio inside the Dynamic Duo's cruiser crackled. "All personnel in the vicinity of 577 Jefferson Street NW, respond immediately," said the dispatcher. "Shots fired inside residence—577 Jefferson Street NW. I repeat, respond immediately. Shots fired inside residence. All units in the vicinity respond ASAP!"

A stunned look shot across Louis' face and he belted himself in the chest with his fist. "Kill a hog's ass!" he muttered abruptly, startling his partner.

Clark gripped the wheel and whipped his head around. "Wh-what the hell is going on, Rich?"

"Five-seven-seven Jefferson. That's the technician's address," Louis replied without hesitation.

"Technician? What damn technician are you talking about?"

"You know, the pretty model," he said staring his partner down. "Ms. Tomay, the CSI you don't really care for."

"Ain't this a bitch," Clark gruffed. "Isn't she the one that wouldn't give you the time of day? Let me find out your Canadian-ass stalking women on the low," Clark insinuated bluntly.

"It's not what you think." Louis waved off his partner's remark.

With a lighthearted chuckle, Clark reached out and activated the emergency siren. The Crown Victoria lurched forward when he mashed on the gas pedal.

He turned to Louis. "Hey, buddy," he began slyly, "if stalking is your thing, don't let me cramp your style. But if I were you, I'd take a more direct approach. You're a nice-looking guy. You shouldn't be having any woman problems. What's the deal?" he inquired, arching his eyebrow.

Louis glared through the windshield, his sights locked on the road up ahead. "That's enough, Will," he expressed, sounding snide. "I'll deal with the women in my life the way I see fit. Right now, let's concentrate on getting to this crime scene."

"Okay buddy, you got it." Clark snickered and gunned the engine. The unmarked cruiser accelerated with ease as the obnoxious detective pointed the vehicle in the direction of Uptown.

When they arrived, two empty squad cars were parked with their red and blue lights flashing. The cruiser slowed, and both men's gaze went wide when their eyes came upon a black Mercedes truck parked in front of the residence. They stared at one another with startled looks.

"Are you thinking what I'm thinking?" asked Clark, jamming the brake. The Crown Vic skidded to a halt in front of the black SUV. Both doors flew open and the men emerged with guns drawn.

Just as the pair rounded the vehicle, another squad car rolled up on the opposite side of Jefferson.

Clark motioned to the officer. "Hey, buddy, I want you to run the plates on this black Mercedes here. I need a name and address, ASAP," he ordered before turning and trotting off up the steps hurriedly to catch up with his partner.

At the top of the stairs, both men approached the open entrance with caution.

"Homicide!" Louis announced strongly. "Is anyone hurt? Does anyone need assistance?" He poked his head inside and took a quick look around. The coast was clear, so he rushed in with Clark trailing right on his heels. They darted across the open foyer, scanning the vacant living room and dining area, then took up position at the bottom of the stairs.

"Homicide!" Clark yelled out. "Is anyone hurt upstairs? Does anyone need assistance?"

"All clear upstairs!" a male voice hollered out. "Officers Ready and Cross on the scene investigating. C'mon up. We have fatal casualties. Double homicide."

Louis and Clark paused in the doorway leading into the first bedroom. Their eyes fell upon the lifeless corpse of an attractive African woman sprawled across a large canopy bed that sat in the center of the room.

Officer Ready was standing just inside the doorway. He turned and extended his hand. His handshake was firm and unyielding. Considered the misfit of the 4th District, with his tall lumbering stature, blonde rugged beard, and orange curly bush.

"From the looks of this crime scene," Officer Ready began, offering his critique on the scene, "the victim's purple-tinted lips and the lacerations around her neck ..." He stopped short, looked from Louis to Clark, stroking his chin and added, "It's pretty safe to say the young lady here was strangled to death."

Reserved looks exchanged between the detectives. They knew the officer was trying to be helpful, but this was their area of expertise. They felt Officer Ready was infringing on their territory.

"Um … Officer Ready," Clark said politely, placing a hand on his shoulder. "I think me and my partner here should take it from here, buddy. Maybe you can go help out the other officer."

Ready shook his head. "No," he stated defiantly, "I think you need to go help out the other officer. Now that crime scene, I believe, is far beyond … uh, how do you say? Far beyond my qualification." He held his ground, regarding both men with a stern gaze.

Clark was extremely apt when it came to reading between the lines, and he gathered from Officer Ready's demeanor that the other victim's condition must have been in really bad shape. For the uniformed officer to challenge them like that took a lot of gall. Clark just nodded to the officer and tapped Louis on the shoulder on the way out the room.

Something in the blonde-headed officer's voice unnerved Louis. His instincts were revved up on heightened alert. He turned from the corpse on the bed and stared toward the open room at the end of the hall. He could feel something askew in the air. His palms suddenly became moist. He watched Clark march off down the hall. Louis hesitated, trudging behind him with a growing sense of pessimism.

"Mother of God," Clark gasped, standing in the doorway, taking in the grisly crime scene.

Louis was in utter shock. He felt his teeth clinch in rage as a strong sense of loss overcame him. He gazed at the woman's headless corpse for several moments.

Officer Cross, who resembled a high-school student, with his boyish good looks, long micro-braided hair and rakish frame. He turned to the door and introduced himself. His persona was surprisingly poised, in total contrast to his young appearance. His strong handshake gave the men a glimpse of his strength and overall disposition.

"That's the way we found her," Officer Cross explained. "Handcuffed to the leg of the bed, totally nude, with her legs spread eagle, as if the killer actually staged the crime scene, ya know?"

In that instance the subordinate's naiveté was exposed. Clark proudly intervened.

"My boy," he said displaying a haughty grin, "that's exactly what this crime scene represents." He kindly took the officer by the wrist and led him into the hall. Clark stepped around and clasped his hands behind his back. His authoritative swag was on front street as he studied the room from the doorway with Louis and Cross.

"What we're baring witness to is a perfectly staged horror show by public enemy #1," Clark said condescendingly.

The trio stood framed in the doorway shaking their heads at the bloody carnage that lay before them.

Outside, the quiet tree-lined landscape quickly transformed into an active crime scene. An army of marked and unmarked police cruisers, CSI vans and teams of news vehicles with towering satellite poles extended from their roofs clogged Jefferson Street.

Louis and Clark were standing at the top of the second-floor landing discussing the crime scene when Clark was accosted by an overly anxious and pudgy rookie charging up the stairs.

"Here you are, sir," said Officer Leeky. His fat little hand offered the Detective a white piece of paper. "This is the information you requested, sir." A dumb grin appeared on Leeky's face, as if he had made a major accomplishment.

It took Clark a full two seconds to realize what the officer was referring to. When it dawned on him, he immediately snapped up the paper.

"Thank you, son," he said, peeling open the folded paper. The information on the paper put a wide, cheesy grin on his dark, shiny face. "You're sure this name and address is correct?" He watched the short, hefty man's head bob up and down in response.

Louis was impatient. He stood with his arms folded, tapping his foot.

"Well, partner," he muttered, sounding annoyed, "don't leave me hanging. What's the good news?"

Clark straightened his hat before responding. "Okay, does the name Jovan Rising ring a bell?" He studied Louis' facial expression, waiting for an answer.

Louis thought for a moment, and his right eyebrow shot up suddenly. "Isn't that one of the names mentioned in that DEA report you somehow got a hold of? I'm not for certain, but isn't he one of the suspects that benefited from that botched drug sting on the Lorton-Morton projects?"

Sporting a crooked grin, Clark conceded. "Right on the button, Richie boy." Feeling jolly, he gave Officer Leeky a congratulatory slap on the back for a job well done. "Thank you, Officer Leeky. This information you've provided us with is extremely pertinent, and I would appreciate if you could keep this between us three." Clark eased his arm around Leeky's shoulder and leaned in his ear. "You see, there's a leak in the department, so you can understand where I'm coming from, right, buddy?" He gave

Leeky a knowing look, as if only the three of them were privy to the information.

The stout little man looked Clark directly in the eye, returned the smile and agreed without question.

A satisfied grin pierced Clark's lips. "That's what I'm talking about," he said, turning to Louis. "Alright, let's go Rich. We need to move on this, fast." The burly detective was agile for a man his size. His 270-plus frame descended the long staircase, quickly and efficiently.

Clark stopped outside the driver's door. "We have to secure a jurisdictional warrant and put a team together, and we don't have a lot of time," he said, shrugging off his trench. He climbed behind the wheel. "This here is our collar, Rich," he said, his tone more serious now. "Trust me on this; I wouldn't steer you wrong."

Louis didn't respond. Trusting Clark so far yielded many benefits, but it also brought its fair share of liabilities. Louis shook his head and peeled off his trench before climbing in.

"Rich," Clark pressed on, "are we clear on this? You know this collar will put us back on top. Whoever closes out this case, not only will they be rubbing elbows and hobnobbing with the chief, but they'll be doing it up with the mayor and his buddies too. Catch my drift?" He winked and flipped on the siren. "So let's get ready to bust some ass!" Clark said, feeling alive for the first time in a long time.

Closing this case would get a big monkey off their backs. The way he saw it, solving this case would put the Dynamic Duo back atop the departmental pedestal where they once reigned. Yeah, he was hell-bent on seeing this case through to the end.

Chapter 22

The sound of automatic gunfire erupted from upstairs. Ray wasn't faking—he let the Feds know that he meant business.

"We got women hostages in here!" he roared with conviction. "You fuck with us, and all them bitches dying tonight!" Another burst of gunfire ripped the air.

Downstairs in the main room, the front door eased open slightly.

"Muthafuckas!" Nutso squeezed the trigger. A violent burst of gunfire ripped through two floodlights. He laughed and slammed the door. Before he could move, a wave of slugs tore through the frame around the smoked bulletproof glass.

"Muthafucka! I'm hit!" Nutso screamed, then fell to the floor. He felt an intense pain race through his entire body. The left side of his torso was riddled with gaping bullet wounds. "Ay, Dude," he grunted in a fit of panic, "I need help!" His brawny frame collapsed on his stomach.

A few seconds later Nutso heard someone scampering in the dark.

"Aww, man!" Dude gasped. "You seriously fucked up, champ!"

Nutso reached out and jerked Dude by the collar. "That's why I called you for help," he said though gritted teeth.

"What's going on?" Biggie came crawling in on all fours.

"Can't you see?" Nutso retorted sharply. "Muthafucka, I'm hit!"

"C'mon, Big, we gotta get him outta here," Dude instructed. "Let's move him to the back room."

Dude steadied him on the right, while Biggie positioned himself on the left. Together they hoisted Nutso's mammoth frame to his feet. A gut-wrenching moan jumped from his mouth with every step he took.

Another volley of automatic gunfire resonated from the upper level, followed immediately by the sound of laughter. Ray's laughter stopped when he spotted the women that were supposed to be locked up in the pool house scampering across the grounds, running and ducking for cover right into the arms of the law.

Ray's jaw dropped as he watched his only ace in the hole slip right through his fingers. He could feel his heart deflate in his chest. The writing was on the wall, and he could sense the end was near.

But Ray had one more trick up his sleeve, and this would be the perfect time to try his hand. A minute later, Ray stepped through a secret archway and descended a rear staircase.

After placing Nutso in the back room on a sofa and actually seeing how bad his wounds were, the boys began having second thoughts. They both agreed that now wasn't the time to back out. They had made their beds, and now they would have to lie in them.

Reluctantly, Dude and Biggie prepared to continue the battle. Both men crept toward the main room. They had stopped in the archway to reload their guns when a violent barrage blasted the front structure, catching them both off guard.

Dude dashed through the archway as bullets exploded behind him. Miraculously, he managed to duck and dive and roll to safety.

Still standing in the archway like a deer caught in headlights, Biggie's oversized frame was struck in a flurry of gunfire. He felt the sudden explosion of heat tear into his chest and stomach. The force pushed him backward, and he stumbled in pain. Small baby cries dribbled off his lips as he doubled over.

"Big! No!!!" Dude cried out. "Get down!"

Biggie never heard him. The big fella was consumed with pain and the darkness invading his soul. He was in another world.

Another flurry of gunfire exploded through the main room. Dude recoiled. His bottom lip quivered at the sight of Big. Witnessing his partner's death psychologically crushed him.

Biggie felt something heavy pound on his chest. It felt like a blow from a sledge hammer. He was too far gone to realize he had just taken the full blast of a sniper's round in the chest, right though his heart. Slowly, he could feel himself evaporating, his soul being swept away by a massive wave of darkness. A moment later, Biggie's hefty frame crumbled to the floor with a heavy thud.

The sound of a car's engine reverberated. Dude looked startled and baffled all at once. "What the fuck?!? That sounds like a goddamn car!?!"

Inside the four-bay garage on the lower level, Ray cranked up the engine to his pearl-black Porsche Carrera, and hit the remote for the garage door. He could sense his pulse rate soar as he watched the door roll up in slow motion. A chilly breeze whipped in the open bay, swirling like a miniature tornado.

"This is it!" Ray said, feeling the tension in his chest tighten as he sat behind the wheel, a .50 caliber on his lap. He stared out at the pitch-black landscape before him. He could see the jagged silhouette of wooded land far off in the distance.

If I can just make it to the woods, he silently breathed, *I'll be home free.*

He reached down and jostled the gear shift into position, then popped the clutch. The black Porsche shot out of the garage like a rocket on wheels. Headlights off, he rolled across the dark, open expanse, moving away from the estate. Ray could see the start of the slope, which gave him just enough hope. He held his breath and gunned the engine in an attempt to close the distance as quickly as possible.

If I could just make it to the drop off, he prayed., *I'll be in the clear.*

Suddenly, the dark landscape around him was bathed in bright light, and the sound of gunfire resonated in the air.

"Oh, shit!" Ray's entire body cringed in fright. He felt like a target in a shooting gallery. Instinctively, he jerked the wheel, and the car banked hard to the right, moving away from the floodlights. Clumps of earth spewed high in the air as the Porsche peeled out across the grassy knoll, leaving a deep swath in its wake.

Ray turned on the headlights while trying to straighten out the wheel. A boulder popped into view on his left and an old wooden shed appeared on the right.

"Whoa!" Ray grunted, knowing he had overcorrected on the wheel. He braced himself for impact.

The Porsche smacked hard against the boulder and ricocheted to the right, bouncing harmlessly against the side of the shed.

Echoing in the dark distance, the sound of voices were getting louder. Time was short, and Ray wasted none of it. He bolted from the car, and attempted to go left. Bullets ripped the ground in front of him. He sprinted off in the opposite direction until the sound of bullets whizzed by his head, prompting him to dive head first to the ground for cover.

Crawling on hands and knees, Ray made his way toward the shed. It was locked! He bounced to his feet and started kicking on the door in a futile attempt to break it down. He paused, whipped out a .50 caliber and pressed the barrel against the lock.

Boom!

The lock disintegrated, and he lunged through the door just as floodlights illuminated the area. Basking in the bright glow from the spotlights, Ray froze in the middle of the floor. His right hand fell to his side, still clutching the pistol. The expression on his face was a combination of total shock, horror and disbelief. He covered his mouth with his left hand and gagged at the horrific scene.

The hellish display inside of the shed was an assault on the mind. The floor of the shed was spotless, save for the decrepit wooden shelves filled with lab jars. The contents inside the jars blew Ray's mind.

Each glass jar was filled to the brim with liquid formaldehyde, preserving the grisly assortment of human body parts floating inside, as if awaiting release from their glass tombs.

A woman's head was inside the first jar that caught Ray's eye. He thought he recognized the dead face glaring at him, and a chill raced up his spine. She resembled Jovan's girlfriend Malaysia. But this woman's eyes were hazel.

A voice in the distance shouted, "Freeze! Drop your weapon and put your hands in the air! Do it now!"

Ray's senses were consumed by the horrid sight before him. The verbal command didn't register in his brain. A moment later, a gunshot rang out, and Ray thought someone had whacked him in the back with a bat. The force pushed him forward, and he staggered, clutching at the sharp pain in his chest. Suddenly, Ray was short of breath. He looked down and gaped at his blood-stained hand and the growing crimson stain in the center of his lime green Polo cardigan.

"Oh my God," he groaned in horror, "I've been shot." He turned slowly, his gun dangling carelessly at his side.

Boom! Boom!

Two more shots split the air. The first slug blew a golf ball–size hole in the right side of Ray's head. The second slug crippled his right lung. He wobbled on his feet for a couple seconds, then withered like a dying flower in the middle of the floor.

DEA and ATF agents swarmed the shed.

"What-the-fuck?!?" A commanding agent stood in shock in the doorway. "Everyone stand clear!" he ordered.

"Secure this scene and fall back! Get forensics down here, ASAP! We got multiple homicides!"

Cordel Smith moseyed up to the shed and got a nice eyeful from the doorway.

"Humph ... looks like a storage shed for body parts," he commented offhandedly. "These boys are knee-deep in homicides."

Chapter 23

In the distant recesses of his drug-tainted mind, Jovan heard Malaysia's muted croak of death. He also could see her head floating bodiless in the dark. A weird sensation surged through his body. He wondered why his penis was feeling so sore. Felt like a tight piece of virgin pussy had taken a ride on his rod.

A vision suddenly jumped out at him. He saw those wicked blue eyes and the blonde hair. Angel's imposter stood over him with a syringe dangling from her fingers. He could see her kneeling down beside him, stroking his penis with this crazy gleam in her eye. Without warning, she jabbed the needle deep in his erect penis!

Jovan's eyes sprang wide. His upper torso jack-knifed into a sitting position.

"Oh my God!" he mumbled, feeling anxious and bewildered, his eyes darting around in the pitch-black space that surrounded him. *Where am I*, he wondered, feeling lost and confused. He tried to move, but his hands and legs were still bound.

Something moved overhead, and his head shot skyward. He could hear the faint sound of voices drifting through the thick cover of blackness just above him. He strained to make out what they were saying, but he couldn't.

His heart jumped suddenly when he heard the sound of footsteps moving across the black space overhead.

Seconds later Jovan heard a doorknob rattling somewhere in the distance and the echo of a door creaking to his left.

Light appeared suddenly, and he made out the outline of a door about ten feet away. That's when he realized he was locked in a separate room somewhere. Wherever he was, he was sitting on a hard and uncomfortable elevated surface.

Seconds later Jovan's heart jumped with excitement when he heard a familiar voice.

"Please, you don't have to do that. Remember, he is my husband, and I still love him no matter what."

Angel! Hearing her voice was music to his ears. Jovan's eyes probed expectantly, focused on the door. "Please, baby ... please get me the fuck outta here," he mumbled under his breath, hoping and praying for his wife to rescue him. "God, please get me outta here."

"Your husband. You still have love for him? Stop being a fool for that no-good piece of shit!"

Jovan shuddered. His heart dropped to his feet when he heard the coarse undertone in the other woman's voice.

"Oh, no," he moaned. A pang of trepidation stabbed him in the gut like a dull blade. "That crazy-ass impostor bitch!" Her voice was unforgettable.

Natasha went on to say, "Get yourself a real man. You can do a helluva lot better than that dirty

dick nigga! If it's the sex you hooked on, then say that. But other than a good fuck, what's he worth? What good is he?"

There was a long, silent pause before Natasha added, "Nothing! That's what I figured. That nigga ain't worth the pain and misery that he puts you through on a daily basis. When was the last time you felt any love from that man?

When was the last time you were able to let your guard down and feel true happiness and love with that man?" Another long pause. "That's what I thought. I rest my case."

The effect of the crazy woman's words filled Jovan with fear and dread. *Why didn't Angel speak up for me? I can't face that dangerous bitch again. Especially not all tied up like this.*

"Angel! What the fuck are you doing?!?" Jovan bellowed, anger and panic etched in his voice. "Get me the fuck outta here! Get me away from that crazy bitch!" He felt himself start to hyperventilate.

Silence momentarily fell over the room. Then he heard soft whispers outside the door.

The sound of Natasha's laughter broke the uncomfortable silence. She laughed hysterically at the top of her lungs, then stopped abruptly. The room fell silent again until the sound of keys jingling in the door broke the quiet.

Startled, Jovan's gaze went wide, and confusion and fright overcame him. He suddenly felt his restraints start to loosen a bit.

"Shit," he muttered, finally sensing a sliver of hope from his pressing predicament. Jovan strained with all his God-given might.

The door swung open, and light instantly filled the room. The eruption of light on Jovan's nude body ignited his senses, and he recognized instantly where he was being held: the laundry room in the basement of his home!

A dark silhouette of his wife's curvy coke-bottle figure stood in the doorway, naked.

OMG! He stared at her, breathless. A familiar rush of lust overcame him as he savored every inch of her delicate physique.

"Do you like what you see?" she said. Angel's wicked tone sounded unnatural to him. She didn't sound like herself, which prompted him to watch her closely.

As Jovan eyed her, he noticed the shimmering blades laying on the carpet beside her French-pedicured toes.

Natasha watched Jovan's facial expression fluctuate. The fleeting glimmer of lust evaporated. Fear was now laced with absolute horror. She observed him, gears churning in her mind.

She slowly reached down and drew the machete and serrated blades off the floor. Jovan watched her with trembling eyes. A bloody image of Malaysia's head popped in his mind. He couldn't help but feel a deep sense of loss for the death of his Thai girlfriend.

Natasha used the edge of the machete to flip on the light. She grinned slightly, gliding toward him like a sinewy tigress.

The imposter!!! Jovan blurted inwardly. "What the fuck is this shit? Who the fuck do you supposed to be, huh? And what in the hell do you want with me?"

Natasha enjoyed the look of fear on Jovan's face as he sat helplessly atop the stainless steel table in the center of the room. She paused at the side of the table, twirling the serrated blade in her right hand. She turned her eyes toward his lap, where his prized organ lay undisturbed.

"Mmph, mmph, mmph," Natasha sighed. "What a waste." She faced him and leaned over his lap. "Jovan, did you really think you could get away with fucking around on my sister and not pay a price for your dirty deeds?" She shook her head. "Mmph, mmmph, mmph."

Jovan recoiled. "Your sister?!?" he snapped, glaring defiantly. "What kind of goddamn games are you playing with me? Angel doesn't have any goddamn sisters! You're trying to make yourself look like my wife with all that fucking makeup, the wig, the contacts. Who do you supposed to be? Her long-lost twin, huh? You crazy-ass-bitch!"

Somehow Natasha managed to keep her cool. She met his hostile leer without flinching. "You're calling me a crazy bitch?" She stared him in the eyes. The feeling to end his life was downright intoxicating. "Do you realize how many women's lives have been destroyed because of your infidelities?" She could see his chest heave. The anxiousness in his breath deepened. "Their deaths are attributed directly to your actions. Your hands are drenched in their blood," she growled. Her tone lowered to a guttural rumble, and her crystal-blue irises sparkled with pure hatred.

Jovan felt himself momentarily transfixed by her ominous gaze. Her sapphire orbs were incisive and tense.

"You crazy-ass bitch!" he snarled, his fear yielding to his anger. For an instant, his eyes flashed death. "I dare you try to blame me for anybody's murder! I've killed muthafuckas for far less than that. You got me fucked up! If you don't—"

"If I don't what?" Natasha interrupted. She took a menacing step forward and placed the sharp tip of the blade against his manhood. "Do you think I give a fuck about you? I'm your worst nightmare, and I'm here to stay!"

Jovan's exasperated look only served to fuel her fire. Natasha got her rocks off inducing panic and fear. She craved the feeling it gave her soul.

Chapter 24

The Dynamic Duo stood at the foot of the road leading to the Rising residence. They gazed down the quiet cul-de-sac. One way in, one way out. The spot was perfect for a raid.

Clark watched the small crew of agents he handpicked for the raid position themselves along the perimeter of the road. They could have the entire house surrounded in thirty seconds flat. Only thing now was to wait for the go-ahead phone call.

Louis moved up the pavement in Clark's direction. He waved his partner to the side. "I need to speak with you in private, Will," he said, his tone urgent. Clark noticed Louis wringing his hands. That was a sure sign that something wasn't right.

"Hey," he said, tapping Sgt. Gain before walking off, "keep your infrared trained on the house. Holler when you see the slightest movement from any window."

Louis waited off to the side, gazing up at the full moon, watching it shimmer in the dark horizon. He heard the sound of hard heels walk up behind him and stop. Louis did an about-face. He stared in Clark's eyes and spoke in a steely tone. "I just got a call from headquarters. I.A.D. is en route to our location." He hesitated. "Will, what would internal affairs be doing on an active crime scene? Do you recall anything like this ever happening in the past?"

"I.A.D.?" Clark murmured, puzzled. "You sure about that? They're en route to this crime scene?" A fleeting look of concern flashed in his eyes. He quickly covered it with a cold laugh. "I'm not sure what's going on, Rich. As far as my experience goes, I've never witnessed or ever heard of internal affairs intervening on an active crime scene. That's a new one on me. That makes me wonder, Rich—what in the hell is internal affairs up to?" The question lingered in the air as both men pondered their next move.

The sound of running water filled the quiet calm in the basement. Just outside the laundry room, Natasha stood over the bathroom sink peering at her reflection in the mirror. The woman staring back at her was strong, evil and demented. It was time for her to come out of hiding and show the world the new breed of woman—the kind that doesn't take any shit off no man.

She removed the wig and contacts, stuffed them inside a compact medical bag and tossed the bag in the bathroom cabinet under the sink. She splashed soap and water on her face like she was trying to wash away some type of diseased rash.

When Natasha finished, she studied herself in the mirror like she was seeing herself for the very first time and laughed quietly under her breath. It was time.

Sensing her enter the room, Jovan looked toward the door. He choked, coughing abruptly at the sight of Angel. *Angel!* He was flabbergasted.

"Thank God, Angel! Where did you come from?" he whispered, straining to see behind her. "Can you come help me please before that crazy bitch comes back? Who is that bitch? Telling me she's your fucking sister!" Jovan began to feel woozy. His vision was blurry. "What are you doing? Okay, enough with the bullshit! I seen that crazy broad kill some—"

Jovan stopped short. A bothered look covered his face. "What in the hell?" It was as if he noticed her for the first time. "Why you walking around naked like that crazy broad?"

She quietly closed the door. "Don't worry about that. That's why I'm here, to help you," she said slowly, her lips starting to quiver. "I'm here to make sure that you're at peace with yourself and God," Angel told him, wiping tears from her eyes. She gave him a half smile.

Jovan's emotions swirled in a windstorm of confusion. "What? Make sure I'm at peace with God?" His brow furled deeply, his mind struggling to put everything together. "What the hell is that supposed to mean?"

Angel shook her head. "I'm so sorry, Da. I didn't want this for you! Please, believe me," she sobbed openly. "I still love you. I'll always love you," she cried out, burying her face in her hands.

Jovan watched Angel fall to her knees. The sight of the knives laying on the floor next to her rocked him. At that moment, the steel-gray duct tape on his hands split. His eyes bucked wide, but he was aware of the unstable situation his wife and her friend posed.

Angel's voice changed. "Tonight, you reap what you sow," Natasha declared, her tone dark and grim. She wrapped her hand around the black leather handle of the machete and rose to her feet like a dark spirit. Natasha viewed herself as the ultimate oracle of death.

Jovan stared at her, paralyzed. Absolute disbelief leaped off his face. The innocent vision of his wife shattered in a million pieces inside his mind.

"Your sins will be cast out and righteousness restored!" Natasha said, her grin taking on a demonic twist. Her hand shot in the air, brandishing the blade as if holding a mighty sword. She brought it down with a forceful roar, aiming for Jovan's feet. "You fucking whore!" she hissed, full of hate.

The sharp blade cut through duct tape and flesh as if it were cutting through a stick of butter. It landed against the steel table with a hard clank.

Jovan moaned in agony when he felt the blade pierce his ankle and foot. A disturbing image of his foot being chopped off flashed in his head. When he glanced down to see the damage she had inflicted, he was surprised to see that his injury was nothing more than a superficial wound.

"Bitch! You fucked up now!" he lashed out, staring her dead in the eye. He knew instantly Angel was beyond the point of reason. Her gaze was hollow. Empty. Psychotic.

Natasha stood erect, unmovable. The deadly gleam in her eye struck fear in Jovan's heart. That intensely startling feeling invoked an epiphany. His mind imploded with vivid images of death. All those horrible nightmares of his sexcapades and all his women and the full scope of Angel's bloody carnage was incomprehensible.

"Oh ... my ... g-gosh!" he stammered. "What in the world have you done? What have you become?" A ghastly expression exploded on his face. "Who the fuck are you?!?"

A sea of blue police lights enveloped the dark cul-de-sac. The Dynamic Duo and their agents burst through the front door of the Rising home, guns drawn. The agents immediately fanned out and searched the first level. Nothing.

Clark gave the signal to split up. They quickly divided into two teams. Louis led the first trio. He gave a few hand gestures, and the dark dressed men ascended the dimly lit staircase.

Clark signaled for the second squad to follow his lead, and they prepared to descend the basement stairs. As the trio slowly crept down the staircase, each man silently wondered why they had proceeded to carry out a raid without knowing if the subject was home.

Just as Clark planted his foot on the last step, a murmur of voices drifted from somewhere deep in the basement. Clark's hand shot in the air on impulse, signaling the men to hold their positions. They listened for a second, trying to decipher the words and lock in on the location.

The voices were coming from deep within the basement's interior. The trio moved silently, darting through the entertainment room and the adjoining weight training room. Within a few moments, they came upon a small hallway with a closed door at the end.

Clark gave the signal. His subordinates moved into position on both sides of the door, guns at the ready. Clark was in front. He readied himself, preparing to smash down the door.

He put three meaty fingers in the air. When everyone was set, he started the countdown—three … two … one!

He launched his burly frame into the door, and it caved.

"Freeze! Hands in the air, now!!!"

Jovan was in a daze. The drug from the syringe had really done a job on him, he realized, feeling his strength waver as he engaged in a heated struggle with his totally gone-mad wife. He managed to escape his adhesive bonds in the nick of time, just as Angel unleashed a fury on him that surprised him in the worst way ever imagined.

Now Jovan found himself in a fight to save his life from the woman he wed. He couldn't believe what was happening.

Angel! My Angel is actually trying to gut my ass like a fish!

"Aaarrgh!" Jovan yelled in pain when Angel sank her sharp canines into his wrist like a mad dog. "You fucking bitch!" he spat bitterly. He wanted to inflict her with the same pain, so he forced her over his lap, and bit down hard on her arm.

"OMG!" he cringed and spit when the pungent taste of blood stung his taste buds.

Natasha whipped her head around and shot him a wild-eyed stare that rattled him.

"You dirty-dick muthafucka! Angel and the world will be better off without you!" she hissed, scathingly. "You fucking whore!!!"

Jovan swallowed hard when he saw the madness in her eyes. Then he heard a voice echo around the room. It sounded like the police. When he turned to look, he felt this excruciating pain irrupt in his groin, and he knew in that instance he had fucked up by diverting his attention away from his wife.

The pain was unimaginable. A blood-curdling shriek blasted the air as Jovan screamed from every core of his being. He looked down and saw his penis was gone, detached from his body!

A thick fountain of blood bubbled up and gushed from the open wound as he stared in utter shock. A second later the sound of gunfire rang out, but Jovan was unfazed by it. He felt a powerful pounding on his back and the sudden sensation of searing heat spreading inside him. But that was nothing compared to the pain he felt in his groin and the shock of seeing his wife as she backed away from him, firmly clutching his prized organ in her hand.

Jovan sensed the darkness evade his soul, and for a split second he was scared. Then he realized he had nothing to live for now. The stark realization deeply saddened him. He conceded, *My life is over.* And he opened himself up to death, welcoming it with open arms.

Chapter 25

The headline story splashed across the front of *The Washington Post*:

"Hidden Horrors Discovered in Posh Potomac Estate Police Kill Suspected DC Serial Killer Attempting to Escape Dragnet"

The follow-up story making major headlines this morning read:

Police Kill Second Suspected DC Serial Killer In Clarksville, MD
Foiling Attack on Wife's Life

The dawning of a new day appeared on the horizon, warm sunlight caressed the lush rolling green hills of Potomac, MD. The narrow stretch of Lake Potomac Drive, which ran the length of Ray Leon's property, afforded passersby a clear bird's-eye view of the intense police presence covering the grounds of the estate.

About sixty yards out from the palatial structure, a thirty-foot sky-blue tent had been erected by a team of FBI agents and served as an on-site lab with the wooden shed, all its gory content and surrounding ground area were shrouded in secrecy beneath a sky-blue translucent veil.

The entire scene resembled something straight out of an X-Files movie – giant plastic tent with an army of plastic-suited agents scouring the grounds for the slightest inkling of evidence to boaster the infamous DC serial killer case.

Earlier in the night, soon after Ray Leon was shot and killed, and the crime scene surrounding the now infamous shed was sealed off, a special SWAT team arrived in preparation to storm the estate. At the last minute, when Dude realized he was the last man standing, he quickly decided to give up. He lay down his weapons and walked out the front door with his hands held high. Detectives and SWAT converged on the house immediately. They found the injured Nutso inside clinging to life. He was given emergency assistance, then whisked away to a nearby hospital.

A team of DEA agents frisked Dude, cuffed him. They were hustling him toward an awaiting transport vehicle when Agent Cordel Smith stepped in and grabbed Dude by the arm.

"Hey, your name Dude, right?" Cordel said with a pointed finger to his face. A beguiled look flickered in the agent's eye. "Remember me?" he asked, massaging his palms. "I was gonna hook y'all up with the big Miami cocaine connect. Looks to me like y'all had bigger fish to fry. You might want to think about putting a bug in my ear because what you're going down for is far greater than anything I could've imagined." Cordel paused and leaned in Dude's ear. He whispered, "C'mon, Dude, give me something I can work with. Help yourself out. Because these boys here are trying to fry your ass." He sucked his teeth, taunting him, imitating sizzling meat.

Dude gave him a harsh look, then leaned back and spit in his face. "Suck my dick!" he snarled, catching Cordel and his buddies off guard. Dude laughed at him when he cursed and shrank away in disgust. "Yeah, put that bug in your ear! You fucking rat-ass bitch!" He railed as the team of agents ushered him away, chiding and admonishing him.

Chapter 26

After the gun smoke cleared ...

At the Rising home in Clarksville, Louis and his subordinates rushed down the stairs, stumbling as they went, when they heard the sound of gunfire ring out from below. By the time they arrived on the scene, it looked like Clark and his men had everything under control.

Louis and his men stared wide-eyed from the doorway at the dead man lying across the stainless steel table, naked and bleeding profusely. He knew by the amount of blood, bullet wounds were totally out of the question.

On the opposite end of the room, they spotted Clark comforting a distressed woman. No doubt she was the victim. Clark wrapped his coat around her. It was quite apparent that she was on the verge of having an emotional breakdown; the woman was sobbing and trembling uncontrollably. Clark was doing his best to comfort her.

"That's our man?" Louis posed the question to Sgt. Rogers, a lumbering blonde European who would have you believe that he was George Clooney's cousin. Rogers was busy examining the label on a pill bottle, turning it over in his hand. Rogers nodded while pondering the significance of his discovery. He pulled open the brown duffle bag. It was filled with dark-orange pill bottles, all with a prescription label for J. Rising.

"Hummm ..." Rogers sighed, mentally choreographing a puzzle in his head. "That's Jovan Rising," he muttered carefully. "I think we just stopped him from killing his wife. But somehow she managed to extract his male organ from his body." Sgt. Rogers couldn't conceal the troubling spirit brewing inside. *Why are so many empty pill bottles being stored in this bag?* he mused quietly.

Louis did a double take. "What was that?" he said.

"Clark! Louis!" A heavy baritone rumbled through the room, followed by a team of young and diligent agents all sporting crisp dark suits with too much starch and cropped army haircuts. They looked fresh out of the academy, ready to jump off a bridge if ordered to do so.

Louis' and Clark's gaze moved to the IAD commander as he strode in the room. His entire being demanded respect and everyone's undivided attention. The commander was broad and tall with a coffee-colored skin tone and a thick mane of jet-black curly hair. His eyes were piercing—glistening black marbles that stared through you like you were a transparent oddity.

When Commander Shane Holt got involved with an IAD case, that was a sure sign that something major had transpired. And whatever violation had been committed, the commander's presence signified a foregone conclusion: The consequences and repercussions of those acts were already set in motion. Any and all excuses, reasons, and defenses were null and void at that point.

"Relieve detectives Clark and Louis of their service weapons and shields," ordered the commander, an intense look sparkling in his eye. He glared at Clark, beaming with anger, then announced, "Gentlemen, you are both under arrest at this time."

Jaws hit the floor! Clark was appalled. "What the hell is this all about?!?" he protested.

Holt stepped forward and fixed him with a gaze clearly meant to intimidate. "You know damn well what this is about!" his voice boomed. "I dare you to play dumbass with me!" he warned. His eyes glistened, black like oil. "You can try and fuck with me if you want. Your ass will be cursing the day you graduated the police academy, 'cause I will make your ass pay longer and harder than your corrupt little mind could ever fathom!"

Louis said nothing. He nodded and counted himself lucky. He had allowed Clark to influence his decision to plant evidence on the Whimple twins. That was really the extent of his misbehavior. But Will on the other hand— Louis caught a whiff of his shady side, and he knew his partner was involved in some deep underworld dealings, to say the least.

Commander Holt motioned for the detectives to be taken away, then turned to Sgt. Rogers. "Sergeant, " he began, his voice firm, "this crime scene is your baby now. So I expect you to treat is as such." When he finished, the commander made eye contact with the victim. There was something in her facial expression that struck him as odd.

"Where's the medical personnel for this woman? Can't you see that she's in dire need of medical attention?"

Natasha stood against the wall, feigning shock, watching the entire episode unfold step by step. She turned on the tears when needed and shivered and sobbed on cue like she was a trained actress, acting her part perfectly.

Inside, Natasha was laughing her butt off. But that couldn't dull the overwhelming sensation of Angel's heart shattering like glass. The death of Jovan simultaneously pierced Angel's soul and strengthened Natasha's reserve.

Meanwhile, outside in the driveway, Commander Holt's shiny black Suburban sat idling quietly. The black SUV was the only one on the scene and served as a reminder to the investigating task force that the head honcho was on the premises.

Observing the crime scene from inside the vehicle's tinted interior, Tony Woo sat incognito, gazing through his thick specs, examining the comings and goings and demeanor of each and every agent involved with this high-profile criminal case.

Chapter 27

The following weekend, Tony Woo sat behind his desk at DC police headquarters. Several stacks of thick file folders sat neatly on his mahogany desk. Each folder was crammed with evidence and information pertaining to the high-profile DC Serial Killer investigation.

Emblazoned on the face of each folder in bold black letters were the names of individuals directly or indirectly involved with the serial case: Ray Leon, Jovan Rising, Will Clark, Rich Louis, Malaysia Tomay, and Angel Rising.

A knock sounded on the door, interrupting Tony's train of thought. He looked up and called out. "The door's open! Come in!"

Commander Holt stepped inside. He acknowledged Tony with a slight nod.

"Mr. Woo, I take it that you have completed your report on the serial case?" The commander's authoritative presence seemed to take hold of the office. He secured the door, then eased his broad tailor-suited frame into the vacant chair beside Woo's desk. Holt crossed his legs, leaned back, and made himself comfortable.

"Well, the floor is yours," the Commander said, the corners of his mouth turned up. "I expect you have a full critique of this matter," he said with a raised brow. "A concise totality, I presume?"

Tony was leaning back in his plush leather wing chair, his index finger tapping quietly on his wired frames. He stopped, plucked the glasses off his face and set them aside. A quiet inflection glowed in his keen, slanted eyes.

"Well, commander, I am somewhat of a totalitarian, wouldn't you say?"

Both men couldn't help but grin and acknowledge the good-humored logic behind Tony's words.

Commander Holt insisted Tony start with Ray Leon's file. His name had sat atop DC authority's "Most Wanted" list for ages. Here sat the top forensic specialist with disturbing information on how Ray and a select group of top-level drug suppliers were able to operate with longevity and impunity because of a departmental mole: Lieutenant Will Clark.

"The rise of Ray Leon began when the Carl Davis, the drug kingpin from Hanover Street, was arrested by federal authorities approximately ten years ago today. Carl's removal from Hanover spurred the emergence of Ray Leon and Jovan Rising. Yeah, that's correct. They were drug dealing buddies and their history together spans more than a decade," Tony Woo announced proudly.

"Sounds pretty interesting," Holt interjected. "Please continue."

"Well, about five years ago, Mr. Leon and Mr. Rising had a falling out of sorts." He hesitated. "Remember that bloody shoot out inside the Four Seasons Hotel?"

Holt thought for a moment. "Yeah, the big drug boy from Virginia. What's his name?" He snapped his finger. "Tony Percy and his crew got wiped out."

"His street name was T.O.," Woo corrected. "His body was found a block from the hotel. Definitely a drug hit. Word on the street was the Rio Brothers ordered him scratched. That was never confirmed. But anyway, T.O. was Jovan Rising's cousin. He wanted to avenge his murder, but Ray didn't want any parts of it, so they parted ways. Jovan filled his cousin's shoes in the Northern Virginia drug market, while our boy Mr. Leon skyrocketed on the DC scene. Enter Lieutenant Will Clark. That P Street raid where twenty kilograms and two hundred thousand dollars was confiscated from the house garage— evidence inventory records shows fifteen kilos and twenty thousand dollars was turned in. Mr. Gavin, the drug lieutenant for the P Street crew, his attorney revealed that twenty kilos and two hundred thousand dollars was the amount seized. That was until Ray Leon's attorney entered his appearance and disputed said amount. At the time Ray was the controlling figurehead for that particular area of the city. His drug territory stretched from the Trinidad section of NE clear over to the LeDroit Park community in NW. Suddenly all papers read fifteen kilos and twenty thousand dollars as the exact amount seized. Ray Leon and Will Clark forged a secret bond from that date forward."

Holt cut in, "Don't tell me. Let me guess. Clark was acting commander in charge of the P Street raid, right?" He watched Tony Woo affirm his suspicion. "Okay, what about Louis? When does he come into the picture?"

At the mention of Detective Rich Louis, Tony's demeanor softened. "Well, commander, Louis has the smallest part in all of this. His involvement centers around the attempted framing of the Whimple twins. His actions in that case were exacerbated dramatically, I believe in part due to Clark's extremely persuasive nature. I think we both can agree on that." Woo took a breath before going on. "When I provided them with the false Aniline evidence, it didn't take long for them to run with it. The actions of Louis were disappointing, but we have to take into account the Clark factor. Louis is pretty much a stand-up guy, so I'd appreciate if you could show some leniency in his penalty deposition."

There was a long pause before the commander finally replied.

"That will be duly noted. I'll give it some thought." His mood was engaging and extremely inquisitive. Holt made a polite gesture for Tony to continue.

"Okay ..." Tony huffed, reading from another folder. "Ray Leon and Jovan Rising—both men's DNA was discovered in the wood shed where the human remains were stored."

The declaration surprised Commander Holt. "Am I missing something here?" He sounded decisive. "When did they become partners again? What's the time line? And what do you suppose sent them off on this mad killing tantrum? I mean for Christ's sake, they're drug dealers." The commander tossed up his arms, baffled.

Tony flipped through another folder and pointed out a passage that he had highlighted, and to Holt's surprise, the dates in the report suggested that Ray and Jovan had reestablished their dealings right around the time of the first woman's death. As he read further into the report, Holt noticed a pattern—the men were in the habit of prowling the city's top nightclubs together. The pair worked in tandem, picking up women like a tag team and whisking them off to discreet locations in the wee hours of the night. The pair's favorite destination was highlighted: 11235 Lake Potomac Drive.

"Looks to me like you're putting together a very complex puzzle." Holt glanced at Woo, then his eyes drifted to the folder resting near his arm. Malaysia Tomay was the name stamped on the cover. The commander changed gears.

"Tell me, Woo ... how in God's name did your newly acquired CSI tech become involved with this Rising character?" The idea seemed to really bother him.

The mention of his colleague caused Woo to wince. He immediately exchanged one folder for the other. He gazed at the folder, a pained look in his eye.

"From the information I was able to gather, sir," Tony shook his head and groaned uncomfortably, "Ms. Tomay and Mr. Rising have been an intimate item for quite some time now. Ms. Tomay was pregnant at the time of her death. And DNA concludes that Mr. Rising was the father of the unborn child." Woo eyed Holt expectantly, awaiting his reply.

Holt fired him a scandalous look. "Your highly regarded CSI was frolicking around with a married drug suspect and became pregnant?" *The audacity of her!* he thought to himself. *What happened to her integrity?* he wondered, his bushy eyebrow arched with anguish.

Woo nodded. "I understand your concern, sir," he told him with a sturdy look. "Someone either dropped the ball during her screening process, or she put on one helluva poker face."

Holt's eyes narrowed. "What are you implying, Mr. Woo?" The expression on the commander's face was absolute skepticism.

Woo directed Holt's attention to information that revealed Malaysia Tomay was receiving inquiries from an inside DEA source highlighting the investigation into the Ray Leon organization. They also discovered a departmental GPS installed on two of Mr. Rising's vehicles, and files downloaded from Ms. Tomay's PC revealed she was keeping close tabs on Mr. Rising.

Commander Holt looked both pleased and concerned. "So what precipitated such a violent murder? Both sisters decapitated. But why?"

Woo sensed the rising surge of intrigue in Holt. "Sir, I'm not one hundred percent certain, but Mr. Rising may have been involved with both sisters." What Woo said had a weird, appealing logic to it, but it was just conjecture. "And the evidence we've collected thus far suggests that Ms. Tomay might have been attempting to blackmail the suspect, which in turn set him off."

Skepticism appeared on Holt's face in the form of a deeply etched brow.

"What about the other body found at the Tomay residence? Where did she come from?"

Woo's eyes turned hazy as he dropped his head back and stared up at the ceiling. He breathed a frustrated sigh. "The woman's body you're referring to—her name was Ms. Eujami Obey," he began, quickly gathering his composure. "She was last seen in public leaving Love nightclub with her girlfriends in a stretch Hummer limousine, accompanied by both suspects and their crew. The same night, mind you, detectives Clark and Louis apprehended Antonio Whimple outside Love. And the last people to see Ms. Obey alive were her girlfriends, who stated she was spending the night with our man, Jovan Rising. That was the last anyone heard from Ms. Eujami Obey, until her body was discovered at said residence."

Chapter 28

The Abduction

It was just before dawn, when Jovan held open the passenger's door of his Benz coupe. He pulled Eujami tight against his body and kissed her passionately before stepping aside and waiting for her to get comfortable in her seat. He wore a satisfied grin as he hurried around and hopped in behind the wheel.

A moment later, the sleek roadster made its way down the road. Jovan sat at the wheel with a pleased look on his face, savoring the sight of his new African pussycat. He couldn't help himself—baby girl was hot! The stylish cream Gucci dress she wore with the high split was enticing.

Jovan reached out his hand. The tips of his fingers brushed lightly along her soft, chocolate thighs. *Damn!* he thought greedily. *I should've got one last shot of ass before I took her home. Damn!*

"So, you have a good time tonight, baby?" he asked, drooling over her thighs. Sensing her eyes on him, his gaze slowly rose to meet hers.

Eujami already had Jovan locked in her sparkling gaze. The look in her eyes and the sunny smile she wore were enough for him. "You have to ask? Oh, I know what it is—you like hearing praise for a job well done." A knowing grin graced her innocent face.

He looked on, and a triumphant smile exploded on his face. He gently took her hand in his and placed a delicate kiss in her palm. A small moan escaped her mouth as she reached out with her free hand and caressed his cheek.

Eujami gazed at Jovan, her eyes swooning now. "Oooh! I gotta watch myself with you," she admitted fondly.

Jovan chuckled. "If you don't know, you better ask somebody," he boasted and flashed a toothy grin. "'Cause I'm the nigga that'll blow your mind."

About fifteen minutes into the ride, Eujami requested a bit to eat. Jovan whipped his coupe into the first McDonald's he saw, on River Road. The drive-thru was open, but the line was too long. He parked his ride and asked Eujami what she wanted to eat. Before he got out, Eujami planted a hot, juicy kiss on him.

"Thank you," she whispered in his ear as she sank down in the seat and watched him walk away. His swag turned her on, and she knew it was only a matter of time before she was in love with this man.

Eujami was busy listening to the thought-provoking lyrics to the song "If I Could Turn Back the Hands of Time" by R. Kelly when a midnight-blue BMW SUV eased into the vacant parking slot beside her.

Malaysia greeted Eujami with the kindest smile she could muster.

"Excuse me … are you familiar with this area? Girl, I am so lost."

Eujami was more than happy to assist the lady. "Sure, I can help you. Where would you like to go?" She hopped out when she saw the woman trying to read one of those oversized fold-out road maps. She leaned into the passenger's window. "What's the address you're looking for?" Eujami asked, smiling.

Malaysia smacked her lips and began, "Oh, girl, silly me. My address book is on the backseat, right by the passenger's door. If you don't mind, could you grab it for me?"

Without saying a word, Eujami stepped to the rear door and pulled it open.

"There's nothing on the seat," she said, peering inside. "Are you looking for this red notepad on the floor? It's right behind your seat."

"Yeah, that's the one," she said, grinning cunningly. "Could you grab that for me?"

Eujami tried but couldn't reach the notepad, so she climbed across the rear seat and leaned over. "Got it!" The cover page fell open. Clean white paper was all she could see. Eujami frowned. "Are you sure this is the address book? 'Cause it's—" She was cut off by a sudden jolt of electricity when Malaysia reached over the seat and jammed a stun gun in the crook of her neck, incapacitating her.

Seconds later, the BMW truck left the parking lot unnoticed.

Jovan walked out sipping on a hot cup of coffee in his right hand and clutching a McDonald's bag in his left. The moment he stepped outside he noticed his car was empty. His pace slowed dramatically as he approached the car. His eyes warily scanned the parking lot for Eujami before he climbed in behind the wheel.

He immediately dialed her cell phone. The voice mail picked up on the first ring and he really got annoyed.

"Alright, shorty, we had a good night, so what's up with the early morning games?" Jovan said in a low monotone, his gaze carefully roaming the landscape outside. He sat back in his seat, pulled out his McGriddle sandwich and chowed down for the next twenty minutes waiting for E to show up. When he finished with his meal, Jovan gave the parking lot one last visual inspection.

He huffed. "Alright, shorty, I ain't for the games," he grumbled sourly to himself. "I don't know what kind of bammas you used to dealing with, but I'm not the one," Jovan professed, looking troubled and confused. He pushed the start button for the ignition and rolled out.

♛ ♛ ♛ ♛

Commander Holt felt a little chill. "Jesus Christ!" he groaned. "These guys give a whole new meaning to the phrase Lady Killer. I mean, what in the hell got into these two? Why did Rising stash Tomay's head in the goddamn freezer at his house?"

As if on cue, Tony Woo pointed out a disturbing fact. The autopsy that was performed on Jovan revealed extremely high levels of a new cutting-edge narcotic called Oxyline present in his system. The narcotic was so new to the field of medicine, he couldn't find any material or information in which to reference the drug's effects or side effects. The stash of Oxyline confiscated from the suspect's basement was untraceable. Field scientists were in the process of dissecting the narcotics elements and component makeup.

Woo flipped open another folder. Referencing the information in the file, he attempted to shed a different light on the case.

"Sir, the two suspects in our custody ... uh ... Mr. Curtis Day, aka Dude, and the other guy still hospitalized over at DC General, Mr. Nathan Fay, aka Nutso—these two individuals deny any knowledge of anything being stored in the shed. They claim to have never seen a soul enter or exit the shed. In their statements, they both refer to the shed as 'the old shack down the hill that no one paid any mind.' Quote-unquote."

"And you're taking them at their word? Two seasoned drug dealers slash killers. Hell, for all we know, these two living suspects could be involved with the whole sordid scheme." Holt locked eyes with Woo. "You don't strike me as being naïve, Woo. So don't let the gravity of this case cloud your better judgment. Believe me when I say, all eyes are on this case. The implications in this matter—the ramifications will be felt far and wide."

The commander's conviction struck a chord in Woo. His final words were meant to uplift the forensic specialist. "Woo, this case is how dreams are made."

"Your point is duly noted, sir," Woo answered firmly. "And I will be doing all that is in my power to bring to justice to any and all parties who have direct or indirect knowledge of these unspeakable crimes. Because there is still one unknown variable that I haven't been able to track down as of yet, and that's the mystery footprint discovered inside the shed. It doesn't match any of the known suspects' footprints."

Holt recognized the troubled look on Tony's face. "What are you implying, Woo? There's another person who has knowledge pertaining to the contents that were housed in that shed? And the two scumbags in custody have been eliminated? You're one hundred percent sure it's not one of theirs? So some other depraved scoundrel is involved in these sick acts of violence? Well, Woo, I don't care what you have to do. I want that lowlife piece of garbage off my streets!" A noxious flame ignited in his eyes.

Commander Holt paused, then leaned forward. Changing gears, he asked, "What's this I hear about a shallow grave that was discovered at the Rising residence? Who's handling that matter? Because I need to be brought up to speed, pronto."

Woo hesitated. "The corpse out at the Rising place," he began carefully, "well, sir, that's also included in my caseload."

"Oh?" Holt was surprised. "Is that a fact," he responded, exaggerating each word. With a cautiously optimistic expression on his face, the commander continued, "So you've decided to take on all aspects of this case?" Holt's hand went up when Woo started to speak. "I have no problem with that, Woo. You're an extremely capable and responsible agent, and to me I would say you have proven your worth a hundred times over. I can definitely vouch for that. Besides, I want to keep as much of this case as possible in the department. Fuck the Feds!"

Holding his emotions in check, Woo was all giddy inside. Hearing such praise from the commander was rare. This was one of those unforgettable moments that he could reminisce about and relish until his heart was content. This would make for a perfect memo, one Woo could file away under the special events category in the back of his daily journal.

"Well, I'm waiting, Woo," Holt said and leaned back in his seat. "Bring me up to speed about the corpse," he demanded coolly.

"Yes, sir," Woo answered proudly, then produced another file from the top drawer. "Well, concerning the deceased buried at the Rising residence," he began, skimming the folder's contents, "approximately sixty yards from the boundary line at the rear of the property in a small cluster of trees, one canine cadaver hound signaled Agent Crawford to the presence of a corpse. After further investigation, a mummified corpse was exhumed and identified; the deceased was a young woman by the name of Natasha Lopez."

The commander grimaced. "Sick minds are made for waste. I want the sick fucko responsible for this identified, along with the unknown perp. Understand?"

♅ ♅ ♅ ♅

Nightmares Become My Reality

.   The sound of slow, methodical breathing surrounded Angel as she waited patiently in the dark.

Ding dong!

The sound of the doorbell invoked that dark, icky feeling she hated.

Ding dong!

She huffed irritably, popped four Oxylines in her mouth and swallowed hard.

Three seconds later, the front door to the Rio residence creaked open slowly. "Hello! Rafael, it's me, Natasha!" The attractive French-vanilla vixen with crystal-blue eyes and a flowing blonde mane appeared in the doorway. Her attitude was overzealous and arrogant as if she owned the world.

"Rafael, I brought that special gift I promised you!" she said, stepping inside the foyer. She hesitated and pushed the door shut behind her. She stood poised in the foyer, the shiny red patent-leather Valentino bodysuit she wore hugging her curvaceous frame like a latex glove. Her long legs bowed back in a provocative stance. She looked like a high-class runway model perched atop a pair of matching five-inch Valentino stilettos. A hand-crafted black leather handle protruded from the red silk sheath she placed on the burgundy and gold sofa cushion.

Natasha peered across the living room, pushed her red Valentino shades up on her forehead, slung her matching Valentino bag over her shoulder and placed her hand on her hip. She huffed and purposefully strode forward.

"Rafael! I don't like playing games, and you know that! I got your fuckin' text message. So your wifey Angel leaving your ass? Good," she smiled surly, sauntering through the living room. "Now I can slide my pretty ass right up in this camp. Shit, that dumb bitch must've bumped her damn head. Leave all this? I'd kill me a bitch first," she voiced aloud to herself as she poked around.

Natasha walked to the bottom of the stairs.

"Rafael! Are you coming down? 'Cause we need to sit down and discuss our future like you said in your text message. I know you're not getting cold feet!" she yelled. She paused when the scenic view outside the bay windows in the kitchen caught her attention.

Natasha turned her hips slightly. "Daaamn," she gasped. "I just love everything about this fucking house," she mumbled to herself and rushed over to the window to get a better look at the sprawling wooded landscape.

From the moment Natasha entered the house, eyes were on her. Angel stood quietly inside of the first-floor coat closet, peering through a small crack in the door, watching the whore as she took stock in her home and inspected her personal space.

My husband wants to leave me for this ho, Angel raged inwardly. Her mind refused to except Rafael's blatant violation of their marriage vows. *'Til death do us part, Rafael! You sorry excuse for a man!!!*

Angel swallowed hard, hyperventilating as she watched the scarlet-clad ho scrutinize the décor in her family room. She suddenly felt nauseous, and her head was starting to spin.

"Oh, God ..." She shook her head violently and silently cursed Natasha for destroying her marriage.

"Bitches like you don't deserve to live. Y'all bitches don't deserve life," Angel hissed under her breath, totally incensed and crushed at the same time. "Why Lord?" she whispered, her eyes filling with tears now. "How could you let a whore destroy my life? My marriage?!?" Angel felt her heart consumed with hatred. She could feel the dark evilness inside of her pulsate with an unholy life force of its own making. It surged forward and coursed through her veins, invading her entire being. Slowly. Gradually. The force consumed her.

"Rafael!" Natasha called out from the bottom of the stairs. "Well, since you can't bring your ass down here, then I'm bringing my pretty ass upstairs!" she told him as she marched up the carpeted staircase.

A minute later, the door to the coat closet glided open. Angel emerged from her hiding space, totally nude. Her facial expression was blank. Empty. The look in her eyes was dark. Hollow. Trance-like.

She walked across the living room floor and cast a cold, contemptuous gaze down upon the sheath. She reached down, firmly grasped the handle and picked it up. Angel striped the silk covering off and glared at the polished chrome machete. "4 Ever Yours — NATASHA" was engraved in the chrome just above the leather handle. Angel's grip tightened instantly on the handle with such force, the whites of her knuckles showed.

"Natasha." Angel heard herself mumble the name, but her lips didn't move. She could see herself walking toward the stairs, but she wasn't moving.

"Natasha, " she muttered again, but it wasn't her speaking. Angel watched herself slowly climb the stairs, but it was as if it were someone else, like she was in some weird dream.

"Natasha!" a demonic voice growled when she reached the top of the stairs. Angel felt her mind teetering on the brink of sanity.

"Natasha, it's you and me forever," Angel heard the strange voice utter a moment before a thick, smoky black cloud descended upon her and swallowed her whole.

Chapter 29

The Setup

A white Mercedes coasted along the narrow, winding stretch of Lake Potomac Drive. Every few seconds Natasha's eyes went from the road to the Sony laptop sitting on the passenger's seat. The blinking black dot she was concentrating on had stopped moving just up ahead on Lake Potomac Drive.

"Yeah, I see your dirty-dick ass," she said aloud to herself when she rode past the estate and caught sight of Jovan walking up the front steps wearing his favorite snow-white leather Redskins jacket and cap. She watched him disappear inside the grand estate.

She also recognized Ray's BMW parked outside along with a black Dodge Charger.

"So this is the big Potomac playboy mansion you and your boys be hanging out together in, having those freak-ass orgies I've been hearing about," she voiced with cynicism and a corrosive sneer. "This is the place where you bring all your whores to fornicate. You and your boys think this is a safe haven, huh? Well, we're gonna see about that."

It was a week later under the cover of night when Natasha returned to the Potomac estate. Her laptop showed that Jovan's car was parked just off Bladensburg Road at the trendy Oxygen nightclub.

"Partying with your little hoes," she smiled, pulling up to the entrance of 11235 Lake Potomac Drive in a navy van. She stopped at the top of the driveway and cut the lights. The only light on inside the estate was a dim glow emanating from a few of the windows on the first level. The circular driveway was vacant, and she knew all Jovan's men were out partying with him.

The van proceeded down the ivory driveway in total darkness. It rolled past the front entrance, across the wide driveway. Sixty yards out from the estate, the van backed up to a worn wooden shed.

Donning an all-black ensemble, Natasha alighted from the van and moved quickly to the rear. She pulled open the double rear doors. Inside were a number of gallon-size milk containers filled with formaldehyde, clear glass lab containers encased in bubble wrap, and a number of small, personal-size coolers in assorted colors.

Natasha had her sights set on a dark red cooler. She pulled the cooler toward her and removed the white lid, elated. She gloated over the contents.

The missing head of Malaysia's younger sister, Mariah, lay inside the cooler. Her decapitated head was grotesque, staring back at her with a hellish, deadpan gaze, as if she were looking up from hell.

Mariah's head was embedded in a white crystalline powder that resembled white sand. Its purpose was to preserve human tissue.

Natasha glanced around the dark landscape. The sounds of nature emanating around her seemed to spark a deep, dark force that surged from her core. The feeling was a robust burst of energy that made her tingle all over inside.

"Yeah, Jovan, you and your dirty-dick niggas think y'all can fuck any and every slut that shakes her ass in your face," she spoke in a cold and distant voice. "Well, I'm sorry to have to rain on your parade. See how y'all like your hos when they're in pieces. Sex and death … damn, what a helluva turn on!" she said as she forced open the shed door with a crowbar and began the meticulous task of unloading her grisly collection of mutilated human remains.

❀ ❀ ❀ ❀

"Whatever it takes. Whatever I have to do, sir," Woo countered with a serious glare, "I will identify the unknown culprit in this case. There will be no stone left unturned, and this case will be solved. You have my word."

Holt stared at Woo a long moment and then reached for one of the folders. His hand landed on Angel Rising's file.

"So what's the deal on the suspect's wife?" he inquired, flipping open the folder.

Uncertain, Woo hesitated before answering. "Um, I'm not sure just yet. I was, uh, saving her file for last, and I haven't been able to get around to her yet. But she's next on my list, rest assured."

Holt fixed Woo with a devilish grin. "Mrs. Angel Rising," he muttered, more so to himself. "Now that's what I call a beautiful woman. I can't believe that bastard husband of hers was actually going to kill her. Now she's left with the task of picking up the pieces and moving on. That beautiful woman's a widow now, and I can tell she's not used to being alone. I could see it in her that this incident really dampened her spirit." He paused. His eyes moved from the file to Woo. "Hey, I think she's going to need some downtime to recover from this hectic episode. I'll just keep her folder with me. She doesn't need to be hassled about this so soon after the incident. I'll do my own little checking up on her. She probably needs a strong shoulder to cry on right about now."

The commander tucked the folder under his arm and rose to his feet.

Woo was caught off guard by the commander's words. He didn't dare say a word; he concurred with a nod and watched the commander pull a pen from his suit pocket.

"Woo," he began, scribbling on a small note pad, "I expect a full report on my desk early Monday morning. Everything you briefed me on and anything you left out. This here is my personal cell number, and you can reach me anytime you need. Keep me abreast of any new developments, ASAP." Holt lingered for a second. "This folder here—keep this between you and me. I'll handle everything pertaining to Mrs. Rising." He shot Woo a knowing wink, then headed for the door.

From the blank look on Woo's face, Holt knew the man was another ace in his pocket. Woo wanted access to the special circle within the department. And to get there, all roads led through him. Commander Holt was the rising star of the Metropolitan Police Department.

Chapter 30

A Nightmare So Real, The Bitch Had To Die...

The entire lounge reeked of musk, sandalwood and Ferragamo. Hints of Prada, Issey and Gabbana were mixed into the cool, carefree atmosphere as the sound of Sade's soothing vocals serenaded the crowd with her timeless song "Kiss of Life."

Across the room, a chocolate-colored woman wearing a white leather bodysuit that highlighted every inch of her 36D-24-37 package with eye-popping effect. She was looking at herself in the mirror, shaking her ass, dancing sleazily.

The woman's jovial mood seemed to intensify when a suave-looking man dressed in a crisp white Valentino suit walked up behind her and wrapped his arms around her waist. He greeted her in such a provocative way Angel felt a twinge of excitement bubble between her legs watching them.

A look of recognition flashed in Angel's eye when the couple started across the room. She watched breathlessly, almost falling over when Jovan and her best friend, Jo Jo, stopped in the middle of the floor and embraced in a hot, passionate kiss.

Jo Jo made eye contact with her, slightly turning her hips. Her dark eyes flashed devilishly as she glared at Angel and flipped her the finger. The couple tossed their heads back and laughed facetiously before walking off hand in hand.

"What-the-fuck!!" Angel sprang upright to a seated position. She scratched her head. Her eyes darted around the family room. She was totally perplexed. It took her a minute to collect herself.

When she was together, Angel swung her legs over the side of the sofa. "Dirty freak-ass bitch!" she cursed as she stood, her emotions in a whirlwind of confusion.

Angel could feel the rage within her mounting, its presence, powerful and all consuming.

"Oh, Lord," she breathed, fearful. This was the preemptive vibe she felt just before the blackouts. Angel immediately snatched the pill bottle off the coffee table and popped two Oxylines.

She whirled on her heels and stared at herself in the mirror. There was a savage eagerness about her that startled her. Angel stood quivering as a blanket of darkness slowly engulfed her mind.

Her face contorted and twisted. The expression on her face was pain. She eased her hand over her mouth to stifle a sigh. Suddenly a disgusted grunt sounded from her mouth as she turned and strode toward the pantry. Reaching inside, she retrieved her favored tool of death: her prized machete with the black leather handle.

Moments later, inside the garage, a brand-new winter-white Mercedes-Benz CL-600 with shimmering platinum rims was purring quietly, ready to hit the road.

"Jo Jo. What are you doing, honey? Oh, you relaxing at home, huh? Well, that goes for the both of us, 'cause I ain't doing shit either. I am lonely, though. You feel like going out for a drink, just to get out of the house? You know your black ass itching to see my new Benz. Get your dark ass together. I'm on my way over."

She dropped the iPhone on the passenger's seat and flipped down the visor. Natasha's piercing blue eyes shone with a caginess that displayed her reckless self-indulgence. She styled her honey-blonde tresses just so and blew herself a kiss.

"You fuck me, bitch, I fuck you twice," she declared, feeling a pervasive touch of evilness surging in her heart.

The garage door glided open revealing a sun-drenched driveway. The Mercedes rolled out, glistening in the afternoon sun like a streak of white lightning. The car's tires gripped the asphalt and propelled the sleek-looking ride along the road with ease.

Natasha sat at the helm, looking like a princess, donning her sheer white Dolce and Gabbana blouse with a matching scarf and shades. There was a devious gleam in her eye that belied the happy-go-lucky smile she wore as a front.

Crude images of a bloodied Jo Jo danced mirthfully in her head to the sound of Sade's "Kiss of Life" playing on the Bose sound system. Picturing Jo Jo beg for her life brought comfort to Natasha's soul and ignited her dark evil spirit to new heights.

Today, Satan wore white Dolce & Gabbana, drove a sparkling white Mercedes-Benz and looked like an Angel.

Chapter 31

The smooth jazz melody of Maysa floated through the immaculate interior of Jo Jo's stylish African-themed home.

Across the living room, positioned five feet from the rose-tinted patio window, Jo Jo sat at her mini-bar, donning a skintight milky-blue Gucci short outfit.

Jo Jo's mood was carefree and full of spunk. Lounging on the bar stool – her head, neck and upper torso were undulating and swinding in rhythm to the sweet sinuous instrumental.

She paused, took another sip of White Zinfandel and savored the taste of the sweet, flavorful wine before letting it trickle down her throat. The sudden sound of the doorbell ringing prompted Jo Jo to stop her groove in mid-motion.

"Angel! Girl, if you don't bring your ass in here!" she shouted over her shoulder, swinging and swaying again to the music. "When you start ringing my damn doorbell? Got a new ride, now you wanna get all brand new on a bitch. I wish you would, ho!" Jo Jo concluded with a lighthearted chuckle.

Jo Jo took another gulp of wine, then set the wine glass on the bar next to a half-empty bottle of White Zinfandel.

A reflection appeared on the rose-tinted window and caught Jo Jo's eye. She hesitated, her vision focused on the white silhouette hovering behind her.

"What's up, girl? You sneaking up on a bitch without speaking," Jo Jo said, her gaze never moving from the reflection on the window. "What's on your mind, Angel?

And, please—I don't want to hear nothing about a man. I'm in celibacy mode. After all the bullshit you just went through, you should be too."

A flash of silver moving in the air above Jo Jo's head caught her attention, startling her. "What the hell? Angel, what are you—" The words died in Jo Jo's throat as she twisted on the stool.

Sheer horror exploded in her eyes when she made eye contact with the blue-eyed demon wielding the chrome machete overhead.

"Fuckin' whore!" Natasha hissed ferociously and brought the machete down with brutal force.

Thunk!

The blade struck Jo Jo's forehead, dead center, with a force so powerful it sliced through her skull as if it were a cantaloupe, snapping her head back in a violent whiplash motion. A death croak escaped Jo Jo's mouth simultaneously as fresh blood bubbled up from the deep contusion in the center of her forehead. A second later, Jo Jo's body fell limp. Lifeless. Dead.

The sight of fresh blood put a sadistic grin on Natasha's lips. Acting off compulsion and a spiteful will, she tugged on the leather handle and pried the blade loose from her skull. Blood spewed sickly from the deep wound, spraying Natasha in the face. A sadistic smirk creased the corner of her mouth. She cocked back with the machete— swoosh! One powerful swing separated head from torso. A calm, demonic serenity settled upon her as she lifted Jo Jo's decapitated head in the air, admiring it as if it were a trophy.

Angel's eyes popped wide awake. She clutched at her chest, gasping, trying to catch her breath.

"Oh my God!" she breathed, a ball of nervous anxiety brewing in the pit of her gut. "Why do I keep having these nightmares?" She cried out in a voice filled with exasperation and fright. "Oh, Jo Jo, I miss you so much." Angel tried unsuccessfully to stem the tide of emotions swelling up within her.

She sat up in bed. Her eyes were a cloudy brown now, full of tears. "Why do I keep seeing you die over and over in my dreams, Jo Jo? Lord! What have I done to deserve this kind of torture?!?" Angel screamed out, the tension in her voice deeply stirred with sadness and confusion.

Frustrated, she tossed the burgundy satin sheets off her, swung her legs over the edge of the bed, slipped on her fluffy white slippers and stood. On the way to the bathroom, Angel wrapped her white silk robe snug against her body and hugged herself tightly as she rounded the bed and crossed the zebra-skin rug.

Once inside, Angel perched her bottom on the vanity stool. She cast her eyes on the gold-plated case with the dancing angels emblazoned across the surface. The case sat on the left edge of the vanity, and she swore the shimmering case was calling out to her.

Angel couldn't help herself. Without thinking, she reached for the case, slid it to the center of the vanity and glared at it. Looking at the outer shell, Angel felt torn inside—one part of her yearned for its contents, needed it, couldn't function without it, while the other part harbored contempt and ill will toward the contents in the case. She loathed the feeling of inadequacy and dependency that came with the contents of the case so much she felt like the contents were actually controlling her.

Slowly, little by little, inch by inch, Angel's hand crept closer and closer to the case—until her resolve totally gave in. She took hold of the golden case with her left hand, and flipped open the lid with the right.

A stash of potent pink Oxyline pills greeted her eyes. Her right hand instantly began to tremble as she brought it over the case and reached inside. With trembling fingers, she fished out two Oxylines and quickly shoved them in her mouth.

Filled with anxiety, Angel felt her heartbeat quicken and her pulse rate soar. Her eyelids fluttered aggressively. There was a possessed look when her eyes rolled up in her head. She felt a sudden arctic chill coast down her spine the moment before paralysis set in.

Soon after, Angel's mind, body, and soul went completely numb and a total sense of chaotic euphoria swept through her core. Her mind plunged into a deep, dark mental space.

Chapter 32

One year later, on a clear summer's morning in Northwest, DC, smack dab in the middle of Rock Creek Park, a middle-aged Austrian woman was out enjoying her usual early morning jog. Her name was Sherry Haegal. She was a pale Caucasian woman with a rakish build and short, curly hair. On this particular morning, Sherry's normal jogging route was under construction. A large black and yellow detour sign loomed in her path and forced her onto a previously closed off foot trail. It was easy to see by the expression showing on Sherry's pale, emaciated face she was utterly pissed by the disruption to her daily routine. With a sense of growing reluctance evident in her every step, Sherry tramped along the uncharted jogging trail, her instincts on heightened alert, her eyes and ears tuned to every movement and sound within her vicinity.

Sherry came to an abrupt stop when she heard what sounded to her like animals growling and hissing. She focused her attention on this huge dark-gray boulder surrounded by a mangled cluster of brown leafy shrubbery sitting about thirty feet off the trail.

Sherry's inquisitive nature got the better of her, and she decided to investigate the animal noise. With caution in her step, Sherry crept stealthily across the leafy terrain. Within seconds, she found herself standing before the massive gray stone structure. Sherry was 5'8" tall. Standing a foot from the boulder, looking skyward, she figured the big rock had to be at least six feet tall.

The heated scuffle sounded intense, like a battle was going down on the opposite side of the boulder. Sherry tiptoed around the giant rock, like a peeping Tom on a mission. Gradually, a pair of red-tailed foxes came into view, both animals involved in a heated tug-of-war, tussling over a human tibia, the shin bone. The two foxes were so consumed with their battle over the prized skeletal find, neither animal was aware of the human intruder.

A sense of amusement and calm came over Sherry when she spotted the warring foxes. She smiled at the sight of them just as the thought occurred to her to snap their picture. Sherry plucked her camera phone from the holster on her hip and started snapping away.

Wow! That's quite a big bone, sherry said to herself while snapping pictures of the dueling rascals. She hesitated suddenly. Her eyes bucked wide when the image of a human skull appeared on the cell phone screen.

Sherry stared at the screen, disbelief and bewilderment written all over her face, as she lowered the phone. What she saw caused her entire body to go rigid. The grisly skeletal remains of a human corpse lay scattered amongst the leafy landscape, like a secret burial ground had been unearthed.

######

DC homicide detectives converged on Rock Creek Park in full force. Specialized teams of detectives and CSI agents selected specifically for this crime scene were busy dissecting the wooded terrain in search of evidence.

The newly crowned chief of police, Commander Shane Holt, led the investigation with his right-hand man Tony Woo, the new chief CSI inspector. Tony seemed to reside close at the commander's side wherever he appeared.

Standing on a slight ridge, Commander Holt's sturdy 6'5" frame commanded attention as he assessed the crime scene and scrutinized his team of special agents as they poked and prodded every square inch of the forested ground within the perimeter.

Commander Holt eyed Tony Woo as the short, pudgy man trudged up the hill towards him.

"How's it going, commander?" Tony greeted him, slightly out of breath.

Stroking his smooth, hairless chin, Holt responded curtly, "I'm peeved at the moment, Woo." His eyes were focused straight ahead. "Murder scenes put somewhat of a damper on my day no matter what the situation."

Woo looked up at the commander. With his pudgy right hand he secured his gold wire frames on his round face, then gave a quick nod.

"Oh, I can truly empathize with you on that, commander," Woo said. "Because the only satisfaction I get from my job is when a suspect is apprehended, tried, and convicted. That's when I'm able to feel some measure of satisfaction for my hard work."

Commander Holt gave Woo a sideway look. He really didn't care one way or the other how Woo felt. His main concern was keeping the capital city safe.

"Well, Woo," the commander grunted, "from what you've gathered thus far, can you give me a brief synopsis of the situation?"

Tony Woo stared out over the flowing crime scene with a strained look creasing his brow. He clasped both hands behind his back and exhaled.

"Well, sir, you've been informed, this area isn't the kill zone; it's the dump site." Woo looked hesitant for a second before proceeding. "The victim is a Jane Doe, and she was murdered in an extremely brutal fashion." The muscles in Woo's jaw line flexed out of frustration. "The skull, before it was beheaded— there's evidence of blunt-force trauma to the forehead and upper frontal region of the skull, right at the point where the hairline and forehead meet. Don't quote me on this, sir, but it appears that the perpetrator may have attempted to scalp the victim."

"What did you say?" Holt snapped. "The victim may have been scalped? You're referring to an Indian-style scalping? That's what you're telling me, Mr. Woo?" The commander's tone was incredulous.

"Sir, that would by my initial inclination," Woo explained, attempting to leave himself a little wiggle room, just in case. "But like I said, don't quote me on this. I would have to do a complete analysis of the victim's skull and the injuries. But initially speaking, yes, I would have to say it looks to me like someone used some kind of tool on the victim after administering the fatal head shot with an extremely sharp object, an ax or sword. After the kill, the perp proceeded to behead the victim. The scalping took place afterwards. That's my hypothesis."

The commander huffed loudly, frustrated. "What are we dealing with here, Woo? You know I don't like surprises, and I damn sure don't want to be blind-sided by some wacko we allowed to run rampant through the streets of Washington. Shit, Woo, the city is just getting back to normal after that bloody debacle with those drug-dealing psychopaths, Jovan and Ra—" Holt stopped short when a dreadful thought occurred to him.

Both men turned and faced each other. They looked troubled.

"I know what you're thinking, sir," Woo spoke quietly, "and I seriously doubt that's the case. It's been an entire year, and not a peep."

"What in the hell are you saying, Woo?" Holt's tone dripped with cynicism. "It's been a whole fucking year, and we're still nowhere near identifying this mysterious and elusive suspect who we know has knowledge of the body count inside that creepy Potomac shed. That head case is still out there somewhere, Woo, and until that wacko is identified and taken off the streets, the serial case remains a top priority. Are we clear on this, Mr. Woo?" Sparks were flying from the commander's dead-serious gaze.

Chapter 33

A flurry of stars sparkled across the dark-blue skies over Washington, DC on this beautiful Friday evening in the Nation's Capital.

The city's gridlock seemed to yield with grace when the glossy white Mercedes-Benz coupe came gliding effortlessly along the 14th Street corridor as if the expensive German sedan owned the road.

The mesmerizing, velvety smooth vocals of Maxwell's "Pretty Wings" filled the plush Mercedes cockpit with an emotional vibe.

Perched behind the Mercedes wheel was a picture of class and beauty. Ms. Angel Rising was vibrant and full of life. Her bright eyes twinkled as she cruised by the glowing streetlights lining the concrete sidewalks. Her long, silk black tresses framed her soft butterscotch face and cascaded pass her shoulders like a satiny waterfall.

It was easy to see that Angel was in full bloom tonight. Her disposition exuded energy and playfulness. It was a special occasion. Today marked Angel's one-year anniversary as a bona fide widow and single woman.

Exactly one year ago Jovan Rising was murdered in their Clarksville home while attempting to take her life. In order to cope, Angel blocked the entire episode from her mind. Her subconscious refused to acknowledge the facts.

Angel sighed and said, "Hallelujah! Thank you, Lord!" A pleasant smile lit up her face as she bobbed her head in slow motion, grooving to the hot, sensual melody.

A minute later, just before entering the traffic in Washington Circle, the clean white Mercedes coasted to a stop when the traffic signal flashed red.

Angel immediately flipped down the visor. It's mirror lit up, and she smiled at her reflection before reaching over the armrest and grabbing her powder-pink Chado Ralph Rucci bag off the passenger's seat. She placed the bag on her lap and drew out a stick of platinum-pink Burberry Lip Mist and applied a fresh coat to her full, puckered lips.

"Humph ... I'm looking good and feeling good tonight," she spoke aloud to herself while inspecting her lips, which were soft, moist, and luscious. She smiled at her reflection in the mirror, satisfied.

"I have to thank my girls Dee Dee and Nina for getting me out of the house tonight. I have to say, I'm feeling one hundred percent better already. And I haven't even gotten my drink on or my dance on, let alone my freak on. Oh, Lord!" she giggled, feeling a twinge of embarrassment.

Angel's moment of self-reflection was disrupted by the soft vibration on her hip. She tapped the screen and her fuchsia-colored iPhone blinked to life.

"Dee. What's up, girl?" Angel dropped the lip color in the bag and tossed the bag on the passenger's seat. "Girl, I'm coming. I'm right at the traffic circle on 14th Street now." The signal flashed green, catching Angel's eye. She mashed the accelerator.

"Chill out, girl, and tell them pressed bammas in the Ultra Lounge that Angel is on the way!" She sounded full of herself, giggling, tickled to death by the thought as she navigated the traffic circle.

After the circle, traffic slowed again at the 14th & K streets intersection. The Mercedes made a right turn on K Street and hit a metal log jam.

Angel jammed on the brake pedal and huffed. "What the hell?!? All this traffic so late in the evening? Damn, I thought rush hour ended hours ago," she complained, venting her frustration with a long honk on the horn.

The Ultra Lounge was located at the epicenter of Washington's notoriously busy and crowded K Street business corridor in the heart of downtown. In DC's infamous "red-light district."

Wedged between towering office buildings, the Ultra Lounge had a rich eloquent appearance, with its glazed white façade and chrome-plated glass entrance. The Ultra Lounge had a certain wow factor that captivated the senses.

Inside Ultra, the atmosphere was up-tempo and tasteful. The décor was a lavish, contemporary mix of onyx-topped bars, frosted-glass tables made to resemble ice carvings, and shimmering black marble floors.

Elegant dark leather Dusseldorf lounge sofas ran the length of a glass wall on the left. Large plasma screens adorned the walls on the right, inside the exclusive VIP suite, where the privileged ballers openly flossed their wealth.

DJ Trini was mixing it up on the ones and twos. He had the crowd on the dance floor winding and grinding to Jerimah's "Birthday Sex."

Angel was feeling it—the sexy music, the sexy crowd, and the alluring atmosphere. She took her sweet time, taking it all in, as she slithered amongst the thick mass of gyrating bodies.

Suddenly the familiar face of Dee Dee came into view. "Angel! Angel, girl!" Dee Dee screamed, beaming with excitement. "If you don't get your ass over here, girl!" She donned a playful smirk, her hands perched on her hips.

Angel and Dee Dee met in college. they were "sorority sisters for life." They coined the phrase and tossed it around whenever they were together.

Dee Dee called herself DC's top diva and had no qualms letting anyone know. Her government name was Debra Noble. She was a successful real estate investor who was heralded as one of Washington's top realty brokers. Her résumé was impressive.

In the business arena she was known as Ms. Debra Noble; she was Dee Dee to her close friends. Dee Dee was an over-the-top attractive cinnamon-toned live wire who favored Gabrielle Union. She had long copper-colored hair, soft brown eyes and an extremely wild and untamed cougar-like attitude.

Angel materialized from the crowded sea of bodies. She looked absolutely stunning, like a pretty pink rose in bloom. Angel was impeccably dressed in a rich pink Chado Ralph Rucci pantsuit that was tailored to her coke-bottle frame. She wore a pair of hot-pink alligator stilettos from Jimmy Choo.

"Hot damn, ho!" Nina shouted, bolting off the sofa. "If I didn't know you myself, I would've mistaken you for one of those pretty super models on the cover of Vogue!" Nina's hefty frame stumbled left and right as she rushed around the table. She belted out a wicked laugh when she miraculously remained on her feet without spilling a drop of champagne from her glass. She wobbled over and leaned on Dee Dee's shoulder for support.

"Angel, girl you look like new money! Don't she Dee?" Nina said loudly and offered up a quick toast before gulping down the entire glass.

With an inquisitive smirk smeared on her lips, Dee Dee eyed Angel up and down, tilted her head slightly forward, and said offhandedly, "Girlfriend is shining. Looks to me like Angel got some new dick in her life. Ain't that right?" Dee Dee's lips scrunched into a tight sneer. "C'mon, Angel, spit it out. What's his name? This new nigga's ass you tappin'?"

Angel flashed her pearly whites and replied easily, "Dee Dee, girl you so crazy. You already know Jesus is the only man in my life right now."

"What?!?" Nina gasped. "You mean to tell me you gotta piece of divine ass you be tappin'!" Nina and Dee Dee high-fived and laughed at her comical remark.

"Nina!" Angel wore a controlled expression, but her eyes, the window to the soul, flashed death. "Don't go there with that bullshit!" she warned.

"Angel!" The familiar high-pitched voice that was Ronnie chimed. "What's up, girlfriend? You coming over to say hi to me and your long-lost sister?" The butter-pecan Halle Berry lookalike waved from the lounge sofa, gesturing for Angel to come join them.

Angel eyed Dee Dee, then Nina. "Excuse me," she said gruffly. Her tone changed dramatically. "Ronnie and Renee are waiting for me." She slung her designer bag over her shoulder and cut a path between the stunned pair.

A cautious murmur rolled off Dee Dee's lower lip. "What in the world got into her all of a sudden?" questioned Dee Dee, as she watched Angel strut over to the sofa where Ronnie and Renee were sitting.

Noticeably unnerved by Angel's response, Nina said quietly, "I'm not sure Dee, it's probably nothing. Just keep in mind this last year has been nothing but hell for our girl. Ya know, how would you feel if your husband was trying to kill you, and in the same breath you witness his death?"

It didn't take long for Nina's words to register . The look in Dee Dee's eyes softened. She turned to Nina and responded with an earnest face. "Nina, girl, I feel you on that. Angel has to be a strong woman to deal with that, 'cause I seriously doubt that you or I, or any other woman for that matter, would've been able to recuperate from such a devastating ordeal so soon without some type of long-term mental or psychological scars."

The sobering reality was reflected in both Dee Dee and Nina's facial expression. A genuine heartfelt concern radiated in their demeanor as they stood watching the friendly interaction between Angel, Ronnie, and Renee.

Ronnie jumped to her feet, beaming, her arms spread wide. "Come here, Angel!" She greeted her friend with an emotional hug. "Girl, you looking good!" Ronnie said and took a half step backward. The sincere adoration showed in her disposition. "How have you been doing? Everything okay with you?"

Angel exchanged pleasantries briefly with Ronnie, then eased onto the sofa next to Renee, anxious to speak to her childhood companion, who she hadn't seen in years.

Renee Gray was a gorgeous Cover Girl model and Angel's longtime next-door neighbor and childhood friend. They'd known each other since Kindergarten. On their first encounter, they realized the uncanny resemblance they both shared with one another. All the little boys in their kindergarten class would swear up and down that Angel and Renee were sisters. Since both girls lacked any sibling companionship, they decided to enter into a sisterhood pact. From the very first day in kindergarten, Angel and Renee considered themselves sisters.

Besides their family, who'd be the wiser, they figured. They looked so much alike, no one outside of their families dared doubt the girls' charade.

Renee bloomed into a gorgeous, statuesque China-redbone with deep, probing black eyes and bone-straight jet-black hair that fell to the delicate crease in her back. Renee's demeanor was deceptively shy. On the outside she gave the impression of a sweet, coy, demure woman. A select few—bad boys with bling-bling and deep pockets—were privy to Renee's naughty nature. They were allowed to enter into her sexual realm. They got the privilege of experiencing the salacious undercover freak that lurked just below the surface.

Soon after graduating high school, Angel and Renee's charade came to an abrupt end. Renee's clean, attractive appeal caught the eye of a top modeling talent scout. Three months out of high school, Renee accepted a lucrative modeling gig. Before the ink on the contract was able to dry, Renee was whisked away to start a world-wind modeling career.

Tonight would be Angel and Renee's first face-to-face encounter since the two were separated the summer following high school graduation.

Angel placed her designer bag on the sofa next to her and crossed her legs, ladylike. "Well …" she breathed, flashing her pretty teeth in a smile. "Surprise, surprise. What brings you back to DC, sis? A little birdie told me that Renee Gray was too good for us folks in the District. What's up with that, huh?" Angel inquired, sucking her teeth in a rude, taunting way.

Renee smirked, but didn't bother to answer right away. She cut her eyes at Angel and readied her full ruby-red lips for the glass of Rose Moet she held an inch from her mouth.

"Yeah, it's nice to see you again too, sis," Renee uttered softly. "Cheers," she added, turning the glass up to her mouth.

Without saying a word, Angel watched Renee as she drained the champagne from her glass, then set the empty flute on the table beside the silver ice bucket.

Angel couldn't help herself, but she had to admit, *Damn! Renee had it going in!* She silently hoped Renee didn't recognize the envious look on her face. Renee was beautiful. She was dressed in a black Gucci wrap dress that fit her well-sculpted body like an expensive silk glove.

Angel and Renee finally made eye contact. For all of three seconds the gorgeous pair locked eyes, and for a brief moment both women were hurled back in time to a place where Angel and Renee were happy-go-lucky teenage girls again, without a care in the world.

Suddenly, unprompted, as if on cue, both Angel and Renee cracked up laughing. A floodgate of mixed emotions ignited the air between them: joy, sorrow, and, pain were unleashed after being suppressed for so many years. The play sisters embraced one another in a tearful, emotionally charged reunion they felt was long overdue.

"My beloved Angel," Renee said in a tone brimming with delight. "I see adversity hasn't changed you one bit. 'Cause you're still the flyest bitch on the block!"

A modest smile touched Angel's lips. "You're full of it, you know that, Renee? I seen your pretty red ass on the cover of *Bizarre* last month dressed in that bad-as-shit black Escada dress with that bad-ass Gonzales croc handbag!"

"What? You're referring to this Gonzales handbag?" Renee answered, nonchalantly twirling the expensive designer bag in the air for Angel to feast her eyes on.

Angel didn't attempt to conceal the surprise and envy on her face.

"Oh ... my ... gosh!" Angel gushed, breathless. "That's the croc handbag from the magazine cover!"

"You like it, sis?" Renee said casually. "Here, it's yours." Before Angel could reply, Renee set the handbag on her lap and gave her a warm, affectionate smile.

Angel's right hand jumped over her mouth. She was speechless. She stared at the black crocodile handbag, utterly mystified by Renee's generous offering.

"What are you saying, Renee?" Angel asked in stuttered breaths. She couldn't resist the overwhelming temptation to touch the luxurious black crocodile bag. She brushed her fingers lightly across the fine reptilian contours and shuddered. "Renee," she began in a hushed, measured tone, "you're giving me a fifteen-thousand-dollar handbag?" Her eyes beamed. She was elated.

Renee chuckled. "More like seventeen-five, sis" she corrected while refilling her champagne glass. "But who's counting?" She waved it off as if the trendy, high-price handbag was irrelevant.

Dee Dee made an unwelcome interruption. "Sorry, girls, for disrupting your sisterly bonding session," she said, casting a shrewd look upon Angel. "But this handsome specimen of a man here is my police friend and the new chief of police, Mr. Shane Holt. He tells me that you two know one another. Is that correct, Angel?"

Dee Dee made it quite apparent to anyone paying attention that she had a thing for the sharply dressed man in the navy Christian Dior suit. She stood at Holt's side hanging on his bicep looking like a pressed groupie.

It was obvious Angel didn't want to be bothered with anyone at the moment, let alone some man she couldn't recall. She was busy indulging her feminine senses with the expensive prize Renee had just given her.

The tone in Dee Dee's voice caused Angel's smile to turn into a tight sneer.

"What is it? I don't know what you're talking about," Angel uttered drily, never taking her eyes off the handbag in her lap.

Renee glanced up. "Oh!" she gasped, pleasantly surprised when she saw the tall, dark, handsome gentleman standing in front of their table. She reached over and tapped Angel lightly on the knee. "Um, Angel ... I think someone is here to see you." A warm smile spread on Renee's face when Shane made eye contact.

Angel responded with an agitated huff. "Is it too much for me to sit here for a minute and just—"

Her words got caught in her throat when she caught a glimpse of the chocolate hunk standing poised before her, his pearly whites glistening from ear to ear.

Shane moved around the table, exuding a heavy dose of untamed masculinity with every gesture. "Hello, ladies." He greeted the twosome with a cordial handshake. "It's a pleasure to meet you beautiful young ladies, especially you, Ms. Rising." He paused, holding Angel's hand in his. Shane gazed deeply into her eyes, soul searching.

Angel felt her heart skip a beat as she watched the handsome stranger step around the table, confidence and charisma coming off him in ripples.

Before Angel could react, his presence was upon her. Shane's masculine aroma permeated her nostrils with the rich fragrance of Salvatore Ferragamo and a potent dose of super-charged testosterone.

Locked in a soul gaze, something undeniable and compelling radiated strongly between them. Angel could actually feel his presence reaching out to her, mentally seducing her. The ominous sensation frightened her and set off alarms in the back of her mind.

She whipped her head around and shot the man a look so unsavory Shane immediately backed off.

"Excuse me, but do I know you from somewhere?" she asked, frowning as she looked him up and down.

Rubbing his hands together, Shane pulled his head back, closed his eyes halfway and let out a cautious growl. "Mmmmrrr." Skepticism squeezed from his lips. "Ms. Rising, before you get defensive, why don't you think for a second? We spoke on the phone some months back. I'm Commander Holt from the Metropolitan Police Department. Remember me?"

The light in Angel's eyes went bright, but she concealed it. She sat there and thought for a minute about what he said, then shrugged. "Sure. I remember the conversation. So you're telling me that you're the commander responsible for the slaughter of my husband? You're the reason I'm a widow?" She answered in a seemingly subdued voice.

Shane exhaled an audible whoosh of breath to expel the sorrow he felt for her. "No, Ms. Rising." His tall frame moved next to her. Everyone watched as he perched himself uncomfortably on the edge of the leather sofa as if he couldn't quite relax until he explained things to her.

He stilled himself as he looked Angel right in the eye. Mindful and polite, he said, "Your husband wasn't slaughtered. He was shot while attempting to kill you, Ms. Rising. I feel you've probably blocked out the devastating event from your mind. But I'm sorry to say what I've just told you is the honest-to-God's truth."

Angel put both hands, palms down, on her thighs to still herself. She shook her head. "No," she murmured, sounding unsure and feeble. She cradled her head in her hands, her body bent as she sat grieving, unable to get her mind around the idea of Jovan trying to kill her. "But why? Why would my husband do that to me?"

Out of nowhere, vague images began to trickle through Angel's mind—a fuzzy image of Jovan's nude, bloody, and dickless corpse lying spread-eagle atop a silver metal table, like he was a piece of butchered meat.

The disturbing image resonated in Angel's mind. Suddenly, the room and everything in it started to spin. She felt like she was on a merry-go-round. Her chest rose and fell. She hyperventilated as she leaned back against the sofa, her eyes fixated on the ceiling.

"Angel!" Renee called out in a panic-stricken voice. Without thinking, she grabbed Angel by the shoulders and shook her. "Angel, get a grip on yourself!"

Angel clutched the edge of the sofa with both hands. Her fingers were dug in like hawk talons. Her eyes darted left and right. She looked nervous, jittery, and discombobulated.

Her breathing slowed down, and she could feel a sense of calm gradually settling in and comforting her. As if emerging from a fuzzy dream, she noticed the strange, unsettling looks plastered on the faces of her girlfriends and the stunningly handsome Shane, all gathered around, staring at her.

Embarrassment pushed aside the calm Angel was starting to feel. "What's going on?" she stammered, confusion swirling in her eyes. "Why are you all looking at me like that?"

Slowly Dee Dee lowered her right hand from her startled mouth. Her concerned expression was mixed with shock and confusion, clearly unnerved by the episode.

"Girlfriend," Dee Dee began, kneeling in front of Angel and placing a hand on her left knee, "I'm not absolutely sure," she told her friend in a quiet, calming tone, "but I think you just had a nervous breakdown."

"Excuse me, ladies," Shane interrupted, clearing his throat and signaling for the waitress. "Give Angel some room please. She needs air." He paused, whipped out a handkerchief from his suit pocket and started to fan the her. "You're close, Debra," he continued, "but your friend just suffered a minor anxiety attack. This club scene and the surprise revelation coupled together may have been a little too much too soon. Would you agree, Angel?" Shane said with a warm smile.

The concern in Shane's voice was refreshing, Angel thought. Something she hadn't felt in a long time from a man. When Angel gave it some thought, she realized that since her husband's death, she hadn't been in the company of a real man at all.

Oh, how she missed the strong presence of a real man and the special attention he gives to the woman of his desires. That tender touch and feel of a man, the sensual, loving, and passionate way he caresses and holds and loves that special woman he places high up on a pedestal, above all others. *Ooooh!* The thought gave her goose bumps.

"Thank you for your kindness and concern. What's your name again? Shane?" Angel spoke up suddenly. The calm meditative expression seemed a bit out of place. "Thank you, Shane, but I'm feeling a little better now. Besides, I don't want to spoil anyone's good time."

"Girlfriend, your health is a lot more important than anything we got going on here," Nina said seriously, waving her right index finger in the air for emphasis. "So don't start that Ms. Prissy shit with us. If you ain't right, say you ain't right. We understand, and we got your back, like always."

Shane sat listening as each woman took her turn expressing her heartfelt concern for Angel. He couldn't help himself from indulging his manly senses with the impossibly gorgeous, classy, sexy woman sitting beside him with a smile so vibrant she lit up the entire room.

I have to have her! he pondered quietly. His eyes absorbed every quirk and facial gesture, the soft texture and sway of her long, silky black hair and the sensuous contours of her shapely physique. Angel's tantalizing J'adore fragrance was giving Shane fits.

There was something else going on here. Shane's intuitive nature was nudging him in the gut, but he was so infatuated with Angel's radiant presence, his feelings gradually allayed themselves.

Without saying a work, Shane eased down on the sofa and enjoyed the interplay between the group of chatty woman. *I must say,* he voiced silently, *everything went as expected tonight.*

He gave himself a congratulatory pat on the back. The goal of making his presence known to Angel was a success in his mind.

The meeting with Debra Noble had served its purpose. He wouldn't dare attempt to separate Angel from her friends tonight. Although the tempting thought had crossed his mind, he quickly pushed it aside. *Nope, not tonight,* the voice of reason spoke quietly. *Tonight I'll play the perfect gentleman. I'll allow Angel's comfort zone to accept me, then I'll put my irresistible charm to work on her.*

Angel was highly vulnerable now. Shane was certain of that. She yearned for the love and affection of a good man—desperately needed it, he figured. His intuition revealed to him that Angel would make the perfect second wife. Shane did his homework on her; he checked her background, employment history, educational history, and finances.

Yeah, Holt gloated quietly, *Angel is definitely prime for the vacant position.* He concluded with an ominous contemplative grin scrawled on his lips. Without uttering a word, Shane poured himself a glass of champagne, leaned back, crossed his legs and relished in the moment.

Chapter 34

The following evening under a spotless summer sky, Angel was home relaxing on her spacious rear deck, enjoying some much needed downtime by herself, watching the sun set on the horizon.

A rose-colored wine glass half-filled with red Spanish wine was cupped in Angel's right hand. She looked hot and sassy standing at the deck railing, swaying her hips slowly from side to side in rhythm to the soft sounds of Corinne Bailey Rae's "Breathless." The songstress's soothing melody provided Angel with some much-needed peace.

Angel sang out loud with Corinne to a pair of blue jays snuggling a few feet away on an elm tree branch. Her gentle voice drifted on the warm summer's breeze:

> *I get so breathless when you call my name*
> *I've often wondered, do you feel the same?*
> *There's a chemistry, energy, a synchronicity*
> *When we're all alone*
> *So don't tell me you can't see what I'm thinking of*

Suddenly, the phone rang, disturbing Angel's quiet solitude. She sighed and pulled her black silk Victoria's Secret robe she wore tight gainst her skin and made an about-face, twirling on the heels of her furry black slippers. In four short steps, she swiped the cordless off the gold satin pillow on the end of the lawn chair.

"Hello." she said, topping the spirited greeting with a sunny smile.

How can I enlighten you with my presence?"

She jumped, startled when she heard the voice of a strange man on the other end.

"Hearing your lovely voice, Angel, " Shane answered, smoothly, "I feel considerably blessed."

"Mr. Holt?" Angel quipped, suddenly recognizing the strong baritone emanating over the phone. She frowned, and said, "How did you get my home phone number? This number is new and unlisted," she stated frankly.

"How soon we forget," Shane responded with a lighthearted chuckle. "I am the chief of police with a pretty sizable law enforcement contingent under my direction and a number of discretionary measures at my disposal. For instance, I have this massive computerized phone registry down here at headquarters to do with as I see fit. Like accessing beautiful women's unlisted home numbers?" He paused, waiting for her reply.

There was an uninterrupted silence for nearly a minute.

"Hello? Ms. Rising, are you there?"

Angel collected her thoughts. "I'm not sure that I'm feeling this," she said in a tone dripping with shrewd skepticism. "Sounds to me like borderline stalking. And, a man in your position?" She frowned.

Holt smiled at the insinuating remark. "Now, Angel," he began, his voice taking on a lighter note, "you're a beautiful, young, intelligent, and vibrant woman." He hesitated, admiring his own reflection in the vanity mirror hanging on the wall above his glazed black mantel. He went on, "A man in my position doesn't have to stalk. And I'm sure you are well aware of that."

He stopped short, grinning at himself. Then without warning, an arrogant snicker jumped from his mouth. He made a weak attempt to stifle the unintended snicker but failed.

"I'm sorry," he instantly apologized. "Let me stop fooling around before you think I'm a real ass."

"Too late for that," Angel muttered, grinning. "Oops. My bad. I didn't mean to interrupt you."

Shane smirked. "Well, anyway, Debra gave me your new number after a little persuasion on my part."

"Is that so?" Angel sounded suspicious, wondering what his angle was.

"Yes," he voiced defensively. "I'm being totally honest with you, Angel," he said seriously. "I told Debra that I wanted to make up for the incident last night at the club. I feel partly to blame for that whole episode with you, and I would like to have the chance to make it up to you … if you can find it in your heart to allow me the chance."

Angel thought for a moment. Visions of Shane drifted in her head. *Tall. Dark. Handsome. Baby-smooth skin. Muscular. Ooooow!*

"Make it up to me?" Angel's response was deliberate and cautious. "Not that I'm saying yes, but hypothetically speaking, if I were to, uh, agree to some form of allowing you to make it up to me, what would that entail? I'm just a little curious." Angel took a seat on the lawn chair, swung both legs up and placed them atop the satiny pillow. She leaned back and gazed up at the darkening sky.

Shane sensed a changed in Angel's emotionally charged armor. This was the chance he had been hoping for. Now it was time for him to shoot straight for her heart.

"Well, Ms. Lady," he said and began painting a picture of an enjoyable and fun-filled day out on the town, just the two of them. Their day, he explained, would kick off at a horse-riding stable in Laurel, Maryland, where'd they spend a couple hours trekking through the woods on horseback. Afterwards, they would make a pit stop at the fancy Timbuktu restaurant in Elkridge, Maryland, for a scrumptious lump crab cake lunch. From Elkridge, Shane would follow Angel back to her Clarksville home, where'd they'd take a quick shower and change into their evening attire.

Afterward, the couple would travel south on I-95. Angel would insist on driving separate vehicles; she would be glamorous behind the wheel of her gleaming white CL-600 Mercedes coupe, while he looked debonair cruising in his silk black Cadillac Escalade ESV. Both vehicles would head for Fort Washington, Maryland, where the sparkling National Harbor Resort complex was located along the edge of the Potomac River.

The highlight of their outing would take place later on in the evening at the fabulous Belvedere Lobby Bar.

Angel would look utterly breathtaking in her fiery red off-the-shoulder Oscar de La Renta dress, which accentuated her curvy frame with eye-popping perfection.

She'd be sitting at the table, quietly sipping her wine. It'd be easy to see how a man could fall deeply in love with this woman. Angel was the epitome of beauty, and baby girl would have put her stamp on it for their date. Her creamy butterscotch complexion would be so radiant. Her natural beauty would be captured like the Mona Lisa in the famous Rembrandt by the soft glowing candlelight dancing in the center of the table. The warm light would glisten in her eyes like liquid pools of amber.

Shane gazed across the table as if he was in a trance. A wave of pure excitement washed over **him** as he savored the beauty of the woman seated across the table from him. His right index finger reached out and touched the cold perspiring glass in front of him. With a slippery grin and cagey gleam sparkling in his eyes, Shane leaned over the table, his eyes peering deep into Angel's.

"Angel," Shane spoke in a deep rumbling whisper, "you are so unbelievably gorgeous. I've never met a woman quite so intriguing as you."

The corners of Angel's mouth turned up, her smile beamed exuberantly.

"Oh, that's so very sweet of you to say, Shane," she replied quietly. *Damn, this nigga got it goin' on!* Angel admitted to herself, fascinated by this handsome charismatic man. *Has God finally sent me a man who matches me inside and out?*

"I must say, I find you very interesting also, and I'm so glad I came out with you today, Shane, because God knows I would've been cooped up in that big ole house of mine, all by my lonesome."

As if cued, Shane moved his right hand across the mahogany wood table and gently caressed her hand. "All by your lonesome," he uttered, sounding doubtful. "As beautiful as you are, Angel, I'm having a very hard time believing that. But if you're telling me the God's-honest truth—oh, no, we definitely can't be having that." His tone took on an air of firmness. "I'm just what the doctor ordered. A healthy dose of me in your life and the word 'lonely' will be a distant memory."

Oh, my, Angel thought, gazing at him, starry-eyed. *He has a way with words. A girl like me could sure use a man like Shane in her life.*

Angel lowered her eyes, focusing now on the lacquered wood. She said, twisting her lips, "You're just what the doctor ordered, huh? Shane, we just met. One day getting to know a person, that's nothing at all. You don't know what tomorrow will bring. You may hate my guts come tomorrow."

Without hesitation, Shane gently squeezed her hand and expressed adamantly, "Angel, you could be with a person for just a day, an entire year, or ten long years. And guess what? You still may not know the person. I'm a very intuitive man," he explained, pressing his left hand firmly against his chest. "I can be with a person for one minute," he voiced, strongly, "and know their soul. It's my job to know people. I don't mean to toot my own horn, but I'm damn good at what I do." He straightened up in his seat and adjusted the expensive olive-colored Fendi button-up he wore.

"Now getting back to you, Angel," Shane said, softening his demeanor. "The first time I laid eyes on you I felt our souls touch, and at that very moment I knew this day right here would come. Low and behold, here you are in the flesh, and your innocent beauty has literally taken my breath away. You don't know it yet, Angel, but there's something bigger than the both of us at work here. There's a purpose for us coming together the way we have, and I truly believe the reason we will discover is profound." He exhaled. "I can't say right now what the reason is because it's a mystery to me," he conceded with a casual shrug. "But there is one thing that I am certain of: I'm having a wonderful time with you. And I'm hoping that you will allow us to spend a lot more time together in the very near future. You know, let's just go with the flow, Angel, see what lies ahead for you and I to discover. My intuition tells me there's something special that awaits us."

Angel stared across the table at Shane. A swooning gaze twinkled in her eye. For the first time she didn't know what to say. Suddenly, like a romantic scene playing on a movie screen, the soft, heartfelt melody "A Woman's Work" by Maxwell floated from the restaurant's speakers and filled the place with a deep, emotional vibe.

"That's my favorite song," Angel mumbled under her breath but loud enough for Shane to hear.

"What a coincidence," he replied, extending his hand. "A Woman's Work" is my favorite song also."

Shane cradled Angel in his arms, their bodies pressed tightly against each other, moving slowly and sensually as one. Angel and Shane slow-danced to the sweet, flowing music.

"Shane," Angel whispered, gazing up at him, "It's hard to believe that a man in your position doesn't have a wife. Never been married?"

"Excuse me?" Shane answered abruptly, a note of brashness boding in his voice. "I never said that I wasn't married or didn't have a wife. I'm a married man, Angel, and my wife's name is Mrs. Yolanda Holt. But my wife and I have been separated for the past six months. I thought you knew that, Angel."

Angel was completely floored by the revelation. Her heart dropped.

"What!?!" she snapped viciously, her whole body flashed rigid, anger and hate spewed from her eyes. "You're married!?" she hissed scathingly as she burst from his arms and shoved him with all her strength.

"Get the hell away from me you whore!" she spat. Her hateful tone spewed like bile from her mouth. "Who in the hell do you think you are?! What kind of woman do you take me for?!? I don't indulge in those kind of sick, filthy games!" she concluded, her eyes simmering deadly. Angel spun around like a dangerous tempest and stormed off across the restaurant, snatching up her Gonzales croc bag on the way out the door.

Angels' abrupt tirade left Shane both stunned and completely dumbfounded. He stood fumbling in the middle of the floor like a bumbling idiot. Shane swore he caught a glimpse of something else in Angel's expression, something destructive and full of rage.

He took a deep breath and shook his head. "Damn Angel," he sighed somberly. *Baby I can see that you've been devastated by the men in your life,* he voiced silently and gave an agitated look to all the nosey patrons looking his way. *After a healthy dose of Shane in your life, I'm sure you'll come around just fine,* he boasted confidently. Standing tall, he stuck out his chest and moved with poise through the restaurant. "All my women do, and you're no different from all the rest. You gonna love me," he said aloud. Shane tossed two crisp Benjamins on the table without breaking stride and bopped toward the exit.

Chapter 35

A large gathering of dark clouds rolled across the horizon, covering the entire length of the Clarksville skyline. A powerful bolt of lightning ripped a swath across the dark gray atmosphere, followed instantly by a loud, thunderous roar so strong the ground trembled in its wake.

A split second later the darkening heavens above Clarksville opened up like the red sea, unleashing a deluge on the wide, rolling green landscape.

Heavy rains pelted the lengthy driveway leading to the front of Angel's estate. Just inside the driveway, three *Washington Post* newspapers lay untouched in their cellophane packaging. Off to the left, next to the bronze cobblestone with the Rising name etched in the stone, a long bronze metal mailbox was stuffed full of mail, an obvious sign of Angel's three-day hiatus.

Since storming out on her date down at the National Harbor three nights ago, no one had seen or heard anything from Angel. It was as though she had fallen off the face of the earth.

Inside Angel's palatial estate, a dark, eerie calm seemed to pulsate within the structure like some sort of unholy spirit had taken possession.

Upstairs, on the second level, soft candlelight radiated just inside the doorway of the master bedroom. Angel's newly renovated bedroom was a display of flawless feminine grace with a splash of stylish panache—the lavish pink-ivory Jaipur furnishings were breathtaking. They set the bar for high-class middle-eastern decorum.

Scattered around the bedroom like sacrilegious impromptu props for a dark, secret ritual, a number of thick, black blocked-shaped candles were all aglow. The vibe emanating in the room was something strange and voodoo-like.

Along the bedroom's private hallway leading to the master bathroom, more black candles glowed on both sides of the hall, illuminating the path into the dark granite suite.

Voices echoed ominously from within the shadowy interior of the bathroom. They sounded like two women discussing a dilemma about a man.

"Angel, are you out of your damn mind?" Natasha asked, disgusted. The eerie glow cast from the candlelight on the vanity gave Natasha a haunting glow. Her intense blue eyes were unmoving, glowering at her reflection in the vanity mirror as she sat perched atop Angel's vanity throne.

"Shane's a married man!" she snarled insidiously, her teeth grinding violently, causing the muscles in her jaw to bulge with aggressiveness.

An abrupt flash of lightning ignited the dark wooded landscape outside the window. A split second later, thunder cracked the sky above the house and made the foundation shudder.

A concerned gaze fell across Angel's face. "He confessed to me about his marriage. They aren't together anymore; he's separated from his wife." The strain on Angel's face softened when she spoke.

"Separated? Do I look that damn gullible?!?" Natasha forced an awkward smile. "Well, if that's the case, there shouldn't be any problem with me adding a layer of assurance to the mix. A little something to make sure the both of them stay separated for good. If you truly want

Shane and want to be with him, the wife has to go. What's her name? Yolanda Holt? Yeah, that bitch can kiss her ass good-bye!" she expressed point blank, grinning devilishly.

Another bolt of lightning electrified the sky as Natasha rose to her feet and moved across the tiled floor.

Kaboom! A booming thunder crack rocked the foundation the moment she exited the bathroom.

$$\psi\,\psi\,\psi\,\psi$$

The following day, an updraft of cool mountain air surged east across the region, sending a cold chill through Natasha's body as she stepped from the silver Cadillac CTS.

Mmmm, the warm sun feels so good on my face, she thought to herself, slipping on a pair of black D&G shades. Instantly, Natasha's gaze zeroed in on the woman in the beige Donna Karen pantsuit rushing across Connecticut Avenue. A moment later the woman disappeared inside of the jewelry boutique Bailey, Banks, & Biddle.

Natasha pulled her honey-blonde tresses back in a ponytail, ducked her head against the wind, and marched across Connecticut without so much as a glance toward the oncoming traffic.

The jewelry associate standing behind the counter looked sleepy when she greeted Natasha. "Our time is running short this evening, but how may I be of help to you?" said the skinny redhead associate. She pushed the thick bifocals snugly on her face and checked her watch, annoyed.

Natasha rolled her eyes at the pale-faced woman, mumbled something inaudible, then spoke up, "Don't worry about me, sweetie. I'm here to check out your inventory for a purchase I'll be making at a later date. So you can go back to what you were doing before I arrived." Natasha moved on down the counter and mumbled, "Lazy, good-for-nothing bitch." Her shade-covered eyes remained focused on the target in the Donna Karen suit.

The store manager, a short gray-haired German woman dressed in a crisp navy sports jacket and matching skirt, emerged from a rear office. She brushed her thin, silvery bangs off her forehead and smiled pleasantly when she recognized the attractive Bahamian woman with the long, sandy locks and impeccable cinnamon complexion.

"Welcome, Mrs. Holt," the manager's voice said from across the store. "It's so nice to see you again. How may I assist you this evening?" The woman moved toward Mrs. Holt and joined her at the counter. "Oh, my," the manager gasped, her lucid, gray eyes wide with excitement. "That piece you're wearing—that's a wonderful Konstantino necklace. Where did you acquire such a fine piece, if you don't mind me asking?"

Yolanda turned from the counter and lowered her head so that she was looking over the top of her tortoiseshell Donna Karen frames.

"Now, Abby," Yolanda began with a broad smile, "you've known me long enough to know that something as trivial as that doesn't matter to me one bit," she said, fingering the exquisite platinum necklace. "I got the charm and necklace from Jason of Beverly Hills."

Abby chuckled lightly and replied, "Silly me, I should've known."

After purchasing a set of platinum earrings, Yolanda turned right outside the boutique and proceeded across 12th Street.

Trailing not far behind was Natasha. She walked outside and paused on the sidewalk. A sinister scowl jumped on her face as she watched Yolanda walk down the block.

"Okay, where are we off to now?" she muttered curiously and flashed Yolanda an evil glare. She looked left and right, whirled on her heels and continued her pursuit.

About forty feet away, wedged in a small alleyway between a pair of skyscrapers, a cranberry red BMW 750 sat idling quietly in the shadows. The Beemer's driver was slouched incognito, hidden behind the car's tinted windows. He instantly focused his attention on the woman wearing the all-black jean outfit and gave her a mystified stare when he noticed her tailing the police chief's wife.

The driver smirked and plucked a red cherry Tootsie pop from his mouth. "So what's the deal with you baby girl?" he said with a crooked grin twitching at the corner of his mouth. "Where your sexy ass come from, and what move are you trying to bring my folks?" His cold, black eyes glistened eagerly as he wondered about the light-skin vixen with the honey-blonde hair. There was something dark and sinister about her that intrigued Chevar and piqued his interest.

In DC, being a "burner" means you have the ability to make people despise you. Chevar Robinson was a burner. Any situation you threw at him, he would find a way to turn it negative. That's how Chevar got his rocks off.

Chevar adopted the nickname Mr. Bad Ass, a title he relished and carried with overbearing bravado and arrogance. It was easy to see why people called him a burner.

A bona fide menace to society, Bad Ass was the leader of a rouge and violent crew of stick-up boys from Uptown DC. He, along with his hard-core cronies, formed an illicit criminal enterprise dubbed CIX, which stood for Criminals In eXistence.

As he ascended through the ranks of DC's underworld, Bad Ass' reputation hinted at a darker side. He was a domineering, compulsive agitator with a violent temper and warped sense of right and wrong.

He also had an insatiable thirst for knowledge and power and became a stout advocate for the powerfully choreographed book "The 48 Laws of Power" by Robert Greene. Every calculated move he initiated, Bad Ass implored the 48 Laws with voracity.

Meanwhile, outside on Connecticut Avenue, the predator was stalking her prey. Natasha kept a safe distance from Yolanda; she didn't want to draw any attention to herself and lose her element of surprise.

While in pursuit, Natasha began to formulate a demented plan in her head about how she was first going to render Yolanda unconscious, then take her to a discreet location where she would have time to open up Yolanda's chest cavity using the new scalpel Angel recently purchased.

A crazed look penetrated Natasha's gaze as she envisioned her hands and forearms soaked with Yolanda's blood after digging in her chest and pulling out a bloody, beating heart. The anticipation of Yolanda's death made Natasha moist between her legs.

Suddenly, out of nowhere, the cranberry BMW swerved right off Connecticut onto 10th Street, right in Natasha's path.

The luxury sedan came to a screeching halt directly in front of Natasha. "Oh, shit!" Chevar gasped, feigning surprise. He quickly lowered the passenger's window and spoke up apologetically. "My bad, baby girl!" He could see the fire of a lioness burning in her blue eyes. "I didn't see you until the last second, baby. You okay?" She stood with her arms folded aggressively, tapping her foot.

Natasha's face twisted into a mask of anger. She looked down Connecticut and watched her golden opportunity fade in the distance.

"You stupid muthafucka!" she growled disgustedly. "Look what you've done!"

Chevar could see rage and frustration simmering in the pretty woman's face. It was time for immediate action. The driver door's swung wide. Before she could react, the handsome, caramel mass of muscle emerged from the BMW and swept around the car like a gust of wind.

Chevar's disposition was cool and poised as he strode right up to Natasha. Before responding, he adjusted the heavy diamond and platinum link dangling around his neck and casually brushed the wrinkles from his Redskins Pro Bowl Santana Moss jersey.

Chevar cocked his head to the side. "Damn, baby girl!" he beamed. The former Howard linebacker's muscles twitched and jumped with every movement he initiated. "Mmph, mmph, mmph ... I would've jumped in front of the next speeding car if I had harmed a hair of your luscious anatomy. Real talk, baby girl."

When Natasha caught sight of the bulging muscle mass moving around the car, a powerful wave of euphoria and adrenaline swept through her body. The masculine 6'3" figure hovered over her, his deep-set eyes peering into hers. Natasha felt an instant surge of power radiating from this man. Confidence and misogyny and something profoundly sinister beckoned her. His overbearing presence rocked Natasha's core.

The smooth thug had her tripping. She was feeling emotions inside of her that she never knew existed. Her whole attitude changed. She went from intensely enraged to being slightly perturbed.

Natasha took a deliberate step backward. She slowly eyed the stranger up and down while carefully slipping the pearl-handled straight razor cupped in the palm of her right hand into the pocket of her Roberto Cavalli jeans.

She blushed slightly and took a deep breath. "You would've jumped in front of a speeding car for me?" She was tickled by his silly remark. "Y'all niggas are just alike, you know that?"

Chevar smirked. "Oh, yeah? That don't sound too cool." He leaned against the hood, stroking his smooth chin. "What you insinuating by that remark? C'mon, I'm all ears." His voice was heavy when he spoke.

Natasha didn't answer right away. She allowed the silence to linger uncomfortably. Her silence was deceptive. She was always careful not to utter a single word without something to elevate her personal stance.

Without warning, she looked him right in the eye. She was calm and collected. "Y'all niggas are full of shit," she said. She whirled on her heels and headed back the way she had come.

"What?!?" Chevar grunted, totally baffled by her response. "So you just gonna leave me hanging like I'm some off-brand nigga, huh?" He tossed his hands in the air. "What's up, baby girl? Can I get your name and number? Anything, shorty!" He bounced off the hood. "I'm Chevar! Ask about me!" he announced loudly.

Natasha giggled as she walked away. She glanced back over her shoulder and made eye contact. "My name's Natasha!" she shouted, feeling a strange tingle in the pit of her stomach.

Chevar rushed around his car and hopped in. "Natasha, huh?" he said to himself. "I don't know what it is about you, Natasha, but I'm definitely feeling you, baby girl."

His instincts were jumping like a gauge on a Richter scale. That's when Chevar knew the woman he had just encountered wasn't your average woman. He could feel it. *Natasha is the type of bitch a man comes across only once in a lifetime. She is that Bitch, more treacherous than she is beautiful,* he told himself.

Chevar stared after her. "It's all good, baby girl," he said candidly. He hit the gear, mashed the gas, and belted out a loud roar. "You don't know me, but you will soon enough, 'cause you haven't seen the last of me. I'm that nigga, Natasha. I'm Mr. Bad Ass!" he howled like an alpha wolf as he sped along 10th Street like a bat out of hell.

Chapter 36

Later on in the evening ...

    The big empty room was eerily devoid of life. Its stark white walls and ceiling gave the room that icky hospital feel, except for the lacquered wood floor that was virtually spotless.

    Angel entered the vacant room. The sound of a whirling ceiling fan drew her eye to the ceiling. A deep frown fell across her brow when she noticed tiny red splotches splattered the length of the ceiling.

    "What in God's name?" she muttered curiously, her voice drifting off when she caught sight of something odd attached to the end of the fan blade, whirling nonstop through the air.

    Angel stopped in the center of the room. Without realizing, she wished for the ceiling fan to stop. As if telekinetic forces were surging from her form, the ceiling fan hit the brakes and came to an abrupt stop.

    Angel's eyes popped wide like silver dollars. Scared, she smacked herself hard across the mouth with her right hand and stared in horror at the hideous object dancing overhead.

    Malaysia Tomay's head was dangling grotesquely from the fan blade by her blood-covered hair. The beauty in her face was evident no more, as she gazed downward, as if locked in a perpetual face-off with the devil himself. A pain-filled, soundless scream was frozen in time on Malaysia's face, like she was suffering in eternal pain and damnation.

Angel heard herself screaming at the top of her lungs, but she couldn't bring herself to move. I'm paralyzed, she thought. Suddenly, Angel watched a single teardrop of blood appear on the rim of Malaysia's eyelid, then cascade down her rough, dry cheek. For a split second, the gooey red teardrop dangled right on the edge of Malaysia's chin before falling.

The bloody teardrop fell in Angel's mouth right down her throat, prompting her to gag and shriek in absolute horror.

Angel's eyes rocked wide open. A look of utter fear and worry was plastered on her face as she splashed erratically in her hot tub in an emotionally charged and physical struggle with herself.

"Father God, help me please!!!" she screamed out, terrified.

Chapter 37

The next afternoon …

When Detective Mecca Tomay walked into DC police headquarters, all eyes focused on the drop-dead gorgeous Thai model with the sparkling gray eyes. Mecca was a stop-and-stare brunette, curvy and statuesque. She was vivacious, unpredictable, and extremely inquisitive.

"Excuse me, Sergeant Ready," Mecca said, reading the bearded desk sergeant's nameplate. "I'm Detective Mecca Tomay on transfer from Miami-Dade. There should be a one o'clock meeting scheduled in your log book for myself and the chief of police." When Mecca spoke to the sergeant, her voice sounded warm and polite. The balmy smile she wore was perfect.

Sergeant Ready warmed instantly to the attractive brunette standing at the counter. It took him a second to gather himself. He paused mid-sentence with his mouth agape, his mind drawing a blank.

"Uh … Miami-Dade is coming here?" he mumbled absentmindedly, his expression both awkward and embarrassed.

Mecca was amused by the desk sergeant's bumbling response. She was used to it. "No, sergeant," she replied kindly and leaned over the counter. She skimmed down the log book. "Here it is, sergeant." She scroll down the columns with her right index finger and stopped on line 19.

Sergeant Ready studied the column. "Hmmm, a one o'clock meeting," he read aloud. "Detective Tomay and the chief—" He stopped short, took a quick glance at his watch, and looked up at the woman. "Detective Tomay? Oh, boy. Corporal Elliot, come here and man the desk while I escort our guest," he ordered his subordinate. "Welcome to Washington," he smiled and extended his hand.

The office for the chief of police was a spacious, square room with dark wood from the floor to the ceiling. On all sides, a vast repertoire of books filled the towering bookcases to capacity. Dark berber carpet covered the floor. And to give the office that handsome executive feel, a large dark mahogany desk was centered in the rear of the office.

A knock sounded at the door. "Come in!" Commander Holt said. The heavy oak door opened without making a sound.

Sergeant Ready stepped in the office. He could see the chief seated behind his desk, a manila folder open in front of him, its contents spread out across the desk.

"Commander Holt? Sir, you have a meeting scheduled with Detective Tomay from Miami-Dade," Ready announced, speaking in a voice that lacked authority.

The commander's interest was roused when he heard the name Tomay. His eyes moved off the desk and peered toward the door, and the woman in the dark brown Yves Saint Laurent pantsuit. She stood poised in the doorway. Tall. Curvy. Confident.

Oh, yeah! the commander said to himself, brimming with excitement as he rose from his desk to welcome the new addition to his homicide division.

"Detective Mecca Tomay," Chief Holt said, moving toward the door. "Welcome to Washington. I'm Shane Holt, Chief of Police." He greeted Mecca with a handshake and a welcoming smile.

"Well, detective," Holt began, taking a seat behind his desk. "You're making a major move coming up here from the sunshine state. Let me tell you, DC can get pretty nasty at times. You sure you're up to the task?" His brow arched to a sharp point. "I'm asking you this because I don't want you to get cold feet at the last minute after preparations have been made and all parties are ready to move forward on this matter." The commander's demeanor was professional and calm, his hands folded easily on top of the desk.

Mecca started to speak, then changed directions. She hesitated, shifted in her seat, and crossed her long legs—left over right. She placed both hands—left over right—on her knee and leaned back in her seat.

She looked the commander right in the eye. Sir, you know as well as I do that I have an objective. For you to insinuate anything remotely possible as to me backing out, getting cold feet, or having second thoughts—I feel offended by your remark, sir." Mecca paused to catch her breath. She sighed heavily before adding, "I transferred to Washington to catch a killer. Moreso the sick ass who killed my sisters. So let's cut out the bull, stop wasting precious time, and get down to business." Her calm disposition spoke volumes.

Commander Holt smiled inwardly. That was precisely the reason he allowed her transfer to go through. Who better to hunt down a predator than a victim's vengeful family member? And this family member just happens to be one of the top homicide investigators in the field. The fact that Mecca Tomay was extremely pleasing to the eye was just a bonus.

"Considering the case and killer that you're referring to," Holt countered smoothly, "we have considerable ground to make up, detective. But with your dedication and expertise, I'm certain everything will eventually work itself out."

Mecca's eyes traveled the table and landed on the open manila folder. "Is that what I think it is, commander?" She sounded uneasy.

"Are you certain that you are mentally and physically prepared to take on this matter? Don't get me misconstrued. Your credentials are first class. You're well trained and versed in your field. But the factors contained in this case—" Holt paused and put on his serious game face. "Let me warn you, detective," he began. He hesitated, then took a deep breath. "They are far beyond the norm and way outside of our customary boundary lines."

A cautious vibe suddenly emanated in the room. They both exchanged uneasy looks. "You are aware that if you take on this case you will be working under the guise of total anonymity? This operation is covert, and you will be reporting solely and directly to yours truly—me," Commander Holt said, leaning forward on the desk for emphasis.

There was a long silence.

That's what I've been waiting to hear, Mecca thought. With a curt nod, she replied, "Besides you, sir, who else will be working along with us in this covert operation?"

Commander Holt eyed the stunning beauty seated before him. It was a struggle for Shane to hold back his lustful urges, his inner beast that was clawing and scratching and salivating over the alluring beauty.

"Tony Woo, our chief CSI inspector, will be your personal CSI contact and liaison," Holt informed, giving her an odd look. He continued, "Inspector Woo will fill you in on all the gory details. Pay close attention to the manner in which your sisters were slain." He paused and shook his head. "Why did I make that statement? Don't ask. I don't know my damn self. That's at the top of your agenda. Well, anyway, your partner for this operation will be Detective Nadia Dozier, one of DC's finest, I must say," the commander declared, sounding like a proud father. "This operation is dubbed Black Hole, otherwise anonymous to any other inquiring minds. Are we perfectly clear on this, detective? No one beyond the small group I just indicated knows anything about the hunt for the mystery predator. As far as homicide and the FBI are concerned, this case is closed. And I'd like to keep it that way."

"That's duly noted, sir," Mecca responded with an impervious show of emotions. "Now, with that said, I'm extremely anxious to examine the particulars in this case. Also, I would love to meet my new partner. I hope she doesn't mind giving me a tour of the infamous Potomac shed of horrors."

"Well, I'm pretty certain that she wouldn't mind taking you on an exploration of the crime scene. That would provide you both some much needed bonding time." A sly grin parted his lips. "Where will you go from there?" he inquired, sensing there was much more going on inside that pretty little head of hers than she was letting on.

Mecca thought for a moment, then said, "Once I'm finished with my examination of the crime scene, I had planned to call it a day. If by any chance you need to get in touch with me, I'll be staying at my sister's house on

Jefferson Street." Mecca was surprised how little emotion she felt when she mentioned the place Mariah and Malaysia lost their lives.

Mecca and Commander Holt both looked at one another for a moment as if there were something more to say, but apparently there wasn't.

Commander Holt reached for the telephone. "Detective Dozier should be in her office," he said, dialing her extension. "She's thrilled to be a part of this operation and to have you as a new partner." He gave Mecca a perceptive wink and a smile. "Detective Dozier," he said into the receiver and pushed the manila folder across the desk toward Mecca. "Guess what. Your new crime partner is right here in my office, and she's anxious to take a ride out to the Potomac grounds with you. Will that be okay with you?" He placed his hand over the receiver. "Take a look at the crime scene photo. I want you to get a feel for what you're up against and what's ahead of you."

Mecca scooted to the edge of her seat and leaned over the desk where the folder lay. She held her breath and pulled the photo spread toward her. *OMG!* Her breath caught in her throat when she laid eyes on the gruesome display. Mecca forced herself to breathe as she quietly perused the hideous snapshots of mutilated female corpses captured in different stages of savagery and mutilation.

Nausea struck Mecca in the pit of her stomach, and the sudden urge to gag overcame her as she stared at the bloody photo spread. The images were a sickening display of pure human carnage.

In Potomac, MD, a charcoal-gray Dodge Charger came barreling down the winding stretch of country road that was Lake Potomac Drive.

Five minutes later the brawny hunk of metal pulled into the driveway leading to the now infamous Potomac estate.

Mecca pushed the passenger's door open and stood at the top of the glazed concrete driveway. She took in the breathtaking landscape of lush rolling hills spread out before her like a tranquil green oasis. From the first whiff of crisp, clean air, she knew the entire area was prime real estate.

About sixty yards out from the estate, Mecca took notice of a rickety wood shed that was completely out of place, hovering in its own green space. The worn splintered structure was more suited for the pastures of some worn-out horse farm somewhere in the country, not here in upscale Potomac, MD.

The car horn sounded, breaking Mecca's reverie. "C'mon, you can't get an adequate feel for this place from up here," Detective Nadia Dozier said as she got out the car. Warm sunlight caressed Nadia's soft, chocolaty face when she leaned on top of the car. Her long black locks covered her left eye, giving her that sexy, saucy Naomi Campbell look.

"From up here the scenery looks so beautiful and tranquil," Nadia said with a casual sweep of her arm. "But the horrors we've uncovered on these grounds ..." She scrunched her nose and shook her head. "Believe me, detective, when I say it will blow you away."

Two minutes later both women were standing outside the shed. Mecca looked anxious and quiet. "Would you like to do the honors?" Nadia asked, producing a set of keys from the front pocket of her navy suit jacket. She jingled the keys in the air, her brown almond-shaped eyes focused on Mecca's facial expression, waiting.

Without a second thought, Mecca plucked the keys from Nadia's hand, ripped down the yellow crime scene tape stretched across the shed's doorway. She fidgeted briefly with the keys until she found the one she was looking for.

Mecca unlatched the heavy-duty cast-iron lock and disengaged a pair of dead-bolt locks. She glanced over her shoulder, took a deep breath, and pushed the wooden door wide open. The aged wooden frame creaked and whined, giving both women instant chills.

Mecca paused in the doorway, allowing her eyes to adjust and focus on the dark, dank interior. The only sign of light inside was the sunlight filtering in through the open doorway.

Inside the aged wooded structure, a strong stench of stale air assaulted the ladies' nasal passages. The dinky wooden enclosure was musky and humid –grimy mole-infested walls seemed to emanate an eerily haunting aura with a silence so deafening it rattled the human senses.

Mecca stepped across the threshold and paused briefly before proceeding the length of the shed. She stopped at the far wall and pivoted on her four-inch Jimmy Choo stilettos.

"Detective Dozier," she began with an obvious look of contemplation. Her eyes darted around the dim enclosure, absorbing every angle, inch, and crevice in the twenty-by twenty foot shed.

Mecca exhaled, then said, "If I'm not mistaken, all the murder scenes which took place indoors were staged, weren't they?" She took a quick breath and continued. "If that's the case, then who's to say this crime scene right here wasn't staged by the perp? Catch my drift?"

A hesitant frown creased Nadia's brow. "What? I'm not following you."

The look Mecca gave Nadia was thorough and precise. "Think about it for a minute. As crafty and meticulous as these predators were, searching out the scent of their prey, and methodically hunting them down. Why slip up and leave one solitary footprint in such a place as this, where all the trophies of their sins were housed?"

Mecca paused when she recognized the poignant expression growing on Nadia's face. "Detective Dozier," she forged on, blunt and to the point, "I strongly believe the footprint found at this scene was left here on purpose to lead us on a wild goose chase. That's my initial inclination. The footprint we have in our possession doesn't belong to our killer."

Nadia's almond-shaped orbs glared defiantly in response. "Well, that's just fucking great," she huffed sourly. "From the prospective you just gave, we're back at square one, and the mystery man we're looking for is once again just a figment of our imagination."

Mecca nodded. "Yeah, girl," she said, her voice dropping a few octaves. "There's a real psycho running loose in DC," she declared with a peevish smirk.

A strong sense of concern permeated the air between the two women. They looked at one another, staring in total silence. The seriousness and urgency they now faced was an uphill battle, a harsh and volatile journey that was bound to get a lot nastier before it got better.

Chapter 38

A perfect crescent moon glowed brilliantly in the cloudless midnight sky over Washington, DC on this blustery summer night.

Racing along the freeway on North Capital, a shimmering burnt-orange Nissan 350-Z dipped from left to right, changing lanes effortlessly as it maneuvered the road.

A buxom redheaded white girl named Gail Saunders was commandeering the sporty coupe. Her overconfidence was displayed in the way she punched the throttle and whipped the wheel like the hot and sassy female driver Danica Patrick.

"If you like it, then you should've put a ring on it!" Gail belted out Beyonce's tune at the top of her lungs and slapped the dash. "Ain't that right, girlfriend?!?" She smiled at the lone photo adorned to the center of the dash. Her BFF Monica Dolce smiled at her from the photograph.

Gail figured that was the least she could do to honor the passing of her childhood friend. Gail was floored the day Monica's mother phoned to say Monica had made special arrangements to bequeath her prized sports coupe to her.

As soon as Gail received ownership of the Nissan, she immediately fixed the colorful airbrushed photo of Monica to the dash and made a solemn promise to Monica and herself, that the two of them were road dawgz for life and they would be riding together forever.

The sleek-looking coupe came careening around a sharp bend in the road and throttled down fifty yards before banking a hard right at the intersection of North Capitol and Hawaii Avenue.

A minute later, the 350-Z was parked at the curb under a dim street lamp. Gail turned off the ignition and fished her BlackBerry from her colorful Benetton bag. In the side-view mirror Gail caught a fleeting image of a silver Cadillac as the sedan bent the corner and disappeared.

Gail quickly typed in a couple of e-mails, telling her new boyfriend good night before she climbed out, and made her way to the rear to gather her shopping bags.

Overhead, the dim street lamp began to buzz and flicker as if sending out a warning to the unsuspecting Gail, who was bent over the rear hatch busy collecting her shopping bags.

A few feet away, a dark silhouette moved silently in the shadows. Cloaked from head to toe in black and gray camouflage garb, Natasha resembled a dark phantom warrior prowling the landscape for its enemy. She crept up on her victim without making a sound. She paused when Gail suddenly stood erect, fidgeting inside of her Benetton bag.

The sight of her caused Natasha's blood to boil. Snapshots fired off in her head. Painful memories of Gail and Monica laughing at Angel inside the restroom of McCormick & Schmick's taunted her.

Without warning the evilness in Natasha raged out of control. "Whore." The fine hairs on the back of Gail's neck turned brittle when she heard the strange voice whisper in the wind. Before she could react, the metallic gleam of a polished straight razor appeared in Natasha's hand and cut swiftly with deadly precision, slashing through the air.

The first strike penetrated Gail's jugular, preventing her from screaming. Blood instantly spewed from the wound, and the ghastly sound of Gail gurgling and choking on her own blood echoed in the air. The second strike pierced the nape of her neck. The next two strikes were deep mortal gashes. They penetrated her trachea and Adam's apple. Natasha was in her element, hitting the helpless woman with strike after deadly strike.

Several strikes later, Gail's body lay twitching on the pavement in a fresh pool of blood. Natasha squatted over her and proceeded to do the unthinkable act only a demented mind was capable of doing. She placed the straight razor to the base of Gail's nose and peeled her entire nose off her face. A thick reservoir of blood oozed profusely from the mangled gaping hole in the center of her disfigured face.

A wicked, sadistic laugh resonated in the night as Natasha melted back into the shadows, her dark form vanishing like a ghost in the night.

ψ ψ ψ ψ

Hours later ...

A thick veil of fog lifted from Angel's eyes. It felt as though a curtain had been pulled open in her mind. Out of nowhere, this strange white girl with bright red hair materialized from the fog like a ghost. The foggy image sparked a strong feeling of caution inside of her.

Wait a minute, a small voice in the back of Angel's mind spoke up. I know this woman. But where from, she quipped, feeling a weird sensation come over her.

Danger!!! The word leaped to the forefront of Angel's mind and startled her. She could feel the woman was in immediate danger, that something sinister was stalking her. Angel could feel it so profoundly it sent a cold shiver up her spine.

Suddenly, in the blink of an eye, something went horribly wrong. The white girl was on the ground, wounded and terrified. Angel looked on, speechless, gazing at the stream of blood oozing from a number of deep gashes dotting her neck like death tattoos.

The white girl stared up at Angel, her eyes screaming out to her, pleading for help, but it was too late. Death had come for here. Agony, pain, and turmoil enveloped her soul as she fought with her last dying breath to stave off her impeding death.

A silvery flash startled Angel. She jumped when the sharp razor swept across her view. What in the hell?!? A voice blasted in her head when the hideous image appeared to her. Angel shrieked and recoiled when she laid eyes on the mangled corpse lying on the pavement.

The image was horrid. The white girl's nose-less, bloody face was glaring up at her. Dark red goo oozed from the deep lacerated fleshy crater in the center of her deformed face.

A strange voice whispered, "Gail."

Angel turned rigid with fear and shot up into a seated position in bed.

"Oh, Lord!" she said nervously, clutching her favorite rose-colored cashmere quilt tightly around her as she stared off into space with a scared, baffled look plastered on her face.

"Gail?" Angel whispered quietly to herself. "Who is she? Where do I know her from? The question Angel asked herself infringed on her mind, like a poisonous ameba feasting on her psyche.

Chapter 39

1A.M.

At the intersection of Hawaii Avenue and Fort Totten Drive, a vast sea of red, white, and blue lights electrified the night. A massive gathering of law enforcement and first responder vehicles were jammed in the intersection.

A woeful, distressed cry shattered the air, and twenty-eight pairs of eyes all turned to see the murder victim's mother collapse from the devastating reality of never seeing her only child alive ever again.

"Uh, that would be Mrs. Saunders, the victim's grieving mother," Lieutenant Barnhart said casually to the chief.

Lieutenant Barnhart was a ruggedly handsome man who sported the perfect tan all year round. He was another transfer, uprooted from the San Francisco Bay area. His sandy brown hair was short, spiked, and stylish. Barnhart swore he was the quintessential ladies' man.

Commander Holt held his breath and his eyes turned grim. He felt Lieutenant Barnhart's emotionless response was inadequate. Yes, of course situations such as murder scenes required a measure of professionalism and control of one's emotions, he surmised. Each murder scene was uniquely different from the next. But when taking into consideration the human devastation and the magnitude of this particular murder scene, Holt felt the situation warranted a measure of humbleness and humility, especially towards the mother of the murder victim.

Holt gave Lieutenant Barnhart a hard, disapproving stare—"Lieutenant!" Holt grunted, gritting his teeth. "Report to my office by 0900 hours today. I believe it would be in your best interest that we sign you up for sensitivity training." The commander spotted Tony Woo in the crowd and walked off.

"Sir?" Barnhart said, scratching his head, looking disgruntled. "Sensitivity training?" he grumbled under his breath, daring not raise his voice and question the chief. He wondered who had pissed him off tonight. *Probably got dissed by one of the cunts earlier.*

When the commander turned back to Barnhart, the lieutenant's eyes were narrowed and his lips were pressed in a thin, crooked line. Holt was satisfied as he skirted the crowd of law enforcement officials gathered in the middle of the street, and walked right over to Tony Woo.

When the Commander approached, Tony was crouched beside the black body bag, holding the corpse. He was unaware of Holt's presence. His focus and attention were totally consumed with the dastardly deed perpetrated with such hate on the young, helpless woman.

"My favorite chief inspector," Holt said good-naturedly. "You don't know how good it makes me feel to see that my better half is taking control of the situation." Tony Woo knew the voice speaking to him—it was the cheery mood that threw him for a loop. "So what's your synopsis thus far, Tony?" inquired the commander, flattening his silver silk tie. His eyes latched onto Tony with a peerless, unnerving stare.

Tony Woo rose to his feet, straightened his navy Pierre Cardin blazer and pushed his gold frames snugly on his nose. "Ahem!" He cleared his throat and folded his meaty hands behind his back.

"Well, sir," Woo began, launching into his crime scene analysis, "our victim sustained major damage to her jugular, the kill zone. Also, her larynx, her trachea, and clavicle were critically lacerated. I'm talking deep, mortal lacerations. So deep, it was as though the perp was attempting to decapitate her."

A subtle groan fell off Holt's bottom lip. "And, the removal of her nose? What kind of depraved act does that signify? Some kind of sick, satanic ritual or initiation going on here?"

Woo leaned back against a maple tree. His gaze swept the periphery of the crime scene, searching, dissecting, and analyzing in a three-dimensional configuration like a super human computer, every angle and pathway leading to and from the point of attack.

"I'm not sure what this falls under," Woo responded carefully, "but the name Jack the Ripper jumped out at me when I examined the body."

"Jack the Ripper?" Holt retorted dryly. "What's that supposed to mean?"

Woo kept a keen eye on the chief. The cheery mood when he stepped on the scene was all a front. The man standing before him was genuine.

Without saying a word, Woo put his right index finger in the air. "Please ... allow me, sir," he said with a shrewd-no nonsense expression. This was Tony Woo's domain. He needed—no, he insisted—on having full reign in order to garner adequate and swift results.

"To elaborate on what I've incurred thus far, I believe it's safe to say the perp we're looking for in this murder has a medical background of some sort," Wood said. He paused and gave the commander a disconcerted look. "Something else about the victim jumped out at me." He winced before adding, "The victim's name ... Gail Saunders. She was a close friend of Monica Dolce, sir."

Commander Holt shook his head and shrugged.

Woo's shoulders stiffened. He clicked his tongue. "Monica Dolce lived around the corner at The Heights apartment complex. She was the third victim to die in the killing spree orchestrated by Jovan and Ray."

Commander Holt cringed. "You have to be shitting me," he grunted, resting his right hand on Woo's shoulder. Anger and discontent flared in his eyes. All of a sudden Holt needed to sit down.

"I wish that were the case," Woo answered plainly, "but I'm sorry to say it's not, sir."

"Tony, if there's a smidgen of truth to what you're saying," Holt began, then paused momentarily. "My God, Tony, the missing nose—that's the son of a bitch's calling card! Have you contacted Nadia and Mecca about the situation?"

Woo gave a quick nod. "They've both been notified, and they're en route to the scene now," he assured the commander.

"Reroute 'em," Holt ordered. "We'll brief them down at headquarters." He stopped short. His eyes were strained and bloodshot. "I want that sick son of a bitch, Woo!" He snapped out and slammed his fist hard against the tree. The commander leaned in Tony's ear and snarled, "Do you hear me?!? At all cost. I will sell my soul to the devil if I have to in order to solve this case and get this psycho fuck off my streets!" he stated vehemently, his deep-set gaze cold and unnerving, like a man teetering on the edge.

Chapter 40

First Strike

The sun glowed brilliantly in the clear blue sky over the capital city on this perfect Saturday afternoon in upper Northwest, DC.

Over in the posh Palisades community, at the corner of Edmonds and McArthur boulevards, this impeccable lavender and white ranch-style home stood out like a sore thumb. This unique residence held the title as the most flamboyant home on the block.

At the front gate visitors to the residence were greeted by a pair of red and white striped candy cane poles at least eight feet tall. The words "Candy Land" were draped in rainbow letters between the decorations. The home's immaculate lush green lawn was peppered with larger-than-life candy ornaments. The colorful landscape was reminiscent of a scene plucked from Willy Wonka's Chocolate Factory.

Inside the Candy Land residence, the king of the castle, Goldie, DC's top pimp, ruled his territory with an ironclad fist. Goldie's way was brutal—women were initiated with forced orgies called cherry parties. Goldie took them seriously, often choreographing the action like a movie director. Goldie led his harem by intimidation and mind control. Other tactics included encouraging teamwork and setting goals. Goldie had a God complex. When he was coaxing a new inductee into the mix, he'd use his infamous introductory line: "I'm gonna make you love me." And he would in his own twisted way. Goldie had this inner power that frightened people, and with that he took cold advantage of his followers.

A slinky Jamaican sex kitten paused in the doorway of Goldie's master bedroom suite. "Daddy-Goldie," she began sweetly, "your friend, Mr. Juelz is here to see you. Would you like me to have him wait for you in the den, or would you like me to escort him to your jungle?"

The soft melody "Te Amo" by Rihanna wafted through the room. Seated on what Goldie referred to as his throne, a rich scarlet leather high-back wing chair positioned in the center of his jungle-themed oasis, Goldie brought to mind Rick Ross wrapped in an exquisite satin magenta smoking jacket, donning a pair of dark Ray Ban shades and puffing on a big Cuban cigar.

At the moment Goldie was in director mode—totally focused, scrutinizing a pair of salacious platinum-blonde snow bunnies, getting down and dirty for him on his octagon-shaped bed, twice the size of a regular king bed.

"Can't you see Daddy-Goldie's attention is elsewhere at the minute," Goldie answered, sarcasm heavy in his voice. He glanced off to the side and caught the Jamaican girl with an icicle glare.

Uncertain, she forced an awkward smile. "Oh, I'm sorry Daddy-Goldie," she instantly apologized. "I'll send Mr. Juelz away." She started to leave but froze in her tracks. Her eyes widened with fear and dread when Goldie wheeled around. "You dumb-pussy heifer!" he chided scathingly. "You send Juelz away and I'll have these two ladies here tie you up and punish every exposed orifice on your body!"

Sixty seconds later, a lean 6'7" form filled the doorway. His name was Juelz Odom, the feared boss of the dangerous A-Team gang.

Juelz paused for a second before entering Goldie's domain. He flashed a devious smile when he laid eyes on the naked duo frolicking on the bed.

"Hell yeah, they gettin' it in!" Juelz cheered, stepping in the room. "Are those freaks for me?" He swung his long, dirty-brown dreads over his left shoulder and waited for a reply.

Nigga, you already know," Goldie grinned, sucking on his Cuban cigar. "My pussy is your pussy. All the pussy you see has a price tag attached to it somewhere, ya know." He pulled the cigar from his mouth. "Poppa Goldie needs a brand-new Jag," he added with a crooked grin. "You think a man in your position can help somebody like me out?" Both men eyed each other for a split second before cracking up.

Outside in the back alley behind the Candy Land residence, two jet-black BMW 745s rolled to a stop. In the rear cabin, gazing through the tinted window, Bad Ass looked fierce, like a man with a serious bone to pick with someone.

"We're ready, boss," the driver spoke up suddenly. He was a big, black, greasy-looking bear of a man named Midnight. He reached in his waist and pulled out a fully loaded Calico. He glanced over at the man riding shotgun, his ugly, beady-headed partner, Nightmare, who was busy loading slugs in a magazine for his Tec-9.

Midnight looked up at the rearview mirror, his sallow eyes focused on Bad Ass. "You ain't gotta get your hands dirty, Bad Ass. We got enough men and firepower to handle these bammas."

"Yeah, I know that's right," Bad Ass replied matter of factly. "But I didn't come along for the ride. You should know me by now, Midnight. I don't make a move unless there's something major for me or my crew to gain in the process."

"Okay," Nightmare said and slammed a fully loaded magazine in the submachine gun. He twisted in his seat. "I'm ready to peel some wigs!"

Bad Ass looked the dark, scary henchman in his funny-looking cockeye and flashed him a toothy grin. "Check on Murder and his crew," he directed, twisting in his seat. He peered through the rear window, spying Murder behind the wheel, his mouth going nonstop. "Tell Murder we ready to roll. Ask him who's staying behind for lookout?"

Midnight had his Iphone out before Bad Ass could finish. He loved to text instead.

"Yeah, Bad Ass," Midnight said, reading from the phone. "Trouble the designated lookout. Murder and the crew say they ready for blood spill!"

"Okay, men, " Bad Ass said, taking a deep breath. "Y'all know what time it is. You heard the man. It's blood spill time!"

Bam!!! The side door leading to the kitchen suddenly burst open and slammed hard against the wall. A hairbreadth later, a gang of gun-toting bandits in dark fatigues rushed in, guns waving wildly in the air.

Midnight took the lead. He was frightening. His burly black frame loomed like a grizzly bear in the center of the kitchen. "All you bitches," he barked aggressively, spit flying from his mouth, "get the fuck down on the floor, now!"

Terrified shrieks filled the kitchen as a handful of scantily clad women caught lounging around the dark granite island were totally stunned by the surprise invasion.

The women gaped in horror as the bandits shoved guns in their faces, snatched them by their weaves, and forced them to the floor.

"Get down and stay down, bitch!" The vicious orders were barked over and over again.

Midnight, Nightmare, Threat, and Dabo didn't bother with the women in the kitchen. As soon as Murder, Cut-Throat, and Screw had the situation under control, they immediately moved in, spreading throughout the house like a tactical squad with the intent on capturing the target.

The four enforcers marched out of the kitchen and made a beeline for the living room. The men smiled when they stumbled upon a trio of half-naked, glossy-lipped women sipping pink champagne, smoking hashish while lounging on pink suede sofas like they didn't have a care in the world.

Menacing black-clad goons with big black guns came out of nowhere. Startled gasps swept through the room. The women's eyes bucked wide and jaws smacked the floor. The high they were enjoying evaporated instantaneously.

On cue, the stocky Mike Tyson–looking dude named Dabo snickered as he broke formation from the group. His job was to round up the ladies in the living room and herd them into the kitchen with the rest of the women.

Midnight, Nightmare, and Threat continued the search, moving deeper into the home. Seconds later the men came upon a long, vacant rear hallway with a number of uncharted rooms on both sides.

After a quick search of each room, the men came up empty-handed, no target in sight. The enforcers huddled in the hallway. Their main focus now was the closed black door at the far end of the hallway. The men stood silent, listening to the music pulsating from behind the sturdy black frame.

Twenty seconds later ...

Brrrrack!!! Automatic gunfire shredded the black door frame a millisecond before Midnight's size 17 Timberland boot kicked the door frame off the hinges.

"I dare your bitch ass!" Midnight growled venomously, the barrel of his automatic Colt-M4 swaying back and forth between Goldie and Juelz. "Pull your gat, nigga, and watch this chopper push your shit back!" he threatened.

Nightmare and Threat stormed in the room. "Oh yeah," Nightmare grinned, exposing a mouthful of crooked, jagged, yellow-stained teeth.

Threat whipped out his cell phone and hit the speaker button. "Hey, Bad Ass," he shouted into the phone, "come straight to the back room. We got the whole package on lock, 'caught the bammas gettin' it in with a couple snow bunnies!" A morbid sense of joy bubbled in Threat's voice when he spoke. Today was a good day, he admitted quietly, realizing the significance of nabbing Goldie and Juelz together. These bammas were the first pieces to a puzzle CIX were putting together.

The enforcers caught Juelz with his pants down, literally. He had his Red Monkey jeans pulled down around his ankles getting some mean headpiece from a pretty blonde snow bunny when Midnight charged in the room.

Bad Ass' favorite cherry-flavored Tootsie pop was marinating in his mouth as he paced the master bedroom with a slick, ominous grin, like a sleeky carnivore sizing up a potential meal. His gun-toting trio stood around watching him with psychotic intrigue swirling in their eyes.

Goldie and Juelz sat butt-naked on the edge of the bed, hands tied behind their backs. The two snow bunnies had been since removed from the bedroom, banished to the kitchen with the rest of Goldie's harem.

The pimp looked totally perplexed. His eyes shifted nervously, his nostrils flared, his forehead drenched in sweat.

Juelz had a crazed look in his eye. His jaw muscles twitched erratically as he cursed himself for allowing CIX to catch him slippin'. *Fuck me! I know better than to roll dolo like that!* he admonished himself.

Bad Ass was amused at the naked pair seated before him. He smiled inwardly when he recognized the frustration etched on both their faces. "Y'all know y'all fucked up, right?" Bad Ass said, standing in the middle of the floor, a facetious grin tucked in the corner of his mouth as he cast a dark gaze on the Tootsie pop twirling between his thumb and forefinger six inches in front of him.

Bad Ass snickered and cut his eye. "Yeah, y'all bammas know you fucked up, don't you?" He looked around at his men and laughed.

"Pssst ... you and you weak-ass crew can suck my dick!" Juelz spewed hotly. "Fuckin' with a nigga like me ... Y'all bammas just signed your own death certificate. I'm a made man, top dawg 'round here! A-Team gonna slaughter y'all bammas slow!"

Bad Ass laughed mockingly and said, "You one fool-ass nigga, you know that? I think you might even believe that dumb-ass shit you spittin'." He cut his eyes on Midnight and grunted, "Mr. Juelz Odom." He drew on the name, taunting the man, then chuckled. "If you're A-Team's top gangsta, what you robbing for?" Bad Ass tossed out the bait, and Juelz bit— his reaction sealed the deal. Bad Ass noticed the slight tremble in his eye when he asked about robbing.

"That's right, Juelz," Bad Ass said. He was calm and collected, facing the naked pair. "We know all about the home invasion, the kidnapping, and the heavy stash of cocaine y'all bammas took off them lames out in PG last week. How do I know? Y'all bammas beat us to the lick!" Bad Ass stopped and stared at the black leather duffel bag sitting at his feet.

"You see," he said. He crouched over the bag and pulled the gold zipper open. The strong aroma of nitroglycerin stung his nostrils, prompting a sly grin. "If everybody in the game would just play the part they were meant to play, you know? Stay the fuck in your lane and don't step on nobody else's toes. Like for instance, robbing muthafuckers you ain't got no damn business fucking with!"

Bad Ass stood up straight and turned. Dangling from his left hand was a new roll of duct tape, gripped in his right was a full stick of dynamite. The dynamite jumped out at them. Goldie's and Juelz's eyes bulged from their sockets.

"I should chop your bitch ass up and feed y'all sorry muthafuckas to the homeless!" Bad Ass said, standing over them. "'Cause when you fuck with my money, you fucking with my emotions. Ain't that right, men?"

"Damn skippy!" Midnight agreed without hesitation. He was so anxious to draw blood, he couldn't keep still, shifting from his left foot to the right, like he had ants in his pants. "And don't nobody fuck with your emotions!" Midnight added with emphasis.

"What?" Bad Ass cocked his head. "Get it right, soldier," he corrected. "I'm all about the loot first." Bad Ass kneeled down and took a knee in front of Juelz. "It was fifty bricks, right?" His eyes were on Goldie when he spoke. "I'm gonna ask this question only once: Where the fuck did y'all stash my coke?"

"Don't both you bammas speak at once," Threat chimed from his position at the door.

Bad Ass put his hand up for silence. "Let me handle this." He reached up with both hands, grabbed Juelz by the throat and snatched his lumbering frame off the bed. "Bring your bitch ass here!" Bad Ass slammed him violently on the floor and growled. "Slaughter me slow, huh, bitch!" He cocked his arm back. Crack! He smashed Juelz in the face with a powerful right hand. The sight of blood seemed to send Bad Ass over the edge. He went punch-drunk on the bamma, pummeling him with a barrage of hard right punches, putting every ounce of his weight behind each punch. Every blow was a vicious head shot.

Bad Ass didn't stop throwing punches until Juelz's face was beaten to a bloody pulp. He grinned, satisfied with his work, watching Juelz's eyes roll around in his head and flutter weakly. He was on the verge of unconsciousness.

Bad Ass jumped to his feet. "Gift wrap his bitch ass!" he ordered. Midnight and Nightmare sprang into action. They proceeded to wrap duct tape around Juelz's exposed torso, then placed the stick of dynamite in the crease of his back, dead center. They taped the dynamite in place and made sure it was snug and secure.

Goldie stared in horror. "What the fuck are you doing?!?" he stuttered, flabbergasted by the thought of what they were intending to do. "C'mon, fellas, I know y'all can't be for real!" His voice cracked as he attempted to stifle the tears collecting in his eyes. "Dawg, it's not that serious! Please! What the fuck are you doing?!?"

Sporting a snide grin, Bad Ass said, "If you don't wanna see your brother blown into a million tiny pieces right before your eyes, I'd advise you to give up the location. Where's my fuckin' coke?!?" Bad Ass extended his right hand. he palmed Goldie's face and squeezed. "Yeah, that's right, your secret's out the bag. I know you and Juelz are brothers. So what's up? Are you your brother's keeper?"

Goldie tried to collect himself. He took a couple of deep breaths. "Look, man ..." He was hyperventilating, attempting to talk and breathe at the same time. "I don't know—"

"Nightmare, light the goddamn stem," Bad Ass said through clenched teeth. "I ain't got time for this bullshit!"

Nightmare and Midnight shared a smile as Nightmare produced his favorite grenade-style butane lighter. His thumb pressed down on the fake pin, and a blue flame sprung up from the sprout with a quiet hiss.

"Goddamn it! Wait a minute!" Goldie screamed, hysterical. His face contorted and his head swung left to right on a swivel. "You want the coke!?!" he stuttered with a lisp.

Juelz groaned in pain as he struggled to raise his head off the carpet. "Don't tell 'em shit," he mumbled in a daze, his voice both fragile and barely audible.

Bad Ass' head whipped around. His dark pupils dilated into sharp needle points. He gave Juelz a twisted look, shifted his weight to his left foot, cocked back with the right, and delivered a whooping kick to his groin. Bam! A gut-wrenching groan emanated from Juelz's mouth as he trembled from the excruciating pain that seized his body.

"Oh, yeah, that felt good right there," Bad Ass snorted. "Now, what your big black pimp ass gonna do, huh? Give up the coke or watch the fireworks?"

Goldie was in utter shock of the situation unfolding before him. He could feel the evilness growing inside of Bad Ass as he looked upon the man, and it made him tremble inside.

"I know where the coke at!" Goldie cried out. "Please, I'm begging you ... If I give you what you want, you have to promise me that you gonna let me and my brother go."

"Alright, you got that," Bad Ass responded prematurely. "But you have to give me the location, the number of bammas at the spot, and the layout of the whole joint. You got that?" Bad Ass gloated. A savage gleam shone deep in the oily black pools that were his eyes.

Five minutes later, Threat was backing out into the hallway, followed by Nightmare and then Midnight.

"No!!! You can't do that! You promised me! Please!" The sound of Goldie's terrified screams made you cringe inside. "No! No! Please! I'm begging you! You can't do that! No! Please! No!!!"

Bad Ass strolled out of the bedroom. He had the cagey swag of a devious street player as he stepped to the head of the pack and signaled for his men to follow.

Goldie's cries rang out from the bedroom, echoing along the hallway. His cries gradually faded into nothing when they reached the far end of the hallway.

Bad Ass walked in the living room. Kaboom!!! A solo blast rocked the foundation. The residual impact was a powerful concussion that rattled the internal framework of the entire house.

"Lord!" The Jamaican girl shivered. "What in God's name have these men done?" She stared around the kitchen looking petrified.

Nervous, jittery, fretful expressions appeared on the face of every woman held hostage in the kitchen. Skittish whispers drifted in the air as the women looked to one another for strength and support.

"Alright," Murder grunted, "don't start no shit!" he warned, waving the barrel of his prized chopper like he was about to open fire. Murder lowered his weapon when he noticed his phone vibrating on his hip. He read the screen: Dirt Nap Time!!! Murder's red-tinted eyes grew dark, as if an evil spirit had taken possession.

He glared across the dark granite island, his demeanor warped. Deadly. Psychotic. "Muzzle up!" he ordered with a wicked grin.

Dark, sinister looks flashed on the faces of Dabo, Cut-Throat, and Screw. Without uttering a single word, each man produced a customized silencer from a hidden pocket and attached it to the barrel of his chopper.

A cold stab of fear ignited the atmosphere in the kitchen and stayed there. "What in God's name are you doing?!?" a dark skinned girl with a neon pink hairdo snapped. "They have silencer," a petite Asian girl cowering in the far corner gasped in horror."

"Fuck this shit!" a voluptuous Puerto Rican name Mia hissed loudly. If anybody was going to make a stand and show courage in the face of adversity, it would be Mia. She was Goldie's lethal bottom bitch. She was gutsy, the type of bitch that would bite the head off a rattle snake if it challenged her.

Suddenly, Mia vaulted off the floor, rambling and irate. "You muthafuckas come up in here with your fucking guns and think you can push us around!" She lashed out at the man closest to her, Cut Throat. Her head bobbed and weaved in attack mode.

Cut Throat was shaped like a gorilla, compact and big-boned with a nose that sat on his face at a sick angle—a souvenir from his street battles.

A glimmer of amusement showed in Cut Throat's facial expression as he watched the Puerto Rican woman vent. In the twinkling of an eye, the amusement was gone. As soon as Mia stopped mouthing off, Cut Throat cracked a dark smile, aimed his chopper, and pulled the trigger.

Phumph! Phumph! He pumped two silenced rounds into Mia's head. Blood and brain matter splattered across the clean white tile a half a second before Mia's corpse crashed to the floor.

Cut Throat set it off. Murder, Dabo, and Screw opened fire on the women with utter disregard. It was like shooting fish in a barrel.

The scene left behind in the kitchen was absolute hell. This was the tip of the spear, and the CIX leader, Bad Ass, was already planning the next bloodbath.

The Candy Land residence in the Palisades community would forever be haunted by the souls lost here today. These killings would go down in the annals' of DC's history as one of the bloodiest days on record. The horrific bloodbath would be dubbed the Candy Land Massacre.

Chapter 41

The hellacious murders discovered at the Candy Land residence were incomprehensible. The human carnage was nauseating, reminiscent of a setting taken right out of the infamous mob assassination from the Valentines' Day Massacre.

Instantly, the Candy Land investigation was deemed high priority, taking precedence over every ongoing investigation. This was the sort of investigation detectives dreamed about solving, referring to it as "star status," the coveted diamond collar for the lucky detective who cracked this case and apprehended the suspect. The detective's career would take an automatic vertical leap, landing him or her at the top, where DC's elite law enforcement dwelled.

The Candy Land property was bursting at the seams with a staggering collection of law enforcement personnel.

Outside, inquiring eyes were drawn to the ominous black Suburban with the pitch-black windows navigating towards the front driveway.

Holt alighted from the SUV, confidence and decisiveness billowing from his dark-suited form. His confident nature was absolute. You could feel it in the air the moment he stepped on the scene.

Holt's sidekick, Tony Woo, climbed out on the passenger's side. His wide, porky frame was in total contrast to Holt, but the stout, steely nature Tony implored gave you an entirely different perspective on the age old adage *don't judge a book by its cover.*

The department's favorite swashbuckler, Detective Rich Louis, made his presence known to the two top cops the moment they stepped foot in the front door.

"Chief Holt! Inspector Woo!" Louis got their attention and hurried over to greet them.

After a severe reprimand for the indiscretion he was involved with his ex-partner and now infamous homicide Detective Will Clark, referred to now as federal inmate #898504, residing at the Federal Penitentiary in Terre Haute, Indiana.

The punishment Detective Louis received amounted to a slap on the wrist, thanks to the intervention on the part of Tony Woo. Louis always made it a point to show his gratitude to Tony for going to bat for him, literally saving his ass and his career.

Louis felt small under the gaze of the commander. He was fidgeting with his signature handlebar mustache as he relayed his take on the situation.

"From what I've observed so far, this has all the trappings of a major gang hit in the worse way imaginable."

Both men greeted Detective Louis with quiet, probing looks.

The Chief responded in his usual assertive way. "The deceased consist of ten women and two men. Is that number correct, detective?" His brow lowered, giving his deep-set gaze a more potent expression.

A look of uncertainty showed in Louis' face. "Well, sir, we don't have confirmation yet on the last victim," he said, brushing a loose tuft of blonde hair off his forehead. "He's en route to the emergency room as we speak."

"'Nough said." The Chief made an impatient gesture toward the detective. "We need to examine the bodies and any witness statements." He stopped short, signaled Woo with a slight nod while sidestepping the detective. He looked back over his shoulder. "Detective, you gonna lead the way?" he said with a wave of his hand, offering Louis a surprise invite to accompany them.

He didn't have to ask twice. Louis jumped at the chance to oblige them. He moved so fast, his right foot lost traction on the bright red carpet, and he almost lost his right shoe, but Louis quickly regained his footing, then took lead, escorting both men into the proverbial dead-zone.

The stench of death in the kitchen was overwhelming and intense. The ghastly scene tugged at your stomach and smacked you in the face, galvanizing your senses the moment you laid witness to the human devastation and loss of life that took place within these walls.

Ten young, attractive, vivacious women's lives were taken in such a vicious, callous, and extreme way. Their lifeless corpses strewn around the kitchen like some sort of demented Art Escape exhibit meant for hell.

Holt sighed deeply. "Okay, Louis." He paused to adjust his black silk Ralph Lauren tie. His piercing gaze swept the bloody crime scene, assessing the human loss. "Give us a quick rundown on what you have thus far."

A flock of homicide detectives were loitering in the kitchen. The second the chief walked in, his presence sparked an air of nervous anxiety. The crowd turned at once and immediately parted like the Red Sea, making a clear path for the commander and his sidekick.

"This one here, sir," Louis said, kneeling beside the voluptuous Puerto Rican sprawled on the kitchen floor with two searing bullet wounds in her forehead. Louis continued,

"Take notice of the burn pattern around the entry wound." He gritted his teeth and glanced up at the commander and Tony Woo. "She was shot at point-blank range, the first to go," he added, crawling to his feet. "Once the first shooter drew blood, the rest of the team didn't hesitate to get in on the action. What you're laying witness to is a virtual human shooting gallery, and these women were the targets," Louis concluded with a sweep of his hand.

Chief Holt's demeanor stiffened. He leaned in and took a closer look at the Puerto Rican's corpse. He turned and made eye contact with Tony and huffed, "How many shooters were involved in this massacre?"

Louis looked to the chief. "So far we've identified four different calibers of some very high-powered weaponry," he responded evenly.

"That's just wonderful," interjected Tony Woo, rubbing his dry, meaty paws together. "Where's the second crime scene? We were informed that some sort of explosion went off? Is that correct?"

Louis' shoulders dropped. "Yes," he breathed slowly. "Follow me, gentlemen. This is not a pretty sight, so prepare yourselves."

The stench of blood and burned flesh was so heavy in the air, the noxious fumes assaulted your nostrils the moment you stepped in the hallway leading to the master bedroom. The stink in the air was so foul your stomach instantly bubbled and churned on the verge of vomiting.

From the doorway, the degree of carnage inside the bedroom literally took your breath away.

"What in God's name—" the chief began. He winced when he caught sight of the burnt clump of disfigured flesh lying on the scorched carpet. "Is that another woman's remains?" Rage and disbelief exploded on the chief's face.

The unlucky soul had been blown to pieces. The body was ravaged by the explosion. Blood, guts, and limbs were scattered across the entire circumference of the room, from floor to ceiling. Every inch of space was tainted by the victim's remains, coated in crimson body fluids and shredded body parts.

The men examined the blood-drenched room from the comfort of the hallway, peering inside at the wreckage. Upon initial analysis, the burnt clump of bloody flesh resembled neither a man nor woman. The disfigured corpse looked more like an abomination, a hideous eyesore, something inhuman spawned from hell.

Louis gave a dejected look and shook his head. "Taking into consideration what we have to work with, sir, we've been able to identify the gender: It's a John Doe," he voiced with a measure of uncertainty floating in his voice. "Now, putting a name to the John Doe—you both can see, that's going to take us some time."

Tony Woo's pudgy frame wavered back and forth in the doorway. He looked on the verge of charging in and having his way with the grotesque figure. Anarchy and devastation brought out the best in him. His energy level ratcheted up to a strong ten when presented with chaotic situations, and Tony Woo loved it.

"Chief!" Tony spoke up abruptly, looking like he was about to bust a vein. A mixture of excitement, anxiousness, and agitation swelled in his disposition.

"I need to go in there. Louis, get me a plastic coverall, pronto!" Standing on the sideline watching the forensic team scour the hellish enclosure was too much for Tony. He needed to be in on the action.

Chief Holt got a charge out of watching Tony suit up. He put on transparent coveralls and trotted onto the death stage.

Instantly, Tony Woo morphed from a sideline observer into the main character on the set. His commanding prowess was on display the moment he entered the room. This was Tony's domain, and he let it be known.

First, he cleared the room, ordering the team of forensic technicians to retreat to the hallway. He walked to the center of the room and stood poised, his piercing gaze sharp, pervading, incisive. Tony scanned the blood-tainted terrain, visually and mentally dissecting, reassembling, and analyzing every square inch and crevice.

"Look at Tony," Holt said, leaning casually against the door frame with his arms folded over his chest. "He's in his zone now. Watch the master go to work." His tone was admirable, sounding like the proud father giving praise to his son.

The chief's head bobbed up and down. "I want everyone to pay close attention," he said to the CSI team gathered in the hallway. "Notice how every move he makes has a purpose and focused agenda. Inspector Woo is literally a one-man forensic team," the chief chuckled. "That takes the utmost dedication," he added as an afterthought. "Oh, yeah, I guess that's why he's the chief inspector, huh?"

The belittling remark didn't go over well with the CSI team waiting in the hall. The chief hit a nerve with much of the team, inciting some harsh glares, but no one dared say a thing.

The team wisely kept their mouths shut and kept a close eye on how the inspector operated. He was meticulous, scrutinizing and procuring each and every piece of evidence, from the most miniscule to the obvious.

It would be hours later when the CSI team finally admitted to themselves, in private, while watching the inspector and the methodical way he manipulated and processed the crime scene, they actually recognized a couple of his signature forensic maneuvers that were the inspector's known trademarks. The CSI team said they felt like they were witnessing a live theatrical performance portrayed strictly for their eyes only. The team agreed it was a memorable and intriguing learning experience.

Chapter 42

It was high noon in Washington. The bright sun hovered over the Nation's Capital like an infernal glow in the crystal blue heaves.

Twenty-four hours after the grisly Candy Land massacre, a *Washington Post* newspaper lay undisturbed on the passenger's seat inside Holt's Cadillac Escalade. The headline was emblazoned across the front page in bold black letters:

Gangland Massacre Erupts in Upscale DC Community

In Georgetown, the commander's glistening black SUV maneuvered through the slow-moving traffic clogging the famous stretch of M Street.

"Son of a bitch!" Shane growled. He gave a long, uninterrupted honk on his Caddy's horn for at least twenty seconds before he let up. "C'mon, people! What's the hold up here?!?" His left arm dangled out the window. He slapped his door in frustration.

"DC has to have the sorriest bunch of drivers in the whole fucking east coast!" He stared up at the rearview mirror and vented some more. "There's no accident, no construction, no goddamn emergency whatsoever on M Street, so why is the traffic so goddamn bad!?!"

Shane peered ahead at the immovable log jam and relented. "Okay," he murmured under his breath and tightened his hand on the steering wheel. He leaned back in the seat, arched his head against the headrest, and closed his eyes. This was a new calming method he learned from his nympho sex partner, Sergeant Dashia Webb. In her free time, Dashia freelanced as a certified masseuse. The method she had shown him was supposed to help soothe anger, anxiety, and irritability.

Shane slowed his breathing and counted backward from ten. He opened his eyes, slapped the wheel, and hissed, "Dumb shit don't work!"

While he sat staring at the newspaper, something outside, something red caught his eye. Shane peered out the open passenger's window. *Angel!* His eyes bucked wide, complete surprise and elation jumped on his face.

A scarlet-clad Angel emerged from inside a posh day spa. She lingered for a minute in the doorway when the owner spoke to her.

She looks absolutely gorgeous standing there, Shane thought, admiring her beauty. The sun's rays caressed her face, highlighting her soft, gentle features. Angel was picture perfect, angelic, in a flowy silk mini-dress, slim cropped pants, and flat sandals by D&G. When she moved, Shane swore he was watching poetry in motion. "Wow!!!" he gasped in awe. He quickly caught his breath, reached up, and flipped down the visor mirror. He slipped on a pair of dark Aviator lenses, re-adjusted his pink silk tie, fished a bottle of Ferragamo cologne from the center console and sprayed on some fresh smell good.

Next, he tapped the gas and eased the Escalade close to the lime-green Taurus SHO waiting in front of him. Shane stopped, leaving a paltry six inches of space between the vehicles' bumpers. He put the gear shift in park and activated the vehicle's hazard lights. Shane stepped out looking dapper in a gray striped two-piece by Salvatore Ferragamo. Head up, shoulders back, he strode off making a beeline for Angel.

"Is that who I think it is?!?" Shane said surprised. "Yep, that's my beautiful Angel. How nice to see you again, Ms. Lady, or should I say, Ms. Don't Know How To Answer Or Return My Calls?" He gave her a warm smile and held out his hand. "Please, Angel, allow me this chance to make things right between us. There's unfinished business between you and I, and I'm quite sure you're aware of that." He caressed her hand and flashed a bad-boy grin.

The moment Angel caught sight of Shane stepping onto the curb, there was a bloom in her cheek and spark in her eye. "Oooow," Angel breathed, pressing her hand against her chest. She stared him up and down, her bright eyes oozing with seduction, her ruby red lips pursed provocatively.

Angel's womanly intuition screamed *No!!!* But it didn't register. Her body reacted to the confidence and testosterone exuding profusely from this big, handsome hunk. His aura was strong, and her womanhood was overwhelmed and intoxicated by his presence. The chemistry between them was too powerful to ignore.

Georgetown's swank Peacock Café welcomed the chief of police with open arms. Shane was a regular at the restaurant. His name was enclosed in parentheses on the Peacock Café's preferred guest list.

Angel was thoroughly impressed by the special attention they received the moment they walked in the door of the five-star dining establishment.

Oh, yes! Angel thought. Her jubilation soared. *A girl like me could get used to this kind of uppity first-class treatment.*

She glanced up slowly and smiled when she felt a gentle hand stroke her shoulder. Angel's warm response boosted Shane's ego to another level.

"Everything okay, Angel? You need me to get you anything?" He was being extra polite and attentive to her wants and needs, totally on point today. He put his best face on and had his A-game on front street. The Dark Stallion, his personally selected nickname, would be tappin' that ass in the very near future. *Today, Shane* surmised, attempting to hide the seediness he was feeling inside.

Shane eased into the seat, his dark pupils overflowing with glee, his attitude playful and kind. He removed a gold bottle of Cristal from the ice bucket cradled on a chrome wine stand beside him.

"That's okay, Chloe!" He waved off the bubbly Italian waitress when he noticed her rushing over to assist him. "I got this." He stared across the table and made eye contact with Angel. He instantly felt the air between them move. Something naughty and uninhibited permeated the small space separating them. He lingered briefly before making a playful gesture. He moistened his bottom lip with his tongue. Angel responded with a coy smile, twirling her long black hair around her index finger,

"How about a toast, Angel," Shane said, topping off her glass with a touch of fresh Cristal. He refilled his champagne glass to the rim, set the bottle aside, and raised his glass. "Here's to a beautiful woman. I want to say thank you for making this day a special occasion. Also, I would like to add I'm looking forward to many more special occasions that I would love to share and celebrate with you. Angel, you are a woman to be cherished, to be loved, to be worshipped. Allow me that chance to come into your life and show you the precious jewel you really are." A big Kool-Aid smile burst on his face before he turned up his glass. He could tell by the swooning look in her eyes, the line he just spit was a grand slam. *Yeah, I just fucked her mind with that one!*

The words Shane spoke were so heartfelt and enduring, Angel couldn't stop smiling. Not until she got a whiff of the ultra-sassy Ethiopian bombshell with big doe eyes and a super thick mane of ginger-colored hair. She came strutting through the door in a chic, skintight white Chanel cat suit that accentuated every curve and contour on her luscious anatomy.

Ms. Ethiopia was known to her clients and admirers as Bambi. She was DC's reigning self-made fashionista and superstar diva on the beauty-salon circuit.

Bambi's rowdy diva-like entrance was her established trademark known all across the metropolitan region by every business establishment she and her female entourage frequented on a regular basis.

She pranced up to the pale, bald, overweight m
aster domo who was manning the dining room entrance. Bambi was over-animated when she spoke. Her head twisted nonstop from left to right, and her thick, bouncy hair whipped the air with attitude, sort of like a lion's mane.

Bambi's entourage, a pack of loud heavily lip-glossed young women adorned in an assortment of racy and colorful outfits, followed her.

Bambi and her crew stirred up quite a commotion. No one inside the restaurant was immune to her bitchy ruckus.

Bambi stopped dead in her tracks when she caught sight of Shane sitting in the restaurant. *My Dark Stallion!*

Well, looky here. She had no qualms about making her lewd intentions known to him. She eyed the police chief and flashed him a nasty look that said, Nigga, come get this!

"Who's the bitch sitting with my dark stud?" Bambi whispered to Paris, her best friend and PR correspondent. "Girl, I'm trying to get my fuck on, so you know what time it is—Ms. Prissy gotta go!", snapping her finger.

The moment Angel saw the saucy diva, she knew the woman was a trifling whore, but there was something else about her that sent warning chills through body. Consciously, Angel zeroed in on Ms. Hot Thang without her noticing; subconsciously, Natasha began to stir.

Natasha was all over the lustful look Bambi gave Shane. *You trifling, no-good bitch!* she raged inside.

"Aw shit!!!" Shane mouthed under his breath and grimaced. *No this bitch Bambi not about to undue all the work I put in just to get back in Angel's good graces. She got another thing coming if she thinks she's gonna throw a monkey wrench in my plans. I'll be goddamn!*

Bambi waved to a group of female admirers dining at the center table. "Hey, girlfriends!" she greeted brightly. "I see y'all getting your eat on!"

Bambi and her entourage floated across the room. DC's diva looked and played the part of superstar, acknowledging each and every one of her admiring fans without missing a beat. A minute later, Bambi turned, put a cover girl smile on, and headed straight for Shane's table.

"Well, looky here!" she announced with a steamy gaze. "Mmmph, mmph, mmph. Look, girls, it's my dark knight in shining armor, Mr. Shane Holt." She leaned over, threw her arms around his neck, and purred, "What happened to our little arrangement, boo? You know, the rain check you promised me?" She placed her hand gently against his cheek. "Is there something wrong with you? Because I know you didn't put Ms. Na-Na on the back burner for Ms. Prissy over there." Bambi cut her eyes toward Angel.

For a moment Shane sat saying nothing. He just stared at Bambi with a cold, contemptuous face. Then it dawned on him he could flip the script on this bitch and save the day.

With that in mind, Shane forced an awkward smile and calmly said, "You know what? At first I was thinking the same thing. As beautiful and sexy as you are, what more could a man want?" The move he just initiated was bold and calculating to say the least. In the corner of his eye he could see Angel watching jealously. So he needed to hurry because time was not on his side. Angel looked ready to blow a gasket.

Shane went on to say, "But then I realized you're nothing but a shallow piece of eye candy, and a man like myself needs a woman with substance. You know, one who's grounded and possesses that inner beauty. The kind of woman who shines from the inside out." Shane paused, and his eyes found Angel. And like opposite poles on a magnet, their eyes made contact.

Angel gazed at him starry-eyed, like, *Damn, nigga, I'm loving every inch of you and everything you stand for!*

For the grand finale Shane graced Angel with his most dazzling smile and spoke from the heart. "Bambi, you see that beautiful woman seated across from me? That's what I've found in this wonderful lady. She's a real woman, not some wannabe Barbie who thinks men are her play toys. No, I'm sorry, but you got the wrong man, baby." The bright diamond smile plastered on Angel's face was pure ovation and admiration.

Before Bambi had a chance to respond, Shane's lips turned grim. "Excuse me, miss, but I gotta date with an Angel."

Bambi's mouth fell wide. "You black piece of shit!" she lashed out. Her upper lip curled up, bearing deadly white fangs that wanted to pounce on his jugular. She was hurt and embarrassed, but she didn't show it. The way she lambasted Shane, unleashing a nonstop three-minute verbal rampage that was so vicious and heated, witnesses readied themselves for bloodshed.

After the violent tongue lashing by Bambi, it took a full thirty minutes for the tension in the air to subside and the heated commotion to dissipate.

A little while later, Shane watched Bambi sashay toward the ladies' room. When he turned back, he was struck by the sheer hatred brewing in Angel's demeanor.

"Angel," Shane said, carefully, "is everything alright? You look, uh, different all of a sudden."

"No, I'm okay," Angel muttered softly. She hesitated before extending her arm, brushing her hand lightly against his. She looked Shane in the eye. "It's probably best we get out of here. Besides, I need some fresh air."

Shane frowned skeptically. "Are you sure?" he asked, feeling uneasy. "I told you I'm not about to let no fake-ass freak run me off from nowhere. Remember, I am the chief of police. That has to count for something."

"It's not that, Shane," Angel said looking tired. "I'm just ready to go, that's all." She finished with a weak grin and another sip of champagne. "Besides," she added, "wouldn't you rather we go somewhere with a more intimate setting?"

"Say no more." Shane immediately signaled for the waitress. "Chloe! Check please!"

Quietly, Angel rose from her seat at the table. The light in her eyes grew darker by the minute. "I'll meet you outside, okay? I need to freshen up a bit," she told him, moving her torso away from the table.

Shane hopped to his feet. "You sure about that?" he inquired, sliding around the table to offer his assistance. She kindly rebuffed his advances by turning away. "Don't worry, Shane," she said in a voice barely above a whisper. The darkness was now clouding her mind and invading her soul. "I'm a big girl; I know how to handle my business," she said before walking off. The cadence in her voice sounded eerie, cunning, and fearless. Shane stared after her, a big question mark flashing in the center of his forehead.

The door to the ladies' room swung open and Natasha strolled in humming her favorite Beyonce melody, "To the Left." She cracked an evil grin when she saw the ladies' room was vacant. *Where's that hoe?* Natasha peered straight ahead and grinned devilishly. *I'm here to collect.* She inhaled deeply and caught her scent.

A small grin parted Bambi's lips. "Oh, okay, that's what I'm talking about," she muttered to herself and smiled when she heard the stranger humming her song.

The humming stopped abruptly, leaving an uncomfortable and eerie silence that seemed to hang in the air like a dark force.

Movement sounded from the stall farthest from the door. When the lady stopped in the middle of the song, Bambi's face grew tight.

"Hey, girlfriend," she yelled out, "I was feeling you. Why you stop?"

A dark shadow appeared on the white tile floor beneath the door stall. Bambi's big doe eyes jumped wide. "What-the-fuck?!?" she mumbled. "Who's out there?" she said, smacking her lips. "Paris? Girl, is that you? You better stop playing games," she warned.

The shadow backed off, prompting Bambi to drop her guard. Three seconds later, the stall door burst wide open, catching Bambi totally by surprise. She shrieked in terror, catching a glimpse of a red blur swooping down on her and crashing into her world.

The scarlet tempest blew into Bambi's stall with lightning speed. Natasha showed no mercy on the helpless diva, pounding her with vicious head shots from every angle. She beat Bambi into submission and unconsciousness.

"Bitch, what kind of games you playing?!?" Natasha snarled, hovering over Bambi's beaten and bloodied frame, balled up in the fetal position on the floor. A cryptic grin tugged at the corner of Natasha's mouth. A glistening straight razor appeared in the palm of her hand. She leaned over Bambi and pressed the razor's edge to the base of her eye socket, just under the lip of her left eye.

"Bitches like you don't deserve life," Natasha hissed and began to apply pressure. She froze at the last second when she heard voices outside the ladies' room. "Goddamn it," she grunted. "Today is your lucky day, whore."

A minute later, Natasha was standing just outside the ladies' room running her fingers through her long hair and gazing across the dining room. Her focus was the table where Bambi's entourage was gathered like a herd of promiscuous cattle. The women were teasing and flirting and flaunting themselves to any available male who happened to be looking their way.

"You go, girl!" a short, thick Trinidadian waitress said as she rushed by. She turned just before entering the bathroom. Her right hand reached out and touched Natasha on the arm. With a kind smile, the waitress added, "Your sexy ass—you are killin' 'em softly in that pretty red outfit. I just love that shit!"

Natasha's head snaked around like a cobra in attack mode. Her eyes sparkled with a force so dark and evil, the waitress could feel the evilness radiating from within. The Trinidadian woman shuddered and snatched her arm away. She gasped, feeling her flesh creep with fright.

"I know that's right," Natasha answered smugly. She grinned and watched as the waitress rushed into the bathroom. Satisfied, Natasha focused her attention on the table where Bambi's entourage was seated. She made eye contact with Paris. She gave her a snide wink as she tossed her D&G bag over her shoulder and traipsed off.

Paris looked on wondering, *What was that all about?* For some strange reason she couldn't take her eyes off the woman in red. There was something about her that struck a nerve in Paris. *What is it,* she pondered. *Who is she?* Paris concluded.

Chapter 43

2:18 A.M.

And when we're done, I don't wanna feel my legs, baby...
And when we're done, I just wanna feel your hands all over
me, baby ...

Kelly Rowland's provocative medley, "Motivation," pumped through the speakers while a dark chocolate dancer spread her cheeks in a cornered-off section of the VIP lounge in DC's hot new party spot, Oxygen nightclub.

Bad Ass was showering a salacious pussycat with big-face twenties. Her body-bending gymnastics were wowing the crowd and giving every able-bodied male in her vicinity an instant erection. Regular club patrons threw shade as all eyes focused on the smooth thug with the thick stacks of cash.

The captain of the notorious Criminals In eXistence and his thugged-out psychopaths were partying like they owned the joint. They were chillin' on four dark gray leather sofas arranged in a tight V shape, limiting access from outsiders. There were long smoked-glass tables lined with bottles of Rose Moet, Nuevo, and Patron in front of them and a bevy of sexy rollers—promiscuous, hot, and tempting women, all down for whatever.

A swarthy pair of hulk-like brutes with unnaturally bright eyes stood side by side manning the perimeter. Monster and Killa were twins, and they were stone-cold killers. The intimidating twosome had a murderous reputation and were known throughout the urban jungle as

Twin Peaks—they were seven feet tall. They were very imposing characters with thick, bushy beards and clean-shaven heads. The Twin Peaks had that Suge Knight vibe on front street.

From the crowd, appeared a tall, lumbering dude with a serious acne problem. His name was Block. At first glance, Block, who was an Atlanta native and an enforcer for the Top Soldiers crew, reminded you of Frankenstein, the new 8.0 version. His flashy trademark iced grill glistened like a disco ball every time he smiled.

Block peered across the VIP, his gaze intent on the corner where the private party was jumping off. He smiled slyly when he spied Bad Ass sitting on the sofa enjoying a lap dance from a thick chocolate roller.

Looking like a man up to no good, Block slinked through the lounge, moving in the direction of the Twin Peaks.

Monster and Killa recognized Block on the move and immediately moved in to intercept the enforcer before he could reach the private party.

The Twin Peaks loomed large in Block's path like an impenetrable wall. Monster glared down at the enforcer with a frigid look, his massive arms folded over his chest. His bulging veins coursed the length of his arms, practically bursting through the skin.

"What up, slim?" Monster's deep voice rumbled. "Did you lose something?" Standing next to Monster, Killa's body language was stark, solid as a brick wall. The left side of his lip curled in a vicious sneer. He was on the verge of taking a chunk out of Block's ass.

The two deadly goons bared down on him, but Block didn't flinch. He stood his ground, firm and aggressive.

"Naw, big slim," Block replied, his dirty-south drawl matching the toughness in Monster's voice. "I ain't lose nothing, but since you all up in my business like the Feds, yeah, I'm looking for somebody—your boss, Bad Ass," he said with a bold face and defensive attitude.

A few feet away, a cagey-looking dude with a strong square chin and slanted, shifty eyes sat twirling a cinnamon-flavored toothpick between his lips. Dude was mugging everything moving. His obvious intent was to hurt somebody.

In reality, the promotion of violence was always at the forefront of this perverse psychopath's mind. This mean and angry psycho's name was Loso, Bad Ass' right-hand man and second in command. Loso was revered throughout the underworld as a natural born killer.

As soon as Loso caught sight of Block being accosted by the Twin Peaks, he cracked a seedy grin and motioned to Midnight and Screw.

"C'mon, let's see what this bamma Block got crackin'," ordered Loso, bopping across the carpet. Midnight and Screw followed his lead without question.

Loso eased up beside Monster. "So what's the deal, Block?" he asked, looking devilish, his toothpick twirling between his clenched lips. "This best be good, champ, 'cause you're disrupting our groove. We got pussy on tap tonight, cuz."

Block sucked his teeth. "Yeah, I can see y'all doin' it up real big tonight," he stated casually, taking a quick peek at the action. "Damn!" he stammered under his breath when he saw the chocolate roller had paired up with a sleazy-looking Asian chic sporting a neon-pink Chinese bob and a mouth-watering rack. Both girls were seated on Bad

Ass' lap, giving him a freak show—sucking each other's breasts and trading spit with lewd enthusiasm.

Block rubbed his hands together. "I got word your bossman interested in Lucius and his operation," he implied coolly.

Loso's eyes lit up at the mention of Lucius. He pulled the toothpick from his mouth and stared Block in his acne-riddled face. "Is that a fact," he responded nonchalantly. Loso turned to his comrades and whispered, "Y'all chill right here. Lemme see what this bamma talking about."

Loso stepped to Block and put his arm around his shoulder. "C'mon, step over here to the bar with me, champ. Let's talk about this in private." They both moved to an empty spot at the edge of the bar.

Loso leaned his back against the black lacquered countertop and popped a fresh cinnamon toothpick in his mouth.

"Okay, champ," Loso began with a slick tongue, "spit it out. What kind of info you got on Lucius?"

Having a face to face with Loso was not in Block's plans. He glanced left and right over his shoulder, took a cursory glance at the faces seated at the bar. Nothing. Although there was no immediate threat in the vicinity, Block felt very uncomfortable in the presence of Loso.

"Alright, check this out dawg," Block said looking Loso directly in the eye. He felt a nervous twitch in his gut and tried to cover it. "A couple of my homies caught that sucka Daz slippin' in the hood."

"Daz!" Loso sneered. "Fuck that bamma! You said you had information about Lucius!" His interest and patience instantly started to wane.

"Hold on, dawg." Block's heavy head swiveled left and right, his extra-dry and ashy hands fidgeting nervously. "You do know Daz is Lucius' right-hand man, right?"

"And?" Loso snorted, turning up his wrist. The diamond bezel on his gold Raymond Weil shimmered under the light. "Slim, it's going on 3 o'clock. I ain't got time for this bullshit!"

Block frowned. "What? C'mon, dawg, check this out. " A shiny iPad appeared in his hand. "This joint has to be worth at least five jiggaz." He looked to Loso with a hopeful face.

With a twisted sneer, Loso hissed—"Five jiggaz! For what?" He was both angry and offended. "Don't fuck with me, Block." He shot him a warning look.

"Loso, c'mon now, dawg, I wouldn't do that," Block replied, his body language and tone totally submissive. "Think about it, Loso. Daz is Lucius' right-hand man. He dropped his iPad when he got low after a shootout with my homies the other night. Think about the information you could get from this joint?" he said, giving Loso a knowing look.

A proverbial light bulb glowed in Loso's head. His shifty eyes shone with a deep, intuitive look that gave Block chills.

"Oh, yeah," Loso replied slowly, speaking more so to himself. "Lucius' right-hand man, huh?" He snatched the devise from Block and looked him in the face. "I'll kick you two jiggaz for the joint. Take it or leave it." A sinister grin slithered across Loso's lips when he pressed the "on" button and watched the screen light up.

Block huffed and shook his head. "Two-thousand dollars?" He reluctantly conceded, "Fuck it, give me the money."

Hovering directly behind the sofa where Bad Ass sat, Loso paused for a minute, super-size grin plastered on his face. He couldn't help but feast his eyes on the nasty duo trading bobs, giving mean head-shots to Bad Ass' pulsating male organ.

Loso leaned over the sofa and whispered in Bad Ass' ear, "I'm not trying to bust your groove," he said, captivated by the deep-throat technique the dark chocolate shorty was engaged in. She was like a ravenous sex fiend devouring Bad Ass' erect penis like a seasoned vet. "Goddamn!" Loso breathed in awe. "Shorty got the killer head game!"

Bad Ass' head whipped around. "What the fuck do you want?" he snapped, looking completely irritated. "That shit can't wait?!?"

Loso jumped, a look of surprise written on his face. "My bad, champ. I just wanted to let you know I got my hands on some vital information concerning that bamma Lucius." He said his piece and backed off.

Bad Ass had to take a deep breath and pause, digesting Loso's words and the implications. "Muthafuck," he huffed and took a chunk out of his cherry Tootsie pop. He directed his attention to his lap and shorty's head bobbing motion. Bad Ass shook his head and exhaled. He shrugged off the feeling and grabbed a fistful of midnight-blue hair.

"It's halftime, baby girl," he said looking them both in the face. "Why don't y'all go have some drinks while I'm gone? 'Cause the way you suck dick you gots to be thirsty as hell." He smiled, jumped up, and stuffed his saliva-coated penis in his pants. Bad Ass looked to Loso and motioned for him to follow.

Minutes later, outside the club, Bad Ass and Loso were hidden behind black tinted windows inside Bad Ass' cranberry BMW.

A soft glow emanated from the iPad screen, covering Bad Ass' facial features. He navigated the screen, his excitement and anticipation building by the second.

"Oh, shit! Is this what I think it is?" Bad Ass said, peering at the screen with wide, expectant eyes. He looked like an inquisitive little boy on a wild discovery adventure.

Loso leaned over the armrest to get a closer look at the screen. He hesitated and gave Bad Ass a questionable look. "Hey," Loso said, plucking the toothpick out his mouth. He shrugged and answered plainly, "There's only one way to find out."

Without thinking, Bad Ass handed Loso the iPad. "Say no more," he grunted and pressed the button for the keyless ignition. Both men listened as the engine quietly came to life and purred softly. Before Bad Ass hit the gas, he looked over to his right and chuckled.

"If this what I think it is, Lo, Lucius bitch ass can get ready for a toe tag and a body bag." Hearty laughter filled the Beemer's cockpit as the luxurious sedan rode off into the night.

Chapter 43

2:50 A.M.
Malcolm X Park

Sitting atop the hill looking at the cloud formation as it swept across the black skyline—a full silvery moon hovered in the background with fleeting flashes of lightning illuminating the atmosphere off in the distance. A black shadowy veil blanketed the entire expanse of Malcolm X Park, just inside the park's unique cobblestone walls sat a showcase of large silhouetted figures (a collection of towering elm trees) that seemed to have taken on a life of their own.

Directly adjacent the park, at the corner of 15th and Chaplin, the porch light on a red brick colonial blinked on and the front door opened.

The curvy statuesque figure of a woman appeared framed in the doorway. She lingered briefly, her hands waving about her head, making crude gestures to someone in the background.

The woman stopped abruptly and stepped out on the porch. The bright light revealed a disheveled and woozy-looking Bambi. Her thick ginger mane was a twisted and matted mess. The glowing white cat suit she wore was worn and wrinkled with dark splotches of dried caked blood soaked in the rich fabric.

"Mark my words, Paris," Bambi insisted, her tone both slurred and surly, "whoever that bitch is that done this

to me, she's gonna pay out her ass! You hear that, Paris?
Don't nobody do this to me and get away with it. No, siree."

Paris moved into view.   Her cinnamon-vanilla
physique was wrapped in a creamy silk robe by VS. Paris
walked out on the porch with her friend and took Bambi by
the hand. She pleaded with her to stay the night. It was
obvious she shouldn't be driving or going home alone in her
condition.

But Bambi wouldn't listen; she was too stubborn and
headstrong.   Besides, when was the last time Bambi
listened to anything Paris had to say? Never. In Bambi's
eyes, Paris was nothing but a pretty piece of eye candy. She
used Paris for her exotic attributes, her attractive Middle
Eastern-Black-Mediterranean-white hybrid, deep, dark,
sensuous eyes, and tight, slender, curvy body shape. Men
were attracted to Paris' hot, sexy ass, like flies on shit.
Paris was Bambi's star trophy piece she used specifically to
attract viable male companions right into her treacherous
web of sexual servitude.

Just inside Malcolm X's dark enclosure, submerged
within the night a starving beast suddenly awakened from
slumber. That beast was Natasha rising to claim her next
victim: Bambi.

*Sometimes we're on a collision course with some
unforeseen, ungodly event, and we just don't know it and
can't do a thing to avoid its wrath.*

*Like earlier in the day, when Angel walked of out the
day spa and caught the eye of Shane, who was running late
for a prearranged luncheon because someone miss placed a
case file down at police headquarters. And the traffic jam*

that prevented Shane from making his luncheon date, which was sparked by a fender-bender at the intersection of Wisconsin and P Street, between a redhead, freckled- face teenage white girl driving a solar yellow Volkswagen Beetle and an over-the-hill Hispanic woman donning a frizzy auburn wig, and driving a sky blue Nissan Altima, who got distracted when this scrawny, rangy looking panhandler tried to wave her down to bed for change. Or when Bambi decided instead of going to the Four Season's for lunch, she and her entourage would dine at the Peacock Café.

Thus, setting in motion the coincidental meeting of Bambi and Natasha.

What if Bambi would've stayed at bay and never encroached upon Shane and Angel's space? She would've never ignited Natasha's wrath. Which in turn, caused Natasha to whoop her ass in the ladies' room and her sending Shane on his way, so she could follow the ambulance from the restaurant to George Washington Hospital, where Paris and the rest of Bambi's colorful entourage would eventually show up. Afterward, Natasha would patiently wait for hours until Bambi's release. Then follow her unsuspecting prey across the city into the Columbia Heights neighborhood where Paris resided adjacent Malcolm X Park in the 3-story red brick colonial on the corner of 15th and Chaplin Street.

Natasha leaned against the cobblestone wall, took a deep breath and smiled when she smelled the distinct aroma of rain blowing in the warm summer breeze.

Bambi said her good-byes to Paris and strode off down the porch steps. She hurried along the walkway and out the front gate.

"I'll give you a call as soon as I get home," Bambi shouted, slamming the gate shut behind her. "If I make it home," she added with a playful chuckle.

Slow and unsteady, Bambi sauntered down the sidewalk on 15th Street. She was contemplating a late-night booty call. "Who's ass should I tap tonight?" she expressed naughtily, flaunting her feminine chauvinism with reckless disregard for the male gender.

"Maybe I should call up Derrick's sexy black ass? Or do I have a taste for red meat tonight, like that pretty young Tavon? Stupid-ass Shane would've been at the top of my list tonight. But his bitch ass fucked that up! His sorry black ass will never taste the sweetness between my legs again!"

A magnificent thunderbolt suddenly illuminated the night sky in front of Bambi, stopping her dead in her tracks.

"My goodness!" she stammered, clutching her white Chanel bag tight against her chest. "Let me get my black ass in the car before it rains," Bambi said and immediately began fishing in her bag for her car keys. "Here they are!" She snatched them out and sighed triumphantly.

A polished lilac-colored Jaguar XJ sedan glowed like a soft, fluorescent pearl in the night. The automobile sat alone under a beaming street lamp.

A concerned frown pinched Bambi's brow when she got close enough to see that all four of her tires were flat.

"Oh, hell no!" She glared in disbelief, shaking her head and cursing at the air. "Who the fuck would do some foul-ass shit like that?!?" Bambi bent over to get a closer look at the damage. While she was examining what looked like slash marks, she was startled by the sound of someone whistling in the distance.

The fine hairs on the back of Bambi's neck turned rigid and prickly when she recognized the distinct tune resonating in the breeze. It was Beyonce's "To the Left," the same tone and same pitch as earlier in the ladies' room at the restaurant. *That's impossible!* Bambi said to herself, cringing at the thought.

Out of the dark, Natasha materialized like a spooky shadow prowling the night. She looked cynical, dressed in all black from head to toe, her honey-blonde tresses pulled into a ponytail, her crystal blue eyes icy cold and piercing.

Bambi's eyes jumped out their sockets. She froze, riveted in place. She choked. "What the—who the fuck are you?!?"

Natasha snickered. "I'm your worst nightmare, bitch!" she hissed, sounding dark and sinister. Without warning, Natasha's right hand cocked back and sprang forward in one lightning-fast move.

Bambi felt a swoosh of air breeze by her cheek. She jumped out of reflex and held her breath when she caught a glimpse of something shiny as it shot past her eye and hit the tree behind her. Fear and bewilderment exploded on Bambi's face when she spun around and saw a switchblade protruding from the bark of the tree.

Two more inches and that blade would've been stuck in my ass! she realized, turning to face her attacker. Bambi shrieked when she noticed the woman reaching for something. "Oh, shit!" She took off running like a panicked deer in the night. But she wasn't thinking straight. In her panic, Bambi couldn't get her wits about her. Instead of running to Paris' house, or any house for that matter, in her confusion, she tore off running in the direction of the park.

A sadistic grin perched itself on Natasha's lips as she watched the skittish woman dash off. Natasha gloated and took a quick check of the area. The coast was clear.

"Your ass belongs to me now," Natasha rejoiced. She was a formidable predator and the hunt was on.

Chapter 44

A couple blocks over on 14th and Columbia Road, Bad Ass' cranberry luxury sedan coasted through the intersection. He tapped the brakes and eyed the speedometer as he rolled into the 1400 block of Columbia Road. This was known GHG territory—Go-Hard-Gangstas.

Loso was on point before they hit the block. His .50-caliber Desert Eagle sat on his lap, locked and loaded. Bad Ass flipped open the armrest and drew out a fully loaded Smith & Wesson .40 caliber.

He gave Loso a firm look and grunted, "Remember, Lo, only if necessary. Right now we're in recon mode. A'right." Bad Ass wasn't asking a question, he was confirming his point.

Halfway up the block, a few members of the GHG crew were lounging on the front porch of a shabby old row house, one of the organization's many drug stash joints.

"Fuck you, Popeye!" said an onerous youngin' as he stumbled out the front door and scowled. "I know your bamma ass better have that fuckin' jigga you owe me by tomorrow night!" Knuckles warned his homie, giving him a deadly stare. On the streets of DC, Knuckles had a reputation as a hardcore head busta, the kind of street thug who was quick to clap a bamma just for stepping on his shoes in a club.

"Popeye, you hear me talking, nigga?" Knuckles pressed while the rest of the crew had diverted their attention to a hot-pink Denali sitting on 26-inch chrome rims. The flossy whip was filled with roller, a rowdy bunch of attractive shortys all bobbing their heads and singing off key to Beyonce's "Diva." "Diva is a female version of a hustla ... of a hustla ... of a hustla!" the women crooned loudly and raunchily.

Knuckles hesitated, listening to his homies erupt in a lewd frenzy. He mean-mugged the crew of women in the Denali and swiped at the beads of perspiration dotting his dark, smooth brow. He turned his attention back to Popeye, who was checking out the scene from behind the front screen door.

"Don't take me for no fuckin' joke, slim! I want my cake, and I ain't playing with your ass either!" Knuckles' tall, lean frame seemed to swell every time he became angry. His homies swore they could see heat waves pulsating off his bald head whenever he was heated.

Popeye was easy and relaxed when he stepped out on the porch sucking his teeth. He tossed a quick glance at his homie Knuckles, gave him a nonchalant look, straightened the collar on his crisp white Lacoste polo shirt, adjusted his diamond link necklace, then cocked his head to the side, and slipped on a pair of black framed Black Label shades. Popeye was too cool.

"You need to slow your roll, slim. You getting too bent out of shape over nothing," Popeye shrugged. His dirty red Afro fluttered in the breeze. "Knuckles, you know damn well I'm good for mine. Don't even sweat that. A jigga? Slim, go 'head with that bullshit. That's trick money, slim." Popeye turned up his top lip and gave Knuckles a smirk that reeked of indignation before he stepped off to join his homies at the curb. "Honeys on the block, slim. You should be trying to get your dick wet instead of sweatin' me for some short shit," Popeye said over his shoulder without looking back.

"What in the hell is going on out this muthafucka? All that goddamn hootin'-n-hollerin' and shit!" An authoritative voice boomed through the screen door and caught Knuckles by surprise.

Lucius Foxx stood in the doorway dressed in all black Under Armor and black Armani eyewear. His skin was smooth as a baby's. He had a razor-sharp mustache and goatee. Lucius was the volatile, power-hungry head honcho of the young and vicious GHG drug squad. His smallish build was very deceptive, Lucius was a giant in a little mans' body. When he moved, he brought to mind a black oil slick gliding along the surface, and everyone in his path gave Lucius extra space when he was on the move.

Though his stature was small, one could easily see he wasn't to be fucked with. Lucius was tenacious, fearless, and extremely aggressive. When asked to describe himself, he'd say, "Picture a rabid pit bull, a badger, and a Tasmanian devil all rolled into one."

Standing on the porch, flanked by two mean and beefy enforcers, Nasty and Pin Head, Lucius appeared strong and commanding. It was apparent to inquiring eyes who was running the show.

Lucius' gaze swept east and west along Columbia Road. His sights settled on the pink Denali double parked in front of GHG property. He folded his hands together and licked his lips.

"Mmm ...what do we have here?" He paused and took a heavy whiff of air. "Is that pussy I smell percolating at my front door?"

Knuckles gave an agitated huff and flopped his rear end on the dark green wicker chair leaned against the banister. "Man, fuck them bitches!" he grumbled sourly. "I ain't got time to be fucking with no freaks tonight, Lucius. My mind on my money and my money on my mind," he expressed adamantly.

The utter disdain Lucius sensed coming from his young soldier caused him to hesitate. "You alright, Knuckles?" he cocked his head and asked. "Yeah, I jive feel you on that, youngin—money over bitches. But you gotta know how to balance that shit out," he explained with earnest, as if Knuckles were his son. "In the great words of San Snead: 'If you're not thinking about pussy, you're not concentrating; if you're not thinking about money, you're not living.'"

Lucius reached down and grabbed his crotch. He focused on the pink SUV and said with a devious grin, "Right now, Knuckles, it's time to concentrate. I hear pussy calling my name." He stepped off without looking back.

As soon as the women in the Denali got a whiff of Lucius, they flipped the script—loud whistling and catcalls were directed his way. Lucius was amused and delighted by females' brazen antics. Upon making his approach, he inventoried the selection and locked in on the prize seated at the wheel.

Baby girl was an absolute eye grabber. Ayanna was her name. She was a totally excellent mix of Ethiopian, Filipino, and Spanish blood.

Lucius rounded the vehicle, his two goons nipping at his heels. He propped his Armani frames atop his head and flipped into player mode.

He didn't waste any time pushing up on Ayanna. He eased over to the driver's window, flashed his dimpled smile, and spit game.

"Damn, you are so fuckin' sexy! It's like I'm dreaming. I swear to God, shorty," Lucius uttered in her ear. "Damn, shorty, I'm trying to do the couple thing with you. Ya know, five-star restaurant, Cristal, lobster, candlelight, Victoria's Secret shopping spree, a five-star hotel ... where you can give me a private lingerie show. Just say the word, baby girl. I can make it happen." His lustful gaze crawled down her elongated neckline.

Staring Lucius in the eye, Ayanna was about to answer when she was interrupted by a high-pitch scream. Tires burned rubber on the asphalt.

Lucius spun around, his eyes glaring eastward toward 14th Street. His piercing dark pupils turned into tiny slits, his street senses tingled wildly. Acting off impulse, Lucius whipped out his chrome-plated .44 Desert Eagle.

Startled, Ayanna gasped and covered her mouth. "Oh, shit! Please don't!" she stuttered nervously, her face marked with worry.

A titanium H2 Hummer with blacked-out windows came barreling through the block like a bat out of hell. Automatically, Lucius' grip tightened on his hammer. He was prepared to unleash his DE at the slightest provocation.

There was deep concern in Lucius' expression as he stared at the oversized SUV rolling by. A few seconds later, he felt his stomach lurch, drawing his attention to a flashy cranberry BMW cruising up the street not far behind the Hummer.

Something didn't bode right with the Beemer, and Lucius could feel the uneasiness stirring in the pit of his stomach. His instincts spiked suddenly and his eyes darted up and down Columbia Road. Chatter seemed to rise in the background and touch a nerve in Lucius.

His head snapped back. "Will you muthafuckas shut the fuck up?! I can't hear myself think!" he growled harshly. His men couldn't help but notice the unsettling aggravation brewing in his face. Lucius looked like a man possessed.

There's something about that Beemer, he thought. *I can feel it in my bones.*

Chapter 45

By now dark clouds had blanketed the entire night sky like a thick, billowing mass of smoke gliding noiselessly above the sprawling black landscape that was Malcolm X Park.

At the park's epicenter, the soothing sound of water trickling onto water echoed in the night. Fresh water flowed over the cobble stone edge, cascaded down cobblestone stairs that ran the length of a steep cobble stone structure.

In the shadows just above the water fall, a large cobblestone erection loomed like a solid black wall in the night. By day, this structure served as the park's maintenance storage facility and public restrooms.

At the forefront of the structure, two soaring archways greeted you. The archway on the left seemed a little darker, slightly taller. It was as if you could hear its colorless core breathing, almost panting. In all actuality, the structure wasn't breathing at all; it was the petrified woman cowering within its dark bosom.

Wheezing for air and shaking like a leaf, Bambi used the dark archway to hide from her pursuer.

"Why is this happening to me?" Bambi cried in a fit of exasperation, holding herself, trying to catch her breath and calm her nerves at the same time. She jumped suddenly when she heard something move overhead. She placed her hand over her mouth and held it there as tightly as she could to keep from screaming.

Bambi could hear footsteps coming down the stairs very slowly, one at a time, until they reached the bottom step. Her left hand shot over her mouth. She had to force herself not to scream. She carefully backed up, moving deeper inside the archway. Suddenly, her left heel landed on something unstable. It was something smooth, something metal, and she lost her balance. The piece of metal slipped out from under her foot, and the unmistakable sound of metal sliding against stone resonated in the archway. Bambi stumbled backward, and her back slammed hard against a wooden door. Her body tensed. She cringed inside when she heard the loud ring of metal raking the air. Right away, Bambi collected herself. She spun around and faced the door. Slowly and carefully, she twisted the doorknob and the door creaked open.

Out of nowhere, a whisper echoed in the dark,

"Whore ..."

Bambi stood motionless. Her stomach trembled as the subtle sound coasted down her spine. Her heartbeat vibrated in her ear so loudly she could feel the pounding on her eardrums.

"Fuck this shit!" Bambi mumbled, mustering up the courage to confront her crazy attacker. She took a deep breath and turned around.

Two feet away, Natasha stood poised in the shadows, her ocean blue peepers glowing like a blue flame in the dark.

The little courage Bambi was able to muster shattered instantaneously when madness graced her presence. She could sense nothing but pure hatred and evilness radiating from this woman.

Her fears were instantly confirmed when Natasha reached up unexpectedly and grabbed Bambi around the throat with both hands and squeezed.

"Whore!" Natasha snarled, closing her fingers in a strong grip, and applied direct pressure to the windpipe. "Bitches like you don't deserve life!" she spewed, her lips taking on a wicked twist, enjoying the look of sheer terror and grief screaming silently from Bambi's eyes. Natasha squeezed harder. "Yeah, that's it, bitch. Let it go," she murmured as if the pain she inflicted would somehow quench Bambi's fear.

Bambi struggled and fought with all her might to break free from the crazy woman's death grip. But the woman's strength was unbelievable. She was stronger than a man! Bambi realized as she clawed and scratched and twisted that everything she did was to no avail. The woman's grip was impenetrable, like a steel vise closing on her neck. Bambi felt her strength faltering, her will succumbing. She could sense her soul slowly fading away, like a weak flame flickering in a strong wind.

Natasha got a charge when she felt the boney-like anatomy inside the whore's throat crumble under her touch. Bambi's trachea sounded like Styrofoam peanuts being crushed—a second later Natasha heard a gurgling sound, which she accepted as then a gurgling sound Natasha accepted as Bambi's apology.

The sick gurgling of blood echoed in the breeze and dissipated into the peaceful sound of water cascading down the cobblestone surface and drifting off in the darkness.

Chapter 46

"Bad Ass, that was that bamma Lucius standing in the street!" Loso exclaimed, peering in the side-view mirror to get a good look. "Cuz, we should've clapped them bammas!"

"What I tell you, huh?" Bad Ass retorted quickly and flashed him a cold stare. "It ain't time for that shit," he said while unwrapping a fresh cherry Tootsie pop. "When we go at them bammas, we gotta come correct. Lucius got a serious squad, so we can't sleep on them bammas," he advised, his voice slow and measured.

"True that, true that," said Loso, serious and grim.

The BMW sped up, making a beeline for the yellow traffic signal at the intersection of 16th and Columbia Road. The tires screeched when the sedan bent the corner on 16th, then accelerated and moved south toward Malcolm X Park.

Two blocks later, the glossy BMW made another left turn and traveled east, cruising along the edge of the park.

A shadowy form appeared on the road, seemingly out of nowhere.

"Muthafucka!" Bad Ass grunted as he slammed on brakes. The sedan's low-profile tires grabbed hold of the asphalt and came to a screeching halt.

"You dumb, stupid-ass bitch!" Loso shouted, irate, sparks flying from his mouth in a fit of rage.

Natasha whipped her head around and shot the men a look so unsavory Bad Ass and Loso both were taken aback. They watched her, their eyes wide with surprise. Natasha flipped them off without bothering to look back. She strutted across the street. Her walk was so nasty it gave the men fits as they watched her drift up the block and melt into the shadows.

A puzzling look splashed on Bad Ass' face. "Natasha?!?" he muttered, sounding hopeful but unsure.

"What? You know shorty?" Loso asked, looking dumbfounded.

"You could say that," Bad Ass answered, sounding vague. He tapped the gas pedal. "If that's who I think it is, then you gonna have to take the wheel while I go see what's up with shorty." Bad Ass caught a glimpse of a shadow turning in the alley just up ahead. He whipped the wheel hard to the left and mashed the accelerator.

The BMW rolled in front of the alley and stopped. Bad Ass jumped out when he spotted the dark form walking up the alley. His inner voice screamed a warning, but he was too amped up to listen. His mind and body were focused on one thing: pussy.

Bad Ass was the poster child for glib, self-serving narcissists. Overflowing with confidence, his mind was made up, and he would not be denied tonight.

"Natasha!" Bad Ass called out, peering at the black silhouette standing beside a light-colored Cadillac. "What's up, shorty? Remember me? We bumped into each other a few days ago downtown on Connecticut Avenue?"

Natasha didn't utter a word. On impulse, she had the pearl-handled straight razor out, pressed firmly at her side, ready to strike a fatal blow the moment he stepped foot within her strike zone.

Bad Ass took her silence as an invitation to join her. He grinned and straightened his Louis blazer. "Go 'head and bounce, Lo," he ordered, gesturing with his hand for

Loso to get lost. "I'm gonna roll with shorty, but keep your cell close by just in case."

He stood on the curb and watched his ride pull off before he turned up the alley. A smug grin penetrated his lips when he noticed Natasha waiting by the car for him.

"Yeah, shorty, I know you want this. And I strives to please," Bad Ass boasted to himself with a stout look of self-gratification. He licked his thumb and forefinger and slicked down the fine hairs on his mustache and eyebrows.

Bad Ass' 6'3" frame stood strong and erect. He hunched his shoulders back, put on his lady-killer smile and stepped off. An aura of overconfidence ignited the air around him.

Natasha's body language was keen and composed. She was ready to pounce. She eyed him quietly. One foot at a time, as he closed the distance between them, the clarity in her eyes gradually changed to a frosty, hateful stare. She felt her pulse accelerate. Impulsively, she gripped the razor with such force the muscles in her forearms bulged powerfully. An image stirred from the deepest recesses of her mind, conjuring up visions of a bedeviled man. Tall. Dark. Powerful. Mysterious. The memory stirred a yearning inside her that had her heart doing somersaults.

I'm Chevar! Natasha recalled him shouting out his name. The recognition neutralized her planned attack, like a fire extinguisher dousing a flame the moment before it erupted into something catastrophic.

Without warning, paralysis seized her muscles and caused the straight razor to slip from her hand, bounce off her right foot, and tumble to the bricked pavement.

A stupefied look splashed on her face as she watched the razor land on the ground between her foot and front tire.

"Hey, pretty lady," she heard him say. She pivoted on her heel and swept the razor under the car as she turned to greet him.

In a surprised move, Natasha turned her frustration on Chevar and berated him. "What the fuck is your goddamn problem, stalking me in the middle of the night!? You call yourself a playa, but you ain't got no game! Ain't that a bitch!"

The blindsided verbal assault caught Bad Ass flatfooted, totally unprepared. For a minute, he was stuck on stupid. He took a couple deep breaths and collected himself.

"Hold up, baby," he quickly clarified, "you got me fucked up. Stalking is not in my playbook. Matter of fact, it's not in my DNA, period."

When he spoke, the deep bass in his voice was smooth and silky. It made Natasha weak in the knees.

In a seemingly subdued voice, she answered, "Is that a fact?" Her brusque attitude changed dramatically. "So what you call it when men cruise around the city in the middle of the night and jump out on women? 'Cause if I'm not mistaken, I heard the only thing open after 3 a.m. is a whore's legs and some easy pussy. Is that what you taking me for? Huh, Chevar?" she inquired. Her expression was controlled, but she couldn't hide the devilish twinkle in her eye.

Bad Ass was all smiles on the inside. He was feeling Natasha and the cynical mind games she played. She was dark and mysterious and discerningly shrewd. He couldn't help but think, *Have I found the one woman who truly matches me? Mind, body, soul, and treachery?* He felt completely captivated by her dark presence.

"Some easy pussy, huh," he laughed mockingly. He took a step to close the gap between them. Locked in a heated gaze, Bad Ass made a bold play when he grabbed Natasha's hand in a gentle caress. His penetrating stare swept across her soft, unblemished face.

"There's not a damn thing easy about you," Bad Ass spoke with passion and strength. "In no way, shape, or form. You are the epitome of what a real woman should be. If you were the measuring rod or scale, Natasha, baby, you would no doubt be at the very top of that scale. When I look at you, I see everything they are not. You are the apex of your gender. Baby girl, you are the perfect woman. Strong. Confident. Not afraid to take on anything or anyone. Not a weakness in sight. Hands down, baby, you are the ultimate woman," Bad Ass finished with a satisfied look.

Is this bamma feeding me bullshit or what? wondered Natasha. *If this is bullshit, then he got me!* she conceded glowingly, completely astonished at how profoundly moved she was by this man.

"Hmmm ... I see there's more to you than meets the eye," Natasha muttered, the tone in her voice soft and sly. "I wonder what else is there about you that I'll find attractive."

Bad Ass' eyebrow jumped. "Did I hear you right? You find me attractive, huh?" He frowned and grunted clumsily.

Natasha placed her right hand gently against his chest and felt her body tingle with excitement, like electrical pulses of energy were surging from his form. She willed herself to remain calm, but she couldn't prevent the soft moan from escaping her lips.

"You got me feeling very naughty tonight, Chevar," she said warming up to him. She cut her eyes up at the moon as it peeked out from behind the clouds. Natasha pursed her lips and coyly added, "Look at that, Chevar." She motioned toward the sky. "There's a full moon out tonight, and the moon just brings the beast out of me. I just love how it looks and feels on my skin. Wanna bathe in the moonlight tonight?"

Is she for real?!? a little voice in Bad Ass' head echoed. "Bathe in the moonlight, baby?" he proceeded cautiously, testing the waters. "Well, if that's how you feel, there's a park across the street with a lot of soft green space just calling our name. I'm sure we could find us a nice private spot where you can bathe in all the moonlight you want. And we can get to know each other on a more intimate level." Bad Ass held his breath and looked upon her with hopeful eyes. She gave him a smoldering look. There was no need for words.

It was about 3:30 in the morning, somewhere on the east end of Malcolm X Park. Two evil spirits—Darkness & Death—were about to merge as one, as if they were consummating the spawning of the anti-Christ, the second coming of Satan!

Moments later, the dark cloud cover began to dissipate and break up above the park. Off in the distance, flashes of lightning continued to ignite the night sky.

Natasha was lounging on her back, carefree and naked, gazing up at the moon. Her protruding nipples jutted skyward, resembling dark chocolate kisses tethered atop twin honey-coated mounds of lusciousness that were yearning to be caressed and sucked.

Bad Ass striped down butt naked. Natasha had him aroused, feeling like a youngin' with his nose wide open.

Hold up! he told himself, flopping down on the bed of grass beside Natasha. *I'm a mack. I can't be exposing my hand like that. I have to be in total control of my emotions at all times. That's a must.*

Quietly, Natasha enjoyed the masculine view in front of her. She stared at Chevar's naked body. She got a healthy eyeful of his chiseled physique under the moonlight. His dazzling display of masculinity unleashed a hot, bubbly eruption of juices flooding and lubricating her vagina. Natasha felt something else rumbling just beneath the surface—a hungry, gluttonous spirit invaded her womanhood and sent a warm shiver up her spine. She had to physically hold herself as she waited for Chevar to lie down next to her.

Natasha turned to face him. "I want you, Chevar," she spoke quietly. Her aqua blue pools reached out to him and smiled anxiously. "My body wants you. If I allow you inside me, that's it, nigga. This pussy best be the only pussy you fuck. 'Cause my pussy is sanctified. So don't fuck me if you can't fuck with me and only me. Understand? Can you handle that, Chevar?"

Bad Ass thought about that a minute, then shrugged. "Sure. I can handle that. From here on out Natasha, your pussy will be the only pussy for me."

Inside, Bad Ass was all jittery, but he was so happy to have her hot body next to him he was willing to say or do anything to not spoil the moment. This wasn't the first time he vowed a promise of monogamy, and this wouldn't be the last. *Women*, he thought.

Bad Ass and Natasha shared a smile. He tried to lift his upper torso, and Natasha forced him to the ground. She reached over with her right hand and took possession of his organ, watching it stiffen in her hand. Natasha wet her lips with her tongue, gave Chevar a nasty, steamy glare as she lowered her head to his penis, and proceeded to run her long, serpent-like tongue from its base to the tip of its mushroomed head.

She stopped abruptly and snapped her head back. "What is that smell?"

"What?" Bad Ass groaned. He shook his head back and forth. "I was having a little fun earlier at the club, nothing serious, though. But now I'm with you, and from here on out is what counts, right?"

Her grip tightened on his pulsating rod, and she relented. "Okay, Chevar, you've been warned. Don't start no shit, won't be no shit."

The eerie gravity in her words, the sheer potency struck an odd chord with him. He was about to say something else, but Natasha slipped the head of his penis between her lips, and all thoughts dispersed from his mind.

Natasha devoured his erect penis, swallowing him whole. Bad Ass gasped. He ran his fingers through her hair and met her mouth stroke for stroke.

"Oh, yeah!" he groaned. Fucking Natasha's mouth was a mind-blowing experience. Watching her pull his throbbing organ from her mouth and slather her puckered lips with the engorged head was turning him on. "Yeah, baby!" he moaned excitedly, his eyes wide. Natasha devoured his stiff shaft. She performed a feat out of the man-eaters' handbook when she swallowed his entire eight-inch organ right before his eyes. "Fuck, yeah!" he breathed, utterly elated as he tried hard to hold back for some extended pleasure.

Natasha looked him in the eye and let out a small moan. That was all it took. Bad Ass' gooey load flooded her mouth to capacity. The fact that she never stopped sucking made him more excited. He cracked a smile while watching her swallow him. He was flabbergasted, feeling a wave of pure euphoria wash over him.

Bad Ass looked at Natasha with adoration and a glimmer of infatuation. It was time he got on his A-game. Pleasuring Natasha's body wasn't the only thing he had in mind.

With a look of fire burning in his eye, Bad Ass' deep-set gaze glided along her curvaceous frame. He caressed her soft, smooth skin. He started salivating with an uncontrollable urge to conquer not only Natasha's body, but her sensuality and the wickedness festering at the core of her spirit as well.

He coaxed her onto her back, repositioning her body in preparation for a salacious, erotic pleasure trip into ecstasy.

Slowly, Bad Ass crawled up her body. He savored the soft, supple feel of her flesh merging cohesively with his own as he leaned down and light touched the nape of her neck with his lips. His grin stretched a little broader when Natasha let out a low sigh and shuddered.

"Yeah, I'm feeling your sexy ass!" she growled, her tone sultry but aggressive.

Bad Ass slithered, snakelike, down her luscious physique, deliberately taking his time, leaving a trail of warm, tender kisses and love bites in his wake.

He gave special treatment to selected areas of her anatomy, such as: Natasha's ripe full breasts with their yearning succulent nipples —so sensitive to the warm, affectionate embrace of his lips and tongue. Her taut midriff – he leaned down and kissed and nibbled all around her diamond-studded navel as he made his way down her silken slope. He landed in the perfect space between her creamy thighs.

Bad Ass started marking his territory. He placed three distinct passion marks on her inner thigh. Afterward, he lingered in that perfect space, cherishing and taking delight in her beautifully contoured pussy. In that perfect space he feasted with fevered enthusiasm, utilizing the full scope of his lips and tongue, delicately fondling her hot, wanting pudendum. He kissed, licked, and sucked her clitoris, making Natasha's pearl swell up like a fledgling rosebud in bloom. The proverbial *'Man in the boat'* winked at Bad Ass.

He loved the way Natasha's thighs closed around his head, the way her pussy gyrated and grinded and thrust, smearing his face from cheek to chin with her thick glazed juices.

Sounds of pleasure dribbled and oozed from Natasha's excited lips.

"Yeah, nigga, that's it. Suck my pussy. Eat my pussy like you never ate pussy before," she whispered huskily, squirming and moaning, and cursing. Her eyes were full of unconcealed pleasure, her face was flush with the mood of ecstasy. Her instinctive, dominating nature gloated in the fact that she was also marking her territory.

Bad Ass couldn't stand the anticipation any longer. He needed to be inside her. He pushed away from her creamy vagina, and rose to his knees. With his right hand, Bad Ass commandeered his erect man piece and aimed for Natasha's fleshy, hot love canal.

He gazed upon her, his facial expression animalistic and heated. Natasha cast a look that let him know there was a raging inferno burning in the depths of her loins.

With his left hand, Bad Ass pushed Natasha's right leg toward the sky, with the right, he guided his stiff rod into her hot crevice and slowly entered her body, inch by inch. Once inside her, Bad Ass took his right hand pushed Natasha's left leg against the grass, and balanced himself.

Natasha shivered visibly when she felt him lock her legs in place and give her a full-throttled thrust, plunging his organ deep in her guts. He started to grind against her soft sugar walls. "Ooooow, " she gushed hotly.

A moment later, Natasha lost her breath when she felt him pull out. Suddenly, both hands reached up and palmed his face. "You muthfucka!" she stammered breathless, her eyes wild. "You better fuck the hell out of me!" she demanded desperately.

Bad Ass grinned. "I got this. You just relax and enjoy the ride," he said arrogantly and delivered another hard, deep thrust from the hip. A victory smile slid on his grill when Natasha's eyes rolled back and started fluttering simultaneously with her quivering lips.

In the shadows of Malcolm X Park, the consummation of Darkness & Death had come full circle.

The hidden perils associated with this insidious union was something nobody would want. Society as a whole was ill-prepared to cope with the travesties they were capable of unleashing at any given moment.

Chapter 47

The following afternoon, a loud wail of sirens approaching from the distance went unnoticed by the masses on this particular stretch of 14th Street in Columbia Heights. Pedestrians and drivers alike seemed unfazed by the presence of the charcoal-colored Dodge charging through the intersection at 14th and Park Road, its dark front grill ablaze in flashes of blue and white lights. The Charger's engine roared powerfully under the hood as Detective Nadia Dozier gunned it, whipping the wheel from left to right, darting in and around traffic with confidence emanating in her expression.

"Get the hell out of my way!" Nadia barked, her soft cocoa brow strained with aggression as she glared through the windshield.

"How much further is this Malcolm X Park that were going to, huh, Nadia?" asked Mecca, her light gray eyes glistening from the sunlight as she gazed at the collage of humanity   wandering to whatever destination their individual lives were taking them.

"Not far at all, Mecca. A few more blocks and we'll be there." Nadia's words were polite, but her brown eyes were fierce. Her pupils focused on the road up ahead and the feel of the gas pedal sinking under foot.

Both needles on the speedometer and RPM gauge drifted forward in conjunction with the power surge in the muscle car's velocity and the adrenaline rush that made Nadia's heart start to palpitate.

Nadia Dozier was your classic adrenaline junky. Moments such as this she relished.

Northbound 16th Street, for a three-block stretch, marked and unmarked police cruisers crowded the street outside Malcolm X Park with a massive and formidable show of force.

Blocking access to the park's gated main entrance, a police barricade was constructed along the western perimeter on 16th Street – and stretched east, sealing off all entry points to media and the public. Without valid law enforcement credentials on hand, permission to enter any blockades were met with a staunch – 'No!'

About five minutes later, the Dodge Charger arrived on the scene. Immediately, the two women were greeted by the ruggedly handsome Lieutenant Barnhart.

"Detective Dozier, Detective Tomay," Barnhart said, sounding overly formal. "Please, ladies, if you would follow me. Your assistance has been requested by the chief." He waited for both women to join him and lead the way through the throng of loitering officers.

At the center of the park, a jumble of law enforcement personnel crowded the walkway outside the building that housed the public restrooms. The main focus of the investigation was centered on the building's right wing, just inside the soaring archway.

About twenty feet inside the archway, toward the rear of the structure, the corpse of a woman was nailed to a worn wooden door with two large silver metal spikes protruding grotesquely from her hollowed eye sockets.

Bambi, DC's reigning super diva, was dead. Her cold, bloodied, and bruised carcass dangled stiffly from the door, gripped by the throes of rigor mortis, like a horrible ragdoll ornament decorating the front of the door.

The chief of police, Shane Holt, was on the scene and had the situation under control. This was the first time Detective Tomay had witnessed the chief take command of such a high-profile crime scene. Shane looked strong and powerful, his facial expression stolid as he scrutinized every aspect of this fluid environment. Mecca had a thing for men in powerful positions. For a black man to be in one of the most powerful cities on earth and command with the authority he embodied—and the brother fine as hell! Mecca was more that turned on. She found herself utterly enamored with this man.

Ooooh! Get a grip on yourself, Mecca voiced to herself. *You gotta be more careful around this brother here!* Detective Dozier caught sight of the chief and, unprompted, made a beeline for him.

"Commander Holt," Nadia said and slipped ahead of Lieutenant Barnhart. Both women stood on either side of the chief and gasped when they laid eyes on the horrid sight hanging on the wooden door frame.

"What in God's name?!?" Mecca stammered awkwardly, placing her hand against her chest. She faced the chief, a sharp look of anger and dismay defined in her face now.

"How long has she been dead?" asked Nadia in a no-nonsense tone.

"Time of death was approximately 3 a.m.," the chief responded flatly. His eyes never wavered from Tony Woo, who was meticulously examining and analyzing the corpse and the horrendous manner in which the victim was murdered.

Mecca's mouth suddenly felt parched. Before speaking, she had to swallow hard. "Her eyes are gone," Mecca managed to say. "Did the unsub keep her eyes?"

Tony Woo surprised Mecca when he turned and answered. "Yep. But there's no surprise there, detective," he said matter of factly. "Our perp collects trophies from his victims." Tony keeled beside his black leather evidence bag and carefully inserted the last vials of blood, skin, and DNA evidence he'd collected from the victim and the area around the corpse.

A low grunt dribbled from Tony's mouth as he struggled to stand. He looked over his shoulder and signaled for the forensics team to move in and bag the body.

Facing the commander and the two detectives, Tony peeled the tight latex gloves off his fleshy paws and moved toward the trio.

A worrisome look was evident on Mecca's face. Her eyes moved from Nadia to the commander and made contact with the roly-poly looking inspector.

Tony recognized the stressed outline showing on the pretty woman's face. He clapped his hands together and voiced quietly, "Detective Tomay, looks to me like you have something on your mind that you'd like to share with us."

Mecca scrunched her nose at Tony. "Excuse me?" she uttered off-handedly. "As a matter of fact there is. It's the eyes, sir. The unsub has a fascination with eyes. Your classic nucleator, wouldn't you say?"

"Nucleator?" Tony Woo stuttered, shaking his head. "No, detective." He hesitated and leaned a little closer. "This handy work here is identical to the first victim.

Removed her nose. Remember?" Tony straightened up and turned to the commander. "No siree, our perp is a modern-day Jack the Ripper. He broke three vertebrae when he strangled her. That's hard to do. Believe me when I say, this sicko is beyond human!" Tony lowered his voice just above a whisper. "It's our guy, but keep that on the low."

Mecca gave Tony a strange look. "But, sir ... what evidence do you have that suggests the same killer committed both murders?"

"It's the hands, detective," Tony answered. "Our perp has unbelievable strength but very small hands. Almost like a woman's hands."

Nadia interjected. "How do we know the perp's not a woman?"

"Were you paying attention, detective?" Tony retorted with an irritated smirk tugging at the left corner of his mouth. "Oh, you missed the part about how unbelievably strong he is. It would be virtually impossible for a woman—even the strongest woman in the world—to do the damage he's done. This sicko used his bare hands to destroy this victim. Does that register in your brain, detective?"

Tony's smart-ass remark rubbed Nadia the wrong way. She tossed the portly little man a snide sneer. "The metal spikes in her eye sockets," Nadia began as she leaned forward and caught the commander's eye, "they look like nails!" Her voice was frazzled.

Commander Holt turned to the side. "Railroad spikes, detective," he said plainly. His disposition was robust. His tense gaze swept the archway, scouring the landscape as he pondered the devastating loss of Bambi and the sobering effect of it all. He felt a strong sense of bitterness, turmoil, and revenge billowing inside of him.

Before going on, the chief took a deep breath. "Imagine someone who hates you with the utmost intensity," he said, plucking the words right out of thin air. His attention was drawn to Detective Tomay. "So much to the point that even in death this psychotic individual has the gall to desecrate the victim's body, which devastates the soul, so as to inflict more pain and heartache on the victim's family and loved ones."

The chief took a breath and looked Tony's way. His eyes went flat. "If we look hard enough, I'm sure we'll find a method to this madness. There's an end to this bottomless pit. I'm certain of that." There was a creepy, unsettling tone in his voice when he spoke. Tony Woo absorbed every creepy, unsettling syllable and memorized it.

A male voice spoke up in the background.

"Commander Holt? Sir, the podium has been set up for you to speak to the media. Just say the word. We're ready to go when you are."

The commander changed gears. "Well, Tony," he began as he straightened his navy Christian Dior blazer, "that's our cue. Detective Dozier, Detective Tomay, please excuse us. But don't go far. It's imperative that we put our heads together on this one. You ladies take notice. See how many departments have converged on this one crime scene? The goddamn Feds are here! I'll be damn if they think they can waltz in here and steal my shine. Look, I think it'll be best if we all meet downtown right after I'm finished with my media briefing and tie up a few loose ends here." He glanced at his gold timepiece. "Say around two-ish. See you ladies in my office."

With that said, the chief and Tony Woo moved off in the crowd together.

Nadia and Mecca watched the men walk off, then as if reading one another's thoughts, both women turned at the same time and looked the other in the eye.

"Well, girlfriend," Nadia said, in a much lighter mood, "I guess we can hit the road until it's time for the meeting."

Mecca shrugged. "Sounds good to me. I guess everything we need to know we'll find out at the meeting."

Nadia eyed her quietly. "You're sure about that? Wanna see what he says in the media briefing?"

Not trying to seem too interested, Mecca sensed Nadia wanted out of there. The excitement in the atmosphere had waned, and Nadia longed for something to get her adrenaline pumping.

"Well ... I guess so," Mecca said nonchalantly. "Since we're here, might as well listen to what he has to say." Mecca struggled not to laugh when she saw the dreadful look on Nadia's face.

"Huh? Okay," Nadia begrudgingly relented. "But as soon as he's finished, we're out of here."

Mecca smiled. "I'm with you on that," she said, anxious to join the crowd closest to the podium. Mecca took two steps and turned. "What now?" she frowned.

"Um, I'm not sure," Nadia said, looking curious. "But you sure seemed to change you tune all of a sudden."

"Nadia, if you don't stop your inquisitive mind from analyzing every breath I take, you gonna give yourself a fucking aneurysm," Mecca chided lightly. She did her best to conceal the uneasiness she was feeling under Nadia's scrutinizing stare. "C'mon here, girl," Mecca waved to her. "After you."

Both women strode in step, side by side, and moved from the shadow of the archway out into the warm sunlight. Behind them, the forensic team was hard at work, bagging up the cold, bloody remains of Bambi.

Chapter 48

A dark, murky cloud appeared from nowhere and descended on Angel, swirling all around her and swallowing her whole, like a hungry black hole feasting on a meal.

Slowly, the black cloud surrounding her began to recede. Angel's optical lens gradually came into focus. Suddenly, she was able to make out the blurred image of a woman cowering in the dark shadows of a towering archway.

It was apparent to Angel by the look of absolute fear etched in the woman's face that she was scared to death and hiding, trying to elude whoever or whatever was out to get her.

The scared woman was closer now. Angel could see her carefully backing away in the dark. She stumbled unexpectedly on a large metal spike and fell back against a wooden door.

"Whore!" Angel froze with fright when she heard the cryptic voice whisper in the back of her mind.

Angel kept her eyes steady on the woman as she turned abruptly and faced her head on. Angel was completely stunned when she recognized the face of the woman standing in front of her. She was the trifling skank from the Peacock Café in Georgetown—Bambi!

Angel jumped, surprised when the voice growled again. "Whore!" The infliction in the voice billowed with rage. Angel winced when she saw a pair of hands materialize from the dark. Someone reached out and grabbed Bambi around the throat.

*She felt her heart lurch in her chest. "Lord, no!"
Angel mumbled to herself as Bambi struggled and fought to
free herself from the stranglehold.*

*"Someone help her please!" Angel shrieked,
overwhelmed by the feelings of grief and sadness. She
witnessed Bambi dying right before her eyes, and her heart
went out to the woman. In that last glimmer in Bambi's big
doe eyes, she cried, "Why!?!" A split second later the
agonizing sound of her neck being snapped echoed in the air.*

*Angel's heart dropped when she sensed the life force
evaporating—the air and spirit and energy seeped out of
Bambi's form like vapor dissipating in the atmosphere.*

A sunny early morning light filtered in from the
Italian bay windows and splashed her soft caramel face.

Angel popped straight up into a seated position and
struggled to get her bearings.

"That was all a dream!" she breathed, feeling a sense
of relief and calm come over her. "Thank God it was nothing
more," she murmured, yawning and stretching.

Ten feet across the room, adorned to the wall space
above the cream marble fireplace, the 70-inch Sony plasma
screen blinked on automatically, like it did every day at its
pre-set time.

The sound of the television coming to life prompted
Angel to move. She swung her legs over the side of the
exquisite chestnut-colored Renoir sofa. She placed her bare
feet on the plush carpet and sighed pleasantly when she felt
her toes sink into the soft, luxurious fibers.

"Did I spend the entire night down here?" Angel said
as she looked around the room. She paused and took a
quick peek under the cashmere quilt wrapped around her.

A cold shudder raced through her body when she realized she was totally nude.

That's not like me, Angel thought to herself, drawing a blank about last night. She tried to stand. Her rear end rose about six inches off the sofa, and suddenly Angel felt her entire body cringe with soreness, especially in between her legs. It was extra sore down there!

Angel's legs trembled and gave way. She flopped on the sofa groaning uncomfortably with a disturbed and confused look gripping her face.

"Oh, my Lord!" Angel groaned in pain. "My kitty is sore!" She leaned over and started carefully probing and examining herself. "My kitty-cat ... my thighs. What in God's name happened to me last night?!?" The unthinkable emerged in her mind. *Somebody's been up in my pussy! OMG! They beat it up!* She looked horrified. Her mind twisted and turned in every direction. *Was I raped!?! Did I have a one-night stand?!? Something as significant as that, and I can't remember shit!?! Lord, what is wrong with me?!?* Angel's mind teetered between rage and confliction and embarrassment. "I'm gonna be sick," she mumbled, feeling nauseous and lightheaded.

Breaking news flashed suddenly on the television screen, diverting Angel's attention.

The familiar face of Mark Garvey, the news anchor for Fox 5 appeared on the screen. "Hello. Mark Garvey, Fox 5 news, reporting live. We have breaking news at this hour. There's a news conference about to get underway, and the Chief of Police, Chief Shane Holt will be speaking live. Before Commander Holt takes the podium, allow me to give you a brief update on what I have so far.

At approximately 10 a.m. this morning, a female jogger, while on her normal run through Malcolm X Park in Northwest, DC stumbled upon a woman's body. The victim has been identified as Ms. Naomi Forrest. For those individuals who frequent DC's elite social circles, she was considered a DC icon, a flamboyant celebrity diva who was loved by many and known intimately by one name: Bambi."

Bambi!!! The name exploded in Angel's head and rattled her to the core. She felt herself split in half and then come back together again with one cohesive thought reeling through her mind—*I witnessed Bambi's murder in my dream!*

The news report left Angel slack-jawed. She was both exasperated and shocked. Suddenly, from the dark recesses of her mind, a beacon of light appeared, and the word "whore" flashed over and over and over. The word floated to the forefront of Angel's mind and seemed to take on a life all its own as if it held some vital significance she should be aware of.

Angel wondered if this was an uncomfortable coincidence or if there something more diabolical at play? Again, Angel drew a blank.

Chapter 49

Things were finally starting to look up for Shane. Right after his media briefing he was happily surprised when he received an unexpected phone call from Angel. She mentioned the live news briefing and said she was sorry to hear about his friend Bambi. The incident really upset her.

"Would you mind if I stopped through? Ya know, make sure you're okay?" Shane asked, assuming the answer would be yes, which it certainly was. "Angel, you're sure about that? It's cool for me to come over? Because I don't want to impose on anything you might have already planned." Shane played the part of a perfect gentleman, and Angel ate it up. She was like putty in his hands.

"Okay, Angel, let me finish up here at the park and make a quick pit stop downtown at headquarters, touch base with a few of my detectives, then I'll be on my way." Beneath his strong, authoritative exterior, Shane was jumping for joy.

🌱 🌱 🌱 🌱

The leaves were spectacular, and the sun was shining along a tranquil stretch of Howard County. Shane steered his sparkling Escalade down the winding country road in Clarksville. His facial expression was contemplative. He was mulling over the unstable and quirky behavior Angel displayed on all three of their encounters.

Shane came to the conclusion that the issues prompting Angel's erratic behavior were most likely due to the fact that she was having a hard time adjusting to life as a widow.

"Poor thing. I can see baby girl is definitely exhibiting signs of a woman with post-traumatic stress syndrome," he said. "But who could blame her? Bless her little heart. After being married to a wack job like Jovan ... shit, I'm surprised she's progressed enough to make an attempt to deal with another man so soon after such a devastating tragedy. Lucky me. Then again, I'd have to say my timing was perfect." He looked up in the rearview mirror, smiled, and gave his reflection a big thumbs-up just before he slowed down to make the right turn into Angel's cul-de-sac.

All was quiet inside Angel's immaculate home. But this wasn't your normal quiet; there was something peculiar radiating within the quiet stillness of the home, as if something creepy and ghostlike was blossoming in the air.

Upstairs, the sound of splashing water emanated in the hall and got more pronounced closer to the master bedroom. Interspersed with the sound of splashing water, grumbling voices echoed from the bedroom. They sounded like two people in a heated dispute.

Angel's head emerged suddenly from beneath the bath water. "Don't be so fucking stupid! He's a married man, Angel! I don't want you fucking with him!" The raspy, toxic voice was undeniably Natasha.

Angel's head reared back violently, like she was possessed by some sort of dark, invisible force. She paused briefly, as if she were fighting against the unforeseen entity. A second later, she smacked the water and disappeared below the surface.

There was a long pause. The raging water in the

large oval-shaped Jacuzzi calmed to a slight ripple undulating on the surface. Without warning, both hands leaped from the water and latched on the rim of the tub. Fighting the dark forces working against her, Angel gave a mighty heave and lunged forward. Her head and upper torso exploded from the water and she gasped for air, like a human offspring bursting from its cocoon and taking its first breath of life.

As quickly as the flash of evilness showed itself, it was gone.

"Who in the hell do you think you are?!? Telling me who I can fuck with! You go to hell!!!" Angel shrieked at the top of her lungs, totally outraged.

Ding-dong! The ring at the front door seemed to snap Angel back to reality. She stopped abruptly and stared around the empty bathroom. Her gaze came to rest on the vacant hallway just beyond the bathroom door. She was fixated on the spot as if she was half expecting to see someone standing there.

Ding-dong! The doorbell sounded again. Angel looked hesitant for a brief second, then slapped a smile on her face and rose from the tub.

"Coming!" she said sweetly, her voice emanating from inside the front double glassed doors. Five seconds later, both doors swung open and she glistened like a ray of sunshine beaming in the doorway.

"I'm so sorry, Shane, I didn't mean to make you wait so long," Angel apologized while running a comb through her damp hair. "I had planned on being ready by the time you got here." A warm smile graced her lips. "But you know how us women can be sometimes—we're never ready until everything is just right. Which means we're always late. Especially me."

Shane gulped. "Wow," he said. He slowly stroked his thin mustache, his eyes beaming with excitement. He was star struck. Angel was a vision—sexy, exotic, beautiful. She looked like she just stepped off the cover of *Smooth* magazine.

"You look splendid, just as you are," Shane whispered as lewd thoughts of them getting it in emerged vividly in his mind.

"That's sweet of you to say," Angel replied, turning from the door. "I know you didn't come all this way to just stand there and gawk at me from the front door." She gave an innocent wink and motioned for him to follow. "Come in, silly."

The sheer white silk gown Angel wore caressed her curves enticingly as she floated across the plush gold carpet. She was a slinky siren of irresistibility.

Lust, desire, and hunger billowed in Shane's deep, probing gaze. His expression was wild and uncivilized. His long, drooling tongue wagging, Shane looked more like a love-struck baboon than the egotistical narcissist incapable of love that he was.

Angel led the way to the family room. "What's in the bag, Shane?" she asked, plopping her soft backside on the sofa. "Did you bring lil 'ole me something special?"

Shane flashed his toothy grin her way and placed the white plastic bag on the cream marble coffee table.

"Well, of course," he said, careful not to expose his underhanded intentions. "Me coming here is all about you. But you know that already, don't you, beautiful?" He produced a bottle of red wine from the bag and lowered his head. He announced with a proud grin, "A bottle of the finest Spanish wine in the entire Washington-Baltimore region. Just for you, baby." He hesitated, waiting to see her response, before he set the bottle on the table.

"Oh, goody!" Angel sounded spunky. "Spanish wine—that's my favorite. But how did you know?" she inquired, standing. "Make yourself comfortable while I get the wine glasses."

"Where's the CD player?" asked Shane. "You do like Maxwell? Because I got the 'Best of Maxwell.'" He fished the Maxwell CD from the bag and placed it on the coffee table next to the wine. "I also thought you might like a bite to eat, so I stopped by Crisfield's and got two Oyster Rockefeller and lobster bisque dishes."

"Why, thank you, Shane. That was very thoughtful of you," Angel said, strutting around the end of the sofa, a rose-colored wine glass in each hand. She set both glasses on the table and headed back in the kitchen for plates and utensils. "Oh, and I love me some Maxwell!" she said over her shoulder. "The CD player is over there in the corner, right next to the bar."

Shane loaded the Maxwell CD in the CD player. He glanced around the room, a shrewd sneer dancing on the edge of his lips. His eyes drifted to the marble mantel above the fireplace and settled on the dark gray designer sculpture—"The Thinker." The miniature man seemed to return his cool stare.

He exhaled a satisfied sigh when the soothing instrumental to Maxwell's "Know These Things" swept through the room.

You stood ... as if you knew I'd stay right there
And you shouldn't know these things about me
Abused ... as if your pain would quench my fear

How could you know these things about me?
You shouldn't know these things

A fleeting look of surprise flashed on Shane's face when Angel eased up beside him and simply asked, "Is everything alright, Shane?" Her tone was coy. She oozed sex and sensuality.

He looked at her with the cynical eye of an excited voyeur. At that moment, in a haze of infatuation, he realized Angel was the one. It wasn't just her looks; it was that X factor.

"Looks to me like you've got something really serious on your mind," Angel insinuated quietly, her inquisitive stare probing and feeling him out. "Care to share your thoughts with me?"

He gave her a warm smile before saying, "With someone as lovely as you by my side, of course I have something serious on my mind. You, Angel, are seriously on my mind." This was a critical, defining moment in which Shane could make or break their future destiny together.

Shane stood over Angel. He ran his fingers across her hairline, lovingly stroking her long, soft mane. "What wonderful memories you and I together could create, if only you would allow us to take that journey together." He lingered for a minute, allowing her to carefully consider the intriguing prospects. He went on to say, "You know, Angel, life is not the amount of breaths you take, it's the moments that take your breath away."

He said all those penetrating words women loved and yearned to hear. He was so genuine and heartfelt, so charming and original. Shane was well aware of the power he implored with his words, and he could see the effects working on Angel. Beneath the façade, he detected a deep reservoir of emotions bubbling over.

Shane put his hand on Angel's back and pulled her into him so close he could feel the heat from her breath on his chest and smell the alluring, sweet fragrance of Oh, Lola permeating her hair, neck, and chest.

He sucked his bottom lip and whispered in her ear, "Angel, do you know what you do to me?" He was well aware of his confident swagger and the receptive vibe coming from her. "You make me smile with my heart," he breathed softly in her ear.

Angel's heart fluttered, and her expression was all bubbly and giddy and glowy as she glazed up at him, her sparkling eyes spellbound, like amber pools floating in a daze.

Her woman's intuition warned her that something was wrong, but the hot lava flow brewing lustily between her thighs relaxed any and all mental warnings, red flags, and alarms.

Shane held Angel's body close to him, the way she melted under his embrace – totally relaxed and comfortable – like they were made for each other. Shane sensed the time was right now, so he leaned over and kissed Angel softly on her pink, shimmering lips.

That kiss sparked an emotional fire that had been smoldering between them for a while. It was as if a floodgate suddenly opened and their primal urges were finally unleashed.

The smooth rich melody of Maxwell's "Til The Cops

Come Knockin" set the mood, the tone, the tempo.

Didn't you love the way I rubbed your back, girl?
Wasn't it cool when at first I kissed your lips?
Was it enough to penetrate your dark world?
Were you embarrassed about the way you freaked?
Cuz I wanna hold you
I wanna mold you
If it's alright with you

Shoes and clothes were scattered everywhere along the hall carpet leading to the entrance of the master bedroom. Sensual moans of pleasure drifted from the bedroom and resonated all along the hallway. Angel's flamboyant pink oasis reeked of mandarin and rose-fragranced candles. The smell was soft, rich and inviting.

The atmosphere in the bedroom was extremely heated and super-charged. Its interior was saturated with burning sexual energy. Inside, Angel and Shane's ultimate desires erupted with unabated lust. Their hot, sultry flesh collided and intertwined in a passionate embrace of sexual lust.

Pink silk Chanel sheets spread over a king-size canopy bed served as their erotic playpen. Shane's long dark chocolate frame stretched the length of their erogenous zone with Angel's soft, creamy thighs straddled across his lap, her arms flailing wildly over her head as if she were giving praise to the heavens and the Almighty above. Angel was getting her rodeo ride on, and Shane's rock-hard fuck-stick was her bucking bronco.

Shane's torso rose off the bed. Angel paused, looked down at him, and stopped him, mid-motion. She slammed both hands hard against his hairy, muscular chest and forced him down on his back.

"Just lay back, Shane," Angel muttered in a breathy voice. "Enjoy my body while I enjoy myself doing you." She spoke bluntly, adding an exclamation point by sinking her long fingernails in his hard, thick pecs like a tigress punishing her mate.

Angel jerked her head back suddenly and arched her back almost to the breaking point, then flexed the muscles in her buttocks and pelvic area with a lewd, excited grimace perched on her lips.

A gratifying utter drizzled from her mouth the moment she tightened her labia around Shane's throbbing penis and descended upon him ever so slowly, inch by loving inch. She savored the feeling of his organ invading her body, the mounting pressure she felt probing and pushing against her insides. Her body quivered anxiously from the inside out as she commandeered his penis, aiming for the target—the G-spot. Angel made a direct hit. Her lips fluttered, releasing a sigh filled with pure ecstasy.

Feeling her body soar to new heights of satisfaction, Angel's mind veered off course and ventured into dark territory. Out of nowhere, a disturbing image resonated in her mind. She could see the face of a man hovering over her, a face she'd never seen before. The man was handsome, she couldn't deny. He was tall and muscular with caramel skin and deep, penetrating black eyes, like Shane.

With a cool, mischievous grin slip-sliding on his face, the handsome stranger looked her in the eye. "I got this pussy. You just relax and enjoy the ride," he said in a voice dripping with arrogance and conceit.

The vision streaming in Angel's head was extremely

vivid, as though she was actually there. She could smell the scent of rain in the air. She really thought she was losing her mind when she pictured the stranger climbing atop her, forcing her legs wide and thrusting his engorged limb inside her, pounding her sweltering pussy into submission.

The graphic image galvanized her senses. Angel felt a strong rumble deep in the pit of her stomach and cringed. Her body went rigid, wrecked by an abrupt surge of emotional tension.

Shane noticed the sudden change immediately. "What's the matter, Angel?" he asked, showing obvious concern. "Did I do something wrong, baby?" He rose up on his elbows and eyed her closely. Her eyes betrayed a dark haughtiness he hadn't noticed before.

Angel didn't respond to his question right away. She sat there for a minute and wrapped her arms around her torso, comforting herself. She sat staring at Shane like she was in a trance. But she wasn't looking at him; she was as if she were peering through him.

"I don't know," Angel said, shaking her head slowly. "I started to feel sick all of a sudden," she expressed with a hint of skepticism in her voice.

"C'mon, Angel, I think you should lie down for a minute," Shane said being as helpful as he could in such an awkward situation. "All this excitement might be a little too much for you to deal with all at once," he told her and placed a pillow under her head.

His words seemed to strike a nerve in her. Angel cut her eyes and looked at Shane with noticeable disdain.

"Could you please go downstairs and get me something to drink?" asked Angel, sounding cranky.

She didn't say another word. She watched Shane's

fine black tail hop out the bed and strut across the floor. The moment he walked out the door, Angel turned toward the ceiling and asked herself what in the hell that crazy-ass shit was.

She pondered the whole sordid episode but was left feeling weird and confused.

It's been more than a year now since she was able to enjoy the company and pleasure of a man. Just when she was having the time of her life ...

Angel relished in the moment. The gratification, the fun, the excitement she felt was all gone now. On the fun-o-meter, Angel's high took a drastic nosedive, plummeting from +10 to -10 all in one take. The emotional swing left her traumatized, drained . She was thoroughly pissed and it showed in her facial expression and body language. It was the silent affliction of Angel's womanhood.

Chapter 50

30 miles away in DC ...

It was 3:17 p.m. when Tommy Gunz arrived by escort at the CIX secluded Petworth safe house. To be on the safe side, Midnight parked in the rear alley. He and Nightmare ushered Tommy Gunz in through the rear basement. New faces attracted too much unwanted attention, and Bad Ass always said, "Keep in mind, just 'cause them bammas go hard on the block, doesn't necessarily make them team players. The streets are watching."

This would be Bad Ass' first face-to-face meeting with one of the most ruthless and unpredictable forces on the DC gang scene. Tommy Gunz was known as the hardcore A-Team's assassin.

Upon meeting this noxious character for the first time, it was easy to see the madness lurking in the man's eyes. Tommy Gunz was a bitter and troubled soul. He was a man consumed by his personal misfortunes and failures in life.

At the very top of Tommy Gunz's list of unwanted tribulations, the one thing that ate at his soul like a malignant tumor was the fact that his crew, he unwittingly discovered, had given the okay to replace him. Within the twisted diabolical order of a gang's hierarchy, the only acceptable and respectable way for a living, breathing gang member to be replaced is for the gang member (comrade) who is vying for the position to slaughter his comrade—in the most heinous way possible. But first Tommy Gunz felt a need to create a vacancy in order for the comrade to obtain the position.

Knowing the order had been sanctioned made it that much worse in Tommy Gunz's mind. You see, Tommy Gunz was a bona fide OG, one of a select few still in existence and still putting in work. Matter of fact, Tommy Gunz was the only OG physically able to walk the streets of DC. The remaining OG's were either chillin' with the Grave Digger Mob, resting six feet under, or chillin' with the Walkin' Dead Mob, doing life in the penal without parole. Gangstas called it doing life/no pussy.

Besides the fact that Tommy Gunz was a bona fide OG, he was also the leader of a top-tier squad of assassins, which in his eyes was a blatant form of disrespect. When Tommy Gunz unearthed the plot, it literally crushed his gangsta soul, and he was out for blood, hence the prearranged meeting with the CIX boss, Bad Ass.

The sound of Young Jeezy's "Ballin" reverberated through the hardwood floors in the living room. Bad Ass bobbed his head to the beat as he made his way across the floor and opened the basement door. Donning his trademark black attire, Bad Ass descended a rickety wood staircase leading to the basement level, which he dubbed "the lair."

At the bottom of the staircase, a thick haze of cloudy white smoke saturated the air and filled his lungs with every breath he breathed—Purple Haze, Black & Mild and Wild Sex incense were the odorous aromas stimulating his nostrils.

Bad Ass stopped and stared across the lair, which in essence was the basement transformed into a hip party room, complete with a stage and striper pole. Over in the corner, two topless shortys shot smoldering gazes his way. While up on stage, a well-oiled Ethiopian in a thin gold G-string turned and flexed her shapely rump while her dance partner, a sleazy redhead pinched her nipples teasingly and flickered her extra-long tongue.

Four crew members were lounging on a super-stretch red leather sectional encompassing the small six-by-six stage.

Dabo, Cut Throat, Threat, and Screw were the source of the herbal smoke screen. Each man was puffin' on a fat blunt of crucial with one hand and guzzling a 40 oz. 211 Steel Reserve with the other while their undivided attention was focused squarely on the two freaks getting down on stage.

On the far side of the room, a door creaked open. The light spilling in from the doorway caught Bad Ass' attention. When he looked, he noticed Midnight's big head bobbing and weaving for him. An aggressive scowl jumped on Bad Ass' forehead. He made a short, quick gesture with his right hand, and Midnight's big head ducked out of sight.

Bad Ass watched the dark shadow sweep away the light when Midnight pushed the door shut. Satisfied, Bad Ass stood for a minute, a cool, composed, smug look on his face as he contemplated the meeting with Tommy Gunz. Bad Ass reflected on Law 14 from The 48 Laws of Power by Robert Green.

Bad Ass cut his eyes toward the two topless shortys sitting over in the corner at the bar. He slipped a fresh cherry Tootsie pop from his black True Religion jeans and casually peeled off the red paper wrapping. Watching the topless shortys watch him, Bad Ass tossed them a slinky wink and a smile, slipped the candy between his gums, and stepped off.

Bad Ass acknowledged his men with a grunt and a curt nod as he sauntered across the black carpeted floor and headed for the rear conference room.

The conference room was nothing more than a small walled off area at the far rear of the lair. It was sparsely furnished with two heavy oak tables and matching chairs for crew meetings and strategy planning. A black leather Natuzzi sofa and 40-inch plasma screen were situated at the front of the room, specifically for lounging and getting your freak on.

When Bad Ass entered the conference room, he found Nightmare sitting at the small square oak table in the corner. He was busy puffin' on a beedie, a hand-rolled leaf cigarette imported from India.

At the round oak table in the center of the room, Midnight sat across from Tommy Gunz. Both men engrossed in the XXX video playing on the wall-mounted plasma screen.

Bad Ass focused his attention on the A-Team assassin, Tommy Gunz. He was a monster of a man with a long black ponytail that smacked the small of his broad back. He had three dark tear drops tattooed under his right eye and a thick scar down his left cheek. The scar was glazed dark brown. Aged. His claim to gangsta infamy.

Upon seeing Bad Ass walk in the room, Midnight shot to his feet, followed immediately by the monster with the long ponytail. The OG brought to mind images of a big scrappy-looking silverback gorilla with a bad attitude.

Midnight introduced the men. Although Tommy Gunz was an extremely imposing figure in his own right, he was very much aware of the grossly wicked and tremendously violent-natured man standing before him. Bad Ass was in a league of his own.

"Tommy Gunz," Midnight said with a wave of his hand, "this is the man ... Mr. Bad Ass, the boss of CIX."

Sporting a crooked grin, Tommy Gunz responded with a nod and a firm handshake. "What up, hustler? I've been waiting for this moment for a long time." When he spoke, Tommy Gunz's voice was laced with a raspy undertone, as if he had a touch of laryngitis he was trying to stave off. "The moves you making on the streets of DC are major, and you got some major bammas shakin' in their boots. Feel me?"

Twirling the Tootsie pop between clinched lips, Bad Ass replied with a devious smirk, "I hear that, Gunz, but that's not your motivation behind this meeting, so don't stand there and try to stroke my ego. That's a waste of time, and my time is money, soldier." He gave the OG a stout look.

The moment Tommy Gunz looked Bad Ass in the eye, he immediately sensed the cynicism pulsating deeply in the man.

Tommy Gunz prided himself on being a formidable alpha male, even bragged about it. In his lifetime he could only recall two other occasions where he actually came face to face with this particular type of man, one who possessed that extraordinary characteristic trait that made alpha males wary. These stand-alone men were the ultra-alpha males of the species. In Tommy Gunz's mind, these men were abominations.

Today marked his third encounter with an ultra-alpha male. Tommy Gunz swore there was something odd in the ultra-alpha male's chemical makeup that gave off a specific hormonal scent that his body unconsciously reacted to, causing Tommy Gunz's palms to sweat profusely every time he was in close contact.

Tommy Gunz knew without a shadow of a doubt he could not underestimate the capabilities of the man standing in front of him. He could actually feel the power and darkness in his nature surging from him like some poisonous force about to strike out at any second.

Tommy Gunz fathomed Badd Ass was a rising supernova in their warped and violent underworld.

Fuck him! I'm a fuckin' OG! Gunz voiced to himself with boding confidence. *I'm an underworld star my muthafuckin self!* With that in mind, Tommy Gunz realized he needed to stand his ground firmly when dealing with a man having such diabolical qualities manifested in his nature.

When Tommy Gunz spoke he did so with strength and assertiveness. "Well, Bad Ass, you know my motivation for being here, and I believe you and I both will benefit from this meeting."

Bad Ass plucked the wet candy from his mouth without breaking eye contact. He twirled the white stem between his fingers and sucked his teeth.

"Let's keep it trill, soldier," Bad Ass said in a tone that was slick and condescending. "You need me a lot more than I need you. Because I can tell you this, there's nothing or no one that can stop me from getting back my fifty bricks. Matter of fact, this meeting with you is impeding my progress." He stopped and gave Tommy Gunz a ferocious look that was meant to intimidate.

Tommy Gunz surprised Bad Ass when he didn't blink or flinch. He was completely unfazed.

"Fifty bricks," Tommy Gunz snickered mockingly. "That's it? What if I told you I could double that number? Would I be impeding your progress then, huh, Bad Ass?"

Bad Ass was all ears. "Oh, yeah," he murmured, softening his tone. He popped the candy in his mouth and pulled out a chair. "Have a seat, soldier. You might be of some benefit after all. Let's hear what you got."

"Off the muscle, you already know what I wanna do," Gunz began, taking a seat at the table. "I'm in serious get-back mode, and I'm itching to peel back some A-Team wigs." He cracked his knuckles and gave a dry smirk.

"Yeah, yeah, that's good and all," Bad Ass retorted in a nondescript way, "but I wanna hear more about that hundred keys of cocaine. Who got 'em, and how I can get my hands on 'em? Then we can focus on your little problem. Feel me?" Bad Ass leaned back in his seat and gave Gunz a hard stare down.

A twisted chuckle jumped from Tommy Gunz's mouth. "Little problem, huh man? I like how you put that. But I can tell you that little problem you're referring to has some major playas backing them, and I do mean major," he expressed with a snort.

Bad Ass' frown deepened. "Major playas?" Bad Ass sneered, his tone dripping with sarcasm, his gaze fierce, meticulously peeling away the invisible layers of a mental wall Tommy Gunz had erected as a buffer zone to deal with him.

"So who are these major playas you're referring to, huh, soldier? Why don't you elaborate for me?"

Tommy Gunz smacked his lips. "Check this out, Bad Ass." His upper torso leaned forward over the table. "I'm not privy to that kind of info, ya dig. But check it, you like to make people suffer and so do I. We're in the business of bringing misery to the masses." The way Gunz verbalized his psychotic rationale seemed to make perfect sense in a weird, morbid way. Bad Ass liked what he was hearing so far.

"When it comes to them A-Team bammas," Tommy Gunz stopped short. He brought up his right hand and balled it into a hard, tight fist. Holding it in front of his face, his lips tight, he mumbled, "Dawg, I would love to see them suffer the worst death possible, especially while I'm rollin' on E's. That's the best way to experience murder, up close and personal," he expressed, emotionally, an aura of pure hatred oozing from his core.

For some crazy, bizarre reason, Bad Ass took a keen liking to Tommy Gunz's wily-looking ass. When he looked the A-Team assassin straight in the eye, he could see a determined man with a dark, driven soul. Bad Ass saw a lot of himself in the OG.

"So what you saying, Tommy Gunz? You wanna flip sides and ride with my crew?" Bad Ass responded, a cautious look swirling in his gaze.

Tommy Gunz sucked his teeth loudly. "Naw, hustla, you know I can't roll like that. I'm rollin' dolo. Just call me Mr. Freelance from now on, ya dig."

Bad Ass paused, slowly stroking the fine hairs on his chin. His head bobbed up and down as he weighed his options, the pros and cons of the situation before him.

"Okay, Mr. Freelance," Bad Ass said evenly, taking his statement at face value. Bad Ass' gaze shifted, moving to the corner table where Nightmare sat alone. His big black cocked-eyed ass was firing up another beedie. He looked in Midnight's direction. He was standing at the side of the sofa, a-faking like he was really into the XXX video. Bad Ass knew his ears were tuned to the conversation he and Tommy Gunz were engaged in.

Bad Ass gave Gunz a steely look. "Let's stop fuckin' around. The hundred bricks got my attention. You insinuating A-Team and some major playas got them joints on lock. I don't give a fuck. I want 'em. Point-blank. Who dying for sanctioning your departure? I'm all ears. Those major playas you're referring to … well, in due time, I'm sure we'll eventually bump heads." Bad Ass plucked the Tootsie pop from his mouth and took a hefty chunk out of it before adding, "With that said, it's time we got down to business. Give me the rundown on them bricks, killa." He leaned in his chair, a dark, cunning vibe radiating heavily in his expression, as if some monumental event was forthcoming and he was the only one who knew.

$$\text{🦂 🦂 🦂 🦂}$$

Later that evening …

A full moon floated in the twilight sky over SE, Washington. On the streets below, a raspy, resonant voice rang out the open sunroof of a jet-black 745 parked at the corner of East Capitol and Division Avenue. Dark silhouettes were bobbing in rhythm behind the car's pitch-black windows. Dirty South rap icon Jeezy's song "Gangsta Music" was in the heads of the men seated inside.

The metal clank of a gun being cocked echoed from the speakers, followed by three quick bursts of gunfire— Pow! Pow! Pow!

I'm here now, you old news
Gotta couple Porsche trucks, couple old schools
I line your ass up, push your tape backwards
'Cause I'm a real nigga, and I don't like rappers

The volume inside the BMW cockpit dropped off sharply. Bad Ass put his left hand in the air and said, "A'ight, men, chill out!" he snapped, sounding short. His eyes, peering hard through the Beemer's windshield, focused on the eggshell-white Lexus 430 with the bluish lights rolling down Division Avenue towards them.

Four pairs of eyes watched quietly as the white sedan rode to the corner, made a slow right turn on East Capitol, and parked at the curb in front of a large corner row house.

"Call Murder," Bad Ass ordered. "Tell him strap up, them bammas just pulled up."

In the rear alley behind the A-Team's East Capitol stash house, a coal-black Suburban crept stealthily up the alley. The long black SUV rolled to a stop about three feet from the property line. Murder jammed the gearshift in park.

A second later, every door on the SUV sprang wide and CIX emerged like black-cloaked ninja assassins. Murder crawled out and gave the signal to move in, like he was some sort of brigadier general commanding a synchronized tactical squad.

Bam!

Six A-Team members were caught totally off guard. The back door was kicked it, and they were completely surrounded by a band of gun-toting bandits before the enormity of the situation hit them.

Murder led his men like wicked clockwork. They brought to mind a pack of hungry wolves circling their prey the moment before the kill.

Dark and brawny with uneven pink lips and a thick, nappy bush, Murder wrapped his large mitts around the black rubber handle and trained his Colt M4 on the Mohawk-styled head of an ashy-black Mr. T wannabe name Diesel, the biggest A-Team bamma standing in the living room.

"Go 'head, reach for it!" Murder snarled with a nasty smirk simmering on his pock-marked face. "I dare your bitch ass! Any one of you bitch-ass niggas!"

Cut Throat peered down the barrel of his chopper, a Kahr-K9. He glanced over his left shoulder and gave his partner Screw a cryptic grin.

Screw resembled a human version of a weasel—long, slim, and sleeky with a small, pointed nose and beady little eyes. Screw's dry, bony hands gripped the handle of a large chrome magnum .44. He returned his partner's gesture with a slight nod and a seedy smile while aiming his pistol at a young hotheaded rookie name Skinny.

"Stay your chump-ass right there, and don't move out that chair," Screw directed, backing his words up with a cold, contemptuous scowl.

A thin sheen of nervous perspiration coated Threat's clean-shaven dome. His posture was solid, as he held his automatic chopper, a DPMS-308. His itchy finger hovered over the trigger, anxiously awaiting the order to unleash his fury.

Dabo covered the men closest to the rear hallway. He swung the barrel of his Colt-1911 back and forth between the pair, mouthing, "Ennie … Meannie … Minnie

... Moe ..." The two bammas caught in his sight were jittery, their eyes darting back and forth in every direction, like two skittish bucks about to dash off at any second.

"I wish you bammas would," Dabo growled, giving Threat a knowing wink, letting him know he had the two under control. "Go 'head and try your hand," Dabo dared them, his cool expression deceptively hopeful, a sly sneer tiptoeing around his dimples.

A single voice rose from the A-Team and echoed in the room.

"Okay, everybody chill out and hold the fuck up!" A-Team co-captain, Santana blurted out forcefully. He stared around the room studying the faces of the men holding them at gunpoint. "What's going on? We ain't got no beef with y'all bammas! What's this all about?" he demanded, a look of absolute indignation sprouted on his light-complexioned baby face.

"This about my goddamn cocaine!" a cold voice bellowed angrily from the front hallway. Three seconds later, Bad Ass came strolling in the room, his black-clad form looking both potent and sinister. Trailing right behind him were Loso, Killa, and Monster, each man wearing identical black attire, like they were on their way to a gangsta funeral.

The moment Santana laid eyes on the CIX leader, an icy wave of tension ripped through his core and caused him to tremble.

As if he was casting a spell, Bad Ass narrowed his dark gaze. Santana was locked in his crosshairs. *Oh shit!!!* Santana cringed and cocked his head to one side. "Your cocaine?!?" he said, feeling the oomph of outrage and trepidation collide inside. His voice cracked when the threatening figure walked up to him and stared him directly in the eye. The gravity of the situation rocked him and his mind froze. Santana struggled to say something, but Bad Ass cut him off.

"You knew I would be coming, didn't you?" Sheer loathing and hate radiated in Bad Ass' deep-set gaze. "You had to know I would be here to collect what's mine." Bad Ass' tone was deceptively calm. The dark spark in his eye sent a frigid jolt through Santana.

Apprehension erupted with full force upon Santana. Suddenly a tear escaped his eye and streaked down his cheek. He didn't bother wiping it away. He couldn't because his body was flash frozen in place.

Bad Ass withdrew his half-melted Tootsie pop from his mouth. "I thought you muthafuckas understood how things worked around here. Evidently not, huh man?"

The youngin' seated in the dusty brown chair, Skinny, an arrogant, fool-hearted crash dummy, was trying to impress and earn his stripes. Right now Skinny was getting more antsy and agitated by the minute, sitting in his seat sweating by the buckets. He looked like he had taken a few laps around the anxiety pool.

Unprovoked, Skinny hopped up from the chair, a Glock-21 in hand and spouted, "Man, fuck this shit! These bammas don't scare me!"

Screw and Skinny made eye contact for a split second. Right then and there, they realized each man's life hung in the balance. The fastest man to pull the trigger and hit his mark would live to see another day. The other man would be a faded memory, tossed around in casual street chatter.

In a flash, both men pulled the trigger at the same

time. Two shots rang out in unison, sounding as one. The whites in both men's eyes bucked wide with surprise. A hairsbreadth later, Skinny's eyes dropped to the floor as he watched a big red splotch on the front of his clean white tee grow bigger and bigger.

The bloodstain brought joy to Screw's eyes. A sigh of relief floated off his lips as he watched the reality of death leap off Skinny's young, petrified face. Screw had seen that look many times—the expression of utter shock, grief, and sorrow a man experienced in his moment of profound doom, when death claimed his soul.

Feeling no sympathy whatsoever for the man, Screw aimed for Skinny's heart. A triumphant growl erupted from Screw as he dumped four more slugs in his chest.

The powerful force from Screw's hand cannon pushed Skinny's frail body backward, as if he was shot out of a cannon. His limp body fell back against the chair and flipped, crashing hard to the floor.

Stunned silence swept the entire room as if something mythical had just intered their space. It was apparent by the agonizing looks hanging heavy on their faces, members of the A-Team had never been affected so deeply before this moment. The whole team looked vulnerable. They were rattled and confused.

Members from the A-Team eyed one another, attempting to garner support from their comrades. Should they go for their guns all at once? Maybe make a mad dash for the door? The window? Their eyes drifted slowly toward Santana, each man silently calling out to him for answers, a way out of this mess.

On the opposing end of the spectrum, CIX stood poised in suspended animation. A warped sense of satisfaction surged in their body language. The armed gangstas stood gloating over their brutal strike.

Bad Ass whipped out a polished nickel-plated .50-caliber Desert Eagle, slammed a slug in the chamber, and placed the barrel to the bridge of Santana's sweaty nose.

"What the fuck y'all looking at this chump for?" he hissed, leaning in Santana's frightened face. Without provocation, Bad Ass cocked back and slammed the DE across the bridge of his nose. A sharp pop cracked the air. Santana yelped in pain as his knees buckled from the violent blow and blood gushed from his broken nose.

"This bitch can't help you!" Bad Ass snapped and yanked Santana by his collar. "Get your bitch ass over there!" He slung Santana, dazed and bloodied, into the waiting arms of Monster. He greeted him with a big, creepy grin.

"Yeah, we just getting started with your ass," Monster said, wrapping his enormous arms around Santana and hoisting him in the air like a life-size ragdoll. "C'mon, Killa," he said walking toward the basement door, "let's gift wrap this sucka!"

Bad Ass glared at the face of his enemy with bloodlust billowing from the oily black pools glistening in his eye sockets. A dark aura radiated around his form like the flame of an evil halo.

"You bitches say your prayers. Ain't no more A-Team," Bad Ass professed, the cadence in his voice full of doom and gloom. He eyed his men. "Bad Ass says blood-spill time!" He gave the command, his tone low and sadistic. He did an about-face, turned his back on his enemy, and strode off, heading for the basement.

Soon as CIX heard those deathly words uttered—

blood-spill time—they instinctively morphed into a state of super aggression, salivating and foaming at the mouths like a pack of wild, rabid dogs ready to do bodily harm.

"CIX ready!" Murder grunted, tightening his grip on his automatic chopper. "Three ... two ... one! Drop these bitches!"

An all-out shooting frenzy exploded in the living room. It was absolute mayhem, Armageddon.

The initial plan involved torturing Santana in the basement of the stash house, but that was before the violent massacre in the living room. In their line of work, plans were subject to change on the fly. Bad Ass prided himself on making split-second decisions under pressure. He claimed he was the master of adapting and was quick to boast that high-pressure situations brought out the best in him.

It's all about war, Bad Ass reflected. *The most vital part of these gangstas' lives. The most precious gift I can give to these young head-bustas is a legacy of destruction in their arch rivals: the A-Team, GHG, Top Soldiers, etc. And they give me the opportunity to plant the seeds of death in the next generation. In death, real gangstas endure.*

Immediately following the bloodbath, Bad Ass ordered CIX to vacate the premises. Monster and Killa took care of Santana. The two behemoths bound and gagged him and tossed him in the rear of the Suburban.

Standing just beyond the living room entrance, Bad Ass eyed the human destruction, his gaze devoid of emotion. He stood there inspecting the dead bodies, the blood-stained walls, floor, ceiling, and furniture, the devastation. He could smell the stench of death permeating the air like caustic gases attacking his airways.

Loso appeared in the hallway. He held up a black leather bag. "You want me to, uh, take out the second floor too?" he asked, grinning.

Bad Ass gave him a knowing wink. "Yeah, Lo, bring the whole muthafuckin' house down!"

It took Loso less than five minutes. The entire stash house was rigged from top to bottom with sticks of TNT.

Outside at the curb, Bad Ass climbed in the front passenger's seat. He pulled the door closed and gave one last look at the house before the BMW pulled off.

Loso's diluted sense of humor was on front street this evening. Donning a wide, cheeky grin, Loso produced another stick of dynamite.

"Might as well do the Lex joint," he said, offering the long stick of TNT to Bad Ass. "Fuck it," Bad Ass snorted and plucked the stick of explosives from his hand. "Might as well blow the joint. Them A-Team bammas pushin' up daisies now." He proceeded to snap the lengthy stem by less than half its length and put fire to it. He tossed the flaming stick in the open window as they rolled out.

Two seconds later—Kaboom!!! A powerful blast rocked the block. The large end unit exploded. The entire structure vaporized in the twinkling of an eye.

Half a second later—Kaboom! Another blast rocked the pavement when the Lexus exploded. Every window destroyed, leaving behind a mangled egg white shell sitting half-cocked off the curb.

Chapter 51

The sun had long ago left the sky, setting the tone for a peaceful evening. Angel and Shane were cuddled in each other's arms. The glare from the fireplace calmed their inner spirit and soothed their souls. Shane lay wide awake. A deep, inquisitive haze burned in his eye as he gazed up at the frosted pink ceiling. It had taken him awhile, but he was finally able to get Angel to calm down and relax.

A soft moan interrupted Shane's train of thought. His head slowly rotated to the left as Angel stirred in her sleep. He was perfectly still, waiting for her to settle down and get comfortable. He listened for her quiet breathing to become rhythmic again.

"Okay," he muttered to himself, feeling the relaxation spread through his body. He rose slightly on his elbows. "Damn, lady ... you are so beautiful," he whispered quietly, watching her sleep. "I wonder what makes you tick. I wish I could see inside your mind."

If Shane could see inside Angel's mind, he would be horrified by the level of treachery manifested in her mind, her psyche, and her soul.

At the moment a sense of turmoil seized Angel's mind—she was grappling against unholy forces that were invading her dreams.

"Whore!" A voice brimming with hatred and rage echoed all around her, and like a puff of smoke, the face of Bambie materialized out of nowhere. "Bitches like you don't deserve life!" the voice screamed.

Bambie gazed at her with those big doe eyes, but her eyes were empty, lifeless.

A dark shadow floated across Angel's line of sight,

momentarily blocking her view. The shadow drifted away and with it Bambie's big doe eyes were plucked from her eye sockets. Two large metal spikes sprang from the bloody vacant crater that impaled her skull – the spikes large, silvery edges were round and smooth. Angel could actually see her reflection on the smooth, round mirror-like surface. The woman looking back at her was alien. She looked evil, demented.

"No!!! Please, Lord, help me!!!" Angel shrieked in horror.

Like a stiff springboard, Angel bolted straight up in bed, her eyes stretched wide as she peered across the room as if she had stared death in the face.

Caught by surprise, Shane jumped up to comfort her. "Is everything okay, baby?" he asked, concerned. Shane placed his arm around her shoulder to comfort her. "You just had a bad dream, that's all. But I'm here for you, and everything gonna be alright," he expressed with an endearing tone. His embrace was both strong and caring.

Angel winced, recalling the large metal spikes protruding from Bambie's eye sockets. A shiver snaked up her spine. "What in God's name!" She felt her stomach doing flip-flops, like she was about to be sick. It took Angel a minute before she was finally able to catch her breath and gather herself.

She had to admit it felt good to be held by a man, especially a man of Shane's stature , so big, strong, and protective. As he held her, Angel could feel the trembling anxiety gradually subsiding from her body. She exhaled, and it felt so good.

The ring of a cell phone cracked the calm tranquility

they were quietly sharing. The interruption totally disturbed Shane.

"Fuck!" he hissed, "I have to get that." He reluctantly released Angel from his embrace and scooted to the edge of the bed. When he pressed the touch screen on his cell phone, the words "Emergency Woo" popped up. Shane shook his head with disappointment.

"What's the matter, Shane?" Angel asked, quietly.

A victorious feeling came over him when he noticed the bashful look in her eye and watched her soft caramel skin tone blush all over.

Shane dropped the phone. He swooped over Angel and gently caressed her chin with his right hand, coaxing her face toward his. Heated desire burned in their eyes. There was no hiding the inflection of raw emotions igniting the air between them.

"I love the way you look at me with your eyes, Angel. They sink deep into me," he whispered softly. The emotions in his voice reached out to her. "We are meant to be, baby," Shane said as a grin came over his face. He placed his hand against her soft caramel face. Gently, he traced the smoothness of her skin with his index finger. Angel closed her eyes, enjoying his delicate caress.

"I hope you know what you're getting into messing with a woman like me." Exciting tingles raced through her core when their lips touched. Angel tossed her arms around his neck and thrust her long, probing tongue in his mouth.

Shane was helpless. He couldn't deny the lust, the pure unadulterated craving that pulsated between them. Their bodies passionately clashed and collapsed in a heated embrace on the bed. Shane was anxious. He yearned to savor her flesh, her body, her sweet nectar.

He turned Angel on her stomach and entered her slowly from behind. Sweat rolled down his naked back. His taunt muscles flexed and contracted with every rhythmic stroke and pussy-pleasing pelvic thrust. Passionate groans sounded off, like an overly excited baboon grunting in heat. Shane felt like the mythical beast, and Angel was his prized beauty.

An atmosphere inflamed with lust and desire filled the room. Angel let herself go, mind, body, and soul. She succumbed to utter delight. *Finally!* she exclaimed, giving in to the moment.

The sexual interaction between them was intense. Their spirits seemed to touch with such profoundness, like the two were a kinship of souls merging as one.

An hour later, Angel and Shane were standing at the front door sharing a good-bye kiss.

"If it's not too late, I'll give you a call when I get home," Shane said with a warm smile, then kissed Angel on the forehead before turning to leave.

A look of pure joy and satisfaction danced in Angel's eyes as she watched him walk away. She exhaled. "Lord, what a man," she mumbled, waving good-bye as she watched him climb in behind the wheel. Before the Escalade pulled off, Angel closed the front door and locked the deadbolt.

She moseyed into the family room and started to gather up the dirty plates they left full of food. Angel froze when she heard a quiet buzz. She paused. Her gaze shifted to the white plastic bag on the coffee table. Angel set the plates aside and scooped up the bag.

Before inspecting it she quipped, "Shane forgot his cell phone." She pulled a black Boost Mobile phone from the bag. The look in her eyes changed instantly. Her gaze was shrewd with a hint of defiance when she noticed a woman's name flashing on the screen. *Dashia Webb?*

A new e-mail alert sounded.

Hello my Dark Stallion. Quick note—there's been a slight change of plans for our rendezvous tonight. My sister got into it with her boyfriend this evening and she needed a place to crash for the night. My two nephews and her are staying at my place tonight. Don't worry, we're still on, change of venue. My girl Tammy – Remember her? She's out of town and I have the key to her place. 16000 Massachusetts Avenue – apt. 1244 – the high-rise building on the corner. The key will be under the welcome mat, so let yourself in. See you soon!

By the time Angel finished reading the e-mail, she felt that evil thing awakening inside. A black hole opened suddenly in her head and long, dark tentacles emerged from its core. The tentacles reached out seizing her mind and another kind of evil penetrated her being.

Madness flashed in Natasha's eyes. She rolled her head from left to right. The sound of bones cracking in her neck echoed in the room. She flexed the muscles in her back as she glared hard at the cell phone screen.

"Dashia Webb," she snorted, her upper lip twitching. She sighed when she felt that familiar surge of dark rage ignite her senses. "Nasty slut!" she growled viciously. "I can already taste your death and see your filthy corpse." Natasha's head snapped back. She belted a maniacal laugh that filled the room with her dark haughtiness.

Chapter 52

Shane's black Cadillac truck stopped on the opposite side of East Capitol, directly across from the sight of the obliterated row house. His tall frame alighted from the vehicle. Immediately the pungent odor of nitroglycerin assaulted his nostrils when he breathed in the caustic fumes saturating the atmosphere.

Just beyond the devastation, a wall of fire engines lined the westbound lanes along East Capitol for about one block. At the corner, on Division, more emergency vehicles clogged the narrow street in both directions.

The moment Shane stepped foot outside and got a good look at the destruction, his instincts screamed , *Something ain't right!* There was something askew in the air.

In no time, the commander descended on the crime scene. He singled out Tony Woo, Detective Rich Louis, and members of a newly formed gang strike task force, which Detective Louis commanded. The chief directed the team to a mobile police command trailer for a private briefing.

Inside, Shane stood in the doorway of an adjoining office, watching the men grab a seat at the makeshift conference table in the center of the room.

The cheif drew the team's attention when he shrugged off his dark blazer, slung it over the back of a chair, and took his place at the head of the conference table.

"Well, men, don't everybody speak at once," he said with an obvious chip on his shoulder. He hesitated, turned up his wrist, and pushed up his long black sleeve. "But, uh, the clock is ticking," he smirked, staring at the black face on his Movado timepiece, "and you got less than five minutes to suffice my growing anger, or heads will be rolling—right out the fucking door of this trailer!"

Louis hopped to his feet, stumbling over his words. "Sir, we're in the initial stages of gathering witness statements   and—"

"Save it!" Shane snapped. "Don't patronize me, detective. I'll have your ass clocking parking meters by tomorrow!"

The chief's cold response rankled Louis. He zipped his mouth shut and quietly sank back in his seat.

Lieutenant Barnhart decided to make a go at it. He stood with his palms leaning on the table.

"Well, sir," Barnhart began, looking around the table, "what we've been able to ascertain so far in our investigation—we're in the midst of an all-out gang war."

Commander Holt huffed, "No shit, Sherlock."

The commander's snide remark didn't deter Lieutenant Barnhart. He pressed on with his verbal assessment. "This Southeast residence is highlighted on our target gang listing. It's a hotbed for A-Team activity, sir. And the five bodies pulled from the rubble are presumably A-Team gang members."

Barnhart's Asian counterpart, Lieutenant Bruce Maruchan, was seated to his right. The stocky Asian let his presence be known when he started shaking his head and mumbling incoherently under his breath.

Shane's anger shifted on the beefy Asian sporting the canary diamond in his earlobe. "Lieutenant Maruchan," he spoke firmly, "is there a problem? Do you have something to add, some pertinent information that you would like to share with us? Because by all means, feel free to take the floor."

"Chief, sir," Lieutenant Maruchan said, sweeping a hand through his brown wavy hair, as he rose to his feet. He could feel the cold eye Barnhart was casting his way and paid him no mind. "This was a hit, plain and simple. A viciously planned, blatant, and vital strike aimed at the core of the A-Team's hierarchy." Maruchan returned Barnhart's stare before adding, "Somewhere in the city, we have us a masterful manipulator working an angle. This kind of thing happens all the time in China with the Yakuza."

Shane nodded in agreement. "The Yakuza? You're referring to the Chinese mafia?" he asked with a growing look of interest.

Maruchan smiled. "Yes, that is correct, sir," he answered, standing erect, as if he were about to salute the chief.

"Go on," Shane prompted him, making eye contact with Tony Woo. This was right up Tony's alley. The inspector was intrigued by the inner workings and transgressions of the Yakuza.

The Asian detective was built strong, like an ultimate fighter contending for the heavyweight title. Maruchan gave his crispy-black partner, Barrack Nubi, a knowing look. He straightened his navy blazer and cleared his throat.

"From my experience dealing with these organized crime entities—"

"Whoa!" Barnhart blurted. "Or-ga-ni-zed crime," he said, exaggerating each syllable, slowly and disdainfully. "These uncouth miscreants don't' give a rat's ass about being organized!" he fired back, drily. "These fuckers are monsters. If they can't fuck it, rob it, or kill it, they don't want it! Plain and simple!"

It was quite apparent to Shane and the other men seated at the table that Barnhart was attempting to undermine Maruchan's assessment. The commander wasn't having it. Dissension in the ranks was not tolerated.

"Lieutenant Barnhart!" Shane's voice bellowed, rigid and edgy. "I advise you take your seat. Another outburst like that and you will be dismissed from this meeting. Is that understood?" The commander looked like he was struggling to keep his composure.

His edgy response sent warning chills through the room, and Barnhart knew he better heed the warning.

"Lieutenant Maruchan," Shane said, taking a seat, "you have the floor. Please continue."

Maruchan took a deep breath. "Like I was saying before I was rudely interrupted, these organized criminal entities are known to operate with some objective in mind. That's where we need to focus our energy and resources. We decipher the intended objective, we narrow our suspect pool." Maruchan stopped short and turned to Lieutenant Nubi. " Lieutenant Nubi, care to enlighten the group with your take on the matter?"

Lieutenant Nubi looked up and smiled, revealing a set of perfect white teeth. His teeth were so bright that when he smiled his pearly whites seemed to illuminate his crispy blue-black complexion.

"My pleasure," the long, lanky Nigerian said, standing. "For starters, gentlemen, let's take into account the initial hit—the Candy Land Massacre." Barrack Nubi's strong Nigerian accent rolled across the room as he moved away from the table. "I understand from a visceral standpoint," he said, clasping his hands behind his back. "The attack at the Candy Land residence was strategically planned to take out the A-Team leader, Juelz Odom. They did so in a manner so obnoxious, DC's underworld cringed when they heard the method of death. These individuals didn't just take out the leader, they annihilated him in the most heinous way imaginable. They totally destroyed his existence. After such a deplorable act, what do they do next? These bastards take it up a notch." Lieutenant Nubi stopped dead in his tracks and turned to the chief.

"They immediately attack the A-Team's home base and second tier in command." Nubi's expression grew tense. "I'm willing to bet you a dollar to a doughnut, the culprits left that house with someone or something. Whatever gangbangers are left on the A-Team, they're shitting their pants right about now, running around town like a chicken with his head cut off."

Shane lifted his right index finger. "Let me make sure I got this right, gang war is out of the equation. What we're dealing with is one gang's vicious intent to dismantle and destroy another gang's existence, right?" A look of concern flashed in his face. "Tell me, what would be the purpose behind that? What, get the remaining gangbangers to drop their flags and pledge a new oath with them? Is that what you're getting at here, lieutenant?" Shane's right eyebrow went up in an awkward way.

"No, sir," Maruchan replied. "Their intent is not to gain members," he said, looking straight at the chief. "At this moment, sir, we are not fully aware of their intended objective, but we are in the process of sifting through the evidence and hopefully, collectively, as a team, we will be able to garner some viable intel and take this extremely dangerous character off the streets."

A deep furl appeared on Shane's brow. "Explain to

me, lieutenant, why you're so convinced that these two incidents were spawned by one individual. That baffles me because we know for a fact that a number of individuals participated in both attacks. In light of that, why then would you be so strongly inclined to think there would be just one individual mind behind this so-called plot? Exploding gangbangers, now exploding houses? What's next?" Shane's gaze bounced from Maruchan to Nubi to Tony Woo.

Tony Woo pushed his gold-rimmed glasses snugly on his nose and said, "Probably some form of evil plague will descend on Washington and put us all out of our misconceived misery." He chuckled lightly and leaned back in his chair.

"Cheif Holt," said Lieutenant Maruchan. His no-nonsense tone drew every one's attention. "When it's all said and done and this particular investigation comes full circle, then and only then will Lieutenant Nubi and myself receive the proper accolades that we both deserve. At this juncture, our opinions on this matter are just that. But keep in mind the individual behind this violent upsurge is a single person who is extremely egotistical and manipulative and has an innately violent nature. He's a man with a sick and demented mind. Don't get me wrong, sir, our man has a team of followers doing his work, but he is the controlling faction. The place and time we finally apprehend this abomination?" Maruchan hunched his shoulders. "We are not Gods. Evil falls suddenly. Who should say when it falls?" Maruchan concluded. His eerie dialogue hovered in the room, weighing heavily on each man's mind, like a blade suspended in the air about to drop on their heads at any second.

Chapter 53

The sounds of traffic down on Massachusetts Avenue were muffled and distant. From behind the 12th floor enclosure, Dashia listened to the low mechanical groan blowing in the breeze as she gazed out on the city's bustling nightlife crawling along the urban landscape and its intersecting manmade arteries one hundred twenty feet below.

Sergeant Dashia Webb was a carbon copy of the saucy female rap artist Trina. She was a short, feisty brown-skin bombshell with long, curly brown locks and a ravenous sexual appetite that was out of this world. The hot and tempting sergeant also held the title belt as the police chief's prized piece of pussy, on the low.

A slinky brown silk teddy hugged Dashia's short, bosomy frame as she swung her curvy hips from left to right in a slinky, provocative way, gyrating in rhythm to Keri Hilson's hip melody "Pretty Girl Rock."

Feeling herself and the music, Dashia reached out and snatched the half-empty wine glass off the window ledge as she mouthed the chorus, her full, shimmering brown lips doing their best Keri Hilson impression.

Dashia spun away from the window. She was light on her feet, dancing the two-step across the gold, burgundy, and brown Persian rug in the center of the living room floor.

She stopped in the middle of the room when she noticed herself in the mirror hanging above the burgundy and gold suede sofa. Dashia turned her plump rear end toward the mirror and flipped up her teddy.

"Damn, Dashia!" she said, looking naughty, "you got

one helluva ass on you, girlfriend! A nigga would have to be gay to turn down an ass this phat!" She laughed out loud, took another sip of wine, then danced her way toward the bedroom and disappeared inside.

Once inside the candlelit bedroom, it was pretty much a wrap for Dashia. She told herself she would lie in bed and wait for Shane to arrive. The moment she pulled back the gold silk sheets, she felt a sluggish, woozy feeling coming on.

Dashia polished off her third glass of wine. Before the music was over, the alcohol's effects crept up on her, pulled her down under the covers and off to sleep.

Positioned on the right side of Dashia's queen-size sleigh bed, a burgundy lacquered nightstand was pushed tightly against the bed frame. A square alarm clock sat a half inch from the corner edge. The clock's large red neon numerals floated across its black face. It was 11:46 P.M., and total silence swept through the entire apartment. The sound of Keri Hilson ended about half an hour ago.

Outside the apartment, a shadow appeared beneath the front door. The doorknob turned slowly and carefully, until it could turn no more. Someone leaned against the steel door frame and carefully nudged it open, creating a sliver of space, just enough to get a peek inside.

A cold blue eye peered in from outside. Slowly, quietly the brown steel door creaked open, pausing every few inches until there was enough space to slip inside.

Seconds later a dark shadow drifted silently across the living room floor and made a beeline for the bedroom. The shadow floated through the open doorway, over the carpet floor, and onto the bed where the silhouette came to rest on Dashia's sleeping form.

Clad in a skintight patent leather cat suit, Natasha looked spooky as she hovered in the doorway like the dominatrix from hell.

She cast a sharp gaze upon the woman lying asleep in bed. A look of hellfire burned deep within.

"Mmmm," Dashia said, stirring when she felt the presence of another body climb in bed with her. "Baby, where you been?" she purred coming out of her slumber. "Ooooh," she cooed, excitement building with every breath as she listened to the sound of heavy panting in her ear. "Shane, you sound like a sex-craved maniac ready to tear the fur off my ass!"

A sense of lewd anticipation swelled in Dashia's stomach. She started squirming and wiggling her ass beneath the covers. "Here, baby," she said as she thrust her naked derriere toward her illicit lover, offering her body with a nasty giggle. "Don'tcha wanna slide that fat snake of yours between my phat-ass cheeks?"

Natasha leaned back on the bed, her upper torso propped up on her elbows. She arched her head back, her patent-leather skully brushed against the wooden headboard. She hesitated a split second, held her breath, and closed her gloved right hand over the pearl handle of a razor-sharp switchblade.

The switchblade felt good in her hand. Natasha flexed her hand, licked her lips, and grinned as she stared up at the ceiling. A wicked gleam shimmered in her blue eyes.

She reveled in the moment before taking a life. She loved the feeling of darkness, power, and raw energy colliding like a train wreck inside her.

Natasha exhaled, and a loud sigh resonated in the room. "Whore!" she growled, maliciously. "How this dick feel sliding in your ass!"

The excitement instantly drained from Dashia's face. Her stomach hit bottom as she braced herself and whipped her head around.

Natasha moved with wild abandon. Before Dashia could utter a word, she slammed her left hand over Dashia's mouth and clamped down with such force, Dashia was paralyzed.

"Bitches like you don't deserve life!" Natasha snarled in her ear, and slowly inserted the razor-sharp blade in the opening of her rectum.

Dashia was in utter incomprehension of the situation unfolding upon her. The eyes looking down on her embodied a soul of pure evil and hate. Dashia tried to break free of her grip, but it was too late.

Tears of pain exploded in her eyes when Dashia felt the sharp, excruciating agony tearing inside her rectum, like someone pouring hot lava in her anal cavity. She knew at that moment her life was over.

Lord!!! Please take me away from this devil!!! Dashia's soul cried out for mercy in the last second before her spirit breached the realm of death.

A dark, seedy smirk cut the corner of Natasha's mouth when she felt Dashia's soul succumb to her. "Yeah, that's it bitch," she grumbled, "take all this dick!" She rammed the length of the blade deep in her anus, to the hilt, and twisted it back and forth, relishing the feel of death permeating the air.

12:24 A.M.

"Shhhh!!!" Natasha hushed herself when she heard the front door open.

"Dashia!" Shane stepped inside the apartment and closed the door behind. "Big Poppa is here! Come out here and show me some love, girl!" he said, sporting a wide, expectant grin. His grin faded slightly when a cloak of silence greeted him.

He walked over to the sofa, slipped off his blazer, and placed it across the arm of the sofa. His eyes casually roamed the exquisite interior, taking stock of the expensive Arabian décor dominating the apartment and the half-empty bottle of red wine on the mini bar.

"Pretty nice place your girlfriend has here," he muttered, facing the gold-framed wall mirror. "What she do for a living?" he inquired, loosening his black silk tie. "She better be a company CEO, a bank president, or owner of a Fortune 500 company. If not, then I know she's knee-deep in illegal activities," he remarked, nonchalantly. He did an about-face and headed for the bedroom.

Shane paused in the doorway and looked around the dark room.

"Dashia, you know I don't like it when you drink yourself into a stupor like that. I'm in the mood to fuck. I don't want no goddamn ragdoll I gotta be tossin' around the damn bed," he said as he moved to the right side of the bed. He flopped down on the edge of the mattress and started unfastening his shirt. Shane huffed, "Damn, I thought I made myself clear. Didn't we both agree on this?" He got aggravated when she didn't respond.

"Oh, I get it." He clinched his jaw, snatched off his

shirt, and fell back on the bed. "You're testing me, right?" he said in her ear as he rolled up on her backside. When she didn't respond this time, he really got pissed.

"Dashia! What in the hell is your—" He yanked her by the shoulder. Dashia's head rolled over, limp. She was dead!!!

Shane's eyes leaped from his skull, totally horrified by the mangled, lipless face staring at him with dead eyes.

"WTF!!!" he cursed. He catapulted off the bed in one mighty lurch. He stumbled backward, startled and disturbed. His heart pounded on his chest as he tried to catch his breath. Shane couldn't tear his eyes away from the ghastly sight even though his instincts were sounding off warning bells loud and clear in his head.

Five feet behind him, the shadow in the corner came to life. Natasha's black form moved like a phantom camouflaged in darkness as she closed in on the unsuspecting Shane.

A black slap-jack rose in the air for a second before swooping down and crashing hard on the back of Shane's head. Not once, not twice, but three vicious blows! She cracked him in the head and sent him crashing to the floor, totally unconscious.

"You dirty-dick muthafucka!" Natasha hissed scathingly as she whipped out her switchblade. She stood over him like some sort of dark, threatening she-devil casting her death gaze upon Shane as he lay perfectly still.

A wicked smile burst off Natasha's face in 3-D as she savored the moment before the kill. A second later, she kneeled down beside his head and pressed the sharp edge firmly against his thick Adam's apple.

Natasha inhaled deeply. A rush of pure evilness

aroused her core.

"You piece of shit for a man!" she snarled deadly. "Reap what you sow, Shane, 'cause bitches like you don't deserve life." She pressed on the blade. Her adrenaline pumped hard in her veins and her breath grew deep. A sadistic grin spread on her face as she applied more pressure to his Adam's apple. Natasha groaned excitedly when the blade pierced Shane's skin.

"Bitch!!!" Natasha jumped, startled. "What in the hell are you doing!?! Have you lost your muthafucking mind?!? Get your filthy hands off of him! Get the hell away from Shane. Now!!!"

Natasha's head snapped back, a look of complete shock flash-frozen on her face!

"Oh my God!!!" she stammered, completely astounded, shaken, and confused.

About The Author

R.J. Champ is a self-taught author and native of Washington, DC. His passion and creativity for writing has given him the drive and vision to enlighten the urban genre and its readers with compelling new story lines, plots, and characters that will take the realm of urban street lit to unchartered territories and exciting new regions that have yet to be explored. R.J. Champ's in depth knowledge and life experiences on the inner-workings of the streets has enabled this author to bring to life stories with vivid imagination, and entertain his audience with the hottest cutting edge urban tales-so contemporary-he's labeled his books: "Urban Adult".

For more information about RJ Champ visit his Facebook page: facebook.com/rjchamp

Coming Soon!

DC Bookdiva Publications

#245 4401-A Connecticut Avenue, NW

Washington, DC 20008

dcbookdiva.com

Name: _____

Inmate ID _____

Address: _____

City/State: _____ **Zip:** _____

QUANTITY	TITLES	PRICE	TOTAL
	Dynasty, Dutch	$15.00	
	Dynasty 2, Dutch	$15.00	
	Dynasty 3, Dutch	$15.00	
	Que, Dutch	$15.00	
	Secrets Never Die, Eyone Williams	$15.00	

Sub-Total

$_____

Shipping/Handling (Via US Media Mail) $3.95 1-2 Books, $7.95 1-3 Books, 4 or more titles-Free Shipping

Shipping $ _____

Total Enclosed $ _____

Certified or government issued checks and money orders, all mail in orders take 5-7 Business days to be delivered. Books can also be purchased on our website at dcbookdiva.com and by credit card at 1866-928-9990. Incarcerated readers receive 25% discount. Please pay $11.25 per book and apply the same shipping terms as stated above.